Ann Granger has lived in cities all over the world, since for many years she worked for the Foreign Office and received postings to British embassies as far apart as Munich and Lusaka. She is now permanently based in Oxfordshire.

Ann Granger is the author of four hugely popular crime series, the Mitchell & Markby mysteries, the Fran Varady mysteries, the Campbell & Carter mysteries and the Inspector Ben Ross mysteries, all of which have been highly praised:

'Characterisation, as ever with Granger, is sharp and astringent'
The Times

'Her usual impeccable plotting is fully in place' *Good Book Guide*

'While Ann Granger's novels might be set in the familiar mode of traditional country crime stories, there is nothing old-fashioned about the characters, who are drawn with a telling eye for their human foibles and frailties. Granger is bang up to date'
Oxford Times

'Entertaining and lifelike characters . . . a satisfying and unexpected twist'
Mystery People

'Period colour is nicely supplied . . . This engrossing story looks like the start of a highly enjoyable series'
Scotsman

'The book's main strength is the characterisation and the realistic portrayal of London in the mid-19th century'
Tangled Web

'Murder most enjoyable'
Bournemouth Daily Echo

ANN GRANGER

MYSTERY IN THE MAKING

18 Short Stories of Malevolence and Murder

HEADLINE

First published in 2021 by
HEADLINE PUBLISHING GROUP

First published in paperback in 2022 by
HEADLINE PUBLISHING GROUP

1

Cataloguing in Publication Data is available from the British Library

ISBN 978 1 4722 9021 2

Typeset in Adobe Garamond by
Palimpsest Book Production Limited, Falkirk, Stirlingshire

Printed and bound in Great Britain by Clays Ltd, Elcograf S.p.A.

HEADLINE PUBLISHING GROUP
An Hachette UK Company
Carmelite House
50 Victoria Embankment
London EC4Y 0DZ

www.headline.co.uk
www.hachette.co.uk

To my mother,
Norah Davey Granger,
and my grandmother,
Sarah Davey Martin.

Contents

Contents

Introduction

These tales were written at different times and several years ago. For me, their creator, to find them gathered together now, is like finding myself unexpectedly at a reunion of old friends and acquaintances. The door opens, I walk into the room and there they are, all those characters who jumped out of my imagination. What a motley crew crowds the space. The air is filled with the babble of their voices. 'Where have you been since we last met?' we ask one another. 'What have you been doing?' and in some cases, 'What a surprise to see you here!' If one or two of the characters are secretly thinking, 'Couldn't you have made me nicer? Prettier? Kinder? Cleverer?' – well, they are all too polite to say so. Too late now to change their fate, anyway; and a reunion is no time for grumbling.

I have written all kinds of books in my thirty-plus years as a writer. But, for the most of that career, I've been an author of crime fiction. Authors are readers before they ever set out to be writers, and I've been a lover of books since I was very young. I was lucky enough to have a mother and grandmother who were both enthusiastic readers, so I came into contact with all sorts of books in childhood and many of them, probably most of them, were not intended for young readers. The only children's stories I recall devouring were those with horses in them, such as the wonderful yarns written by the Pullein-Thompson sisters. Their plots always featured nearly as many ponies as characters, and were exciting adventure stories, often with a dash of mystery thrown in. Much later in life I was lucky enough to meet Josephine Pullein-Thompson, and was able to tell her how I'd enjoyed her books.

My grandmother, with whom I spent many holidays, lived in the New Forest. The free-ranging ponies that are so much a symbol of the area roamed much more freely then than now. There was an area of grass before her home and a small group of them would sometimes arrive there and wait at my grandmother's front gate. She always took water out for them, in a galvanised bucket, and they'd form a disorderly queue with the leader of the gang at its head. For me this is another parallel with writing the stories. Characters and plot ideas mill about in my head, slowly getting organised. Some push their way to the front at once; others work their way through the throng and make a later appearance.

My mother liked historical fiction and biographies. My grand-mother, on the other hand, had a liking for westerns and crime fiction. She amassed books from various sources, and was an enthusiastic buyer of paperbacks at jumble sales. A bag of such gleanings would be brought home and tipped out in a heap. Burrowing among them was like treasure hunting. Some of these books were in poor condition but I didn't worry about that. I felt I was reading them in the company of all the previous readers. With books, I was always among friends.

At my parents' home in Portsmouth I followed her example and raided second-hand bookstalls for hardback copies. Before these could be read, they had first to be trussed up in string to prevent the covers from curling, and then baked in the oven at a low heat 'to kill the germs because you don't know where they've been'! This might sound extreme to modern readers, but these were the days before the common availability of antibiotics.

The first crime fiction I recall reading from among those tattered volumes were the courtroom-based investigations of attorney Perry Mason, written by Erle Stanley Gardner, himself a lawyer. Gardner's books are economically written by today's standards. But this does not make them 'short stories' as generally understood.

I came to include short stories among my reads much later. I don't recall either my mother or grandmother reading magazines, where most short stories were to be found. So, I had no memory guide to help in my own efforts when I began to write them myself – except, perhaps, in one respect for which I must thank all those Perry Mason yarns: whatever is going to happen, it has to happen fast.

Creating a short story is a tricky business. Those who have never tried their hands at it sometimes imagine it must be so much easier than writing an entire novel of any kind. This is far from the case, because of the concise nature of the narrative. Like a novel, the short story must have a beginning, middle and an end. There is no room for the plot to wander off down side-alleys and meander its way back to the main narrative. Every word must be relevant.

The characters, too, must step off the page as real people. There is no time to 'get to know them'. The reader must feel he or she recognises them at once and can believe in them. Some of them may strike the reader as pleasant, others as sinister . . . and new acquaintances may not be what they first seem!

For the writer, there is little or no room for error, and the way is strewn with pitfalls. The writer can't take refuge in passages of description. There just isn't space. But the author still has to paint a picture and give the characters depth.

Some of the stories in this present volume are longer than others because they were originally written to be magazine serials. The serial presents a few different challenges. The writer has more space to tell the story, but can't tell it all at once, so each episode has to form a satisfactory whole, but leave the reader wanting to know what happens next.

Sitting down to create a short story is not unlike opening a trinket box and beholding a colourful heap of assorted objects, each representing a character or element in your story. You pick the ones you need and set them down on a chessboard of the imagination. They are all at a crucial point in their lives, and their fate is in your hands. No wonder some of them look a little worried. But for the writer, it can be quite a power trip! I enjoyed writing these brief tales. I hope you enjoy reading them.

Sadly, there are fewer opportunities today for publishing short stories. Magazines are no longer on the look-out for them as they once were. I would therefore like to thank my agent, Isobel Dixon, for believing these tales could be gathered together in book form, and to express my gratitude to my editor at Headline, Clare Foss, for taking up the idea and making it come to pass, seeing the book through to publication.

So, I raise a glass at the reunion to all the old friends who people these tales. They raise a glass in return. (They like a wee dram or a glass of sherry!) 'Really good to see you again!' they call out. 'Happy memories!' And, hopefully, 'Haven't you worn well!'

Ann Granger

A Lady Should Avoid Murder

Amongst Jane Pritchard's childhood memories was a book. It'd belonged to her grandmother and been entitled *Everything a Lady Should Know*. Everyone can recall seminal reading of long ago, and the venerable handbook had fascinated young Jane. Embellished with pictures of a smirking Lady writing little notes or embarking on a visit in hat and gloves, it advised the reader on the correct response to every conceivable situation in which the unsuspecting female might find herself. Armed with rules as rigid as the corsets worn by the illustrated examples, the Lady could sally forth, fearing no man and no social pitfall, to knock 'em dead with her grasp of etiquette.

Ah, yes, dead . . . Unfortunately, as far as Jane could recall at the present moment, the wonderful book hadn't offered any handy hints on dealing with a murderer. Surely an oversight. Allowing herself a moment's daydreaming, Jane mentally composed a letter of enquiry.

Dear Editor,
I have recently made the acquaintance of a gentleman of homicidal tendencies . . . Please advise . . .

Catching herself out in this lapse of concentration, she wriggled on her chair and smiled nervously at the young man sitting opposite her in her tiny living room. He was rather younger than she was, by about eight years, she judged. She was thirty-seven. He was pleasant in appearance except for a sharp look about the eyes, and wore a neat sports jacket and well-pressed slacks. She was momentarily inspired to wish she wasn't wearing cut-off jeans and a washed-out sweatshirt.

A Lady who has taken Trouble with her Toilette will always be at her Ease.

'Shall I make us some more tea?' Jane asked, seizing a chance to get out of the room for five minutes and pull herself together. It was a stressful situation and she ought to be keeping her mind on matters, not indulging in eccentric fancies.

'Thanks very much,' he said, picking up the pottery mug she'd handed him earlier. 'Need a hand?'

'No, thanks!' she replied rather too forcefully and bolted into the kitchen to switch on the kettle.

Tea is taken between four and five o'clock. A selection of plain and fancy cakes should be offered. Napkins are essential.

Jane opened a tin and stared in dismay at the one crushed cracker lying forlornly in the bottom. She dunked the teabag in boiled water and hurried back to her visitor.

'Sorry, no cake or anything . . .' she apologised.

'Never eat it,' he said. He sipped from the mug which had been hand decorated by Jane with comical cats and glanced out of the French windows leading to the back lawn.

'Nice little garden you've got here. I'm a bit of a gardener myself.'

He was prompting her nicely. She took the hint. 'I bought this cottage just about a year ago, after my divorce. I'd been living in

London. But, you see, most of our friends – my ex-husband's and mine – had been joint friends and – well, I wanted to get right away and start over with no ties. I'm a writer. All I need really is my computer and a stack of paper.'

She had a horrible feeling she'd told him this before. Like a child who has rehearsed a piece for a school concert, once interrupted she could only resume by going back to the beginning and starting again.

'I know the cottage is isolated but I didn't – I don't – mind that. I also realised there was a house next door, behind all those trees, but I didn't give a thought to who might live there. I think I imagined at first it was empty. There was no sign of life . . .'

She stopped, wondering if that had been a simple turn of phrase or a Freudian slip. 'I mean,' she went on firmly, 'I hadn't seen anyone going in or out. So it was a real surprise when Mr Warren put in an appearance about a week after I moved in.'

She'd been out in the garden, trying to fix a rotary washing line. The metal post was heavy and it needed someone else to hold it while she wedged it. Otherwise, once it had laundry pegged to it, a good wind would carry the whole lot away like a ship under sail.

There was a rustle from the further side of the nearby hedge, between her property and the next, and without warning, a head popped up like a puppet's from behind a curtain. It belonged to a man of about her own age or slightly older, perhaps forty-one or -two. He had straight, flat mousy hair and a small neat moustache.

'Can I help?' he asked. Of course, he could.

When he'd arrived in the garden and she'd been able to see him top to toe, the rest of his appearance had also been mousy. Small, a little tubby, wearing brownish trousers and a beige sweater. A dark maroon tie was knotted neatly below his Adam's apple. He'd scurried round fixing the washing line with nimble fingers and smiling all the while at her, showing slightly prominent front teeth.

'It's nice to have neighbours again,' he said. 'My name is Harold Warren. I live with my mother.'

Jane replied with a brief word about herself.

'A writer, eh?' said Mr Warren, eyes sparkling. 'I'm a great one for books. I love a good book. I read all kinds, anything I can get my hands on.'

He went on to explain he was unmarried and his mother, with whom he shared the house, was elderly and infirm. She required constant attendance so he didn't work. Jane gathered there was some family money, enough to live on. She supposed his mother must have a pension as well. She thanked him for his help with the washing line and offered him a cup of tea.

He refused. 'Can't leave Mother for long!'

With that, he went back to his own side of the hedge.

A silence fell in Jane's living room. Her visitor sipped his tea. Jane picked up her own mug.

'See much of him after that?' asked her visitor conversationally.

She shook her head. 'Hardly anything. Their garden's completely overgrown and you can't see their house from here because of the trees. The exit from their drive is around the curve in the road and so I wouldn't normally see anyone go in or out, either. I heard the car occasionally, and saw it sometimes when I was walking along the road. I supposed he was going shopping or something. He had to leave the place from time to time. He always waved to me and occasionally let down the window to call out a greeting. We'd exchange a brief word. I felt sorry for him and that he must be an exemplary son. The next time I had any real conversation with him was when he brought me some apples.'

She'd been outside in her back garden, hoeing weeds from a flower bed. There'd been a rustle on the other side of the hedge and Mr Warren's head popped up as before, surprising her into letting out a yelp and nearly dropping the hoe. He'd apologised for giving her a fright and held out a plastic carrier bag.

'Thought you might use some apples. They're only fallers, so you'll have to use them at once. They won't keep. But they're very good cookers, Bramleys. We have more than Mother and I can use.'

'How is your mother?' Jane asked.

'Oh, much as usual.' He sighed. 'Nothing can be done. She's a bit of a trial, poor old darling, but we manage.'

With that, he'd scurried away.

It had been the second time he'd shown neighbourly kindness. Jane felt impelled to respond in some way.

A return Visit should not be made too soon, neither should it be left too long!

She used the apples to make a batch of pies. She froze all but two of them, put one aside for her own immediate use, and set off for the Warren house, bearing the remaining pie as a thank-you gift. After all, he probably didn't do much cooking, not if he had to wait hand and foot on his mother.

When visiting the Housebound, some little home-baked Delicacy is always welcome.

Jane walked up the long, weed-strewn drive to the house. The lofty old trees to either side almost met overhead, blocking out the daylight. It was chilly and damp. Fallen leaves had formed a slippery mulch. Everywhere was silent. There was even a curious absence of birdsong.

The house itself appeared ahead of her with the disconcerting suddenness Mr Warren himself had shown when his head appeared over the hedge. Jane, still holding the pie before her in both hands like a religious offering, stood studying the scene. Had she not known better, she would have believed it deserted. The tall narrow windows were covered with a film of dust. The place clearly hadn't been painted in years. There was a detached garage standing amongst the trees to her right. Indents in the soft soil showed where a car had passed in and out, the only sign of any life. The garage door was shut.

As she approached the front door to the house, she saw that garden debris had piled around and across the steps and clogged the cobwebby cellar windows. She climbed the stone slabs, her feet disturbing the leaf cover which gave a soft shur-shurring sound, and put out her hand to the unpolished brass torque which formed the knocker. The sound echoed throughout the house like a distant clap of thunder.

After a moment she heard footsteps approaching the door. It was tugged open with some effort. It must have swollen shut. A form was dimly discernible on the far side, through the crack. Then it was pulled open wider and Mr Warren stood there in his mouse-brown trousers, beige pullover and maroon tie. He wore slippers.

'Oh,' he said, blinking at her. 'Mrs Pritchard!'

Jane held out the pie. 'I brought this. I thought, as you were so kind and gave me the apples. I made a whole lot of pies, perhaps you'd like—'

'Thank you, yes, you really shouldn't—' he interrupted her. He seemed agitated and reached out to take the dish.

Before his hands closed on it, a door opened in the depths of the dark hallway to the rear of Warren. A female form appeared, silhouetted against the light from the room beyond.

The woman, whom at first Jane couldn't make out clearly at all, began to move quietly towards them. She had a curious, uneven gait and put out her hand to steady herself against the wall. Now Jane could see that she wore a dowdy print dress and rather dirty cardigan. Her hair was grey but abundant and fell loose to her shoulders in long, tangled strands. She had large pale blue eyes which were fixed on the visitor with puzzled wonder. It was impossible to judge her age, but her skin appeared fine and remarkably unlined.

Then the smell hit Jane. An insidious stench of soiled under-wear, sweat and grime-stiffened clothing, unbathed skin. The woman's feet were bare – that was why she moved so quietly – and the unclipped toenails had grown to curl over like the talons of a bird of prey.

Jane's expression betrayed what had happened to Mr Warren, or possibly he'd sensed that someone stood behind him. He whirled round and gave an exclamation which sounded part surprise, part dismay or embarrassment and part anger.

He bustled towards the dishevelled apparition at once and took her arm in a firm grip.

'Now, dear,' he said. 'You shouldn't be out here.'

'Who is this?' the woman asked, staring at Jane over his shoulder with the same kind of wonder. Jane could see now that the pupils of the pale blue eyes were dilated and curiously unfocused.

Raising her voice, Jane replied, 'I'm Jane Pritchard from the cottage, Mrs Warren. I expect your son has told you about me—'

'I haven't got—' the woman began in a peeved tone.

Warren had moved to place himself more fully between the two women. He looked over his shoulder to Jane and said irritably, 'She doesn't understand. It's dementia.' He began to push his mother ahead of him towards the rear room.

'Come on, dear, back to the warm kitchen. You'll catch cold.'

'You've taken away my shoes,' said the old woman, sounding even more sulky.

'No, I haven't,' he retorted with crisp authority. 'You keep taking them off yourself.'

He propelled her through the door at the back of the hall, shut it and scurried back to Jane.

'You see how it is, Mrs Pritchard,' he began hurriedly. 'It's dementia and nothing at all to be done.'

'I understand,' faltered Jane. She didn't know quite how to phrase this, but the woman was filthy and ought at least to be bathed and her toenails clipped. 'Do you have any help with your mother, Mr Warren? The district nurse could call, say, once a week and – lend a hand.'

'No!' he said sharply. 'There's no need!' He made an effort. 'I don't want to sound ungrateful, Mrs Pritchard. It's kind of you to ask. But I can look after Mother perfectly well. Besides, strangers worry her. I'm the only person she'll let do anything for her.'

He made to close the door in Jane's face. She was still holding the pie dish and anxious that he should take it, pushed it forward. The result was that it caught in the closing gap and she almost dropped it. Mr Warren grabbed it in the nick of time.

'I'm sorry,' he stammered. 'I didn't expect— it's not one of her good days. You shouldn't bother. We can manage quite well, Mother and I. I'm something of a cook, if I say so myself.' With a flash of his rodent's teeth he was gone.

'I felt so embarrassed and frankly rather foolish,' Jane told her visitor.

He sat, cupping his empty mug between his palms and watching her intently.

'I hadn't meant to intrude,' she went on. 'Goodness, a nosy neighbour can make life miserable! I had no wish to interfere. But I thought, how dreadful for him. How awful to be shut in there all day long – and all night too – with someone in that state. Of course, it was clear to me he needed outside help, but he would refuse any offer. He was determined to look after her himself.

'You see . . .' Jane hesitated. 'I felt a sort of responsibility for them both. In one way it wasn't my business. But in another, if someone's in need, you don't ignore them, do you? Sooner or later, as I saw it, he was going to have to get some help, and the sooner, the better, for them both. I decided to leave it for a week and then call again.'

*   *   *

During the following week she saw nothing of Mr Warren. On Saturday afternoon, the sun shone so brightly after several overcast days, that Jane decided to go out for a walk. Her book, on which she'd been trying to work, had reached an awkward stage. She needed a break.

Returning to the cottage, she passed the Warrens' drive and, on impulse, turned in.

This time, she decided, she wouldn't knock at the front door. Obviously it wasn't in daily use and on the previous occasion, she'd disturbed the old lady. It was customary, in country areas, to use the back door. She'd forgotten that. She would make her way to the back of the house and tap discreetly at the kitchen door.

The rear of the property was as overgrown as the frontage. Here, years ago, had been a productive orchard, but now the trees – source of the apples he'd given her – were unpruned and grass grew high between them. A shrubbery close by the house had turned into a veritable jungle.

There was a window open near the back door and a movement on the other side of it caught her eye. It was Mr Warren but as she made to signal to him, he turned aside without seeing her and went back into the room, out of sight.

Jane went up to the window and peeped in. Her hand was raised to tap on the glass, but she stilled the gesture.

It was the kitchen all right, large, old fashioned and untidy. Mrs Warren was sitting in a rickety overstuffed armchair near an antiquated kitchen range. She wore the same dirty print dress but a different, though no cleaner, cardigan. Her face gleamed with sweat and her tangled hair clung to her shiny skin. Her large blue eyes were wide open and held such an expression of dread that Jane had to clap a hand to her own mouth to stifle a cry.

Warren himself leaned over his mother and held a glass of water or some other liquid to her mouth.

She shook her head, cowering back.

'Come on!' he ordered roughly. 'Get it down you!'

'I don't want it, Harold . . .' whimpered the old lady.

'You'll do as you're told. I've got to go into the village, right? I'm not having you wandering about while I'm gone.'

'I won't, Harold, I promise!'

He merely pressed the glass to her mouth. 'If you don't drink it,' he said, 'I won't give you any dinner tonight, nor tomorrow, nor even, perhaps, the day after.'

There was no doubt in Jane's mind that he meant it and that this punishment had been employed before. The tone of his voice was unlike anything she'd ever heard in any voice. It wasn't only threatening. It hummed with a barely concealed quiver of exultation, taking pleasure in the prospect of cruelty.

The woman believed it too. Jane watched as she gulped down the contents of the glass, some of it spilling and dribbling down her chin, spotting the print bodice.

Warren turned back towards the window. Jane just had time to duck down under the sill. She heard the sound of running water, the metallic groan of metal. The sink unit must be under this window. She waited for two or three minutes and when she ventured to take another look, she couldn't see Warren. Mrs Warren was in the chair, eyes closed. She was mumbling faintly to herself.

Jane ran back to the shrubbery and concealed herself amongst the bushes. After a while she heard the scrape of the garage door being pulled open and then the throb of an engine. Warren drove out, down the drive, and was gone. All was quiet.

Jane came out of hiding and hurried towards the house. The kitchen door was locked, but the window, thank goodness, was still ajar. She didn't know how long he'd be away in the village, but she wouldn't get another chance to get into the house.

She pulled the window wide open and scrambled up onto the sill.

'Mrs Warren? Don't be scared, please! It's only Jane, from the cottage . . .'

But Mrs Warren was slumped in the chair, apparently asleep.

Jane managed to get over the sink unit and drop down onto the floor. She hurried to the chair and its immobile occupant. Her nostrils were assailed by a sour odour, but she was prepared for it this time and not put off. Gently Jane shook the woman's shoulder but Mrs Warren slumbered on. So close up and in repose, she looked younger, her skin little lined. The grey hair, though dirty, grew thickly. Trimmed and clean it would be quite an asset. Jane frowned and tentatively touched one of the sleeper's eyelids, raising it.

'Drugged . . .' Jane muttered. She straightened up and turned. The glass still stood on the draining board and beside it was a small bottle such as pharmacists use when making up prescriptions. She picked it up. It contained a white, crystalline substance. Its label, which looked as if it had been stuck on some time ago, read 'Chloral Hydrate'.

So Warren had made up and forced his mother to drink an old-fashioned but undeniably effective sleeping draught. It seemed a drastic action. Prolonged use of chloral hydrate had depressive, debilitating effects. If the woman couldn't safely be left alone he had to do something, but this was out of all proportion to any need.

Jane moved across the kitchen and looked into the hall. It was as she'd seen it from the front door on her previous visit; dingy, the carpet worn. A clock ticked quietly, but not here – the sound came through the half-open door to a room on the other side of the hallway. Jane crossed the narrow passage and went in.

It seemed to be an all-purpose living room and study used by Warren. It was warmer and tidier in here than elsewhere in the house. The gas fire in the hearth must have been in use earlier. There were a few books, but not as many as his claim to be a dedicated reader might lead one to expect. There was, however, a large television set and an expensive computer. The other furniture comprised mostly solid, quite valuable pieces including a large Victorian roll-top desk. It was open, showing the ranked pigeonholes and flat writing surface. Warren must have been working on it before he found he had to go to the village. Jane could see that various papers were laid out neatly.

She ought not to be doing this, she knew. But in extreme circumstances, one could only take extreme action. Jane went to the desk and glanced quickly at the papers. They were bank statements and the amounts listed made her blink. A little family money? A lot of family money! But there was only one name printed at the top of each sheet: Harold Warren. Everything, then, was in the son's name.

A prickle ran up Jane's spine and what had been a growing suspicion hardened into chill certainty. But how to prove it? The bank statements didn't do that. If the old woman was senile, then naturally, control of all financial matters had to lie with the son. He probably had power of attorney.

But there were other papers stuffed into the pigeonholes and, with luck, one or more of them might provide more clear-cut evidence. She didn't know how long she had to work before Warren returned. Feverishly Jane pulled out a handful of assorted paperwork and began to riffle through it. Domestic bills for gas and electricity, others from a village garage for repairs to the car.

An envelope slipped from the middle of the bundle in her hand and fell to the ground, spilling its contents. Jane gave a gasp of dismay and knelt to gather them up.

They were photographs. She spread them on the carpet. They were a mixed bunch but here was one, not so very old, which showed a couple. The woman wore a smart two-piece outfit and a corsage of flowers. She was smiling happily at the camera. The man beside her also had a carnation pinned to the lapel of his suit. Small flecks of colour dotted the ground around the couple's feet. Confetti.

The young man in Jane's sitting room stirred. He put his mug carefully on the table. 'So,' he said. 'That's when you twigged what it was all about!'

'Yes, they were wedding pictures. The man was Warren and the woman – even given the awful state she was now in – was the same one he was passing off to me as his mother. But she wasn't his mother. She was his wife!'

'And that's when you contacted the police.' Detective Sergeant Sullivan smiled at long last. 'You acted in the nick of time to prevent a very nasty crime, Mrs Pritchard.'

'Yes, but I can't honestly say I understand all of it, even now. How was he going to work it?'

'Oh,' Sullivan made a wide gesture with his hands. 'It was simple enough. Clever crooks make simple plans. It's a mistake to make 'em too complicated. Warren worked on the assumption that most people believe what you tell them. After all, why should they disbelieve you? He told you she was his mother and you had no reason to suppose otherwise, or that she wasn't, as he claimed, in an advanced state of senility.

'He was a pharmacist in a seaside town when they met. Mrs Beryl Darcy, as she was at the time, was a widow. Her husband's death had left her financially comfortable but lonely. She had no family and, frankly, was in that holiday resort looking for companionship. She found it in Warren.

'He was some years younger than she was. But she'd looked after herself and could afford nice clothes. She didn't see why a younger man shouldn't find her attractive. They married. He probably started feeding her drugs little by little almost at once. She fell completely under his sway. He was able to get her to sign away money and property. Once she'd done that, it only remained for him to get rid of her.

'He bought a lonely house, moved her in, began to dose her regularly so that she didn't know half the time what was going on. He told anyone who enquired that she was his mother who never went out.

'If he'd said "wife", people might have been more curious, wondered why he didn't seek some help. But an elderly parent, well, people accepted a sad situation and that he was a devoted son. In due course, after a suitable time, he'd have told you that

19

she'd been taken into a nursing home and, shortly after that, he'd have reported she'd died. He'd probably have claimed her body had been taken for burial miles away – to her birthplace, perhaps. You would have believed it, why not?'

Jane shivered. Sullivan got up and went to the French window through which they could see Jane's garden and the hedge beyond which lay the tangled vegetation and trees of the Warrens' property.

'He probably intended to bury her out there in the grounds somewhere,' the sergeant said. 'Or under the cellar floor. Somewhere safe. Then, well? He might have just slipped away, gone abroad and started again. Or if he felt secure enough, even cleaned the place up and gone on living there.'

Sullivan glanced over his shoulder to where Jane sat, pale faced.

'You can be sure you prevented a murder, Mrs Pritchard. We got to Mrs Warren in the nick of time.'

'How is the poor woman now?' Jane whispered.

'Poorly but making a good recovery. She knows what happened and is most anxious to meet you properly and thank you.'

'I don't need thanks,' Jane said. 'But I will go and see her. I'm so glad she's all right. What – what will happen to him? I hope they lock him up and never let him out!'

DS Sullivan pulled a wry grimace. 'That's too much to hope for! He'll serve his sentence and then, who knows? Perhaps just disappear, never to be heard of again? But once a conman, always one. They nearly always return to their old tricks. He may decide he knows where he went wrong this time and, next time, aim to get it right!'

Sullivan gave Jane a shrewd look. 'Personally, I think that if he'd got away with it, he would have stayed here and looked about for another victim. There are plenty of women on their own, with a little money, living in quiet spots, lonely.'

His voice died away and he looked expressively around the room.

'You mean,' Jane said dully, 'that the murder I prevented may ultimately have been my own!'

'You're smarter than poor Beryl Darcy Warren,' her visitor assured her kindly. 'But probably, yes, he intended you to be next.'

Sergeant Sullivan returned his gaze to the view from the windows and gave an appreciative nod. 'Yes, you've got a very nice garden here, Mrs Pritchard. Very nice little place altogether, in fact. Don't worry about being here on your own.' He turned back and smiled at her. He was a good-looking young man. 'We'll keep an eye on you!'

'Huh!' thought Jane. She scooped up the empty mugs and marched out into the kitchen.

Everything a Lady Should Know, Grandma's old book, had done its best but it had left out the most important rule of all:

LADY, WATCH OUT!

A Rare Fino

A gentleman, naturally, does not discuss money. That is not to say that, though indisputably a gentleman myself, I don't *think* about money. Prior to the unfortunate events I am about to relate, I'd been thinking about money a great deal. It was very distressing.

I should explain. For some years I had been working on my book: *The Fauna and Flora of the Iberian Peninsula*. I was and remain convinced that when my book is finished and published it will become the indispensable work of reference on the subject.

Originally I dedicated my work to the famous naturalist, Charles Darwin. I even visited the great man shortly before his death in 1882. I travelled down to his family home and gained entry with the greatest difficulty and by insisting that my research was of paramount importance. (I had prudently taken a copy of the manuscript with me to present to Darwin. I was sure he would appreciate that.)

I have to say I was bitterly disappointed in the great scientist. I realise he was old and sick at the time, but I found his manner abrupt almost to the point of being uncivil. I gave him my manuscript. Instead of expressing pleasure, he just said he would 'glance at it if he had time'. He tossed it to one side quite negligently and asked if I wanted anything else. Why yes, I declared, I wished his permission to dedicate the book to him.

'Oh well,' he said, 'if you like. It makes no difference to me. I'm not going to be here when it's published.' He then added, '*If it is published!*'

I went home and struck out the dedication. It is my personal opinion he was jealous of my scholarship.

Naturally, I had had to visit Spain and Portugal often and spend some time there in the course of my research. This had cost money: all my money, in fact. The last of my personal fortune had been spent in this cause some years ago. Since that time I had depended on an allowance paid to me by my aunt Matilda.

My aunt (my late father's elder sister) was a wealthy and childless widow. She lived alone in a large house in Chertsey in Surrey with an elderly cook and maid. There was also a gardener but he must have been seventy if he was a day. Her only companion (excluding the servants) was her pet dachshund, by the name of Oscar.

Oscar wasn't a young dog. His muzzle was quite grey. He was overweight and bad tempered. People talk of a mule or a camel being the most obstinate of beasts. Such people have never had to deal with an elderly dachshund. If Oscar chose to take possession of a comfortable armchair, it was best to leave him there. His teeth were yellow with age but sharp.

As for my aunt, they say people grow to resemble their pets and she had certain characteristics in common with Oscar. She too was elderly (but robust and in good health), stout, rather short in the leg, and very short in temper. Both she and Oscar had a sharp nose and beady eyes.

I had to work very hard to keep on the right side of Aunt Matilda. She could stop my allowance at any moment and if that stopped, my work must be forced to stop too. It didn't bear thinking of. What's more, there was the question of her will.

Now, I had reason to hope that she would leave the lot to me. I had two cousins, it was true, but they were girls and had married, so no longer bore the family name. Only I carried that into the next generation and Aunt Matilda had remarked on it several times.

Not that the cousins had given up hope, oh no! Those women were always visiting her, taking along their awful children, and showering her with little attentions. They particularly chose to do this when I was away studying my subject in Spain or Portugal. I was sure they took the opportunity to undermine me and damage my own chances.

What's more, both cousins had chosen to name their very plain daughters after my aunt (although to my mind, three Matildas in one family make far too many).

Now, Aunt Matilda had one little weakness (if you don't count doting on that wretched dog). She loved a glass of good sherry. As it happened, my research took me to the beautiful region of Spain around Jerez, a name synonymous with that famous aperitif. It is a wonderful part of the world.

This is the Spain of one's dreams. By day one travels through a landscape of castles, great mansions, white-washed villages, and ranches where the bulls for the arena are bred. At night one may relax beneath the stars enjoying the warm, balmy air, the tinkling of guitars in one's ears and in one's hand a glass of that drink akin to the nectar of the gods. For this is the birthplace of sherry. It is a wine which, like the women of the region, has beauty, dignity and grace. It enchants the eye, seduces the nose and the taste is one to be savoured slowly. Roll it around your tongue. Close your eyes and give yourself over to an experience almost erotic in its physical charm.

You should know that the very best sherry comes from grapes grown on chalky soil. The more sandy soils produce an inferior wine. But the truly great fino, ah, that is something so special and so rare that bottles of it are guarded as fiercely as any part of the national heritage of that country, and seldom leave it. However, on my last visit I had been able, in Sanlúcar de Barrameda, to obtain a bottle of this unique creation. A triumph!

I took it home to England and down to Chertsey to present it to Aunt Matilda. I imagined her delight, the excellent impression my thoughtfulness would make. I even considered the real possibility that she might contact her lawyer at once to make me her sole heir.

I found her thoughtful. She greeted me with less enthusiasm than I had hoped. No matter. I produced the bottle of rare fino, confident that would change her mood.

'Thank you, Charles,' she said. 'Just put it on the sideboard.'

This wasn't the reaction I had expected or counted on!

'My dear aunt,' I said, 'could it be that you have something on your mind? Are you not feeling quite well? If that's the case, I recommend a glass of that excellent fino I have just given you. That will buck you up in no time.'

'As a matter of fact,' replied my aunt, 'I do have something on my mind. Just take a look at Oscar, will you? Tell me what you think?'

I turned my gaze unwillingly on the dachshund which sat beside my aunt on the sofa. I stared at him. He stared back at me. I hid my dislike of him. He did not hide his dislike, even contempt, of me.

'He seems much as usual,' I said.

This was true. He hadn't improved. He might have been a trifle fatter, but perhaps it wouldn't do to mention that.

My aunt sighed. 'He's not himself. He's really quite listless. I had the veterinary surgeon call to look at him but he could find nothing wrong. He was tactless enough to mention Oscar's age. I told him, very plainly, I saw no reason why age should affect an animal so well cared for. I shall not engage that man's services again. Yet I do fear there is something wrong with Oscar.'

She stroked the animal's head. Oscar rolled his eyes up at her.

'He is so intelligent,' crooned my aunt. 'He understands every word we say.'

It was difficult to know how to reply. I daren't make the same mistake as the veterinary and mention age: especially as my aunt herself was no longer young.

'Well,' I said, 'you know, dear aunt, that we all of us from time to time suffer short periods of poor spirits and a general feeling of being "down". This doesn't have to mean illness. It is more likely to be the time of year; winter's short days and long hours of darkness, for example. Or a week's bad weather that's kept us indoors and prevented healthy exercise. Oscar just needs a little encouragement and perhaps a tonic designed for dogs. In no time he'll be as right as rain.'

Oscar gave me a look I can only describe as sarcastic. Perhaps he did understand not only every word we said, but also much left unsaid.

My aunt cheered up at once. 'How kind you are, Charles,' she said. 'Thank you for your advice – oh, and thank you for the sherry. It is very good of you to remember I like it.'

I left Chertsey well pleased.

The following week I went down there again. I found my aunt much improved in spirits, quite cheerful. I glanced at the sideboard. The bottle of fino was still there but much depleted. There was only a glass or two left in it. In my imagination, I patted myself on the back.

'It is very nice to see you again, Charles,' said Aunt Matilda.

Better and better!

'I'm very pleased to see you so much happier than the last time I came,' I said. 'Does this mean Oscar is improved?'

I looked at Oscar. He had a curious expression in his eyes. He, too, looked quite mellow but his gaze seemed a little hazy.

'Oh, he's so much better!' replied my aunt enthusiastically. 'And I have you to thank for it, Charles.'

'Me?' I was startled.

'Why, yes, I took your advice.'

I hesitated. 'Er, what advice was that, aunt?'

'About giving Oscar a tonic. That was all he needed to make him quite his old self.' She turned and indicated the sideboard. 'I have been adding a drop or two of that fino you brought me to his food. It's done him no end of good. His temper is much improved and he sleeps like a top!'

For a moment or two it seemed the world stopped. I couldn't believe what I'd heard. Surely I was imagining it? The fino, which I'd brought back from Spain with such delight and presented to Aunt Matilda with such high hopes . . . it had been fed to *a dachshund*? It wasn't possible. But oh, yes, it was. I looked at Oscar again, his hazy expression and unwarranted mellowness . . . the dog was drunk!

My ears filled with a roaring. My brain seemed to explode. Was everything I thought of value and gave to a chosen recipient with hope, to be scorned in this way? Darwin had cast aside my cherished manuscript, openly doubted its fitness to be published. This stupid old woman had treated a rare and great wine as though it were a tonic for dogs! Was the world full of Philistines?

I heard myself ask, through gritted teeth, 'Have you drunk *any* of it yourself?'

She shook her head. 'I saved it for dear Oscar.'

The injustice of it all was too much; the insult to me, to my work and to a great wine, the denigration of all my efforts . . .

In a red rage, I rushed to the sideboard and seized the bottle. I splashed half of what little was left into one of the glasses on a tray there and carried it back to Aunt Matilda.

'Drink it!' I ordered.

She looked alarmed. I must have seemed quite wild. I *was* wild.

'But what about Oscar . . .?' she began.

I didn't allow her to finish. I bent over her. I grasped her jaw and forced her mouth open. 'Drink it!' I screamed at her. I poured the glassful of fino, all of it, between her lips as she struggled and gasped, protesting in a panic.

To give him his due, Oscar tried to protect his mistress. He leapt at me, but his general lack of fitness, his weight and his recent diet of sherry all overcame him. He fell off the sofa and landed heavily on the carpet where he lay, glaring at me impotently.

To prevent the wine dribbling out again, I threw the glass aside, clamped Aunt Matilda's mouth shut with both my hands and repeated my order to her to swallow it.

Still she struggled and then a strange sound came from her throat. Her eyes bulged. She pawed feebly at my hand.

Too late I realised she was choking. I snatched back my hands and tried to revive her but it was too late. Suddenly she was still and I knew she was dead. Her eyes stared up at me in a horrid way with no life in them.

I knew I must not lose my head. I went to the sideboard and poured the last drops of the sherry into a fresh glass. I raised it to my lips and tasted it. Ah! If only for a moment this wine would be savoured by someone who appreciated it.

Oscar watched me all the while, growling in his throat. I took my glass to the little table near to the sofa and set it down. Then I ruffled my hair and ran into the hall shouting for the maid.

'Help! Help! My aunt is ill. Run for the doctor!'

The doctor came quickly but was far too late. I told him my aunt and I had been enjoying a glass of the rare fino I had brought on my last visit when the choking fit overcame her. I indicated my own glass on the table and Aunt Matilda's which had fallen to the carpet. Oscar was sniffing at it with appreciation and trying to lick out the remaining dregs.

I was afraid the doctor would notice the red marks on my aunt's jaw so I offered the explanation that I had tried to save her by opening the airways but it had been in vain. I tore at my hair and clothing. I wailed.

The doctor was sympathetic and patted my arm. 'My dear young man, you are distressed but don't blame yourself! These sad accidents happen so suddenly that unless a medical man is present little can be done. No layman could have saved your aunt.'

The inquest returned a verdict of accidental death. After the funeral my cousins, their husbands and I gathered to hear the lawyer read the will. My aunt had left a paltry three hundred pounds each to my cousins, myself and the two juvenile Matildas.

Three hundred pounds! Was that all? And the same amount to *me*, who carried the family name, as to those two women and their frightful daughters? Even from beyond the grave, Aunt Matilda managed to insult me.

So what happened to the large house in Chertsey and the rest of the money? Would you believe it? My aunt had set up a trust of which the sole beneficiary was Oscar. Oscar, in short, inherited the lot. The trust stipulated that he was to continue to live in the Chertsey house. The cook, maid and gardener would retain their jobs in order to maintain the place and look after the dog. Only when Oscar died would everything be sold up and all the resulting fortune was to be distributed to various animal charities.

It was in the interest of the servants that Oscar lived on for a long as possible. They kept their sinecure jobs while he did. At last, two years later, despite their valiant efforts, Oscar passed away. The veterinary surgeon who examined the body declared he must have been very old, really quite ancient in canine terms.

Oscar had been a lucky dog indeed. Perhaps, after all, the tonic of rare fino had done the trick.

A Trick of the Light

Part One

The frogman was sitting alone, perched uncomfortably on a crumbling wooden stump, once a support for a long-vanished jetty. He was without mask or flippers and had pushed back the hood of his wetsuit. His head was buried in his hands and Hetty Farrell could see only a mop of dishevelled brown hair. The rest of him resembled some stranded and unknown species of amphibian.

She'd just parked her own car alongside the large white van marked *Underwater Search and Rescue* which stood behind them, concealed by a straggly line of trees. However, the frogman wasn't an official police diver, part of the team which had arrived in the van. He was clearly an amateur and excluded from the work in progress at the lakeside.

'I suppose,' she mused with sympathy, 'he's the poor chap who found the body.'

All around them a hive of activity provided stark contrast to his brooding form. A police powerboat, moored at the far end of a narrow, wooden-slatted walkway, was lurching on the water as figures scrambled in and out. A couple of uniformed minions of the Cumbria Constabulary, brought in to control civilians, were parrying questions good humouredly as they chivvied people away from the landing stage. The crowd of would-be boat-trippers, whose excursion had been unexpectedly postponed, chatted, speculated and fiddled with cameras.

At the back of the throng, perched on a natural rise in the ground, the tall, thin form of Bradley Wills stared majestically towards the shining waters of the lake. His lordly gaze took in both the activities of the search team and the sheer slopes of the fells on the far side of Coniston Water. His chin held high and his hands clasped behind his back, he was the personification of aloofness.

The excited onlookers observed him from afar in awe and speculated wildly as to his rank. Some optimistically put it as chief constable and one, losing all sense of proportion, as lord lieutenant of the county. Others had got it right and guessed inspector.

None of them looked at the slender but athletically trim young woman in cord jeans, strong walking boots, thick socks and a pullover, who was striding their way, her bobbed brown hair bouncing about her ears. Just another hiker, they thought, if they thought anything at all.

She had nearly reached Bradley Wills on his hummock and had to suppress a grin. Irresistably, into her head, jumped Cowper's lines:

> *I am monarch of all I survey,*
> *My right there is none to dispute . . .*

Nevertheless, she was well aware that however unheeding the inspector might appear of the crowd, he would be extremely irritated by it. Bradley Wills had a notoriously short temper. At the moment he was freezing out the annoyance. His armour of indifference was likely to be pierced without warning and then Wills's temper would erupt to the discomfiture of all around.

Hetty approached his imposing figure with some caution and cleared her throat deferentially. 'Good morning, sir.'

The inspector unbent so far as to incline his head without actually turning it in her direction.

'Farrell,' he said, apparently to the world at large.

'Yes, sir. I came as soon as I could. Any progress?'

Wills took one arm from behind his back and consulted a large and expensive-looking wristwatch. 'They've been down there long enough.'

A testy note sounded in his voice. At the same time he observed that one of the camera enthusiasts had had the temerity to snap him. That he'd been added to anyone's souvenirs of a holiday in the Lake District proved the straw to break the camel's back.

The inspector's face turned dull red, the muscles around his mouth and jaw twitched alarmingly, he flung out a pointing finger and roared, 'Tell that wretched fellow to stop that at once! I'll impound his camera if he so much as takes another picture, even if it's only of his wife and kids!'

The photographer staggered back in shock, almost dropping his apparatus. One of the uniformed men moved across with alacrity but the photographer had scuttled away before he got there.

There was a shout from the waterline. Another police motorcraft had arrived. A black-clad figure clambered out onto the narrow wooden jetty and pounded along it towards the shore. Shimmering drops of water flew through the air and the wooden slats shivered and creaked ominously beneath his feet. The sense of expectancy amongst the crowd was almost tangible. But out of his watery element, the nearing diver ceased to look formidable, only cumbersome and slightly ridiculous. Nevertheless, the crowd of onlookers parted respectfully before him and much whispering followed in his wake.

The diver lumbered across the stony shore towards Inspector Wills on his hummock, who watched his approach with a jaundiced eye and in silence. The man panted to a halt and gave his report.

'Something down there all right, sir. Can't tell what it is, to be honest. It's rolled up in a big sheet of plastic, tied together with rope and weighted down with some kind of large stone object.'

'Which area of the lake exactly?' Hetty asked. 'I've only just got here. I didn't see where you were searching.'

The diver met her eye and, not impervious to a pretty girl in any circumstances, even the potentially grisly, grinned. He turned and pointed down the long narrow lake. 'Out there, just about where Coniston Old Man overlooks the water.'

Hetty knew the ridge he referred to, so called because someone's fancy had once imagined it resembled a sleeping man lying on his back.

The diver's grin hadn't passed unnoticed by Wills. 'What about the hand?' he snarled.

The diver looked suitably abashed. 'Couldn't be sure, sir. There is something sticking out. Might be part of a hand.'

'Can you get the whole bundle out of the water without further equipment?'

'Should think so, sir.'

'Then do so!' Wills ordered.

The frogman padded heavily back to rejoin the other members of his team. Inspector Wills at last deigned to descend from his hummock and turn his pale gaze on his subordinate.

'Nice day, Farrell,' he said. 'I was hoping to go fishing.' He observed her practical clothing. 'You, I take it, were going walking?' He didn't wait for her reply but looked, if anything, more morose. 'I suppose you could call this fishing, of a sort.'

Activity at the water's edge had increased and the powerboat roared away, leaving twin foaming peaks in its wake.

Hetty did her best to appear as coldly professional as the inspector, but it wasn't the sort of incident she relished. People – divers, fishermen, yachting and wind-surfing enthusiasts – did find things in the lakes from time to time. Sometimes these finds were harmless in themselves, just simply oughtn't to have been jettisoned where they'd been. But just occasionally, the find proved more sinister.

A man in a state of some agitation had phoned the police earlier that morning to report that he'd sighted a strange object on the lakebed.

'I think,' he'd gasped, 'it might be a body!'

So here they all were, underwater search team, CID, uniformed officers, all milling about on this beautiful morning, oblivious of the wonderful scenery. That it was a Saturday, and that both she and Inspector Wills had been called upon by staff shortages to give up their free weekends, more than justified the inspector's bad mood. She didn't feel too happy about it herself.

'It might be a body,' returned Wills cynically, echoing her thoughts. 'Or it might be an old standard lamp or someone's garden rubbish. Don't ask me why they insist on putting these things in the lakes. One would have thought the trouble it took to dump their garbage outweighed any other consideration. They do it to be awkward, if you ask me.'

Hetty nodded sympathetically. 'Who found it?'

Wills sighed and pointed across the shore to the crouched figure of the lone frogman, confirming her earlier guess. 'That fellow, name of Woodley. You'd better go and get his story. And believe me, when we get it out here on land, whatever it is, it had better be worth all this trouble and my cancelled fishing trip!'

He set off purposefully towards the jetty.

Hetty returned to her car and took out the Thermos flask without which she never set out into the spectacular but lonely terrain around them. She carried it back to the shore and approached the figure that still crouched like Rodin's celebrated statue, lost in his own thoughts.

'Mr Woodley?' Hetty stooped over him. 'Would you care for a cup of tea?'

He looked up. He was a youngish man, she judged him in his early thirties, with blunt but not unattractive features. His face was rather red, perhaps from emotion and possibly from the change in temperature. Down on the lake floor where he'd been earlier, it had been very cold indeed. For a moment his eyes stared at her unseeingly, then an expression crossed his face not unlike that of Inspector Wills when he'd spied the photographer.

'Who are you?' he said aggressively. 'Journalist? Local rag? Look, just clear off, will you? I can't be bothered now.'

'Sergeant Farrell,' she told him. 'Cumbria CID.'

He groaned and returned his head to his hands. From within his fingers he mumbled, 'That just about takes the biscuit! Some woman asking damfool questions!'

She was allowing for the fact that he was probably still in shock, but there was a limit. It was true that in rural areas especially, a young woman in her job still occasioned comment. But nowadays it was mostly good humoured and actual hostility towards her had been rare. That it should appear now from this man, a young man at that, both startled and annoyed her. On a less personal level, she noted that his wasn't a local voice. At this time of year, tail end of summer, visitors flocked to the whole Lake District from every part of Britain and indeed, from overseas as well. So the fact needn't be significant.

'If you're the member of the public who reported finding a suspicious object on the lake floor, then you must have expected some questions, Mr Woodley! Are you saying you don't feel you can cope with them just now?' Hetty smiled at him sympathetically, but with a combative glint in her grey eyes.

Perhaps used to being in charge of situations, rather than being organised in any way by others, he reacted as she'd expected.

He removed his hands from his face and squinted up at her. Hetty suspected he was well aware that she'd deliberately made his cooperation a matter of masculine honour. He'd no wish to appear a weakling.

He sat up. 'I'll answer anything you want to ask. Did you say you had some tea?'

Hetty poured out the tea and handed him the steaming beaker. As he sipped it, she took a look at his hands. Well shaped, strong, nicely manicured. She categorised him as senior management or something financial. Outdoor enthusiast he might be, but one who spent his working life indoors and in some comfort.

'Not that there's much I can tell you.' He'd already regained composure and spoke in a clipped, decided way. He'd been genuinely in shock, but he'd recovered. Since he'd had a bad experience down there on the lake floor, Hetty gave him credit for his resilience.

'Tell me who you are and how you came to be diving here today?' she suggested. She sat down on the thin dry turf, fished out her notebook and rested her arms on her bent knees.

He gave a short laugh. 'They say it's a bad sign when policemen start looking younger. I don't know what it means when they start looking prettier!'

Her smile must have frozen because he added, 'All right, all right! Don't glare like that! I'm not being sexist, just tactless.' He managed a wry grin. 'You're not going to charge me with anything, are you? You look as though you're about to read me my rights.'

'With wasting my time, if you go on like this, Mr Woodley.' She smiled as she said it, but her tone let him know she wasn't prepared to put up with any more nonsense along these lines.

He hunched his shoulders, recognising it. 'My name's Ned Woodley. I've a dreary job in London. Given the slightest opportunity I get away from it all, as they say. My godfather lives around here. His name is Felix Crowe. I'm staying with him.'

He pointed behind them down the lake shoreline. 'His house is called Stoney How. You can't see it from here, but if you're out on the water, you can just glimpse the chimneys.'

'I know it,' Hetty exclaimed. 'Or rather, I know of it! It's a statesman's house. I've never been inside it.'

The term, as used in the Lake District, had nothing to do with diplomacy. In former times, a statesman had been a prosperous farmer of considerable importance in the local community. Some of the rambling houses in which the statesman and his extended family would have lived had survived and were of considerable historical interest. Actually to own and live in one . . . Hetty thought of Woodley's godfather with a mix of respect and envy.

'Come over and visit any time,' Ned offered, adding with another wry grimace, 'although I suppose I shall have more coppers on my doorstep, or on my godfather's doorstep, than I need after this!'

'You may find me!' Hetty told him impetuously. 'I'm not one to turn down an invitation to see inside Stoney How!' She recalled that she was supposed to be getting Ned's story from him. She scribbled down everything he'd said so far. 'Can I have your home phone number? Also details of your firm in London?'

'Why should you need that?' He looked startled.

'We may need to contact you again after you've left the district.'

'I see.' He still looked uneasy but reached towards a canvas grip on the ground nearby. 'One of those uniformed coppers fetched this from my car for me. I've got a pile of stuff here, I think there might be the odd business card amongst it.'

The sort of man who, even on an outdoor activities weekend, carried his business card with him. He wasn't to be aware of it, but he had suddenly called up a host of old memories for her.

There'd been a time when she, too, had been a city office-worker, an ambitious high-flyer like many others. Then, one morning, crushed into a commuter train, running late and with the prospect of many such mornings ahead of her, she'd realised this wasn't how she wanted to spend her life. At that point she'd broken out and joined the police. Consternation amongst family, friends and business colleagues had been considerable. Not to mention the teasing, of course. The comic farewell cards depicting red-nosed bobbies. The party at which an improvised office choir had sung 'A policeman's lot is not a happy one' . . .

But her lot, against all the odds, had been a happy one. Although days like today, when grim reality intruded, could cast a blight on things.

'Card,' said Ned Woodley, handing her a small buff-coloured rectangle and recalling her abruptly to the present.

'Thank you.' She took it and read that he worked for a firm of insurers. Perhaps it was as dreary as he claimed. She tucked the card into her pocket. 'Right, so you came here to do some diving? That's your hobby?'

He nodded. 'Yes, I was just fooling around, trying out some new gear. I came across a sort of trough in the floor of the lake. I went down out of curiosity and found more than I bargained for!' Ned swallowed the last of the tea. 'Any more of this, by any chance?' He sounded more human. Perhaps a residue of the shock lingered, after all.

She refilled his beaker. 'Go on.' He must be a good and experienced diver, she thought. Certainly very fit. She eyed him surreptitiously again and revised her earlier opinion. No one tied to a desk five days a week could keep that fit without considerable effort. She was beginning to wonder about Mr Woodley.

'I saw the stone first,' he was saying. 'It looked unusual, not a rock, but a carved affair. That was strange enough. I thought at first it must be a trick of the light. Then, that I'd stumbled on some archaeological wonder! I took a closer look and saw that it was lashed to a big plastic-wrapped bundle, obviously as a weight. I started to get a bad feeling about it at that point. I might just have chickened out and swum off and left the thing, to be honest. But then I saw the hand . . .'

He put down the beaker with an over-precise gesture. 'It was sticking out of a tear in the plastic.'

It took an hour and a half to get the object up from the lakebed and another forty minutes to get it ashore. The crowd had been dispersed by now and fluttering blue and white police tape cordoned off the lakeside area preventing access by unauthorised persons.

The thing lay on the shingle, untidily shaped, long and narrow, wrapped in gleaming wet black plastic and secured top and bottom with rope, rather like a Christmas cracker. One end had been lashed to the 'stone' which, on being brought ashore, turned out, surprisingly, to be an ornamental urn of the sort put in formal gardens.

They'd all gathered round it. Ned Woodley had regained his composure and changed out of his wetsuit into jeans and a sweat-shirt from his canvas bag. He looked younger, perhaps no more than twenty-nine. He was also much nicer looking. That, thought Hetty crossly, was of no importance. This was a police matter, and a serious matter at that.

'There!' Ned exclaimed, pointing.

They all looked. Through a tear in the black plastic, what looked remarkably like fingertips protruded. A silence fell on the group. Hetty braced herself for an unpleasant experience.

A car horn broke the silence with a raucous blast. It announced a tweed-suited newcomer who hurried down the shore towards them, carrying a black case.

'Got here in time?' he demanded in a marked Scots accent as he came up to them. 'Good day to you, Wills! That it?' He nodded at the thing on the ground.

'Who's this?' Ned whispered to Hetty.

'Dr Harris, come to certify – er – you know, that's it's dead – if it's what it might be in that package.' She rallied and went on sternly, 'Routine!'

'But hardly necessary!' said Ned unkindly. 'After a spell down there tied to a stone vase, it's not going to come up dancing the hornpipe!'

'We always try,' she reproved him, 'to show some respect in these circumstances!'

He had the grace to look chastened.

'Let's have a look then!' Bradley Wills decreed, taking charge.

The ropes were removed and the plastic wrapping unfurled. Water ran out in rivulets around their feet. There was a lot of mud and some small stones. Amongst it a body lay revealed to their assembled gaze. No one spoke.

Dr Harris leaned gravely over the recumbent form. 'I see.' His Scots burr became more pronounced. 'And this is what I've come here at great inconvenience to give my medical opinion on, is it? To say nothing of breaking the speed limit to get here?'

He tapped the body on the chest. 'I would give as my professional opinion that it's made of plastic and is some kind of tailor's dummy. Probably last seen in a shop window, modelling the latest in menswear! I suppose you could say it was dead. It has certainly never been alive!'

There was another silence. Bradley Wills raised bloodshot eyes and fixed them on Ned Woodley. When he spoke his voice was very quiet but no one could miss a syllable.

'Is this, by any chance, someone's idea of a joke?'

'I didn't know, how could I?' Ned Woodley protested for the fifth or sixth time. 'The light's very poor at that depth. I had an underwater flashlight but it's not the same. The water and the murk deceive. The bundle was lashed to that stone vase. I saw the fingers poking out and had no reason to suppose it wasn't a body. I wasn't going to mess about with it making sure! I did what anyone would do. I swam off at a speed which ought to qualify me for the next Olympics! I came ashore and phoned the police, as a good citizen should do. What would you expect?'

'Yes, yes, Mr Woodley,' said Inspector Wills. He held Woodley's business card between his fingers and was tapping the corner of it irritably on his desk. 'I don't think we need trouble you any further today.'

'I can go home, then?'

'If you've signed a statement, Mr Woodley. See the gentleman off the premises, Sergeant, would you?'

Hetty and Ned Woodley descended the staircase in silence and made their way to the car park where Ned's Range Rover stood.

'Don't feel bad about it,' she advised. 'You did all the right things.'

'I feel a fool!' he growled.

'Come on! You were right and it was a body – just not a real one. Let's face it, we don't really want to find a dead body in that or any lake! Today's efforts cost money and manpower, but it was just one of those things.'

He was looking at her as she spoke, still scowling. 'That's what you say now. Once I've gone, you'll go back in there and join the others, falling about laughing at me!'

'Believe me,' Hetty told him, 'Inspector Wills has never been observed falling about laughing. He's been known to raise a weak smile at Christmas.'

There was a pause, then Ned gave a husky and decidedly attractive chuckle. 'Thanks for being so decent about it. If you're still interested in seeing Stoney How, come by the house sometime this week. I shall be here until Friday.'

'On a proper holiday?' She was surprised. 'I got the impression you were just weekending.'

He looked slightly embarrassed. 'I had some days owing to me, you know how it is.'

'I lost my weekend,' she said with a sigh.

He was plunged back into consternation. 'Then it was my fault. You must come out to Stoney How tomorrow! Come to lunch!'

She was tempted, and a little surprised he'd remembered the interest she'd expressed.

'What about your godfather? Will he mind you inviting stray police personnel to sit at his table?' Hetty asked dubiously.

'He'll be delighted.' Ned was glancing around the car park. 'Er, where is it now?'

'Where is what?'

'That thing, that dummy and the stone vase.'

'I'm not sure. Stuck at the back of a police garage, I shouldn't be surprised. We'll try and find where it came from. We really

44

feel quite strongly about people dumping their rubbish in the countryside or in our lakes.'

Casually Ned said, 'If you do find out where it came from, could you let me know? I mean, after the fright I had, and all the trouble it caused us all, I'd like to know.'

Hetty considered this. 'I suppose so. But it's highly unlikely we will find out.'

He hesitated then smiled. 'Fine, see you tomorrow!'

Hetty watched the Range Rover drive out of the police yard. A faint frown crossed her forehead as the vehicle disappeared from sight and she pushed back a rebellious lock of brown hair.

Inspector Wills turned from the window as she re-entered his office. 'Off back to London, is he?' His tone indicated Ned hadn't been forgiven for depriving Bradley of his fishing trip.

'Staying a few more days, I think.' She hesitated and decided not to mention the invitation to lunch at Stoney How.

It turned out she'd been wise. Inspector Wills's thin lips twisted in a silent snarl. 'I still don't trust that young man! Might have done it for a bet!'

'Oh, come on—' Hetty began.

'Look into it, sergeant!'

'Yessir!' Hetty picked up Woodley's business card from the desk and retired from the august presence to the outer office.

There she asked, 'Anyone know where that dummy and the urn were stored?'

A short time later, she was in a garage workshop, as she'd guessed. She stared down at the dummy that was laid out on a trestle table.

The urn stood on the floor alongside it. The plastic sheeting which had shrouded the mannequin was folded nearby and the ropes coiled neatly. At some point between revelation at the lakeside and being left ignominiously here, the dummy had acquired the name of 'George'. No one seemed to know who'd bestowed it, but George their aquatic friend now was.

Hetty peered at it. It was lifesize and had artificial but realistic hair and soft eyelashes. She touched them. The limbs could be dismantled and were jointed so that George could be posed fetchingly in a shop window. The surface wasn't shiny and obviously plastic, but made of some sophisticated skin-coloured material with a matt finish. George was even clothed modestly in cheap cotton underwear.

'Going to take its fingerprints, sarge?' asked a passing police driver facetiously.

Hetty ignored him. 'Right, George!' she addressed the dummy. 'If you'll excuse the liberty . . .'

But there was no maker's label on the underwear, which could have led immediately to a particular chain store. George himself, according to a stamp on the back of his neck, hailed from Korea. But again, no manufacturer claimed him by name.

Hetty sighed. The dummy wasn't cheap. A thing like that must cost a lot of money. Only the better stores would have it in their windows. She couldn't imagine any small town shop having such a thing. If they did, they'd take good care of it. She didn't fancy spending unlimited time going from store to store in the surrounding larger towns. If stolen, she hoped the theft had been reported.

But why on earth should anyone throw it in the lake? Hetty glared at the dummy in dissatisfaction. Other than for a prank or a bet? Surely, if that were the case, the culprit wouldn't have bothered lashing it to the stone vase? A joke wasn't a joke if no one knew of it and a bundle on the lakebed stood little chance of being found. It was pure luck that Ned had happened upon it. She didn't believe, no matter what Bradley Wills suspected, that Ned himself would have gone to so much trouble to pull a silly stunt.

She turned her attention to the urn. It was ornate and intricately patterned, also costing a fair bit of money. Expensive garden ornaments weren't infrequently stolen and the urn's loss might have been reported.

Hetty spent the remainder of Saturday afternoon checking through reports of stolen garden furniture and ornaments. Apart from the fact that they seemed to have an active gnome-napper in the district, she drew a blank. With the help of Yellow Pages, she rang the larger stores in the surrounding towns. Most didn't take kindly to being bothered late on Saturday with a query about a missing mannequin and none had lost one.

'Time to go home!' she told herself.

In the corridor, she passed Inspector Wills, also homeward bound.

'I hope,' he announced, 'that at least my Sunday won't be disturbed! I'm planning some gardening. I'm digging out a fishpond!'

He proceeded on his way, unaware that his sergeant had stopped in her tracks.

The heavy-duty black plastic sheeting which had wrapped the dummy was the sort often used to line garden pools! That and the urn together suggested a garden centre.

'Now why didn't I think of that first?' she asked herself.

* * *

Sunday morning saw Hetty out bright and early. It was a beautiful day, the air clean and crisp. All around her, as she drove along, rose the fells, majestic and wild. From time to time the road ran through small wooded areas, but the steep slopes themselves were bare, grassy at the base and soon turning, as they rose, to sweeps of dry brown bracken and outcrops of rock and shale. Black-faced, long-tailed sheep watched her pass. Otherwise she saw only walkers and cyclists. She'd made a list of nearby garden centres the previous evening and was on her way to the biggest.

Garden centres do a lot of business on Sundays, Hetty realised with some dismay. The car park was full. Whole families with children were here. Some people pushed wire trolleys provided by the centre and were obviously intent on filling them with every kind of garden plant and accessory. It wasn't a morning to pester busy assistants with her queries.

Hetty made her way first to garden statuary. There were stone bird-tables and bird-baths. Greek goddesses nestled against plump cherubs. There were graceful lead herons. There were square, round, Grecian and rococco vases and pots. All, Hetty noted from the labels, were expensive but none exactly resembled the urn dredged from the lake. If you couldn't afford these items, there was a cheaper line in plastic, some of it looking remarkably like the stone version. And there, picking his way through it all like a wading bird, was Bradley Wills in a check cap, pullover, body-warmer and disreputable corduroys.

Hetty saw the inspector just in time and scurried away to another area. She found the plastic sheeting in huge rolls and enquired about recent sales. They sold a lot of it, she was told. It would be almost impossible to track down a particular sale unless there had been something unusual about it, an extra-large quantity for example. The assistant was restive and had to be persuaded to chat by being shown Hetty's official identification. He then became defensive and wanted to know if this was going to mean hunting through tillrolls and credit chits. Nothing that had happened warranted such drastic action and Hetty reassured him.

Time was getting on and she had to get to Stoney How by twelve thirty. She retreated towards the exit.

'Farrell? I didn't know you had an interest in gardening?'

Her heart sank. There by the till was Bradley Wills again, a garishly coloured plastic heron tucked beneath his arm. He placed the bird on the counter and stood beside it. The resemblance was uncanny.

Hetty swallowed, 'Not really. I – er –' Wills had made it clear he hadn't wanted his Sunday disturbed by official matters. On a stand nearby was a display of cyclamen plants. Hetty grabbed one. 'I've been invited out to lunch and thought I'd better take a little gift.'

'A cyclamen?' Wills nodded approval. 'Very suitable.'

Stoney How lay at the end of a lane, turning off the main road. It was a broad lane, unsurfaced except for a layer of deeply embedded stones and small rocks. Once it had been a road in regular use by strings of packponies scrambling surefootedly over the fells to the lake and long-lost ferry stage. The modern world had turned traffic elsewhere.

The house was surrounded by a high wall and a protective fringe of trees. Suddenly unwilling to drive straight in, although the gate had been left open, perhaps for her, Hetty drew up under the lea of the surrounding wall, collected the cyclamen from the front seat, and got out of her car.

She walked through the gate into what was more a wide yard than a garden, betraying its farming origins. To her left was a newish-looking garage, a necessary addition but sadly out of tune with its surrounds.

To her right, the house itself stood in a time warp shaded by trees. It was whitewashed and bright, but its irregular shape, the glimpse of a timbered gallery, its tiny windows set in massive walls, betrayed its ancient origins. Everywhere was very quiet.

As she stood there, gazing up at the frontage, the peace was abruptly broken by a loud barking. Automatically she took a step back, because more than one canine voice gave tongue. She was sorry now she'd left the car on the other side of the wall. She might need to scramble back inside it for protection!

Around the garage, from some depths of the garden invisible from here, bounded the origins of the disturbance: a pair of dachshunds. The noise the two of them produced was out of all proportion to their size. One was long haired, coppery in colour, and the other smooth haired black and tan. They rushed up to Hetty, bellowing what might have been either welcome or defiance, she couldn't tell which.

'Hullo!' she called out encouragingly to them, at which they both retreated some distance, still barking furiously. But tails wagged tentatively at the other end. Ears were pricked. Curiosity was taking over.

'They don't bite or anything!' said a clear voice.

A girl of about ten had appeared around the corner of the garage in the wake of the dogs. She had bright red curls and was clad in dungarees and purple boots. 'Copper! Jo-Jo!' she shouted with authority.

The dachshunds fell silent and bounded up, tails wagging furiously now. Copper, the long-haired one presumably, sniffed at the newcomer's shoes. The child turned a candid gaze on Hetty.

'I'm Freddy,' she said. 'Who are you?'

'Hetty Farrell.' Hetty hesitated, feeling rather foolish. She supposed she was expected. Ned had rather tossed off the invitation and he wasn't the house-owner, only a house-guest.

'Are you my brother's latest girlfriend?' enquired the child loudly. Her gaze travelled over Hetty taking a critical look at every detail of her appearance.

'I'm not sure I know your brother . . .' Hetty began.

The door of the house opened and Ned appeared. 'Thought I heard those brutes kicking up their usual racket! Glad to see you found the place, Miss Farrell, or Sergeant, or whatever. I don't know your first name, I'm afraid.'

'She's called Hetty,' said the child. 'She just said so and she also said she didn't know you.' Her stern gaze returned to the visitor.

'No, I didn't,' Hetty defended herself. 'I said I wasn't sure. I didn't know he was your brother.'

Ned intervened. 'How should you? This, then, I'm afraid, is my sister Freddy. You'll have to excuse her.' He ruffled the child's hair affectionately as he spoke, robbing the words of their criticism.

'So,' said Freddy impatiently, 'is she your new girlfriend or not?'

'Not!' said Hetty and Ned together.

Freddy looked mildly disgusted and trailed off indoors, both dogs at her heels.

'Is your whole family here?' Hetty asked, rather worried at the prospect.

'Lord, no. There's a bit of an age gap between my sister and myself, as you can see. Her mother is Dad's second wife. She's an actress and in rehearsal at the moment, so couldn't cope with a kid. Freddy goes back to school next week, thank goodness, but most of the summer she's been here with Felix. She gets on well with him and he doesn't mind her kicking around the place. It gives him someone to cook for.'

Ned ushered Hetty towards the house as he spoke.

'Left your car outside? Bring it in later,' he said. 'Come and meet Felix. He's cooking up the most enormous meal in your honour.'

She was at least expected by the owner.

'Hah! The lady detective!'

A vast, rotund figure with a white beard, swathed in a blue-striped butcher's apron, bore down on her. He brandished a rather dangerous-looking kitchen knife. They had an odd way of welcoming visitors around here, Hetty decided.

'Bearing a cyclamen! How very kind, my dear!'

Fortunately he put the knife down before attempting to accept the plant and shake hands at the same time. 'Felix Crowe!' he said. 'I've prepared for us Chicken Marengo, in white wine with mushrooms and shallots. It was created by Napoleon's chef for the Emperor himself. You have no objection? Good. Ned, open the wine, there's a good fellow. Or perhaps the lady would prefer a glass of sherry?'

Stepping through the front door, Hetty had found herself in a long, straight, oak-panelled hallway. Ned ushered her into a low-ceilinged room with more dark panelling and the remains of a once capacious hearth. A spice cupboard was built into a wall, its door engraved 1767. In the depths of the building Freddy could be heard scolding one or both of the dogs.

'Wine would be lovely,' Hetty said. 'Thank you for letting me come and see your house.'

'I don't open to visitors in the usual run of things,' Felix told her. He sat down heavily on the edge of a, one hoped, robust chair. He picked up the knife and studied its edge. 'Mind you, if anyone's interested and gives me a call first, I'm happy to show a small party around.'

Freddy appeared in the doorway. 'You know that pudding thing you made this morning, Uncle Felix? Well, Jo-Jo's eaten it.'

'What!' Felix rose wrathfully from his chair.

'I got it away from him,' Freddy offered, adding doubtfully, 'Some of it looks all right.'

Felix lumbered away towards the kitchen, promising vengeance.

'Don't worry,' said Ned to an alarmed Hetty. 'That sort of thing happens in this house all the time.'

She relaxed. 'I'm not a great eater of puddings, anyway! The oak panelling in here looks very old.'

'From some time in the sixteen-hundreds. I'll show you over the place while Felix is sorting out the culinary disasters in the kitchen. I thought, later after lunch, we might walk down to the lake. There's a path which starts up here behind the house.'

He smiled at her. Hetty smiled back, reflecting with a twinge of conscience, that Inspector Wills wouldn't approve of any of this.

Lunch, despite the absence of any pudding, was very nice. Felix, it was abundantly clear, was a cook who thought on the grand scale. It was probably a good thing there was only one course, thought Hetty, as she refused cheese and biscuits.

A walk afterwards seemed more than ever a good idea. Her walking boots always travelled in the car, because she never knew when she might have to take to rough terrain. Hetty changed into them, and escorted by Ned, and proceeded by Freddy and the dachshunds, set off down the tree-shaded pathway to the lakeside.

'Is your father alive?' Hetty ventured to ask.

'In America,' he said, without offering any further explanation.

Hetty could hardly press the matter but she was curious. They seemed a slightly disorganised family.

Perhaps Ned guessed what was in her mind, because he went on, 'It's not done Freddy any harm, having so many homes, as it were. If anything, it's made her rather precocious.'

Hetty might have disputed the desirability of any child being shuttled between boarding school and any relative or friend who happened to be free of other commitments. But she'd no wish to start an argument and she was a guest here.

They emerged from the trees, crossed over a lakeside track and made their way down to the water's edge. Both dogs were splashing through the shallows, resembling with water-sleek fur a pair of otters. Freddy followed, her purple boots already equally soaked.

'I'm sorry about that business yesterday,' Ned said. 'You didn't get any lead on the culprit, I suppose?'

'No theft of either mannequin or vase has been reported. I won't give up, not yet, anyway,' Hetty told him.

He tossed a pebble out across the lake. 'You will remember to tell me, won't you? If you find out anything?' His tone was rather too casual.

'Sure.' She glanced at him curiously but he was avoiding her gaze, or so it seemed.

'What's that house down there?' she pointed ahead.

'Greywalls,' he said shortly. After a pause he added with some reluctance, 'It belongs to chap called Erwin van Leeuwen, something of a recluse.'

Ned raised his voice and called out, 'Freddy! Watch those dogs! There's a reedbed just along here.'

The child and the dogs were all out of sight. There was no reply. Ned muttered under his breath and quickened his step. Hetty, with a sense of alarm rooted, she afterwards decided, in her police training, followed.

The shore curved outwards in a shallow headland. They rounded it and came across the reedbed. Freddy, to Hetty's relief, was sitting on the shoreline, one arm cuddled around each of the two dripping-wet pets. She didn't turn her head as they came up, but said in a small voice, 'There's something horrid in the reeds. Copper found it. I don't know what it is, but it looks strange and I don't like it.'

'What? Where?' Ned looked worried. He made as if to walk towards the reedbed but Hetty stepped in front of him.

'My job!' she said firmly. In a low tone, she added, 'Your sister's upset. You'd better take care of her. I'll take a look.'

He watched her go with manifest reluctance.

There wasn't a soul out on the lake, not even a pleasure launch. The fells on the far side were veiled in a mist, reminding Hetty how quickly the weather could change hereabouts. Further along the shore was a dilapidated boathouse. That must belong to the other house, Greywalls. The water lapped softly around the clustered reed stems. It was stirred up and muddy by her feet where the dogs and Freddy had paddled around.

Hetty picked a water-logged branch from the water's edge and used it to part the reeds carefully. There was something dark snagged in them, it looked like cloth.

She moved in closer. It *was* cloth. It was a trouserleg.

'Oh, no,' Hetty murmured.

Bradley Wills's weekend plans, and her own, were truly doomed. Copper had found a body and, this time, it was real.

Part Two

Hetty made her way to where Ned sat with an arm round his sister's shoulders. Freddy must have guessed something unpleasant had happened but, significantly, asked no questions.

With a murmured word of comfort, Ned left her to walk over to Hetty, his eyebrows raised questioningly.

'You'd better take Freddy back to the house,' Hetty said in a low voice. 'I think it's what you found yesterday, only this time for real.'

Ned paled. 'You're sure?' Without waiting for her answer, he attempted to walk past her towards the reedbed. She caught at his arm.

'Nothing must be touched! The fewer people trampling the shore the better. I've got my mobile in my bag and I'll call up help.'

'Could you see – was it a man or woman?' Ned hissed.

'I think, a man. Do hurry up, Ned. We oughtn't to waste time and Freddy might get curious.'

He was still hesitating. It seemed to her that some further question hovered on his lips. But he nodded. 'I won't be long. I'll tell Felix to keep Freddy at home, and get back here as soon as I can.'

When they'd gone, Hetty took out her mobile phone, sighed, and relayed the news of the discovery, finishing with a request to contact the blissfully unaware Inspector Wills in his garden.

The call made, it remained to protect the area from unwarranted intrusion until the arrival of the Scene of Crime team. The boathouse caught her eye. It had an abandoned air. Water lapped around the wooden piles and the slatted gates on to the lake looked locked. She couldn't see the house, Greywalls, but that must be nearby behind the trees. Otherwise, the only house in the immediate vicinity was Stoney How.

This was a tourist area and visitors were many. But the body face down in the water, even at a cursory glance, wasn't dressed for outdoor activity. The impression had been of a formal suit, now sodden, and the heel of a once-smart shoe.

Hetty thrust her hand into her pocket and her fingers touched something stiff. She withdrew a business card, Ned's. She must have slipped it into her pocket when she picked it up from Wills's desk the day before.

Hetty read it, frowning. With some hesitation, she took out the mobile again. 'Hullo? Sergeant Farrell again. Can someone run a check for me? It's on this firm . . .' She gave the name and phone number. 'Yes, I know it's Sunday, but they're insurers. They must have an emergency number. Disasters don't only occur between nine and five!'

And don't I know it? she thought bitterly. Here am I, at four o'clock on a nice Sunday afternoon, theoretically my free weekend, and what am I doing? Standing here with a corpse for company!

Into the mobile she continued, 'I want to know if they still employ an Edward Woodley and, if possible, what his job is with them. Thanks.'

She didn't like checking on Ned, especially when they'd all been lunching together so merrily. But perhaps it was something she ought to have done before.

So here they all were, back again. Divers, police photographer, Dr Harris with his little black bag, a veritable circus. Blue and white tape cordoned off the area. An electrician was busy fixing up lighting, as daylight faded. This spot wasn't accessible by car, all equipment had to be carried down by hand, and no one was in a very good temper.

Ned had returned and was watching from afar. He looked worried but impatient. Photographs and measurements having been made of the body *in situ*, it was being lifted onto the shore. Ned took a step forward and tried to see. More than ever, Hetty had the impression this wasn't morbid curiosity on his part. There was something he was desperate to know.

Bradley Wills had arrived, still in disreputable gardening trousers and a pullover with holes in both elbows.

'What's all this, Farrell? Not, I trust, another dummy?' His head shot forward at the end of his long thin neck like an angry bird about to peck at her.

'Afraid not, sir. Definitely for real this time.'

Wills had spotted Ned Woodley. 'What the dickens is that fellow doing here again? Don't tell me he found this one, too?'

It was time to confess all. That she'd been lunching at Stoney How and that a family pet had led them to the body.

Wills listened in steadily mounting ire until she finished. 'Hardly prudent behaviour, Farrell!' he growled.

'No, sir,' she admitted glumly.

'What on earth did you think you were doing? I told you to

look into this chap's antics. Not go hobnobbing with him socially! I still don't believe he just chanced on that dummy in the lake yesterday! Now I find it hard to believe that coincidence alone brought you and him to this genuine corpse in the water!' Wills was working himself up into a fine lather.

'Yes, sir. I mean, no, sir. I've asked for a check to be run on the company he works for. I oughtn't to have accepted the invitation to lunch. Does this mean I won't be working on this case?'

Hetty asked this with some trepidation. She'd never been taken off a case for any reason. The thought that she might be so now filled her with dismay she found it hard to disguise.

'We'll discuss it later. Let's see what we've got here first. But you showed lack of judgement, Farrell. I'm extremely disappointed.'

Hetty's face glowed, but the inspector was distracted by the approach of Dr Harris.

'I've certified death. It will be up to the pathologist, of course, but even I can see there's a wound to the back of the head he couldn't possibly have inflicted on himself. It seems unlikely to me that he just fell in!'

Within Hetty's bag, the mobile shrilled its call. She retreated from the crowd and put it to her ear. What she heard caused her dismay to increase but also for it to turn to anger. 'Thanks!' she told the caller.

She put the mobile away and made her way to where Ned was waiting and watching the proceedings at the water's edge.

'Mr Woodley—'

He pulled a wry grimace. 'Official, is it?' he asked. 'I'm not called "Ned" any more?'

'Yes, it is official. Ned, I mean, Mr Woodley! Someone has been in touch with your company.'

'Oh.' He glanced again and more apprehensively at Bradley Wills, and then at a preparing stretcher party.

'Ned! I mean, Mr Woodley, at least pay attention to what I'm saying!' He was still trying to see the stretcher, but the body was decently covered over.

Ned sighed. 'All right, Hetty, I know what you're going to say.'

'Do you, indeed?' she snapped. It was difficult to hide how she felt. 'You've been less than frank with me. I suspect you've tried to use me! I was to keep you informed of any police discoveries!'

A mulish expression appeared on his face. 'That isn't so, or not exactly. I'm sorry you feel aggrieved. I couldn't confide in you. It's a delicate matter. I have to be extremely careful what I say in public!'

'Oh, for goodness' sake!' she cried. 'I'm a policewoman! Talking to me isn't the same as talking to just anyone!'

'Why is it,' he asked ruefully, 'that I have the greatest difficulty in thinking of you as a policewoman?'

'You'd better start practising!' was the unkind retort. 'You should know I'm well aware of how to treat sensitive information! You've put me in an extremely awkward situation, Ned, and that's putting it mildly!'

It was no use trying to remember to call him 'Mr Woodley'.

'Your company tells us you work for them as some kind of investigator!'

'That's right, into possible insurance fraud and that kind of thing.' His gaze was taken by Bradley Wills. 'Look, Hetty. Do you have to tell that inspector fellow all this? I'd rather he didn't know.'

'Ned,' she said wearily. 'This is likely to be a murder investigation. Inspector Wills has already made clear his displeasure. He has to know. It seems to me there's an awful lot more you ought to tell us. For starters, just what were you really up to yesterday out in the lake?'

'I swear, it doesn't concern you, I mean, not the Cumbria Force.'

'So it is a police matter, then!' Hetty stared at him in exasperation. 'Ned, you can't keep whatever it is a secret from us! From me! You were clearly interested to know where that dummy came from yesterday. What's more important, you seemed very interested to get a look at that body! Ned, I'm asking you a straight question and I'd be obliged if you'd give me a straight answer! Do you think you might know the identity of that poor chap we've just fished out of the water?'

There was a silence. Ned stood squarely before her and glowered down at her. Then he said stiffly, 'I think it might be the body of a man called Michael Holst.'

'I'm on a case!' Ned admitted.

'Are you, indeed?' said Bradley Wills.

'I wish you'd said so at the beginning,' muttered Hetty.

The three of them sat in Wills's office. It was dark now and the neon strip above their heads buzzed fitfully. The building had that half-empty feel. Most people had gone home. Not so the team investigating the Body in the Lake, as the newspapers would no doubt call it. Although Ned had now made a provisional identification and moves were underway to contact Holst's relatives.

'I've rung my company,' Ned went on. 'They understand the situation here and that I'm about to confide in you.' He hesitated.

'See here, I know you're police officers, but . . .'

Bradley Wills put his clasped hands on his desk. 'Mr Woodley, believe me, I would happily see you charged with obstructing the police! However, thanks to the intercession of Sergeant Farrell here, who has pointed out you've saved us much time by identifying the deceased, I'm inclined to overlook your reticence yesterday. But don't, please, mess us about now!'

Ned gave Hetty a look which was part hunted and part grateful. She tried to keep an air of detachment, but it wasn't easy. Despite a promise to tell them everything, she had a nagging feeling Ned meant to tell them as little as he could.

'The story begins with the revolution in Russia in 1917,' Ned said unexpectedly. 'In the 1920s, large numbers of Russian *émigrés* flooded into Western Europe. Quite a few settled in France, which many of the exiled nobility had visited in happier times.'

'This history lesson is necessary, I hope,' said Inspector Wills dourly.

Hetty, already interested, hoped he wasn't going to keep interrupting. To get Ned talking at all was a start. To interrupt him might be disastrous.

'It's vital,' said Ned in answer to the inspector's question. 'You see, these exiles had been very rich people in Tsarist Russia, but now they were refugees and broke. Many had left large estates behind them and palaces! But the luckier ones had smuggled out their family jewels, and began to sell them, in order to survive.'

Hetty was beginning to see the drift of this. She saw Wills open his mouth and glared at him. The inspector, either startled by his sergeant's audacity, or realising that she was quite right and this was a moment for him to keep quiet, subsided.

'A diamond dealer at the time, called van Leeuwen, bought up a number of these Russian pieces at very advantageous prices, not to re-sell, but to keep. He was a collector. These were fine stones set with skilled craftsmanship, often in flamboyant Imperial taste! Amongst them he bought a complete set of diamond jewellery made for a lady of the Russian court in the 1880s, on the occasion of the coronation of Tsar Alexander III. For that reason, the whole collection got the name of The Romanov Diamonds.'

Ned shrugged. 'It sounded romantic, I suppose. All the pieces were of Russian origin and belonged to the aristocracy so had very likely been worn at court!'

'Do they still exist as a complete collection?' Hetty asked, fascinated.

Ned looked grim. 'If I could answer that, I'd be a happy man.

'The point is,' Ned explained, 'that people with valuable private collections tend to keep quiet about them.'

By now he was sure of even Bradley Wills's rapt attention.

'When van Leeuwen died, his son inherited the collection. The son, Paul, married an Englishwoman. When he died, Mrs Pamela van Leeuwen became its owner. She's lived for many years near Paris. She's childless and the future of the collection has been on her mind. She's no longer young, you understand! She particularly wanted to ensure the collection was kept together. Being English, she contacted a London museum and suggested the collection might be put on display. Should the exhibition be a success then, eventually, the whole collection might be given to the museum.

'Everything was arranged in the greatest secrecy because Pamela van Leeuwen and the museum rightly feared the interest of thieves. It was agreed that the collection should be taken from Paris to London by air, in the care of a man she trusted, Michael Holst. We were approached with regard to insuring the gems in transit. Holst would be escorted to the plane in Paris, and met by a security firm at Heathrow Airport. Customs had been forewarned and special fast clearance arranged. Holst had acted as courier before in confidential matters for various clients. We were satisfied with his employment on this occasion. Only when the gems were safely in this country would the loan be announced. It would pre-empt any idea of their being hijacked en route.'

Ned smiled grimly. 'Or that was the idea! The courier, Holst, boarded the plane and reached Heathrow without problem. He went through the formalities and was met by a security guard in uniform and helmet, escorted out of the building into a special van and whisked away.'

Ned paused dramatically. 'Never to be seen again, poor fellow, until today. Nor, needless to say, has any trace of the Romanov diamond collection been found!'

'Bogus security guard,' said Inspector Wills with a sigh.

'Exactly. The real security team was later discovered tied up in their own van in a lay-by. As insurers, we're faced with paying out a great deal of money. Naturally the company isn't happy. If possible, they'd like to recover the jewellery intact. Of course, the police are working on it . . .' Ned added a little unfortunately. 'But in these circumstances, delicate enquiries have to be made. That's my job.'

The suggestion that official efforts were ever anything but tactful went down badly with his listeners.

'This man, van Leeuwen, who lives at Greywalls,' Hetty asked impatiently. 'Who is he?'

'He's a retired art dealer,' Ned told her. 'A distant relative of the late Paul. Pamela van Leeuwen informed him of her plan to allow a London museum to display the stones. Naturally, she thought he'd be interested! He was more than that. He was strongly against the idea and Pamela had to explain the security arrangements and reassure him that all care would be taken. Unfortunately, she then let slip the possibility that she might give the collection to the museum outright. Erwin van Leeuwen was furious at the idea the jewellery might go out of the family. There was a bitter quarrel and Erwin instigated legal action in France to prevent disposal of the collection, but he was unsuccessful. He isn't, by all accounts, the sort of man to give up easily!'

'As finding the unfortunate Holst in the lake would seem to confirm!' said Bradley Wills grimly.

Ned glanced at him. 'Even before finding Holst today, we had reason to suspect Erwin. He has a strong motive. He also employs a driver/handyman called Stark. A clip of film from a security camera at Heathrow shows the false "security guard". His face is obscured by his helmet, but in build he's very like Stark, who is a bruiser of a fellow, a one-time naval diver who was dishonourably discharged.'

Inspector Wills shifted in his chair and Hetty realised he was about to impart some information, much against his will. 'I should tell you I've seen a confidential memo concerning an important jewel theft in London. And that's still confidential, Farrell!'

Hetty swept his warning aside. 'But has no one officially questioned Erwin van Leeuwen about the theft?'

Ned pulled a wry face. 'Erwin took himself off to Scotland Yard as soon as a distraught Pamela phoned him from France with the bad news! Erwin blamed security at Heathrow, the police, the real security firm, and demanded to know what the police were doing to recover the jewels. He made quite a nuisance of himself!'

'But how about his own movements on the day of the theft?' Hetty demanded. 'Or those of his driver, Stark?'

'They both have alibis!' Ned said promptly. 'A caller at the house saw them both.' Again Ned paused for effect. 'An utterly reliable caller. The vicar.'

'Vicar?' cried Hetty.

'The incumbent of one of the local parishes which, apparently, is raising money to repair the church roof. They are short of the target and the vicar was delighted when he received a message from Greywalls saying that Mr van Leeuwen wished to give a sizeable donation and suggesting the vicar come to the house the following afternoon to discuss details. Naturally the vicar said he would, although the trip would clash with cricket coverage on television. The vicar is a cricket fan! However, he couldn't afford to turn down van Leeuwen's offer, so he set out for Greywalls.

'Erwin had told him that he should park outside the gate and walk up the path to the front door. The reason given was that the drive was newly gravelled and it needed time to settle. That's true. The vicar set off up the path. It took him past the lodge where Stark lives. The curtain of the downstairs window was drawn right back, and the vicar – a cricket enthusiast, remember! – found his attention caught by a flickering TV screen showing the match. He could also see Stark, sitting in an armchair, glued to the screen. The vicar felt rather envious of him! However, he paid his call on

67

van Leeuwen, settled their business, and walked back down the drive. It didn't take long and when he passed by the lodge, the match was still on and Stark still watching it. The vicar hurried home as fast as he could, to catch the final period of play on his own set. The vicar swears to all of this and I don't think we can doubt his honesty.'

'Now we come to your own activities, Mr Woodley,' Inspector Wills said. 'I presume your purpose for being in this part of the world is to investigate Erwin van Leeuwen, and not, as you told Sergeant Farrell, to visit relatives.'

Hetty flushed.

'It was partly true!' Ned insisted. 'I wanted to see my sister.'

'So why were you messing about in the lake?' Wills countered.

Ned's manner which, until this point, had been briskly frank, became – to Hetty's eye – decidedly shifty. He stared at the paperweight on Wills's desk and said, 'I thought I might be able to get up to the house from the lake, take a look around. I took my diving gear with me and went down to the shore. I swam up to the boathouse, but Stark suddenly appeared and started working inside. As my plan was frustrated, I decided to try diving in the deeper part of the lake, just for my own amusement. I had a lot of new gear and I wanted to try it out! That's when I found the – that dummy.' Ned grimaced. 'I swear, I didn't know it was there and I really had a fright! There was no way I could tell it wasn't – wasn't a real body.'

Bradley Wills slapped his hands on his desk, making the paperweight rattle and startling his companions.

'Right! This amateur sleuthing has to stop, Mr Woodley! This is now entirely a police matter and in *our* hands!'

'Hey!' Ned bounced to his feet. 'With all due respect, Inspector, the last thing my company needs is for Erwin – if he does know where the jewellery is – to be scared into doing something drastic! Mrs van Leeuwen's great fear is that the items of jewellery will be broken up and sold. For that reason, she's insisting that secrecy be maintained. The settings could be melted down, the larger stones re-cut and re-set into new jewellery. An innocent buyer mightn't question the provenance. Or there are plenty of unscrupulous buyers. All hope of tracing the Romanov Collection would be gone for ever!'

'That is the second time you've questioned the competence of my officers!' Bradley Wills thundered. He controlled his temper and added, 'You may rely on Sergeant Farrell's tact and discretion!'

'Me?' cried Hetty inelegantly. 'Does that mean I'm not being taken off the case?'

'On the contrary, Farrell. I think you might be the very person to inverview van Leeuwen. Catch him off guard, eh?'

In a silence neither seemed inclined to break, Hetty accompanied Ned to his Range Rover in the police compound.

Once there, Ned at last asked, 'Mad at me, Hetty?' He didn't sound so much regretful, as mildly amused.

'Shouldn't I be?' she countered, chin tilted aggressively.

'I've come clean, Het, honestly.' The abbreviation of her already abbreviated name seemed quite natural on his lips, but Hetty hardened her heart.

Ned could be infuriating, but over lunch that day he'd been funny and entertaining, quite disarming her. Then they'd found Michael Holst's body and she'd found out the true nature of Ned's occupation. Now she didn't know quite what to think, only that she couldn't be sure he wasn't already plotting some further, highly irregular activity of his own.

'I wish I could believe you, Ned,' she said frankly. 'But I still feel there are things you're not telling us. Telling *me*! This is police business.'

'Yes, Sergeant Farrell!'

'Don't make fun of me!' she warned.

'Good grief, wouldn't dare!' Ned returned with such feeling that despite herself, she almost laughed.

Her impulse for mirth disappeared, however, when Ned continued, 'Finding the Romanov Collection is my job, Hetty, and neither you nor Bradley Wills can stop me trying! You must see why I'm so worried that if the police start blundering – sorry, but you know what I mean! If you start asking questions at Greywalls, the jewellery, which I'm sure is hidden there somewhere, will be spirited away to a safer hiding place and we'll never find it!'

'And *you* ought to understand that this is a murder inquiry now,' she insisted. 'That's more important than finding the jewels! If you sneak around Greywalls and are seen, you'll be the one alerting Erwin and attracting Stark's attention! Leave it to me!'

'I'll keep out of your way,' he promised.

'Ned! That's not the same thing! If you cause any trouble, the inspector will blame *me*. Because I lunched at Stoney How, he already thinks I might be prejudiced in your favour!'

'Sadly,' Ned muttered, 'I don't think you are.'

'I'm a police officer! This is my career! I don't want to be taken off the case, Ned. Still less do I want to be turfed out of CID altogether and sent back to uniformed branch! If you interfere any more, either of those things could happen. I don't want you just out of my way here, I want you to go back to London!' She glared up at him beneath a fringe of untidy brown hair.

'Do you really, Hetty?' he asked seriously.

For some reason, as she afterwards glumly reflected, she'd found it very difficult to reply, 'Yes, I do!' with any sort of conviction.

Monday morning dawned bright and clear. Shortly after breakfast Hetty drove to Stoney How.

She was greeted as before by Copper and Jo-Jo, bouncing around her, barking hysterically, but with wagging tails.

No one came to see why the dogs were kicking up such a fuss. The front door was open. Hetty peered in. 'Anyone at home?'

'In the kitchen!' roared a distant voice.

She made her way down the oak-panelled hall. In the roomy kitchen Felix Crowe, today in red-striped apron, presided over Freddy who earnestly rolled out dough. Hetty didn't know whether it was concentration on her task, or something else, which made the child look so tense.

'Ah, the lady detective!' rumbled Felix. 'Just in time for coffee! We're making scones,' he added.

Freddy looked up, her face and clothing plentifully bespattered with flour. 'Hullo,' she said casually and returned to her work.

'Where's Ned? Has he left?'

Although she'd herself urged him to leave, Hetty couldn't help a note of anxiety in her voice.

'He hasn't gone back to London yet. He went out about ten minutes ago, don't know where.'

Felix was busy with the coffee. Hetty sighed. She'd missed Ned by so few minutes. She had no idea where he was now and had the deepest misgivings about his activities.

'I really came to see if Freddy was all right.' She lowered her voice.

Felix glanced at Freddy who was stamping out the scones with a pastry cutter.

'Fine, fine. Hasn't said a word about anything.'

'Felix, that's not necessarily a good thing. It might be better if she pestered us with questions!'

Felix made a warning gesture. 'I know, my dear. But give her time. Can't rush these things.'

'Ready!' called Freddy. The scones, rather uneven in thickness, had been set out on a baking tray.

They were duly transferred to the oven and coffee poured out for the adults. Freddy collected a plastic bottle of strawberry milk from the fridge. She took it to the window, set deep in the massive stone outer wall of the kitchen, scrambled into this sunny nook and began to slurp her drink through a straw. Jo-Jo and Copper began to search diligently around the table for pastry scraps.

Hands cupped around her coffee mug, Hetty surveyed the child. Then she cast a meaningful look at Felix and rolled her eyes in Freddy's direction. Felix interpreted the message.

'There's a very pretty walk up the hill behind here!' he boomed. 'Why don't you take Hetty for a stroll up there, Freddy? You could take these dratted animals with you, from under my feet! I'll clear up here.'

'I expect Hetty's on her way to arrest someone,' said Freddy with relish.

'Not today!' Hetty told her.

Privately she was thinking, *Not unless it's your brother who, wherever he is, is probably interfering in a police investigation!*

She put down her empty cup, 'Come on, then, Freddy! I can spare an hour!'

After all, she had been robbed of her free weekend. Besides which, getting Freddy to relax was a priority.

But Hetty did wish she knew where Ned had gone and, more importantly, just what he was doing.

'Just so long as he keeps away from Greywalls!' she muttered.

Greywalls was to be her next port of call, to talk to Erwin van Leeuwen.

Part Three

The hillside was steeper than it looked. Hetty was a regular walker and used to the terrain but wondered how Freddy would make out. She needn't have worried. Freddy scrambled up the incline with the agility of a mountain goat, her red curls gleaming in the sun. The dogs were having more trouble, their stumpy legs working energetically as they bounced along over the rough turf.

They followed the line of a low drystone wall. There were only the black-faced sheep for company up here and one sturdy, short-legged Fell pony which raised its head as they passed, then went back to tearing at the short dry grass. At last they reached the top and paused for breath by a stile, leaning on the rough stone wall in which it was set.

They could see the lake in the distance, a long thin silver finger surrounded by dark trees. Behind them rose the quaint but imposing contours of Coniston Old Man. Stoney How was immediately below, its tall chimneys poking out of the branches. Hetty's eyes searched for Greywalls and caught just a glimpse of Erwin van Leeuwen's roof.

She felt a stir of unease. Where *was* Ned?

'It's a pity Ned couldn't have come with us,' she said. 'You don't know where he's gone, do you, Freddy?'

Freddy, hanging over the drystone wall, her purple boots dangling, shook her fiery mop. 'Do you like Ned?' she asked in her direct way.

Serves me right, thought Hetty ruefully, *for introducing Ned's name!* 'Yes, of course I like him,' she said robustly but in what she hoped was a casual manner.

Freddy turned her head sideways and studied her. 'He's got a proper job and everything.'

'I know he has!' Hetty was amused at hearing this recommendation on Ned's sister's lips. Although, she thought, 'proper job' wasn't how Bradley Wills would describe the occupation of civilian investigator! The inspector believed such matters best left firmly in the hands of the police.

'He looks quite nice, he doesn't drink or anything, or drive too fast.' Freddy seemed intent on listing Ned's virtues. 'He's a great swimmer and he hasn't got any other girlfriend at the moment. Have you got a boyfriend?'

If Freddy had a career in mind already at her tender years, it was clearly that of matchmaker.

'No, no boyfriend, and far too busy for one!' Hetty told her cheerfully.

Freddy had scrambled onto the stile now and sat atop, her head fractionally higher than Hetty's. A shrewd psychological move, thought Hetty. Ned had been right. His sister's unorthodox upbringing had made her precocious. The little minx was quite the manipulator!

But not of me! thought Hetty determinedly. 'Come on, Freddy, let's walk on. I can't take too much time, I'm afraid. I have to go and see someone.'

'And arrest them?' Freddy asked hopefully. The child's mother was in the theatre, after all. Dramatics appealed to her.

'I doubt it very much.' Hetty turned the conversation. 'Is your name Frederica?'

Freddy grimaced. 'It's worse, it's Freda. I was named after some relation of Mummy's.'

'No one ever likes their name,' Hetty comforted. 'I'm Henrietta and it's such a mouthful! It takes so long to write it out.'

Having found a common cause of grievance, they walked on companionably. Freddy scuffed her toe against a tuft of coarse grass. 'Ned told Felix and me he knew that man in the water.'

'Did he?' Hetty was surprised Ned should have told the little girl.

Freddy made things clearer. 'Really he told Felix, but I was listening outside the kitchen window.'

This child was a handful, quick witted and unscrupulous. Hetty tackled the subject she'd come up here to discuss, head-on. This seemed the best way with Freddy.

'Does it worry you, Freddy? Finding the man in the water? Did you have any bad dreams or anything like that?'

The red mop shook negatively. 'I didn't see him properly. Only his legs. He looked like a Guy Fawkes dummy. Did he fall in?'

'We don't know yet what happened, but we'll find out.'

Freddy's mind had not been detoured from its original track. 'If you find out quickly, and haven't got anything else to do, then Ned is here until Friday. You could go sailing together or something.'

Freddy's guileless gaze fixed on Hetty who found herself blushing. Really, this kid!

'You see,' said Freddy calmly, quite in charge of the situation and well aware of it, 'I think it's high time he got married. You seem nice and he likes you.'

Hetty stopped and obliged Freddy to look up at her. 'Listen here, my girl,' she said. 'It's a very dangerous thing to try and organise other people's lives!'

Freddy was unabashed. 'No, it's not,' she said. 'Not if you do it right.'

Hetty delivered her young friend back to Felix with relief.

'I don't think things are worrying her,' she told him. 'At least, not the things I thought might be.'

'I'll keep her occupied and not let her pester you,' he returned, perhaps guessing rather more than Hetty might have wished about the conversation by the stile.

After verbal fencing with Freddy, tackling Erwin van Leeuwen ought to be a doddle, she thought as she drove away from Stoney How.

Hetty parked by the gate and walked up Greywalls' drive. She took note of the newish gravel. That bit of Ned's story was right, anyhow.

Greywalls was by no means so old a house as Stoney How. Hetty judged its fanciful Gothic style to be Victorian. The lodge, just inside the gates, was of similar design, a cottage that played at being a chapel, with arched windows and crenellated stonework above the eaves. Hetty paused to look in the front window. She could see the television set and a comfortable, deep armchair set directly before it. Another part of Ned's story checked out and found correct. The lodge appeared unoccupied at the moment. Certainly no Stark hove into view, asking what she was about.

She reached the house and tugged at an old-fashioned bell pull. A distant jangling within the house replied.

A woman answered the door. She wore a pinafore and looked like a housekeeper. Hetty gave her name, but not her occupation or rank of sergeant.

A little later she was ushered into Erwin van Leeuwen's presence.

With her experience in police work, Hetty knew that it was a great mistake to assume or imagine anything, before having a chance to see reality for oneself. Even so, she'd made the error of visualising Erwin van Leeuwen, perhaps because Ned had spoken of him with such grim suspicion.

The picture she'd formed as a result had been of a tall, saturnine, sinister figure. In fact, the real person was so different to her fancy that Hetty had to struggle to hide her surprise.

Van Leeuwen was a short, square figure with balding head, its shiny pink crown surrounded with a wild fuzz of white hair. His face, with its plump cheeks and snub features, resembled an elderly baby's. As she entered, he struggled up from his chair to greet her and she saw the stout walking stick he kept to hand.

'Miss Farrell! How may I help you?'

Hetty produced her identification and held it out. 'I didn't show this to the person who answered the door. I thought it better to keep the nature of my visit private for the moment.'

Erwin studied the identity card and returned it. He didn't appear dismayed or surprised. 'I've been expecting the police, of course. I've been hoping some news would have been had of the Romanov Collection? Have you come about that?' His chubby features formed an expression of hope.

'Not directly.' Hetty chose her words carefully. 'Although my enquiry is connected. I've come about the body found nearby yesterday. You heard about it?'

Erwin had indicated a chair and as she sat down, he sank back gratefully into his own seat. 'Oh yes, some unfortunate drowned in the lake. Stark, my driver, came and told me the police had recovered a body not far from here. A summer visitor, was it?'

'We're awaiting the post-mortem results.'

The identity of the victim hadn't been released officially and there ought to be no way Erwin van Leeuwen could know it, unless he was involved. She was interested to see how he'd react when told.

Hetty continued, 'But the man has been provisionally identified as a Michael Holst. I believe you might know that name.'

Erwin's expression was at first almost comical. His mouth fell open and his round blue eyes popped. Then distress took over. 'Holst? Is it possible? Poor Holst? But how can this be?'

'We don't yet know, Mr van Leeuwen. Michael Holst hadn't been seen since leaving Heathrow Airport with a security team which later proved to be bogus.'

Erwin clapped his pudgy hands together. 'I knew it! I warned Pamela, my cousin's wife. I told her of the risk in moving the entire collection, all at once like that! It was so unnecessary, just asking for trouble. But she wouldn't listen to me, such an obstinate woman. I tried to stop her, you know. I took legal advice. She countered with lawyers of her own. It was all very unpleasant.'

'I understand,' Hetty said, 'that you took legal advice when you heard that Mrs Pamela van Leeuwen intended not just to send the jewels to London on loan, but to present them outright to the museum.'

Anger sparked in the round blue eyes. 'You know about it, then. You can't be surprised. No one would be!' Erwin leaned forward. 'It isn't a question of the value of the jewels! It's that the collection is unique and irreplaceable! Where is it now, tell me that! Broken up and disposed of, for all I know. Oh, it's a tragedy!' He waved his hands in the air.

'And so is the death of Michael Holst,' she reminded him.

Erwin stopped gesticulating and placed his hands on his knees. 'Poor fellow, poor fellow. I didn't intend to sound uncaring. But the whole thing, you see, stems from that mad notion of Pamela's to send the collection travelling about. No need for it. My dear late cousin, Paul, who was Pamela's husband, would never have permitted such a folly. The collection belongs in the family.' He tapped his fingers on his kneecaps. 'Now it's lost and poor Holst, too. It cost him his life!'

'Can you offer an explanation as to why he was so near here?' she asked.

If she'd expected Erwin to be thrown by the question, she was disappointed. He gazed at her. 'Isn't it obvious? The poor fellow escaped from his kidnappers and was making his way here, to see me! Either he fell into the water somehow or – or the scoundrels followed him and prevented him from reaching me. This is quite dreadful!' He took out a large handkerchief and mopped his brow.

It was difficult to know what to make of Erwin. His surprise at learning of the victim's identity had appeared quite genuine. On the other hand, he admitted he'd been expecting the police. He'd had plenty of time to rehearse all this.

'Perhaps I could speak to the other members of your household?' she asked.

'Of course!' Erwin tucked away the handkerchief. 'I was about to offer you some refreshment in any case. I'll ring for Mrs Beckett.'

The housekeeper, Mrs Beckett, was the woman who'd opened the front door. She came on a daily basis, she explained, cleaned the house and did the cooking. Mr van Leeuwen was on a strict diet. He lunched lightly, usually fish, and she left him a salad for the evening, when she went home at five thirty.

Erwin listened to all this, nodding and exclaiming, 'Yes, yes!' at intervals.

Mrs Beckett had nothing further to add. She'd heard about the body in the lake and thought it 'a real shame'. The name Holst meant nothing to her.

Hetty thanked her and she left. She refused the sherry Erwin suggested and asked if she might speak to the driver, Stark.

For the first time, Erwin appeared a little unsure of himself. 'Stark? Yes, of course. A good fellow. Very reliable.' He hesitated. 'There's an unfortunate episode in his early life, when he was in the Royal Navy – no need to bring it up now. He made a mistake and paid for it. I've never found him anything but utterly loyal. He's worked for me for ten years.'

Again, it was difficult to tell whether Erwin meant only to defend a faithful employee, or whether he was mentioning this before the police found it out for themselves, thereby defusing the issue.

Erwin hauled himself to his feet again and, using his stick, limped to the far side of the room. Hetty noticed for the first time a row of push-buttons on the wall.

81

'I'm not too good on my feet, my dear, as you see. I had this system put in, simple but effective. Each of these buttons connects to a place Stark might be – the garage, the lodge, the boathouse.'

Erwin touched the relevant switch with a stubby finger as he spoke. 'When I need him, I press the one for where I think he is, or all of them, if I'm not sure. A bell rings in one of the places and Stark knows I want him to come up to the house. Let's see, I think he's working on the car today.' Erwin pressed the centre button.

He retired to his chair and subsided. 'We'll wait a few minutes. If his hands are dirty, he needs time to clean up.'

Hetty's eyes had travelled from the row of call-buttons to a set of watercolour seascapes above them on the wall.

'You like those?' Erwin sounded pleased. 'I was a dealer in my time. Now I'm a collector, like Paul's father, only he collected jewellery. With me it's paintings.'

Was it only paintings? Hetty wondered. Or had the opportunity to get his hands on the Romanov diamonds been too great for his collector's instincts to resist?

'Mr van Leeuwen,' Hetty asked suddenly. 'Before the Romanov Collection disappeared, when did you last see it?'

It occurred to her that if Erwin had a mobility problem, he probably hadn't been to France, where the jewellery had been kept, for some time.

'Oh, some four or five years ago.' Erwin seemed puzzled as to the reason for her question. 'My last trip across the Channel. I visited Pamela in part to discuss the Romanov jewels. I wanted to know what she intended to do with them. I had a feeling, you see, that she was planning to do something. I begged her to do nothing without consulting me.'

'And she did consult you,' Hetty prompted.

'Oh no!' Again anger sparkled in his protuberant blue eyes. 'Not until after she'd made up her mind! Then she just informed me, if you please. Cool as a cucumber. She said she intended sending the collection for exhibition in London. She wouldn't hear of any objection and then I realised she meant more – she meant to present the entire thing to the museum! It was to be put on display as the *Van Leeuwen Collection*, in memory of her husband and father-in-law. She seemed to think that a suitable purpose for it! I stressed how upset both Paul and his father would have been, but she's an obstinate woman. Impossible!'

Erwin van Leeuwen had become quite agitated. He dragged out the handkerchief again.

As he was mopping sweat from his reddened face, Hetty turned over in her mind what she knew of Pamela van Leeuwen. Were her intentions exactly as she'd told Erwin? That she intended only to send the jewels to England as the first move in a plan to create a permanent memorial to her husband and father-in-law? With the loss of the jewels, just how much insurance money was involved? It was something she hadn't asked Ned and ought to have done.

A sound broke into her thoughts, making her jump. It was a discreet clearing of the throat by someone near the door. She turned.

Ned had described Stark as a 'bruiser'. He was certainly a tall man and muscular in build, with straight dark hair brushed back from his forehead. His skin was curiously pale for someone Hetty would have imagined spent much of his time out of doors, and had done so all his life. He was in his forties. But there was a type of complexion like that, white skin and black hair. She had seen it before and it always seemed unnatural to her, although, especially on a woman, it could be striking.

Stark had been staring at her and she was sure he guessed who she was and the nature of her visit. But he only said, 'Yes, sir?' and shifted his gaze to his employer.

'Ah, Stark!' van Leeuwen said fussily. 'Come in! This is Sergeant Farrell. She's come about the body – the poor fellow who drowned in the lake near here. It seems it was Holst. You recall my telling you of Holst? He was the courier who carried the Romanov Collection.'

'Yes, sir. Indeed, sir?'

Stark's heavy black brows rose questioningly but the question remained unasked aloud.

'Were you acquainted with Michael Holst yourself, Mr Stark?' Hetty asked him.

'No, ma'am.' He had a wooden way of speaking and was apparently a man of few words.

'You have no idea why he might have been in this neighbourhood?'

'None, ma'am.'

'You hadn't noticed any unusual activity around here of late?'

Hetty had fully expected Stark to reply 'No' again. But instead the man said, 'As a matter of fact, ma'am, yes.'

Hetty blinked. Van Leeuwen exclaimed, 'What's this? You said nothing to me, Stark!'

'I didn't wish to worry you, sir. I was keeping an eye on things.' Stark's heavy-lidded gaze returned to Hetty. 'There's been a young man with diving equipment messing about in the lake, ma'am. He hasn't the air of a normal tourist and he's been taking a bit of interest in properties along the lake edge, like this one. So I took a bit of interest in him. I fancy he's staying near here, at Stoney How.'

Ned. Hetty suppressed her exasperation. To think that Ned had warned *her* not to alarm Stark or his employer. *Wait till I see him!* she thought wrathfully. This was followed by an even greater desire to know where he was just at this minute!

She looked at Stark, whose white face was as impassive as a mask. Yet there was something lurking in those dark eyes, she was sure. Triumph, that was it. Stark had disconcerted her and he knew it. He had rather turned the tables on her. There was little point in prolonging this visit.

'Thank you,' she said. 'I may need to talk to you again, Mr Stark.'

When Stark had left, she thanked Erwin van Leeuwen for his help and repeated that she might need to call again.

'Any time, my dear!' Erwin hobbled briskly towards the door. 'I would invite you to stay to lunch, but Mrs Beckett won't have cooked for two. Next time, perhaps?'

Hetty declined this offer politely. However, when they reached the front door, she asked, 'May I just wander around your garden? I see it goes down to the lake.'

'By all means. I wish I could accompany you, but alas!' Erwin tapped his stick on the floor in unspoken explanation. 'The garden is somewhat overgrown. When I was a little more agile, I took quite an interest, but there is no one now. Stark trims hedges and weeds the drive, mows the scrap of lawn just to the rear of the house. Otherwise, it's a veritable jungle!'

They shook hands and parted.

The garden was a jungle, all right. The only reasonably tidy area was immediately around the house and leading to the front gate. From the rear of the house to the lake shore, bushes and trees had run riot. Hetty set off, beginning to wonder if she would need a machete to deal with all this!

But there had to be a way to the boathouse and, sure enough, she came upon it, a narrow footpath, twisting between unpruned shrubs and obviously in regular use. She made her way down it.

The coppiced trees closed over her head. It was gloomy, no sunlight permeating at all through the canopy of leaves above. As she walked, she was listening and looking around her, aware that somewhere Stark was about. With luck, he'd gone back to the garage.

From within the tangle of branches and weeds, a twig snapped. Hetty stopped, her heart thumping. She made an effort to pull herself together. A bird, perhaps, or some small wild mammal, even a domestic cat on the prowl!

She moved forward again, more cautiously. The shrubbery rustled to her left. She tried to ignore the sound but spied a movement from the corner of her eye. There was something in the bushes, far too large to be a rabbit or even a rat.

'All right!' she called out sharply. 'I am a police officer. Just come out of there at once!'

There was a silence. Then a louder crack of breaking twigs

signified that the unseen presence was about to make itself known. The wall of undergrowth heaved and swayed before an advance. The bushes parted and Ned Woodley appeared a short distance away, standing on the path ahead of her.

'Good morning, Sergeant Farrell!' He was wearing a disreputable pair of jeans and a dark sweater. His hair was full of grass and leaf scraps and his face smeared with grime. Any police officer but Hetty herself, she thought, would have arrested him on sight.

'I should have guessed!' she exclaimed in a mix of anger and resignation. (Not to mention just a touch of relief.) 'What on earth do you think you're doing here? Apart from trespassing . . .'

'Much the same as you are!' he retorted promptly.

'I have the owner's permission to look around! For goodness' sake, Stark is here somewhere!'

'He's been in the garage all morning, I checked.' Ned glanced towards the distant buildings, invisible from here. 'Except for a few minutes when he went up to the house while you were there. Then he came out again and went back to tinkering with the car. I saw you arrive,' he added belatedly.

'Did you? Then you ought either to have made yourself known to me or taken yourself off, well away, back to Stoney How! If you'd been seen, you'd have ruined *everything*! You do realise,' Hetty added with some satisfaction, 'that Stark is aware of your interest in this house and grounds and has just reported your suspicious behaviour to me?'

Ned grinned. 'Has he? He doesn't lack nerve, does he? Charmless fellow, otherwise. What did you make of old Erwin?'

'I don't know,' Hetty confessed. 'I find it hard to make him out. He was very pleasant and helpful. But beneath it, he's extremely angry about *something*. He declared himself upset about the loss of the jewellery, of course. He blames Pamela for taking the original decision to send it to England. He was also upset when I told him that it was Michael Holst we took out of the water near here.'

'As if he didn't know!' growled Ned.

'I'm not sure that he did.' Hetty frowned. 'He seemed genuinely shocked, and laid the blame for that at Pamela's door, too. Although, thinking it over, he seemed more angered by the theft of the Romanov Collection than distressed by Holst's death, though he expressed his regret.'

She sighed. 'I'm sure he was infuriated by Pamela van Leeuwen's decision to dispose of the collection. It's clear he and Pamela have had a real fight about it and are still at daggers drawn. I wish I could talk to Pamela herself. No chance of her coming over to this country, I suppose?'

'Every chance,' Ned said. 'Highly likely, I would say. Look here, Het, you're a police officer. You don't believe everything people tell you, do you? I certainly don't, not in my line of work. Whatever has been going on, it's been organised from here, from this property! This quarrel between Erwin and Pamela, which Erwin was so keen to tell you about, it could be as fake as the bogus security guard who kidnapped Holst, you know! Designed to lead us all astray.'

'Yes, I do know, thank you very much, Mr Woodley! I'm bearing in mind both Erwin and Pamela van Leeuwen may be lying, either individually or as accomplices.' She tilted her chin. 'And now I'd be obliged if you'd leave the premises.'

'Or your name and address will be taken!' said Ned disrespectfully.

'Just don't think I wouldn't. You're obstructing me in my enquiries!' she threatened.

'If you're going to be like that about it,' Ned informed her, 'I shan't show you what I've found.'

'If you've found anything at all to do with any of this,' Hetty insisted, 'you have to show me or tell me about it!'

Ned's expression grew maddeningly vague. 'Although I dare say I shan't be able to find it again in all this undergrowth!'

Hetty admitted defeat – temporarily, anyway. 'All right, I give in. Roam around here and get caught by Stark, if you must! But I'd like to see what you've found. Please.'

Ned gestured extravagantly into the depths of the coppice behind them. 'Follow me, Sergeant Farrell!'

It had once been a flight of steps down to a landing stage. Stone balustrades bordered either side. Now vegetation had crawled over it, obscuring most of it. Climbing plants twined their way up the graceful balusters. The edges of the stone steps had crumbled and surfaces cracked where weeds forced their way through. But it was just possible to imagine it how it had been, with the water lapping at the foot of it and the spectacular view across the lake ahead.

Nevertheless, Hetty didn't appreciate having stumbled through the coppice, getting as dusty and dishevelled as Ned was, just to be shown a ruined architectural feature. 'Is this it?' she asked rather ungraciously.

'No, *this* is!' Ned told her.

At the top of each balustrade, an ornamental urn had once stood on a plinth. The one on the right was still there, if almost completely overgrown and out of sight. The one on the left was missing.

It was easy to see where it had stood. The plinth was still there and the creepers around it had been torn roughly aside. Ned pointed silently to the surface of the empty plinth. On it was a pale circle of cleaner stone. The urn had been removed not more than a week ago.

Hetty seized the creepers smothering the remaining urn with both hands and tugged them away, to reveal the stone vase beneath. Though obscured by moss, the pattern on it was all too familiar. Without a doubt, this was the pair to the one Ned had found at the bottom of the lake, lashed to the packaged dummy.

'So, Sergeant Farrell,' Ned hissed. 'What do you make of that?'

Part Four

'So the dummy we took from the lake and the stone vase which weighted it down, both came from Greywalls!' Hetty murmured. She wondered what Inspector Wills would make of this. At least, she found herself thinking, it would put an end to his suspicions that Ned had staged the recovery of the mannequin from the lakebed as some sort of practical joke.

'Exactly, so don't tell me Erwin van Leeuwen isn't the mastermind behind all this!' Ned said grimly.

The breeze gusted across the lake and rustled the leaves of the trees behind them. Water slapped against the supports of the boathouse and from within came a creak of wood.

'I'd like to see in there,' Hetty murmured, more to herself than to Ned.

Ned's gaze had followed hers to the boathouse. 'Tried it already. Locked. I might be able to gain entry by swimming round and underneath it.'

That shocked her into a reminder of his presence. 'You'll certainly do no such thing! I could go back to the house and ask Erwin to lend me the key. But on second thoughts, we need to take a proper look around everywhere. I'll report back to Inspector Wills and we'll get a search warrant. Now that you – we've – found this –' Hetty pointed at the pale patch on the plinth where the vase had once stood – 'I think we've got reason enough to request one.'

Ned was looking stubborn. 'I don't like the delay!'

'Can't be helped. Still, they don't know we've found out about the plinth and the missing vase. Look, Ned, you've really got to get off the premises immediately! If we're seen together, the fat's really in the fire. Go now, please!'

Ned fidgeted about, rubbing his dusty hands over his unkempt hair and making himself look wilder than ever. 'You should leave, too, Hetty. Come back with a gang of coppers.'

'I don't need back-up at the present time, thank you! I'll leave about ten minutes after you. That way we won't be seen and I'd just like to take one more look around.'

He was still obstinate. 'I don't like leaving you here alone, Het.'

'I've got Erwin's permission to be in his garden. And I've got my police two-way radio in my pocket.' She tapped her jacket. 'Do go, Ned. The sooner you leave, the sooner I can leave, after you.'

He was finally persuaded by the last argument, although still manifestly unhappy. He nodded and then, the least thing in the world she expected, leaned forward and kissed her cheek. 'Take care, Het!' he whispered.

And he was gone, vanishing into the trees before she could react.

'Hm!' muttered Hetty, rubbing her cheek. 'Let's hope he doesn't do anything like that while Freddy's watching. That really would encourage the little madam in her plans!'

Ned's farewell gesture had been oddly disconcerting. Hetty, originally startled, now felt by turns annoyed and inexplicably pleased. 'Altogether making too much of a trivial thing!' she told herself sternly.

She made an effort to pull herself together. She was here to see what she could find, not to indulge in confused emotional daydreams by ruined staircases, like the love-struck heroine of a romantic novel.

'So stop smirking like the Cheshire Cat, my girl,' she added, 'and get on with it!'

She checked the boathouse and found, as Ned had told her, that it was locked. She peered through one of the ornamental fretted woodwork panels which served instead of windows to admit light, but could make out little. There seemed to be some kind of rowing boat or dinghy in there. She couldn't imagine Erwin out on the lake. But Stark had been in the Navy early in his career, and the boat might belong to him.

She was about to turn away when something caught her eye. Snagged in a crack in the wooden frame was a tuft of reddish hair. The breeze had again rippled the lake's waters and, reaching the shore, caused the hair to waft in the air, catching the light.

Gently Hetty teased a couple of strands loose. It was too thick for human hair and felt too slippery. All at once she identified it. It was the realistic but synthetic hair of George, the dummy pulled from the lake.

Together with the evidence of the missing urn, it now seemed without a doubt that the dummy and urn had been rowed out to mid-lake in the dinghy kept in the boathouse, and tipped into the deep water by Stark's powerful arms.

Hetty took a small plastic envelope from her shoulder bag and carefully slid the hairs into it and sealed it up. 'Exhibit One,' she murmured. She slipped the plastic package into her pocket and turned.

A few yards away, in the shadow of the trees, Stark stood watching her. In his right hand gleamed the ugly snub nose of a revolver.

Hetty's heart gave a painful lurch but she kept an outward façade of calm, even managing a smile.

'Put the gun down, Mr Stark. I'm not a burglar.'

'You're something worse,' Stark said dourly. 'An interfering snooping copper!'

'I have your employer's authority—' she began but wasn't allowed to finish.

'Shut up!' he ordered her in a tone she accepted it would be wise to heed, at least for the moment.

He came towards her and stretched out his free hand. 'Give me your bag!'

It wasn't the time to argue. Hetty slipped her shoulder bag free and threw it towards him. She had briefly – very briefly – considered throwing it *at* him. But that kind of trick, which invariably worked beautifully in films, wouldn't be likely to make him drop the gun in reality. More likely, he'd fire. His white face was fixed with unnatural tension and the look in his dark eyes indicated a mind which was beyond reason. The man was wound up like a clockwork spring and the slightest rash move or reluctance to obey his orders might be fatal.

The bag – and the mobile phone it contained – landed with a soft thud on the leafy ground. She still had her two-way radio, however.

'Jacket!' Stark ordered.

Hetty's heart sank as she realised it was possible, even likely, that he'd been hidden in the trees and listening while she told Ned she had her police walkie-talkie in her jacket. She had played into Stark's hands by sending Ned away. Stark might have hesitated to tackle two of them. On her own, she presented little problem to a ruthless crook.

Hetty slid her arms out of her jacket and it joined the bag on the ground.

Stark relaxed marginally. It was the first encouraging sign she'd had. It didn't last long. He gestured with the revolver.

'Walk!'

She was about to move in the direction Stark indicated when there came an unexpected interruption.

Within the boathouse sounded a loud electric buzz. It startled them both, the revolver jumping dangerously in Stark's hand. The buzz sounded again.

For a moment, Hetty thought it was a telephone, but then she realised what it was. It was the signal that Erwin van Leeuwen wanted Stark at the house. He'd pressed one of the bell pushes she'd seen him use earlier, on that occasion for the garage.

Stark appeared undecided. The bell rang for a third time, sounding, to Hetty's fancy, more irritable.

The man seemed to come to a decision. The wavering gun steadied. 'Never mind that!' he said. 'Just walk, like I told you, little lady!'

'Your boss wants you,' Hetty said.

'He can wait,' Stark snarled. 'You do as I say!'

* * *

They set off along a narrow footpath between the trees. They proceeded single-file, Hetty ahead and uncomfortably aware of the gun held to her spine by the man behind her.

Even so, her brain was racing. The little episode of the bell had told her something about the relationship between Erwin and his driver. Ned believed Erwin van Leeuwen was the mastermind behind the plot, but Hetty thought differently.

She tried out her theory, remarking over her shoulder, 'It's been easy for you to run rings round Mr van Leeuwen, I dare say, with his being lame and trusting you entirely. He has no idea what you've been up to, does he?'

Stark didn't oblige her with an answer and she had to try again, expounding her theory. 'You're the one who thought all this out, aren't you? The fake security guard and the theft of the Romanov Collection? Does Mr van Leeuwen know anything of it? How about the jewels? Does he have them?'

Behind her she heard Stark snort in derision. 'Old idiot! Him? Too busy paying lawyers to quarrel with other lawyers paid by that woman in Paris! The pair of them, squabbling away about a fortune in diamonds, and letting me just sneak it away from under their noses!'

So, thought Hetty. It had been like the thieves in Aesop's fable. Although, in this case, neither Pamela nor Erwin had stolen anything. But they had been so engrossed in disputing ownership of the treasure, a third party had successfully managed to steal it away.

They had emerged from the trees and passed through a gap in a stone wall to find themselves out on the open fell. It rose steeply in front of them. Hetty took a quick glance around. It appeared an utterly deserted spot. She had hoped to see some walkers, even in the distance, but there wasn't a soul. Only a few sheep trotted out of their way as they began to scrabble uphill. She wasn't wearing suitable shoes for climbing and her smooth soles slid about on the pebbly soil. In addition, the breeze blew chill up here and she hadn't her jacket.

Behind her, Stark was breathing heavily. But his physique indicated he was fit; the climb wouldn't bother him enough to distract his attention, or give her any chance to get away from him. She wondered uneasily where they were going.

She resumed their conversation, such as it was. At least she could learn as much as she could and hope for some unforeseen event to turn the tables.

'You were the bogus security guard who met Michael Holst at Heathrow,' she said. 'You fixed up an alibi using the dummy. You set it up in an armchair before the television and told Erwin you were going to watch the Test Match.'

'It was my day off,' Stark said, sounding indignant. 'I was entitled to watch the telly if I wanted!'

'Yes, but how did you know the vicar would visit Erwin that afternoon and see you – I mean, see the dummy?'

Behind her came a hoarse chuckle. 'Easy. That padre, he's famous for being mad on the cricket. As for Mr van Leeuwen, he don't get out much, but he's generous enough, a sucker for a good cause if he hears about it. I suggested he give some money to that fund they got, for the church tower or something. Said I'd call the vicar for him and arrange a visit. I told the padre the evening before that he had to come that next afternoon and then told the old man what time to expect him. After that, all I had to do was fix up the dummy and make sure it could be seen from the driveway outside, switch on the telly and leave 'em to it!'

'And Michael Holst . . .' It was the most dangerous question of all. 'You killed Michael Holst?'

'He was trying to run out on me!' Stark's voice boomed suddenly, loud and angry by her ear.

Hetty stopped and spun round. Stark's white face had gained two dull red spots on either cheekbone, turning his features more than ever into a grotesque clown's mask.

'You were in it together, you and Holst? You were partners?'

'That's what I thought!' Stark growled. 'But he tried to trick me! I got rid of the dummy like we planned. But that insurance investigator went diving out there. He managed to find the dummy on the lakebed! The shore was swarming with police after that.'

Stark's face was sullen and his voice bitter. 'Spoiled everything! Holst lost his nerve – not that he ever had much! He turned traitor on me, reckoned he could say I'd kidnapped him and he'd be believed. I was furious with him and struck out with a boathook . . . Killed him outright. I hid his body in the boathouse; I meant, as soon as I could, to take him out and dump him over the side of the boat, like I did that dummy!'

There was silence. Stark licked his lips nervously.

'But I couldn't plan properly no more. Got a bit panicky myself by then. I just rowed out Saturday night, under cover of dark, and tipped Holst in, thought he'd sink. But he came floating back inshore in the morning and you went and found him in the reeds!'

They moved off again, Hetty thoughtful. They crested a rise and were now descending the further side, down into a broad valley. A stream ran along the bottom of it and nearby was a stone hut, probably built to shelter shepherds. Though it was unlikely it was used for that now, it looked as if someone might recently have repaired it. Hetty suspected they were headed towards it.

Sure enough, they crossed the stream by stepping stones of smooth rocks and turned aside towards the hut. It had a strong wooden door, with hasp and padlock.

'I fixed that up,' Stark said unexpectedly, indicating the lock. 'Had a mind it might come in useful, this place. I wasn't ever sure of that Holst fellow. Thought I might have to lock him up. As it was I had to knock him over the head!'

Hetty said, her voice shaking despite her best efforts, 'If you shoot me out here, the shot will be heard for miles.'

Stark grunted in response. He was hunting in his pocket, but keeping the revolver fixed firmly on her. Hetty watched as he took out a bunch of keys and unlocked the padlock. He pulled the door open. Inside it looked dark and unwelcoming.

He nodded towards the opening. 'Go on.'

She made a last attempt at delay, asking, 'Just tell me one thing. When did you – or you and Holst – start to plan all this?'

Unexpectedly, Stark's set features split in an unlovely grin. 'I had time enough! We went to France, the old fellow and me, about five, six years ago. He wanted to visit that Mrs Pamela van Leeuwen, and I was to drive him.'

Stark's expression turned to one of virtuous disgust. 'We'd no sooner got there, than he and she, they started quarrelling. Didn't seem to care that I – or anyone else, come to that – could over-hear half of it!

'Pretty soon it became clear they were fighting over some

jewellery, some Russian stuff, diamonds. She wanted to go sending it to London, to some museum. Kept talking of making a gift of it, in memory of her husband and someone else. Old Erwin, he was for keeping it "in the family", as he kept saying. By which he meant, if she was going to give it away, she ought to give it to him. Though what he'd do with it, I couldn't tell you! He's rich enough and has got a collection of pictures and statuettes and things already. You never heard the like, going hammer and tongs, they were, shouting at each other and calling one another names.'

Stark shook his head wonderingly at the memory. 'First off, it just struck me as funny. It wasn't as if they were youngsters, the pair of them, to get in such a passion about it. You'd have thought they'd have had a bit more sense. Then I realised she really did mean to send a whole suitcase full of diamond jewellery off to a museum!'

Stark's voice gained a note of horror. 'Can you imagine it? For once, I was on my governor's side. He called her crazy to her face, and I reckon he was right!'

Stark gave another snort of disgust. 'So I thought, it'd be a real waste. I thought what I could do with it. Sell the stuff easy. Even if a fence only gave me half its value, it'd be more money than I'd be likely to see in my lifetime, all at once. Serve 'em right, too – squabbling away like a pair of spoilt kids!'

There was an element of truth in what Stark said, thought Hetty ruefully. Had Erwin and Pamela van Leeuwen acted with more reason and decorum, all of this might have been avoided.

Stark had spent enough time on conversation. He gave Hetty a push through the open door of the hut and slammed it on her.

She heard the scrap of the hasp and padlock being returned and a click as it was locked. Then there was silence.

At least Stark had gone and that gave her time. But how much time Hetty didn't know. It was dark in the windowless hut. A little light seeped under the door and through chinks in some of the stonework. A little also came in under the roof and as her eyes became accustomed to the gloom she could make out the confines of her prison. The stones were rough cut and their surface uneven. The roof, she decided, was made of wooden planks. As the day wore on, the light would fade – even if Stark didn't come back before that. She had to find a way out now.

Hetty shivered. Without her jacket it was cold in here. Activity of any sort would also serve to keep her warm. She rattled the door to check, and ran her hands over the rough walls, her fingers searching for a crack. Even if she found one, it wouldn't help. To work even one of these stones loose would take a very long time and she hadn't any tools. Or, at least, not in the modern way of things. But primitive man had managed very well with stone implements and so could she. Provided she could find a suitable one!

Hetty knelt down and carefully searched the earthen floor with the tips of her fingers. After a few moments they encountered a larger rock, embedded in the soil amongst the pebbles and stones.

It took a while to ease it out, by which time she was sweating and her fingernails torn and the flesh rubbed raw. But at last, with a glow of triumph, she held the rock, about the size of a coconut, in her hands.

But how and where to use it? It would make little impact on

walls or door. There remained only the roof. Hetty looked up at it.

As far as she could make out, the wooden slats were nailed to a frame. It was a simple enough structure. She stretched up, but it was out of her reach. Hetty sighed.

She tucked the rock in her shirt, slipped off her shoes, and by gripping with toes and fingers in the nooks and crannies of the stone walls managed to lever herself up to the level of the roof. Wedged there in a corner, with her back against a wall and her legs braced against the wall opposite, she retrieved her rock-hammer and, reaching up, struck it against a wooden slat just above where it joined the frame.

It was arguably the most difficult thing she'd ever done. The angle at which she had to work lessened the force behind her blows and made her efforts inefficient. Fit as she was, her arms and legs quickly became so tired she felt she wouldn't be able to hold the position long enough to finish the work or, even worse, fall to the ground and hurt herself. Twice she scrambled down to take a brief rest. Each time, driven by the thought of Stark, she climbed up again as soon as she was able and began again. The light was fading fast and when darkness fell, she was sure, Stark would return. She wondered where Ned was and what they were making of her failure to return back at the station. But she hadn't time to wonder about all these things now. Escape was all-important.

Ned hadn't been idle. He had hurried back to Stoney How where his reappearance was greeted boisterously by his sister and the dachshunds.

'You look dirty,' said Freddy critically. 'And you ought to have been here earlier. Hetty came round and we went for a walk. I think she likes you, even though she doesn't say so. I told her *you* liked *her*.'

Ned stooped over her and said in exasperation, 'You've not been trying to marry me off again, have you, Freddy? I've told you before about that.'

'But you do like her, don't you? I asked Felix and he said you did. Felix likes her too, and so do I, and so do Jo-Jo and Copper.' Freddy's tone was one of gentle persistence, determined to make him see reason despite himself.

Ned abandoned the argument and went indoors. Passing a mirror, he caught sight of himself and chuckled. 'The wild man of the woods!' he said to Felix, who'd emerged from the kitchen.

A little later, cleaned up and judging Hetty to have had time to return to base, Ned rang the police. He asked to speak to Sergeant Farrell.

He was told that Sergeant Farrell wasn't in the building. A sense of unease gripped Ned. 'When did anyone last hear from her or see her? This is Edward Woodley, I'm the diver who found the mannequin in the lake. I need to speak to Sergeant Farrell urgently.'

But Sergeant Farrell, it seemed, had been out of contact since earlier that morning.

Ned slammed down the phone. 'Felix! I'm going into town!'

Freddy ran after him. 'Can't I come?' Her features puckered beseechingly beneath her mop of fiery curls.

'Not this time, sweetie. Business!' Ned said grimly.

'What do you mean, Mr Woodley, by deliberately setting out to interfere in a police matter?' Bradley Wills was at his iciest.

Impatiently, Ned swept aside the inspector's displeasure. 'I told you, I was just looking around the gardens, and I found out where that urn-affair came from. Erwin's definitely involved in this! Look, where's Hetty— I mean, Sergeant Farrell? She was going to come back here and tell you all about it and request a search warrant.'

Inspector Wills hesitated. 'Wait one moment, Mr Woodley.'

He walked to the door and called out to someone in an office across the way. There was a brief conversation. Ned couldn't hear the words, but for one phrase when Wills raised his voice.

'Why the dickens has no one told me the sergeant hasn't been in touch?'

He must have realised Ned could have heard this, and returned to slam shut the door of his own office, isolating Ned. The murmur of voices became so indistinct it wasn't possible to tell even who was talking. Frustrated, Ned waited until he heard retreating footsteps tap briskly down the polished corridor. Someone sent to get a search underway, he hoped. The door re-opened and Wills returned.

The inspector's normal formidable calm had almost – if not quite – deserted him. He was breathing heavily, and the muscles around his jaw twitched.

'It seems, Mr Woodley,' he said stiffly, 'that Sergeant Farrell has not returned nor called in and cannot be contacted. We don't know why,' he added with just a touch of embarrassment.

'She's at Greywalls!' yelled Ned, leaping to his feet. 'You've got to go out there. You don't know what van Leeuwen may have done!'

'We – in fact I, myself – shall be going to the house immediately, Mr Woodley.'

Inspector Wills straightened his shoulders. He had been made to look foolish before an outsider. Wills's manner suggested that in due course, he would be calling for bell, book and candle and make the person responsible suffer. In the meantime, he wasn't going to give anyone on his team another chance to put him in a false position with regard to a member of the public!

Ned fixed the inspector with a look so steely that Bradley Wills, unused to being on the receiving end of this kind of resolve, appeared quite startled.

'And I,' Ned told him, 'am coming with you!'

Crack!

Hetty had been on the point of giving up. The slats on which she'd been working for nearly an hour had loosened, but appeared to have been fixed with sturdy masonry nails and breaking through was going to be beyond her. Then, just as she was despairing, the corner slat gave way.

With renewed vigour, she struck upwards again with her stone hammer. The slat sprang upward and there was a gush of cold, slightly musky air. Hetty dropped the stone and reached up with her bruised and bleeding fingers to work at the next slat. It, too, came free, the nail still attached and offering a dangerous spike to be avoided.

'One more!' muttered Hetty.

The next offered some resistance, but Hetty was now inspired and not to be thwarted by a piece of wood. It groaned, the nail holding, then snapped. There was a hole in the roof and she could just, only just, squeeze through it.

It was by no means easy, but she managed it. She hauled herself out into the fresh air and paused, panting, half in and half out of the hut, to take stock.

She had lost track of time. She'd supposed it must be evening because the light had failed. In fact, something else had happened of which she'd been totally unaware.

While she'd been imprisoned, the weather had played one of its not unaccustomed tricks up here. A cold, thick mist had descended, enveloping everything in a silent blanket.

Hetty struggled the rest of the way out, and lowered herself carefully from the roof, releasing her grip and letting herself drop to the ground.

It wasn't far, but she rolled over and scrambled to her feet a short distance away. Had she not known the hut was so near, she couldn't have guessed. It was quite invisible behind the dense veil.

'Oh no!' she whispered, appalled.

Struggling to break through the roof had kept her warm. Now the mist seeped through her cotton shirt, wrapping her in its icy embrace. Hetty knew the wisest thing to do in the circumstances would be to wait in a sheltered spot for the mist to lift. Hereabouts this could happen quite suddenly.

However, she wasn't dressed to remain motionless, generating no body heat. Secondly, although Stark couldn't return to find her in this weather, he remained a real danger to someone else: to Erwin van Leeuwen, who was at Greywalls, blissfully unaware of his driver's treachery.

Stark's carefully laid plans had fallen apart. He had, by his own account, panicked more than once, first killing Holst and later dumping his victim's body so carelessly that it had floated back to shore. Stark now, with the police on his trail, might do almost anything and anyone who stood in his way was in peril. Erwin must be warned.

But her chances of finding her way back to the road were almost non-existent, nor could a rescue party search for her. She had exchanged one kind of captivity for another. The mist that kept others at bay, held her a prisoner on the fell.

Part Five

Hetty hugged her arms about her and tried to recall how far she and Stark had come and over what kind of terrain. The mist confused her sense of direction and she knew all kinds of treacherous potholes and sudden drops lay out there to ensnare the unwary.

The hut was a point of reference – if she could find it again! She put out her hands and took a few tentative steps forward. Her fingers brushed the rough stone. Thank goodness! Hetty put her back to it and knew she faced the direction in which they'd come.

The stream! They'd crossed a stream. She strained her ears and thought she could hear a faint gurgle of water. Setting one foot cautiously in front of the other, she set out towards the sound.

The splashing of water over a rocky bed became louder, telling her she was headed the right way. An icy wetness seeped through her shoe. She drew back her foot, stooped and felt the ground. Her fingers encountered water. She'd found the stream.

She knew it ran downhill to the lake. Drawing on what she'd managed to observe on her climb up here with Stark, she was pretty sure it cut a course skirting the grounds of Stoney How in a wide curve. She edged forward cautiously, well aware that at some point, this watercourse might tumble over a steep drop as some other fell streams did. But she couldn't recall any such waterfall in this area.

She had managed to progress an unknown distance before she realised she couldn't hear the stream's gurgle any more. She dropped onto her hands and knees and crawled forward. All at once, her hands countered an edge of turf and beyond it, empty air.

The stream was now running between banks below her. To go on would be to risk injury. Hetty stopped and began to slap her arms back and forth to encourage circulation as she speculated on what might be happening in her absence.

They must have missed her by now at the station. They would have tried to call her up on her radio and failed. They knew she'd gone to Greywalls. If Bradley Wills suddenly appeared there with back-up, Stark would certainly panic.

Hetty frowned. The mist, which had been a solid swirling mass, now appeared darker at a low level ahead of her. There could be no other explanation of this than – yes! – it was lifting! Even as she watched, the dark strip resolved itself into the hazy outlines of a stone wall.

Hetty leapt up and down, yelling 'Hurray!' Before long, it had lifted enough to enable her to set out again and then, as if by some sleight of hand, it vanished and the way down the fell was clear.

Below her, like the promised land, she sighted the tall chimneys of Stoney How.

The dachshunds, hearing Hetty stumble into the yard, rushed out barking furiously. Freddy wasn't far behind.

She was a practical child and grabbed the blue-featured newcomer by one chilled hand, hauling her into the warm kitchen where Felix, swathed in his apron, presided over a simmering pot of soup.

'F-Felix?' Hetty stammered. 'I need to use your phone!'

'My dear girl!' exclaimed Felix, laying aside his wooden spoon. 'You need a glass of brandy! What on earth has happened to you?' He seized her hands and chafed them between his own broad palms.

'Can't take time to explain now. Where's Ned?' She looked anxiously around her.

Felix glanced at Freddy. 'I rather fancy he went to call on your Inspector Wills.'

'What? Felix, please, *the phone!*'

As she was finishing her call to the station, Freddy appeared carrying a mug of coffee and put it down by her. Hetty put down the phone and picked up the steaming mug gratefully. 'Thanks, Freddy.' She sipped at it and almost scalded her tongue. 'Ow!'

'Where's your coat?' asked Freddy severely.

'Lost it.'

'Never mind,' Freddy consoled her. 'You can borrow one of Ned's pullovers.'

She scuttled away and returned shortly to thrust a bulky woollen garment into her arms. Hetty struggled into it. It came down nearly to her knees and the sleeves had to be folded back several times. It was more like a poncho than a sweater on her.

'Perhaps,' said Freddy doubtfully, 'you'd better change into something else before you arrest anyone, you know.'

'I do hope you're going to take care, my dear,' Felix rumbled. 'None of us here wants any harm to come to you – and one of us, I fancy, in particular!'

'He means Ned,' translated the ever-helpful Freddy.

There were police cars outside Greywalls when she arrived. A constable stationed at the gate monitored entry. He didn't know her by sight and faced with a dishevelled apparition in a huge baggy sweater, he understandably refused at first to let her pass. Her plea that she'd lost her identification fell on deaf ears. Fortunately, another constable who recognised her appeared and vouched for her.

A wrathful Mrs Beckett was standing at the foot of the stairs, arms folded and face set grim with disapproval. From the noises overhead, the upper floor of the house was being searched.

Seeing Hetty, the housekeeper burst into speech. 'I've never known the like, not in my entire life! Trampling over my clean house, pulling out all the cupboards and drawers! Making as much mess as they please and not a word of apology or explanation! Another lot over at Mr Stark's lodge, doing the same there! What kind of folk do they take us for? And what are they looking for, you tell me that!'

Hetty had no intention of telling her that, or anything else at this moment. Instead she asked, 'The inspector?'

'In the drawing room, with another gentleman and poor Mr van Leeuwen. He's not a well man, you know! This is a terrible shock to him. You should know better!' It was clear Mrs Beckett blamed Hetty for the entire upset.

* * *

Erwin huddled in his chair, his pink face crumpled in distress. He looked more than ever like an elderly baby, one who had just been deprived of a favourite rattle. Inspector Wills stood by the row of bell pushes, peering at them suspiciously, and Ned prowled around the room like a caged tiger.

Hetty hadn't given much thought to the effect of her reappearance, but she afterwards reflected that probably never again would she make such a dramatic entrance.

'Hetty!' yelled Ned, diving towards her and clasping her to him in an embrace that knocked the breath out of her. 'You're all right! I've been worried sick! What happened? I told you not to stay here on your own!' He cast an anxious eye over her, frowned, and added, 'Oy, isn't that one of my pullovers?'

'Sergeant Farrell!' Inspector Wills sounded relieved, before adding in his normal clipped tones, 'Where on earth have you been? Mr Woodley! Kindly release my sergeant.'

It was really rather pleasant, being crushed to Ned's chest, but there was a time and place for everything, and this clearly wasn't it.

Hetty detached herself, and gabbled out a résumé of her adventures. Erwin, listening, appeared close to tears.

'I never would have believed it! Stark, of all people! So trustworthy! With me several years . . . Quite out of character . . .'

'Where is Stark?' Hetty asked.

'Done a bunk!' said Ned.

'Eluded us for the moment,' Bradley Wills conceded. 'But he won't get far. We've recovered a revolver at the lodge and it's now unlikely that he's armed.'

Erwin asked plaintively, 'But what about the Romanov Collection? Does Stark have it with him?'

The others stared at him. Hetty reflected that in all the excitement, the loss of the diamonds themselves had almost become overlooked.

'We've no idea,' said Inspector Wills. 'I doubt Stark has them in his actual possession. He left in too much of a hurry to have retrieved them from wherever he'd hidden them. My guess is they're still concealed on the property and he'll return to Greywalls. More than ever, he needs money, and the diamonds represent a great deal of money!' The inspector nodded to underline his conclusion.

Hetty was inclined to agree with him, but was more worried about Erwin than the missing Romanov Collection.

'Will it be safe here for Mr van Leeuwen? With Stark on the loose, even if he isn't armed?'

Erwin bounced in his chair. 'I cannot believe Stark would harm me! No, no. I've known him for years.'

This would be no protection, but no one liked to say so to Erwin.

Bradley Wills cleared his throat. 'Well, Mr van Leeuwen, I suggest we mount a discreet watch. A couple of officers will remain in the house with you overnight. You will be in no danger.'

'Oh dear,' said Erwin, startled. 'I don't like the sound of that at all.'

'A word, Farrell!' murmured the inspector.

Hetty withdrew into the hall with him. Mrs Beckett could be heard in the distance, berating the searchers.

'This is my kitchen! Turning all my pots and pans out! Never heard the like!'

'What do you make of van Leeuwen, sergeant?' the inspector asked in a low voice.

'I think he's quite innocent,' Hetty told him. 'He's rather like a—' She paused, embarrassed.

'Rather like an elderly baby,' Wills finished for her.

Hetty smiled. 'I'm afraid that's just what he reminds me of! In temperament, too, not just in appearance. He's a nice old gentleman. A real eccentric, I'd call him. It was easy for Stark to deceive him.'

Wills nodded. 'I agree. I just wish I knew where Stark has got to!'

'I'm willing to stay tonight on watch,' she offered.

'You will not, Farrell!' Bradley Wills told her crisply. 'You've had enough adventures for one day and after an hour wandering about the fell in the mist, you don't need to sit up all night as well! By the way . . .' He looked even more disapproving. 'Where on earth did you get that dreadful sweater? It's hardly the sort of thing I expect to see any officer of mine wearing on duty. Or off it, come to that!'

'Sorry, lost my jacket!' she apologised.

'Well, get yourself smartened up as soon as you can, Farrell!'

'Yessir.' Hetty's voice became resolute. 'But I'd like to stay here tonight, all the same. Mr van Leeuwen knows me. He's of a nervous disposition. I think he'd be happier with someone he knew around.'

They returned to Ned and Erwin. In their absence Ned had taken the opportunity to remark on the seascapes hanging on the wall. Erwin, delighted to find an admirer of his cherished paintings, was expounding on their finer points.

They were all distracted by the sound of a car horn. It was followed by that of upraised voices. The conscientious constable on gate duty was now attempting to prevent yet another new arrival entering the premises.

A woman's voice, loud and imperious, declared, 'Do stand aside, my good man!'

'What on earth—' began Inspector Wills, starting towards the door. He was too late.

Mrs Beckett threw it open. The housekeeper was clearly in awe, as well she might be. She ushered in a tall, slim, elderly woman dressed in the height of elegance. Her tailored black costume had the look of a leading fashion house about it. Her waved grey hair was styled by an expert. She wore large pearl earrings complemented by a choker of four ropes of pearls. Expensive perfume filled the air.

They all gaped at her. Mrs Beckett, cheeks flushed and eyes sparkling, did the honours. She ignored the others to address her employer.

'Mrs Pamela van Leeuwen to see you, sir.'

Mrs Beckett brought them all tea in what was obviously the household's best china. The housekeeper's air was that of someone who is entertaining minor royalty.

'Would you care for a cup, ma'am?' she asked in hushed tones. Hetty thought that Mrs Beckett just stopped short of genuflecting.

'How kind,' said Pamela, and the housekeeper floated out of the room in seventh heaven.

Considerably more briskly, Pamela asked, 'Would someone mind telling me exactly what is going on here?'

She'd posed her question to the gathering at large. Predictably, they all tried to tell her at once.

Bradley Wills managed to exert his authority, quelling rival accounts and summing up events to date.

Pamela listened in silence and inclined her head. 'Poor Holst. Although, if what you say is correct, he was in on the plot. I was mistaken in him.'

'My company has used him before. We thought he was reliable,' Ned told her.

'I thought Stark was reliable,' said Erwin, gazing sadly into his cup.

Pamela straightened herself, as if to tackle some unwelcome task, folded her hands in her lap and said, 'I have to apologise to you, Erwin. You were quite right. To move the collection, all at once like that, was fraught with danger. The temptation was just too much for Holst and for your driver. One can hardly blame them.'

Erwin became agitated. His protuberant blue eyes blinked rapidly and his cup rattled alarmingly in its saucer. Fortunately, he set it down, just as Hetty was preparing to dive and save the delicate porcelain from being dashed to the floor.

'No, no! My dear Pamela! You shouldn't apologise to me! I should be telling you how sorry I am, so sorry I made such a dreadful fuss. Of course you wanted to ensure the collection stayed together and a museum would be the ideal recipient, a memorial to Paul and his father. Such a good idea and I don't know why I was so – so *vehemently* against it!'

Ned and Hetty exchanged wry glances. A little late in the day, Erwin and Pamela had decided to be reasonable and listen fairly to one another's views.

Pamela van Leeuwen was also sensible of the change. 'We're

both at fault, Erwin. We've behaved like spoilt children. I do hope we can put this behind us, and start again?'

'Of course!' cried van Leeuwen, his pink face shining.

Inspector Wills cleared his throat. 'I'm sorry to add a note of discord, but no one can – er – start again, while the jewellery itself is still missing!'

Van Leeuwen's plump cheeks crumpled and his eyes grew moist with emotion. 'Irreplaceable! Antique jewellery of the finest crafts-manship! Stones of the first water!'

Pamela, of sterner stuff, observed, 'It is certainly a nuisance.'

Footsteps sounded heavily above their heads and Erwin glanced up at the ceiling in a perplexed way. 'They don't think, surely, to find anything in my house?' Horror crossed his plump face. 'Pamela, surely you don't think that *I –*'

'Nonsense, Erwin, of course I don't!' she said.

'I cannot sleep with strangers in the house!' Erwin declared.

They had been discussing the overnight watch and he was proving both awkward and obstinate.

'We could take you to a hotel, Mr van Leeuwen,' Wills suggested.

Erwin's face puckered. 'I hate hotels! If someone must stay, it shall be Mr Woodley.'

'Woodley isn't a police officer,' the inspector retorted.

Erwin reddened and the anger which Hetty had divined lurked suppressed beneath his nervous manner, erupted. 'But it is *my* house, isn't it? I shall have Mr Woodley, who represents the insur-ance company, and Sergeant Farrell, who is a pleasant young woman. Those two or no one at all!'

He was adamant, but in the end, a compromise had been reached. Erwin agreed to accept two constables in addition to Hetty and Ned, provided neither of the strange police officers was in the house.

So one constable was stationed at Stark's lodge and the other at the boathouse. Hetty, inside the house, watched the front approach, and Ned the back. They were in radio contact with one another but so far, nothing had happened.

A faint snore drifting occasionally down the corridor from Erwin's bedroom reminded Hetty she wasn't alone in the front area of the house. But it was decidedly eerie, even so. She glanced at her watch. It was almost three. The wind rustled the trees outside and the woodwork creaked in the changing night temperatures. A louder than usual creak caused her heart to leap in alarm, the door swung open and a voice whispered, 'Hetty?'

'You made me jump out of my skin! You're supposed to be watching the back of the house!' she hissed.

'Yes, I know, but I'm bored and frankly, I'm pretty sure he isn't coming.'

After a moment, Hetty whispered, 'So am I.'

Ned sat down on the floor beside her. She could just make him out in a shaft of moonlight from the uncurtained window, resting his arms on his knees.

'Het? How keen are you on staying in the police force?'

'Very keen!' she said indignantly.

'Don't fly off the handle at me! What I meant was, my company could use another investigator with your experience. We could work together. I think we'd do that rather well, don't you?'

'Working together means not keeping information from one

another. You still haven't told me everything. How did you really come to find the dummy in the lake?'

'Saw Stark go out in the boat.' Ned heaved a sigh. 'The visibility was poor and I wasn't sure what he was doing, but I thought he pushed something over the side. I didn't expect to find the dummy. I thought, if I found anything, I'd find a strongbox. The dummy really threw me. I did think I'd found a body – probably Holst's – an awful shock. But then poor Holst's body turned up later.'

'You should have said you suspected Holst and Stark were in the plot together.'

'I didn't know they were working together,' he argued. 'I thought Holst may have been Stark's prisoner!' After a moment, he added, 'If we worked together, really together in the same interests, the company's, we would share information – and everything.'

She wasn't quite sure what the 'everything' meant. There was a note in his voice that suggested he was thinking of a commitment which went beyond working for the same company.

If so, Ned's plans were running well ahead of any fancies she might have had. Although she had to admit she had indulged in a few daydreams.

'I don't know, Ned,' Hetty said discouragingly. 'I ran away from a job in the city once before.'

'It's not an ordinary city job. I travel about a lot. I never know what I'm going to be called on to investigate next. We'd be together, wouldn't you like that?' He waited hopefully for a reply. Not receiving one, he finished, 'Why don't you think about it?'

She was getting sleepy. It had been a long day and night, and Bradley Wills had been right to doubt she could remain alert till morning.

'I'll think about it . . .' she mumbled.

Ned continued more awkwardly, 'In fact, Hetty, I wanted to ask you something particular. I realise this isn't a good moment, but we never seem to get any moments alone. There's either Felix or Freddy playing gooseberry, or that inspector of yours. Or else you're getting yourself hijacked by Stark. I suppose I ought to have a bunch of red roses and be on one knee, but as it is . . . Hetty?'

A pressure on his shoulder interrupted him and he saw her head tilted to one side and resting peacefully against his arm. She was fast asleep.

'Didn't hear a word, did you?' Ned asked softly. 'Well, some other time, then . . .'

'Stark didn't show up, sir, not a sign of him,' Hetty reported.

She glanced a little guiltily at Ned. She had little recollection of the night's events after the early hours when Ned had joined her at her post overlooking the drive. She'd been awoken by a beam of sunlight to find she'd been fast asleep with her head on Ned's shoulder. Ned had sat, not daring to move for fear of waking her, for three hours and was, he had informed her, 'just about fossilised!'.

'You should have woken me!' she'd wailed.

'Why? Nothing happened.' Ned had sounded a little disconsolate.

It was now a little after eight in the morning and Bradley Wills had arrived to join his puffy-eyed team.

A tap of a stick on parquet heralded Erwin van Leeuwen, resplendent in a black silk dressing gown with scarlet facings.

'Good morning, everyone. You will all join me at breakfast?'

Mrs Beckett had arrived a little earlier and the smell of fresh hot coffee had been filling the air. Breakfast sounded a very good idea. They were not, however, to be lucky.

There was a tap at the door and the inspector's driver appeared. 'Excuse me, sir. Message from the station.' He hesitated, catching sight of Erwin in all his black and scarlet glory.

'Well?' demanded the inspector.

'It's that chap Stark, sir. Uniformed branch have him in custody.'

'What?' cried Erwin.

'The jewellery!' cried Ned, mindful of his company's interests.

The driver shook his head. 'No sign of that. It's a funny business. He was arrested in the police compound just before dawn, trying to break into the garages. They didn't know who he was at first. They thought he was a drunk and put him in a cell to sober up. They only identified him a few minutes ago and got in touch with CID.'

Hetty's tiredness fell away as she gave a shriek which caused all heads to snap round in her direction.

'Sorry!' she apologised. 'But the jewels, they're not here! Never were! We've wasted our time. But I know where they are!'

They were all gathered around the trestle table, Erwin hurriedly dressed, and Pamela van Leeuwen summoned from a nearby hotel. The garage was gloomy and someone had switched on the neon strip light. George, the mannequin, abandoned since Hetty had examined it after its recovery from the water, rested ignominiously beneath a grubby cloth. The covering was now removed and in the pitiless light, the dummy appeared less real and infinitely less attractive.

121

'Puts you in mind of Frankenstein's monster, doesn't it?' Ned remarked.

'It's certainly a gruesome thing,' said Pamela van Leeuwen, stooping over George with a moue of distaste. 'This was recovered from the lake?'

'Stark used it to provide himself with an alibi,' Hetty told her. 'But that's not all he used it for. You see, the head and arms are detachable . . .'

Erwin, leaning on his stick, said faintly, 'You think the Romanov jewels are in that dummy?'

'I think it's very likely,' she told him. 'Right, George,' she added to the dummy. 'I'm afraid you're about to lose your head!'

The head came off easily enough, releasing an odour of lakebed mud, but it was empty, as was the body cavity. The spectators, who had pressed around it excitedly, slumped and stood back with a universal groan.

'Nice guess, Hetty,' sighed Ned, stifling a yawn. 'Pity it wasn't right.'

'Wait a minute!' she urged him. 'If the jewels were taken out of their different cases, how much space would be needed to conceal them?'

He shrugged. 'If they were loose, just bundled up in a piece of oilcloth, oh, very little.'

'Then we try the arms,' Hetty insisted.

The sausage-shaped package had been thrust inside George's right arm. Hetty drew it out with understandable triumph. It was wrapped in plastic bubble-wrap and tied round with string. The plastic was still wet, and the neon light caused it to glisten and lights to play in the air bubbles as if the package contained tinsel.

No one spoke. It seemed even breathing was difficult. In complete silence, Hetty cut the string and unrolled the plastic wrap. As the last sheet was folded back, a gasp went up all around.

The glitter had been no trick of the light on wet plastic. Entangled into a long rope of precious metal and fine stones, at present indistinguishable one piece from another, but gleaming like white fire, the Romanov Collection lay before their eyes.

'Only one piece seriously damaged,' said Hetty. 'It's remarkable, considering the rough handling the jewellery had.'

'The tiara,' Erwin van Leeuwen replied bitterly. 'Cut in three to be made to fit inside the dummy's arm. Stark, the wretched vandal!'

'It can be repaired,' Ned assured him.

They were sitting in the drawing room of Stoney How. Outside it drizzled rain, but here they were all snug sitting around a roaring fire after a splendid lunch cooked for them by Felix. Hetty was enjoying a week's leave which Bradley Wills felt she'd earned.

Possibly the inspector's motives had been mixed. 'You might as well take the time off, Farrell. Woodley is back in the district, and you can keep him out of my way!'

Pamela van Leeuwen had changed her Parisian attire for a more suitable outfit, a tweed skirt and silk shirt, over which she wore an expensive knitted jacket. The casual clothing was a poor disguise. There was something, thought Hetty, about being very rich. An aura of self-confidence and the knowledge that one needn't worry, even if a fortune in jewellery had almost been lost for ever.

'You mustn't fret about it, Erwin,' said Pamela placidly.

'But Stark was in my employ!' Erwin was one of those inclined to wallow in misfortune.

Pamela had no intention of allowing this. 'Cheer up, Erwin!' she ordered. 'All's well that end's well. The collection's recovered and – much more important – you and I are friends again!'

At that, Erwin perked up. 'I've engaged a new driver, did you know?' he asked them. 'A young woman, excellent references. She won't be doing any gardening, as Stark did. But I've found someone else for that.' He beamed at them. 'Pamela is staying at Greywalls for a week or two. I may return to Paris with her, for a little holiday!'

Hetty stood at the window and watched the two van Leeuwens driven away by Erwin's new lady driver.

Ned came up behind her and whispered in her ear, 'What do you think?'

'I think it will work out very well,' Hetty said. 'The problem before was that Erwin had become too dependent on Stark.'

'I didn't mean Erwin's new driver! I meant, Erwin and Pamela. Romance in the twilight of their years?'

'That would be nice, wouldn't it?' Hetty thought it over. 'Erwin struck me as rather a lonely man. I dare say Pamela, for all her money, is lonely too. They'd be good for one another.'

Ned slipped his arms round her waist. 'And what about us? I think we'd be good for one another.'

She was prevented from replying by the arrival of Freddy who surveyed the scene with satisfaction. Things were working out just as Ned's sister wanted.

'It's stopped raining,' she said. 'Wouldn't you both like to go for a walk. I mean, *all on your own?*'

Beneath her mop of red curls, her face was bright with anticipation. Seated either side of her, Jo-Jo and Copper's enquiring expressions were a mirror image of the child's.

Ned gave a dramatic groan. 'You'll have noticed,' he said, 'that my sister isn't subtle.'

'Yes, I had noticed.' Hetty looked over her shoulder and smiled into his face.

'But she does have a few good ideas. How about this walk – all on our own? There is something I want to discuss with you.'

'Yes,' Hetty said. 'I'd rather like that.'

Jo-Jo and Copper, sensitive to atmosphere, beat the floor with their tails in enthusiastic approval.

Chilli, Fireworks and a Little Murder

'I don't know why you're taking so much trouble,' said George Parker.

He was standing in the kitchen doorway. Kate Parker sighed. George would come in when she was busy. She pushed a lock of her greying, untidy hair behind one ear and went to the table. She was a large, competent woman, slow and methodic in her movements. Steadily she stirred chicken pieces in the bowl of chilli marinade but some of the marinade splashed onto her stubby fingers. What a bright red it was, almost like fresh blood.

George came nearer, hands in pockets, criticism written all over him.

Kate said, 'It's Guy Fawkes Night. You know I'm on the organising committee for the village party.'

'Why do we bother with Guy Fawkes Night?' asked George.

He knocked against the dish of salsa his wife had just made. She managed to catch it before it fell.

'Who cares,' he went on, 'that a bunch of lunatics tried to blow up Parliament in 1605? Putting barrels of gunpowder in the cellars was stupid! Of course they were found out and executed. But remembering it this way is uncivilised. Burning a stuffed figure on a bonfire is barbaric and each year there are accidents with fireworks.'

'It's for the children,' said Kate. 'They love the big bonfire.

They cheer when the stuffed Guy goes up in flames. We're making sure the fireworks display will be safe. Kids don't care about the history. They just like the fun.'

'What's that?' asked George next, pointing at the bowl of chicken in the scarlet chilli marinade.

'I'm making chicken fajitas. Each member of the committee is bringing something different. I offered to bring hot dogs, but Julie Wilson is bringing those.'

Kate picked up a kebab skewer, took some chicken strips from the bowl and began to thread them carefully onto the long metal pin.

At the mention of Julie Wilson, George's face had turned as scarlet as the chilli marinade. He fidgeted, took his hands from his pockets, changed his mind and put them back again. He cleared his throat.

'Ah, Kate – you'll say this isn't the right moment. I suppose there isn't a good moment for what I need to say.'

Kate pushed another piece of chicken onto the skewer. 'Must it be now, George? You can see how busy I am.'

'I want a divorce,' said George.

Kate froze. Had she heard correctly? 'What?'

'A divorce!' shouted George.

As the echo of his voice died away, Kate asked, 'Why?'

'Oh, come on, Kate . . .' George had started sweating. 'We're bored with one another. You know it. Don't be difficult.'

She turned towards him, skewer in hand. 'Don't be difficult? Did I hear you correctly? You're telling me you're going to walk out on me after twenty-five years, and I'm not allowed to make a fuss?'

When George knew he was in the wrong he always became belligerent. He jutted his jaw and said loudly, 'If you must know, I've met someone else.'

'Am I to know who the unfortunate woman is?' asked Kate.

'Don't be sarcastic, Kate. It doesn't suit you. It's – um – it's Julie Wilson.'

Oh yes! thought Kate. It would be Julie. Every man in the village fancied Julie Wilson. If rumour was correct, several of them had had their fancies rewarded.

'Don't be silly, George,' she said. 'She's married.'

'She's going to leave her husband. We're in love!' he added self-consciously.

'Rubbish. You're fifty-six. She's half your age.'

'No, she isn't!' he shouted. 'I'm only twenty years older than she is!'

'Don't shout, George. Is this some kind of mid-life crisis?'

In fury, he lunged towards her. He should have remembered she was holding the long metal skewer in her hand. It slipped into his chest as easily as a knife into butter. A red stain spread over his shirt. For a moment, Kate thought it was chilli marinade, but then she realised it was blood.

George stared at her with bulging eyes. He stumbled backwards, either trying to flee or seeking help. But when he reached the door he pitched forward and crashed to the kitchen tiles.

Kate ran to him and, with an effort, turned him over. He was most certainly dead.

Kate sat on a kitchen stool and contemplated George's prostrate form. She supposed she must be in shock. She ought to feel distressed, tearful. Instead, she found herself thinking, 'Bother! This would happen this morning when I've so much to do!'

She hadn't intended to kill George. It was his own fault. If she explained to the police, would they believe her? Probably not. It was then she saw, sticking out of his pocket, a white envelope. She pulled it out and opened it. It was a letter written in George's hand.

Darling Julie,
   I must see you. I'm going to tell Kate today that I want a divorce. Meet me by the old gravel pit at two.

The old gravel pit! It was as if George was telling Kate what to do.

The disused workings were filled with water and known to be a dangerous place. The lonely spot had been fenced off and notices warned people not to swim there. But over the years, the fences had fallen down in places, or been broken down by people going there to pick blackberries, which grew in abundance in the area.

She would drive George to the gravel pit, weight his body and tip him in. He'd sink and no one would ever find him. She'd report him missing to the police and after a while, everyone would forget about him.

She caught hold of his shoulders and managed to drag him to the door which connected the house to the garage.

Getting him into the car was much more difficult. Kate feared she wouldn't be able to do it. But she was a big, strong woman and at last, she had hauled and pushed him into the front passenger seat. She secured him there with the seat belt and considered what to do next.

She looked at the note again. How had George planned to deliver it? Not by post or by going to the house, too dangerous. There must be a pick-up point where he left his messages for Julie, and she, presumably, had left hers for him.

'And I know where it is!' said Kate aloud.

George had been born in this village and attended the infant school. She remembered now that, when they'd first married and returned here to live, he had told her how he and a childhood friend had left messages for one another behind a loose stone in the churchyard wall. He'd pointed it out to her. 'We pretended we were spies!' he'd joked.

George had always been a creature of habit. Kate folded the note carefully and returned it to its envelope. She looked at her watch. It was eleven o'clock. If Julie Wilson was meant to collect this note today, and be at the gravel pit at two this afternoon, George must have been on his way to leave it in the hiding place when he'd stopped by the kitchen and – foolishly – asked for the divorce.

She contemplated his slumped body in the car. It would have to wait there another quarter of an hour. Kate slipped out of the house and strolled, outwardly unconcerned, towards the church. Once there, she looked for the loose stone. Which one exactly? The first two blocks she tried wouldn't move. But at the third attempt the stone slipped out easily.

'Oh yes,' muttered Kate. 'This has been moved recently!'

She put the note in its hiding place and hurried home.

*　　*　　*

George hadn't stiffened yet but he soon would. She had to move him now. But if she drove through the village with him beside her, someone would see. She would have to go by the back lanes. Even so, there was a risk.

Kate fetched a box of make-up items from the bedroom. She rubbed rouge into George's cheeks and ringed his closed eyes with mascara and eye-liner. She powdered his face liberally. She took an old gardening hat and pulled it over his forehead. She wrapped a knitted scarf round his neck and over his mouth. You couldn't see much of his face at all and what you could see was garish and hardly human. Kate put a pair of gloves in her pocket and set off.

She drove through the back lanes without meeting anyone. She was congratulating herself, when she turned a corner and saw Miss Pemberton in the middle of the road. She had no choice but to stop.

Miss Pemberton was elderly and short sighted. She was accompanied by her overweight dachshund, Casper. She approached the car and stooped by the driver's window. 'Hullo, Kate, my dear. What are you doing here?' Her myopic gaze drifted past Kate and tried to focus on the slumped figure in the hat and scarf.

'I've collected this Guy Fawkes,' said Kate. 'I'm just taking it up to the bonfire site. You know there's going to be a competition for the best Guy.'

'That's certainly a big one!' said Miss Pemberton. 'I used to enjoy Guy Fawkes Night so much when I was a child. Now I can't stay outdoors on cold nights and Casper doesn't like the noise of the fireworks, so we shan't be there. I hope it all goes well.'

She walked on. When they were safely out of sight, Kate heaved a sigh of relief. Even Miss Pemberton was wishing her well. It all seemed meant to be.

After that she met no one else on the way to the gravel pit. She parked behind blackberry bushes, bare in November, and pushed George's body from the car. He fell on the ground. She hadn't the strength to pull him any more. Kate managed to roll him to the edge of the pit. She filled his pockets with stones and used the knitted scarf to tie a larger rock to his legs. With a last effort she rolled him over once more – over the edge. He splashed into the water below and was lost to sight. Kate drove back down the road a little way and parked the car behind some trees. Then she walked back to the gravel pit and hid behind the bushes. Disposing of George had taken a long time and it was nearly two o'clock.

Promptly at two p.m., a little red Fiat drove up. Julie Wilson got out. She was a slim, pretty woman who liked to wear tight clothes and had a lot of bouffant blonde hair.

Watching Julie, Kate thought: *She's the cause of everything. But for her, poor foolish George would be alive now. If she's not stopped, she'll do it again, ruin another marriage, bring about another disaster.*

'Georgie?' called Julie. The wind caught at her blonde hair and whipped it up into a golden cloud. 'Are you here, darling?'

Kate tossed a stone towards the bushes which grew on the edge of the pit.

'George?' Julie shielded her eyes with her hand and peered towards the sound. She began to walk towards the spot.

Really, it was ridiculously easy. Julie joined George in the water, having first been struck with a rock by Kate, who crept up behind her.

The keys were still in the red Fiat. Kate pulled on the gloves she had brought and switched on the ignition. A mile down the road was a sprawling collection of semi-derelict cottages built for farm-workers a hundred years before, but abandoned. Hippies had drifted there and taken up residence undisturbed. The villagers blamed the 'people from the old cottages' for petty thefts and vandalism. George, in particular, had written frequently to the council demanding the squatters be evicted.

Kate left the red Fiat with its keys in the ignition near the cottages but just out of sight. It wouldn't be long before one of the hippy community found it. After that, she was confident, it would be moved, hidden and stripped down within an hour.

Kate trudged back to her own car. She was really tired now, but she had to keep going. The fireworks party began at six. She'd be glad when it was all over.

The flames leapt up into the dark evening sky, crackling and spitting out golden sparks. Children shrieked and ran up and down. There was an explosion and a shower of coloured lights burst overhead. The children cheered.

Kate, helping out at the food stall, saw a tall man coming towards her. She'd noticed him earlier, walking up and down restlessly, his eyes searching the crowd.

'Good evening, Inspector Wilson!' she called out.

'Hullo there, Kate.' Julie's husband stopped by her. He looked, she thought sympathetically, worried. He worked at the police station in town but he and his wife had bought a cottage in the village eighteen months earlier.

'Would you like a chicken fajita?' she asked.

'I think I will. They look good.' He handed her the money. 'You haven't seen Julie, my wife, have you? I came here straight from work and expected to see her here. She was going to bring hot dogs.'

Kate shook her head. 'No, she hasn't come. We really need the hot dogs. If I see her, I'll tell her you're here.'

'Thanks,' he mumbled through a mouthful of chicken.

'You're not the only one who's missing a spouse,' said Kate kindly. 'I've not been able to find George anywhere. He went out this morning and didn't come back. To tell you the truth, I'm getting a bit concerned.'

'What?' said Inspector Wilson sharply.

She watched him hurry away. He must know what his wife was like with other men. Now he knew George was also missing, his suspicions would be aroused. It would be all round the village by tomorrow morning that George Parker and Julie Wilson had run off. There would be a lot of sympathy for Kate – and for nice Inspector Wilson, too.

Another man had stopped by the stall. 'Those look nice, Mrs Parker.'

'Councillor James!' she exclaimed. He also lived in the village and served on the district council. George had frequently stopped him in the street to complain about the hippies.

'Your husband about?' he asked as he paid for his fajita.

'I'm afraid not. I haven't seen him since this morning. I don't know where he is.'

He looked interested. Another one to spread the gossip. 'I've got some news for him,' he said. 'The council has decided at last to evict the squatters in the old cottages.'

'George will be pleased,' said Kate.

He leaned towards her confidentially. 'To tell you the truth, we need to demolish the cottages. A new rubbish dump is going to be made out there. We'll be widening the road to take the lorries and draining the old gravel pit— Are you all right, Mrs Parker?'

Poor Connie

Mrs Lorrimer peeped through the curtains. She could see Connie in the garden, cutting dahlias for the drawing-room vases. As she snipped through each stem, Connie twitched the bloom efficiently to shake out the earwigs before disposing of it in the trug. Poor Connie, thought Mrs Lorrimer. She really must do something about her and soon. Connie would be thirty next birthday. Thirty and unmarried. Mrs Lorrimer could not realistically hope to establish her daughter after that.

She had been trying to find a husband for Connie for the past twelve years since Connie's debut in their limited society as a gauche eighteen-year-old. Mrs Lorrimer reflected bitterly on the extraordinary trouble she had gone to and the lack of success which had marked her many efforts. She had driven miles in her carriage (she set her face resolutely against a new-fangled motor car), to leave her card at the homes of ladies with suitable sons. She had arranged picnics and tennis parties. Connie looked her best in a boater holding a tennis racket and could serve underarm with a flourish. Connie in a ballgown was less of a success and had an irritating habit of hiding in the cloakroom on such occasions. Otherwise she was a nice cheerful girl who liked long walks and practical craftwork and had overcome a tendency to guffaw when amusing remarks were made. It was a complete mystery to

Mrs Lorrimer why Connie had failed to 'take'. Other girls found husbands. Plain girls, fat girls, thin ones, girls without any fortune and with buck teeth, flat chests and spots. Why then had it proved so difficult to find a match for Connie?

Goodness knows, thought Mrs Lorrimer despairingly, no mother had tried harder than she had. Local social gatherings exhausted, Connie had been taken up to London for the dear Queen's Diamond Jubilee but although she had enjoyed the sights, she had singularly failed to shine herself at any of the parties to which Mrs Lorrimer had, with enormous ingenuity, wangled invitations. Daunted but not dismayed, Mrs Lorrimer had even, at great expense, taken her daughter to France. But French bachelors had proved disappointingly unromantic with regard to Connie. The memory rankled and Mrs Lorrimer did not feel she would ever quite forgive the French for failing to live up to a clearly unjustified reputation.

However, she was still not ready to give up yet. She came of military family with a tradition of fighting to the last man – or in the case of the female family members, for the last man. Mrs Lorrimer knew her duty and moreover, just a glimmer of one last chance had unexpectedly cast a ray of hope in the gloom. Only yesterday she had met a neighbour in the local draper's. In the course of small-talk this lady had asked, 'Have you heard? Dr Benson has a new young doctor as assistant?'

Mrs Lorrimer grew pale and had all but swayed and grasped the counter for support. A new young doctor? Had Heaven heard her prayer and at last sent an eligible bachelor to their predominantly female neighbourhood?

As nonchalantly as possible, Mrs Lorrimer had observed, 'How nice for Dr Benson. I'm sure his arthritis makes house calls so difficult for him. Is – is the new doctor married?' She had not missed the malicious gleam in her friend's eye at the question – everyone knew how hard she had tried and failed to find a husband for Connie – but for Connie's sake, she ignored it.

'Oh no, unmarried, I believe.'

An unmarried young doctor. Salvation at last! Mrs Lorrimer quite forgot what she had come for and left the shop with three yards of unwanted elastic and knees like jelly.

She had spent a sleepless night forming and rejecting plan after plan. But she had risen that morning knowing what she must do. Mrs Lorrimer disposed herself at her writing desk and penned a carefully composed letter to Dr Benson.

I am aware how inconvenient it is for you to call at the house, but I hear you have a new assistant and I have no objection to the young doctor calling to advise me on my migraine, at three thirty, Thursday afternoon.

That evening she told Connie what she had done.

'Oh, he won't care about me!' said Connie robustly.

Mrs Lorrimer controlled her exasperation with an effort. 'Why ever not, dear? You don't look almost thirty.' She studied her daughter. 'On the other hand, you don't look eighteen. We shall have to make the best of you, Connie. And don't, please, pretend not to care. Of course you would like to be married. All girls would.'

Connie's round, good-natured face flushed and became miserable.

I do hope she isn't going to wear that long face when he comes! thought her worried mother.

They spent the whole of the following morning preparing for the new doctor's call. Connie was roused from her bed at six for her hair to be washed and tied up in rags to make it curl. Her best dress was carefully pressed. The maids were ordered to polish the hall and have the drawing room spotless. Cook was instructed to make her special seedcake and to set out the best china when the new doctor should, professional visit concluded, take his tea.

'Indian and China,' ordered Mrs Lorrimer. 'And the silver teaspoons.' It would do no harm to let the young man see they were comfortably off and Connie was not without 'expectations'.

No London production had a cast better rehearsed in its lines or more carefully stage directed.

'I shall sit in the corner,' said Mrs Lorrimer, 'and when he is announced I shall say, "Do come in, Doctor." You will stand by the window displaying your right profile which is your better, and what do you say?'

Obediently Connie replied, 'How kind of you to call on Mama, Doctor. I am so grateful.'

'Yes, but don't chant it like that. And don't look like a frightened rabbit nor, for goodness' sake, grin! Just look demure. You may cast him a shy smile. I'm sure, in my day, girls knew these things by instinct!'

As the morning passed, Connie's hair was brushed, piled up over scratchy horsehair pads and secured by twenty-seven pins. Her fringe was crimped, filling the bedroom with the odour of singed hair. Her sturdy figure was crushed into a sprung-steel (guaranteed rustless) corset which tilted her agonisingly into a

Grecian Bend. Daringly her nose was powdered. (It did have a tendency to shine.) She knew her lines backwards and had strained her eyeballs casting demure looks at the mirror.

'You look very nice, dear,' said her mother, genuinely pleased. 'So don't, Connie, muff it this time, please.'

The hour approached. The doorbell sounded in the distance. Footsteps clattered on the hall parquet. The parlourmaid appeared with a very red face and whispered in awe, 'It's the new doctor, ma'am.'

'Announce him, silly girl!' hissed Mrs Lorrimer.

'Dr Harris!' declaimed the parlourmaid, staring fixedly ahead.

'Do come in, Doctor!' called Mrs Lorrimer graciously.

A figure filled the doorway, black bag in hand. 'Good afternoon, ladies!' said Dr Harris cheerfully. 'I'm very pleased to make your acquaintance, Mrs Lorrimer. Dr Benson has given me your case notes. Let's see what we can do for you! I would like to say, if I may, that I appreciate your asking for me specially. So many people, including many women, alas, are prejudiced against women doctors.'

Dr Emily Harris pulled off her gloves and raised Mrs Lorrimer's limp wrist to take her pulse, apparently oblivious to the patient's bulging eyes and mottled complexion. 'My goodness, you do have a remarkably rapid pulsebeat, Mrs Lorrimer. Yes, take it from me, we women doctors are here to stay!'

It could not be expected that the visit was the success Mrs Lorrimer had hoped for, other than medically. Dr Harris prescribed powders for Mrs Lorrimer's headaches. Mrs Lorrimer sat motionless and silent as Dr Harris, over seedcake and tea, spoke briskly and with amazing assurance of the cottage she had bought locally and of her hopes of a growing professional reputation. It came as little surprise to learn that Dr Harris espoused both Votes for Women and something called Birth Control of which Mrs Lorrimer thanked her stars she had been brought up in ladylike ignorance. As for poor Connie, her mother quite forgot her and gave a start when her daughter's voice suddenly burst out, as Dr Harris rose to take her leave, 'Oh, let me show you to the door, Doctor!'

Mrs Lorrimer wondered if it was worth signalling to Connie not to bother. She noticed with surprise and annoyance that Connie's round face shone with enthusiasm and she looked almost pretty. As if it mattered, now. But Mrs Lorrimer was past caring. Fate was against her.

Connie and Dr Harris walked to the gate. Parked in the road was a shiny new motor car surrounded by a troop of inquisitive small boys who scampered away at the approach of the two women. Dr Harris dropped her bag into the back seat, tied on her hat with a scarf, jumped up athletically into the front seat and prepared to take the wheel herself.

'I suppose you wouldn't care to crank the starting handle for me, Miss Lorrimer?'

'Oh, yes, please!' cried Connie and scuttled to the front of the car. She stooped and grasped the metal arm, heedless of grease and dust on her best dress. As the engine roared into life, she returned to the side of the vehicle and gazed up at the doctor.

'Dr Harris . . .' Connie's face glowed scarlet with exertion and emotion. 'Do you think, I know you must be busy, but might I visit you at your cottage, perhaps one evening?'

There was a pause, broken only by the juddering of the engine. Dr Harris regarded Connie thoughtfully. As their eyes met, an unspoken communication passed between them. The doctor smiled.

'Yes, Miss Lorrimer. Do please call one evening. I'm sure we have a lot in common.'

Blind Date

It is hard to refuse a good friend, especially when the friend is trying to do you a good turn.

'I know how upset you've been since you broke up with Roger,' said Daisy in her cheerful and tactless way. 'But you're not helping yourself by just moping about. You must come to the party.'

'What party?' Emma asked suspiciously.

Outside the Banbury streets were cold and grey, but inside the restaurant it was warm and welcoming. Around them was chatter and bustle, the chink of china and the smell of food. The waiters scurried about with plates of pasta. From time to time a cork was pulled from a bottle of wine with a satisfying *pop!*

Just at the instant Daisy mentioned the party, Emma was twisting her fork in strands of spaghetti. She suspected that Daisy had chosen the moment because Emma was concentrating on eating, and Daisy hoped to make what was clearly a prepared speech without interruption.

'I don't want to go to any party,' said Emma through a mouthful of spaghetti.

'Yes, you will, when I've told you about it. Because it's Halloween, it's going to be a costume party.'

'I particularly don't like costume parties.'

'But this one will be tremendous fun because it will be *themed*, you know, anything to do with ghosts or witchcraft. I'm organising it,' added Daisy.

'I hope it's a success, but leave me out of it.'

Daisy looked reproachful as only Daisy could. 'Darling, I'm trying to help.'

Emma felt guilty and apologised. 'I know you're trying to be kind, but I don't need people to be kind. Look, if I go to this party, there will be two types of people there.'

Emma ticked off the categories on her fingers. 'One: people who knew Roger and me when we were together and will be embarrassed to see me on my own. They won't know what to say to me. I won't know what to say to them. Two: total strangers. I don't fancy spending my evening with total strangers, whether or not they're dressed as devils or the Grim Reaper! Again, I won't know what to say to them and I won't be interested in anything they say to me. I'm just not in the mood, Daisy.'

'Ah,' said Daisy cunningly, 'but you haven't heard yet where the party is going to be held! It's at Farlington Hall.'

Emma had to be impressed. Farlington Hall, near Stratford-upon-Avon, was a vast country house which had been turned into a hotel. Its architecture was a riot of Victorian Gothic and it had a ruined medieval chapel in the grounds. To hire a large room there for a party must be expensive. She said as much to Daisy.

'It's all right,' said Daisy airily. 'The firm is paying for it.'

'Business must be good,' Emma said.

Daisy beamed at her. 'So, you'll come?'

Fearing it was a mistake, but tempted, Emma said, 'Well, all right, then.'

That was when Daisy moved in for the kill. 'Wonderful! And you can meet James!'

'Who is James?' squawked Emma so loudly people at the next table turned their heads.

'He's a real sweetie. You'll like him.'

'No, I won't,' said Emma quickly. 'I won't like him and he won't like me. I gave up blind dates when I was sixteen. Blind dates never work.'

'I've told him all about you,' Daisy went on blithely. 'He's dying to meet you.'

'No, Daisy!'

Daisy leaned forward confidentially. 'I've had this marvellous idea. Because Farlington Hall isn't far from Stratford-upon-Avon, I suggest costumes with a Shakespearean theme for you and James. Hamlet and Ophelia. What could be better? Hamlet is always seeing ghosts and has that long speech about a skull. Ophelia drowned herself, so you'll make a suitably spooky pair.'

'Has James agreed to this?' asked the horrified Emma.

'Yes, he thought it was a great idea.' Daisy sounded confident. But then, Daisy always sounded confident.

Emma's relationship with Roger had lasted almost ten years. When they broke up, they gave the usual reasons. 'We got together too young.' 'We don't have much in common.' 'We have different ambitions.'

Their friends said, 'Don't look on this as the *end* of something; look on it as the *beginning* of something new.'

It was much easier to give good advice than to take it. To start a new life required courage. It meant resuming single habits after years of thinking as a pair. It meant taking risks.

'And I will!' said Emma to herself. 'I *must*. I'll go to Daisy's Halloween party and I'll meet this James. It will be an adventure.'

That was why, on Saturday evening, Emma found herself looking into her bedroom mirror, studying her reflection critically. For her Ophelia costume she had hired a long dark green velvet gown and entwined a wreath of ivy around her shoulder-length fair hair. She had powdered her face and wore a very pale lipstick so that she looked ethereal. She was quite pleased with the result. What the as yet unknown James would make of it, that was an open question.

She had to hitch up the skirt for the long drive from Banbury to Farlington. The night was very cold and clear. The stars sparkled overhead like diamonds and the moon gave a silver sheen to the fields to either side. There would be a sharp frost before morning. By the time she reached Farlington Hall, the car park beneath the trees was almost full and she had to park at the side of the main drive from the gates to the house. She got out and stood in the dark, hearing the trees rustle around her and feeling the chill wind ruffle her hair. The lights streaming from the hotel's gothic windows invited her to hurry towards it. But as she approached, the dark mass of the building with its towers and pinnacles loomed over her, and would have been daunting if she hadn't been able to hear music and general hubbub. Emma passed through the porch into the main hall where a fire blazed in the huge open hearth. She felt nervous but also tingled with a not unpleasant sensation of anticipation. Perhaps it would be fun, after all.

The party was already in full swing. There was every kind

of costume imaginable. Devils, witches and Grim Reapers certainly, even someone wearing a round orange pumpkin head. *I bet he's hot in that!* thought Emma. Another guest wore a skeleton suit of white bones painted on black Lycra. There were all kinds of scary monsters, three Count Draculas with fangs, and even an angel in a billowing white gown scattered with silver spangles. She had cute little feathery wings pinned between her shoulders. But it was impossible to spot a Hamlet in the throng.

What did Hamlet wear, anyway? Some sort of sixteenth-century costume, doublet and hose, a ruff, that sort of thing, Emma supposed. She wondered whether James was as embarrassed at agreeing to this charade as she was.

'Darling! Lovely to see you!' The angel swooped on Emma in a cloud of glittery gauze draperies. Emma might have guessed the angel would turn out to be Daisy. Only Daisy would go to a Halloween party dressed as an angel.

'Just mingle,' advised Daisy. 'Help yourself to a drink. I haven't seen James yet but he'll be here soon. Just keep an eye open for Hamlet.' She fluttered away, all draperies and wings.

Emma did her best. She drank a glass of wine and then, because she was driving, prudently changed to orange juice. She danced with one of the Count Draculas. Unfortunately conversation was interrupted when his fangs fell off. Emma left him crawling about on the floor between people's feet, looking for them. By now it was unbearably hot. Bodies jostled against her. Feet trod on hers. There was no sign of a Hamlet and, worst of all, she recognised the guest in the skeleton suit as one of Roger's tennis partners. Desperate to avoid him and to get some air, she squeezed and apologised her way through the crowd and back into the main entrance hall.

There was no one at the reception desk and only one other person besides herself. He was sitting on the main staircase, dressed as Hamlet.

'Hello,' he said to Emma.

He had a nice voice and he looked really very dashing in that padded black velvet doublet and the crisp lace ruff. He had tousled brown hair and one of those lop-sided grins which Emma had always found irresistible.

'I've been looking for you!' she exclaimed. 'I'm Ophelia.' She held out her hand. 'This costume is Daisy's idea, not mine! How did she persuade you?'

He rose to his feet and took her hand, bending gallantly over it. 'She was so enthusiastic, I couldn't say no.'

'I didn't see you in there earlier,' said Emma, indicating the party room.

He shook his head. 'I've only just got here. My car broke down and I had to come by train and taxi. Then I had to go upstairs and find somewhere to change into my costume. I couldn't travel on a train like this!' He patted the doublet and laughed. 'So that's why I'm so late.'

'I see. It was good of you to make the effort to come in those circumstances.' Emma looked around. 'Where's the skull?'

'Skull?' he looked startled.

'Yes, doesn't Hamlet usually carry a skull? I mean, not in the whole play. But whenever you see pictures of him, he's always got Yorick's skull. *To be or not to be*, and so on.'

'Ah,' he said. 'The skull. Yes, I – I lost it.'

'Where?'

'To tell you the truth, I left it on the train – in a plastic bag.' He looked at her apprehensively as if he feared she would lecture him.

Emma giggled. 'That will be a shock for some other poor passenger!'

Just then a gong sounded.

Hamlet looked relieved. 'Supper, I think,' he said. 'Let's go, Ophelia. I'm starving and if we don't beat all that lot to the table there will be nothing left.' He grabbed her hand and they plunged back into the throng.

Later when they had edged their way from the supper room with laden plates, they went back to the hall and both sat on the staircase to eat.

'Do you work for Daisy's firm?' asked Emma.

'Yes, in the accounts department.'

'My job's pretty routine, too,' confessed Emma. 'I work in local government. I sometimes dream of giving it up to do something exciting and different. But it's not so easy.'

He nodded sympathetically. 'The career I really wanted didn't pay enough,' he said. 'I gave it a try but after a year, I had to give it up. I was a conjuror.'

She put down her fork and turned to him in surprise. 'Really? On the stage?'

'Not the stage, just performing in clubs. Sometimes the audience was a good one and sometimes there were two or three drunks who made a nuisance of themselves. Most of all, I enjoyed being hired to entertain at children's parties. Kids love the tricks. I used to "find" coins in their sleeves and white mice in their pockets. They'd shriek the place down and come back for more. And,' he added, 'I got to share their ice cream and jelly! But it didn't pay well, as I said, and regular work was hard to get. In the end, one has to eat.'

'But you tried,' Emma told him earnestly. 'That's the most important thing. You had the courage to try.'

He looked at her steadily for a moment, then said quietly, 'Thank you for that.'

They went back to the party firm friends. The evening was getting noisier and even more boisterous. Emma danced with Hamlet. Then the skeleton, Roger's friend, lurched up and took her away. Luckily he was so drunk by now that he didn't recognise her. Then Hamlet reappeared and rescued her. They danced again, before she was claimed again, this time by a masked executioner. That was a bit scary and she was glad to see Hamlet reappear, pushing through the crowd towards her. However, quite early, about ten o'clock, he began to look anxiously at his wristwatch.

'That's not sixteenth century!' teased Emma.

He gave his rueful grin. 'I'm really sorry, Emma, but I'll have to leave soon. It's because I have so far to go. I have to get back to the station and then catch a train. Even after that, it will take another twenty minutes to get home. Will you excuse me a minute? I'll go and phone a taxi to take me back to the station.'

'Oh, I can give you a lift back to Banbury,' she offered immediately.

'Thank you, but sadly I live in the other direction. I live on the outskirts of Birmingham. I took the train to Stratford-upon-Avon and a taxi from there to here.'

'Oh,' said Emma, knowing she sounded as disappointed as she looked.

Hamlet pushed his way through the partygoers and was lost to her view. But about ten minutes later, he was back, looking very worried.

'I can't get a taxi, not to come all the way out here. They're all booked. It's a busy night.'

'I've got my car,' offered Emma. 'I can't drive you all the way to Birmingham, but I can at least give you a lift to Stratford-upon-Avon station.'

'Would you? That would mean taking you away from the party. I don't want to do that. And it's quite a long way.' He seemed quite jittery now, looking around him.

'It won't take us more than fifteen minutes. As for the party, I can always come back. But as I've got to drive home to Banbury, I probably won't.'

'Right,' he said. 'Thanks. Look, I'll just run upstairs and get out of this costume. Meet me in the hall, by the staircase.'

He soon came running down the staircase, now wearing jeans and a leather jacket. He still managed to look quite romantic. He was carrying a small case which he held up. 'My costume.'

'I've got to drive in mine,' said Emma. 'It never occurred to me to change into it here.'

'I only did it because of coming by train.' He looked in the direction of the party. 'I ought not to go without saying goodbye and thank you to Daisy.'

'I'll go and get the car,' Emma suggested. 'I had to park down on the drive, but I won't be long. You'll have just enough time to go and find Daisy.'

'Right . . .' He looked at her helplessly and held up the case again. 'I can't get through that mob carrying this. You couldn't take it with you to the car? It's not heavy.'

He disappeared back into the party and Emma found herself holding the case. She walked past the young woman night clerk who asked pleasantly, 'Going already?'

'I'm afraid so, but it's been a lovely evening.'

'Good. I hope we see you again.' Hotel staff always said that.

Emma hurried down the dark, tree-lined drive. It was now very cold and she was shivering by the time she found her car. She was not the only person to have parked so far from the house. There was another car, pulled over well to the side under the trees and hardly visible.

She put the case on the back seat and drove back to the front entrance. He was there, standing in the doorway, looking at his watch again. He came hurrying towards her, scrambled into the passenger seat and slammed the door.

'It's all right,' Emma assured him. 'The trains must be running up to midnight at least.'

They made a hasty farewell before the station at Stratford-upon-Avon.

'It's been a really great evening,' Hamlet said. 'May I ring you? On Monday?'

'Yes.' Emma fumbled in the glove compartment and found one of her business cards. 'Here you are, that's my office number but if you ring before five thirty I'll be there.'

He tucked the card into his pocket, leaned into the car and kissed her chastely on her cheek. 'I'll ring Monday.'

With that he was gone, running into the station.

* * *

Daisy rang the doorbell the following evening, Sunday.

'Darling!' She collapsed onto Emma's sofa and gazed up at her. She looked like someone who had been up all night and hadn't been behaving like an angel for all of it. 'I am so sorry!'

'Sorry?' Emma asked, puzzled. 'What for? You were right. I had great fun.'

'Oh, good . . .' Daisy hesitated. 'You haven't lost anything then – purse, credit cards, jewellery?'

Emma shook her head. 'Why, should I?'

Daisy threw out her hands dramatically. 'Other people did.' Seeing that Emma still looked puzzled, she went on, 'What time did you leave?'

'Early, just after ten. I had to take—'

Daisy interrupted her. 'Ah, then you weren't there when the discoveries were made. It was about half past ten when people started missing things. First one person and then another, and then everyone started checking and – oh, it was chaos! The police say it was professionals. They say there must have been at least two of them and they were probably in costume, so we didn't notice. One worked the room, lifting anything he could from people's bags and pockets. He even took wristwatches and jewellery. He got my necklace! I'm so upset and furious. I can't think when he took it. The only time I can think it possible is when some chap came up to say goodbye because he was leaving early. He gave me a hug and kissed me. The police say that's probably when he slipped the catch undone and took it from my neck. The nerve! I didn't feel a thing. He must have been a real magician. He slipped the watches off people's wrists and they had no idea. One person lost a Rolex! The police think he gave his haul to a partner to carry out for him, someone who looked really innocent.'

Daisy swept aside a troublesome lock of hair which had fallen into her eyes. 'And I'm sorry about James, too. He rang up this morning and said he had a cold and that's why he didn't go to the party. I ask you, what a feeble excuse.'

'But – but he was there . . .' Emma whispered. As Daisy had been talking, a feeling of dread had been creeping over her. 'He was dressed in his costume . . .'

A padded doublet, probably full of hidden pockets.

'Not James, darling. I told you, he didn't turn up. It must have been somebody else. Didn't he give a name?'

'I called him Hamlet,' Emma said lamely. 'I gave him my business card, so that he could ring me.'

Yes, she thought. *I* called him Hamlet. He didn't say he was Hamlet. He just wore a sixteenth-century costume, so I deduced . . . He *didn't* have the skull. Left it on the train, indeed! I ask you, who could forget a skull? I talked to him about Daisy. I asked if he worked in Daisy's firm and all he had to say was yes. He was also quick to say he worked in the accounts department. Every firm has an accounts department. He didn't have to know what kind of firm it was. When I offered to drive him to Banbury he immediately said he lived in the opposite direction. Of course he wanted to leave early and saying he had come by train was an excuse (just as it was an excuse for his arriving so late). But perhaps, when he got to wherever he had left his car, it wouldn't start. It was a very cold night. He was trapped there at Farlington and he began to panic. So he came back with that story of not being able to get a taxi and I, of course, offered to drive him and obligingly carried the swag past the receptionist. I don't know where he went after I left him at the railway station. Oh, Emma, you do have a lot to learn!

Daisy had brightened. 'I'm so glad you met someone you liked. What does he do for a living?'

Emma said slowly, 'He's a conjuror.'

'Oh?' said Daisy. 'That's different! Do you think he will ring you?'

Emma shook her head. 'No, no, I don't think he will.'

A Step into Danger

A five-part serial featuring crime writer Emma Durrant

Part One

Emma clung to her seat as Mr Collins's ancient Land Rover bounced down the hill into Sidmouth, the need for self-preservation momentarily replacing the finer points of the perfect murder with which her mind had been wrestling for some weeks now.

'Here we are, m'dear!' Mr Collins brought them to a juddering halt. 'Sorry I can't wait around to take you back!'

'Don't worry, and thank you very much for the lift.' She scrambled down, thankful to have her feet on solid ground again.

'I want to keep on the right side of you!' he bellowed through the window. 'You might be plotting to kill me off!'

She was used to that sort of humour at her expense. They exchanged waves and the Land Rover roared away, scattering holidaymakers like sheep. Emma picked scraps of straw from her jeans. Above her head, seagulls wheeled and screamed raucously and to either side people clustered in relaxed fashion round postcard racks and ice-cream stands. She, however, hadn't come to the South Devon coast to relax but to work on a new book, with a deadline to meet. But perhaps it was the sea air or just too much peace and quiet or simply a niggling resentment that everyone else seemed to be on holiday. Whatever it was, writer's block had struck.

What was needed to dispel it was the company of another, someone to bounce ideas off so that, like Mr Collins's vehicle, they leapt away in unexpected directions. She was looking forward to Damian's arrival. His presence might be just the answer.

At the bus station someone else was already waiting at the spot where Damian's National Express coach was due in. A stocky, youngish man in a short-sleeved shirt was leaning against the low stone wall. He was scowling with concentration at a folded news-paper. She noticed he was studying the crossword. As she passed by him, he glanced up and treated her to a sharp stare, before taking a biro from his shirt pocket and carefully filling in the answer to a clue.

Emma hoisted herself onto the wall. The stiff salt breeze picked up strands of her long brown hair and wrapped them around her eyes and mouth. Absently she plucked them away and, tucking them ineffectually behind her ear, took out the letter which she had brought along in order to have her sister there in spirit.

It was brief, little more than a note. There was a round stain in one corner and, even now, the paper smelled faintly of paraffin. She pictured Bridget, hot and sticky, scribbling it in a snatched moment, swatting away flies and trying to blot out the incessant wails of sick babies and their desperate mothers. 'We're very grateful to you,' her sister scrawled. Bridget, who did so much against such odds for others, was thanking her. Emma felt the familiar unwor-thiness as she tucked the tattered scrap of paper away.

'Excuse me!' The man had tossed his newspaper into the litter bin. 'You are Emma Durrant, aren't you? The crime writer? I thought I recognised you from the picture in the local rag. It said you'd taken a cottage down here for the summer.'

She had expected a query about the bus timetable. Taken aback, Emma mumbled assent. Her heart had sunk. His voice and face were friendly but there was an alertness about him which heralded, in her experience, a spate of questions about being a writer.

'Isn't getting published very difficult these days?' he went on, adding frankly, 'I ought to confess I never read detective stories, or watch them on the box. They irritate me. They're far too fanciful. Most detective work is routine with a lot of form-filling. There are standard procedures to be observed.'

'You certainly seem sure of that!' said Emma frostily.

He was undeterred. 'Now, take the hero. The police detective seldom has a free hand and he's generally an ordinary sort of chap. In books, detective inspectors always seem to be eccentrics. But then, the books aren't about real life, are they?'

'No,' snapped Emma, 'they're works of fiction. That's what they're supposed to be – stories. I can make my characters any way I want 'em.'

She cast a despairing look at an approaching bus, praying it would be Damian's. Yes, she could glimpse him, standing in the aisle and partly obscured by a dumpy woman in an extraordinarily brightly patterned dress.

'Excuse me!' she said, sliding from the wall and dusting off the seat of her jeans. 'I'm meeting someone off this bus.'

She moved away but he followed. 'Really? I've just put my mother on one of these buses. She's gone to visit a friend.'

It was obvious he wanted to see whom she'd greet. Fine, thought Emma grimly. Then he was about to get a surprise!

The dumpy woman in the bright dress was clambering down and haranguing the driver about her suitcase. Damian hovered halfway down the steps behind her, scowling as only a thirteen-year-old boy can. Catching Emma's eye, he raised a hand in laconic salute and rolled his eyes heavenwards.

For the first time, Emma's companion appeared disconcerted. 'Your, er, son?'

That really was the last straw. She was twenty-seven, for pity's sake! Did she really look like the mother of a great lanky lad like that? Damian had shot up since the last time she'd seen him. His arms were sticking out of the ends of his sleeves.

'My nephew!' Emma snapped.

'I thought he couldn't be your son. On holiday?'

Perhaps it was easier just to give him the information he clearly wanted. He might then go away.

'His parents are overseas. It wouldn't be convenient for Damian to join them so he's coming to me for the summer.'

That was enough. No need to explain about the gap in age between her sister and herself or the clinic Bridget and her husband were struggling to run in a country racked by warring factions and famine.

'At boarding school, is he? Poor kid,' he said sympathetically.

There was hardly any need to answer that because Damian had rescued a bulging holdall from the luggage compartment and was approaching them. His regulation haircut, old-fashioned tweed jacket and grey flannels announced that he came from an educational establishment which prided itself on Tradition. More surprisingly, the woman in the bright dress had come with him.

'Hullo, Auntie Em,' said Damian with a tense smile. 'This is Mrs Pugh.'

Mrs Pugh was of indeterminate age though of striking appearance.

Emma thought she resembled nothing so much as a large parrot on its perch. The dress was patterned in scarlet poppies on an ivory background. The wearer had matched them with vivid red lipstick and a free hand with the blusher on heavily powdered, plump cheeks. She sidled up, unsteady on stiletto heels, in a manner that was at once bold and ingratiating. Her sharp dark eyes, above an arched nose, assessed them with a mixture of curiosity and cunning.

'Damian and I,' she declared cosily, 'have become great friends!' Her assumption of familiarity was unjustified and made a bad impression. Damian's face was a study in frustration as she smiled and patted his arm.

Damian showed that his parents were paying those fees for something. 'It's nice to have met you, Mrs Pugh. I hope you enjoy your holiday.' The words were expressed courteously, whatever his inner feelings. He held out his hand.

Mrs Pugh clasped it with her heavily ringed fingers. 'He's been telling me all about himself! You must be the auntie he's come to visit!' The sharp gaze was turned on Emma as Damian gently but firmly freed his hand. 'Mrs Durrant?'

'No! Yes! I am his aunt, but I'm—'

'And this will be Mr Durrant!' exclaimed Mrs Pugh, turning on the man beside Emma.

It would be hard to say which of the two addressed looked the more appalled. 'We're not married!' exclaimed Emma. 'He's—'

'Oh? Well, I'm broad minded, dear! You have to be these days, don't you?'

There was a fortunate interruption. A robust cry came from a thin woman in slacks and a weather-proof jacket. 'Felicity! Over here!'

'There's my cousin. Well, bye-bye, Damian. Nice to meet you and your aunt and uncle!'

With a flourish of her plump hand, she departed at last, teetering on her high-heeled sandals and trundling her case behind her on a set of wheels.

Damian erupted like a simmering volcano. 'She was an awful woman! She sat by me and asked questions non-stop! I mean, really personal, embarrassing questions! She wouldn't give up till she got answers. She just asked and asked! Talk about nosy! And grinning away at me all the time with her mouth but not her eyes, do you know what I mean?'

'That couldn't have been much fun,' sympathised Emma. 'No one likes answering personal questions.' She darted a meaningful glance at the man beside them, as she hoisted Damian's holdall with both hands. It felt as though he'd packed a load of bricks. 'We'd better get a taxi. My car developed terminal problems and I couldn't afford to replace it. The cottage is way out of town.'

'Listen, let me give you a lift!' offered her unwished acquaintance, reaching for the holdall.

She swung it away before he could kidnap it. 'No, thanks! I wouldn't think of troubling you.'

She was rid of him at last. As they made for the taxi rank, she informed Damian, 'You may have got lumbered with Mrs Pugh, but I got stuck with a man who thinks I write rubbish!'

'Bet he wasn't as bad as Mrs Pugh. Do you know what, Auntie Em?' Damian went on ferociously. 'You ought to put her in one of your books, as a victim. I'm surprised no one's murdered her!'

* * *

161

The cottage was down a narrow twisting lane bordered by high hedges. The lane led to Collins's farm and there were no other near neighbours. Although it had been considerably renovated by its owners, with a new thatch and white-painted walls, the cottage retained a ramshackle charm which had not been sacrificed to picture-book perfection. It did not, alas, have a garden, only a backyard with a building formerly an outside privy and now a shed. There was just enough space for a couple of flower beds on either side of the front door. They were planted with red roses. Earlier in the year, purple aubretia had climbed over the low dry-stone walls which divided the cottage from the lane. One of Emma's first jobs on taking up residence had been to cut it back. It had looked dreadful when she finished and she'd feared she'd killed it. But now it was sending up a mass of small green leaves.

Damian lugged his holdall through the narrow doorway and gazed about him. 'Where do I sleep, Auntie Em?'

'I'll show you. You know, Damian,' Emma said thoughtfully. 'Now that you're older, perhaps you could call me just Em or Emma. I mean, when you were little, it was all right, but now—'

'I understand,' said Damian. 'You don't want people thinking you're older than you are.'

'Nonsense!' said Emma. 'Your room's up here.'

She led the way up the spiral staircase. Damian inspected the tiny room with the ceiling only inches above his head. 'Great! I'll be down as soon as I've changed. I'm boiled alive. The school insists we travel kitted out like this. I mean, it's embarrassing!'

Emma went back downstairs, reflecting that in one's early teens one is so easily embarrassed by everything. Her heart sank. He wasn't going to like the bike. Not one bit.

When Damian clattered down the spiral stairs a little later, he was a boy transformed, clad in well-worn denims, a T-shirt and trainers, indistinguishable, except for the haircut, from any of his contemporaries.

He looked so cheerful that Emma decided this was a good moment to explain about the bicycle.

'Not having a car at the moment and being stuck out here, I had to organise some transport for us,' she began. 'I had kept my old bicycle, so that was all right for me, and luckily, Mrs Collins up at the farm was able to lend me a bicycle for you. You'll have to amuse yourself, Damian, because I'm just starting on a new book.'

'What sort of bike?' asked Damian suspiciously.

'Perfectly serviceable, if rather old. It's not a mountain bike or anything. Mrs Collins had it – had it put away.' Mrs Collins had found it in a barn in amongst a pile of agricultural scrap and frankly, it looked it. It was a cumbersome contraption with huge squeaking wheels and sit-up-and-beg handles. The frame was awesomely solid and the whole thing incredibly heavy.

'Where is it?' asked Damian in hollow tones.

'Outside in the shed.'

He went out. Emma began to set the table, waiting. She didn't have to wait long. He was back, pale with shock.

'It's an antique! I can't go riding about on that. People will see me! They'll laugh themselves sick.'

'It only wants cleaning up. Look, it's better than nothing, all right? It's that or shanks's pony!'

163

Damian sank down and put his head in his hands. 'First Mrs Pugh, now a Second World War bike! Mum always says troubles come in threes. Wonder what the third thing will be!'

Emma adopted a brisk tone. 'Don't exaggerate! I checked the brakes which are fine and bought a bell and headlamp. Now, then!' She opened the fridge. 'You know I'm vegetarian, don't you? But there are bacon and sausages for you here and hamburgers in the freezer. You can cook them yourself.'

The thought of food roused Damian from his gloom. He came to peer over her shoulder.

'What about the pizza with the olives and things? That looks nice.' He turned a reproachful gaze on her.

So they divided her vegetarian pizza between them, after all.

'I hope,' said Emma, 'that you are going to eat those meat things, considering I went against all my principles to buy them!'

'Honestly,' said Damian, 'you're so squeamish about meat and you write about dead bodies all the time. That's a double standard!'

'Don't you start,' she said. 'I've had enough criticism this morning!'

After lunch, Emma retired to her typewriter but not to work. She rested her chin on her hands. Any criticism niggles and she'd not forgotten the scorn expressed by her acquaintance from the bus station. Her stories weren't realistic, was that it? Yet things happened daily stranger than any struggling author could invent!

Damian had gone to inspect the bicycle again. Now his face appeared at the window. 'Got any bike oil?'

'Under the kitchen sink . . .' murmured Emma.

A moment or two later, he was back again. 'Got any rags and a screwdriver?'

'Same place . . . I'm trying to concentrate, Damian! Just look around till you find what you want!'

'Sure, sorry, thanks.'

After that she was free to expend as much mental energy as she wanted but her mind was fixed on her words to the man at the bus station. She had retorted that she could make her characters any way she wanted them. So she could. But thinking it over now, she began to wonder, not for the first time, why she had become a writer and if the seeds hadn't been sown in childhood.

Her sister, Bridget, had not only been much older but clearly brilliant. Their mother had been told she was unlikely to have more children, but after many years, Emma had come along, a 'change of life' baby as it had once popularly been called. She had grown up very much in the adored elder sister's shadow. Bridget had qualified as a doctor, married a fellow student, and together they now ran a mother and baby clinic in the face of desperate odds in a land afflicted by drought, disease and war.

Emma had always known there was no way she could emulate this shining star of a sister. She had taken refuge in books and from that had progressed to writing them. Now she wondered if she had turned to writing because it allowed her to arrange her world as she liked it and turn her back on a real world which made her so unsure of her own worth. Yet writing seemed a mere frivolity compared to what Bridget was doing. Her sister was saving lives where only death had loomed, giving hope where there had only been despair, facing danger when others had fled. Emma, on the other hand, sat here in a snug little cottage in peaceful countryside with the only dangers those created in her head and transferred to paper.

Eventually, she got up and went to make a cup of tea and see what Damian was doing.

He had completely dismantled the bicycle and was crouched amongst its component parts, smeared liberally with oil and totally engrossed. By early evening, he'd reassembled it, buffed up and shining, and rode it proudly up and down the lane, ringing the new bell. The wheels no longer squeaked but whizzed round, purring softly.

Emma was impressed. 'Tell you what,' she said. 'I'll take a break from the book tomorrow. We'll take a packed lunch and ride along the cliff. I'll show you the Smugglers' Stair. It's similar to the Jacob's Ladder steps in Sidmouth, but situated in a more remote spot and there are far more steps.'

It was a fine breezy morning when they set off. Emma took the precaution of tying back her long hair. They were each provided with a can of Coke, an apple, a packet of crisps and a sweater.

'We should be all right today, but the weather can change round here. When the mist comes down over the hills, it comes down fast.'

They rode up the lane as far as the farm where Mr Collins was just driving out his cows. They stopped, surrounded by curious beasts, for Damian to be introduced. The cows snuffled wetly and the farm dog, recognising Emma, put his muddy paws up on her jeans in greeting.

'You got that liddle old bike cleaned up, then?' said Mr Collins, resplendent in dungarees and gumboots and leaning on the nearest cow for support. 'Looks a fair treat!'

Damian beamed.

After that they saw no one. A track off the lane led across the headland to the cliff edge and the path which ran for several miles along it. The sky above was a brilliant blue. To their left, the land dropped away with horrifying suddenness, red rocks and soil descending to a stony beach where the sea rolled in with a constantly changing pattern of white foam. There was just one boat, bobbing out there, when they stopped to survey the view and take a breather.

'The Smugglers' Stair is just a bit further on,' Emma explained. 'It's made up of one hundred and twenty-three steps. Nobody knows who constructed them. They're partly carved out of the cliff and partly built. They lead down to the beach. There's a cave down there where, so they say, contraband was stored. The smugglers were then supposed to have carried it all the way up the Stair to the top of the cliff. Frankly, I don't believe it! When you see the steps you'll understand why. Even if a hundred and fifty years ago they were less eroded and safer, no one in his right mind would stagger up them carrying a barrel!'

'Could we climb down?' Damian asked with interest.

'The council installed a handrail. But we couldn't get the bikes down them.' Emma didn't add that she wasn't really keen on heights.

She made to ride on, but Damian still had one foot on the ground. 'Look!' He sounded shocked and incredulous.

Emma put up her hand to shield her eyes. The land sloped down ahead of them and the path turned and twisted, shielded by overhanging rock. And in the distance, on the path, was a figure, brightly coloured scarlet and white.

Damian's pointing hand shook with emotion. 'It's her! I don't believe it! It's that woman – Mrs Pugh!'

'Are you sure? It's a long way off and it would be a bit of a coincidence!' Emma argued as she squinted into the sun.

'Of course I am! I told you Mum says misfortunes go in threes! How did she get up here?'

'Probably from the other end of the path. It comes out above the town and visitors frequently walk out from there as far as the Smugglers' Stair. You know, it does look like her. I wish we had binoculars.'

'I don't need binoculars,' Damian insisted. 'It's her, all on her own!'

'Is she?' Emma frowned. A curve of the path and a jutting rock made it difficult to see properly. Certainly only the one figure of a woman in a red and white dress was visible. Whoever she was, she kept turning her head away from the sea and the view, as if she carried on a conversation with someone beside her.

'What do we do?' Damian asked in despair. 'Go on? We're bound to meet her. Honestly, of all the rotten luck!'

Emma considered. 'I can't see Mrs Pugh climbing down a hundred and twenty-three steps to the beach and all the way up again. She's just not the type. She'll just look over the edge and then walk back to the town. We're in no hurry. We can turn off here and ride up over the headland and find a place for our picnic. Then we can come back later when she's gone.'

They sat under a hedge in the sunshine and ate apples and crisps.

'It's nice here,' said Damian, lying back and putting his hands under his head.

'I hope it's not going to be a boring holiday for you. Have you heard from your mum lately?'

'A couple of weeks ago. They don't get much time to write letters. She said not to worry about them. The fighting's not going on in their area just now. They're just getting the refugees, hundreds of people coming every day to the feeding station and, of course, all the babies are sick, so that's where Mum and Dad come in. Although sometimes the people hide the sick babies away at the back of stuffy tents. They think that if they take the babies outside in the sun, they'll die, so they don't take them to the clinic. Mum has to go crawling round the tents looking for them.'

'I wish I had Bridget's dedication,' Emma said simply.

'Do you?' Damian sounded enigmatic, and for some reason they didn't mention his parents again.

When, about an hour later, they returned to the cliff path, it was empty. They arrived at the Stair and dismounted.

'We could put the bikes under that hedge,' Damian said excitedly. 'No one would see them, not that there is anyone, anyway. Then we could climb down. Come on, Em! It won't take us long.'

He sounded so enthusiastic it was difficult to refuse. Emma put aside her own instinctive reluctance. They lugged the bicycles over to the hedge to conceal them and began their precipitous descent.

Emma went first, already slightly dizzy and holding tightly to the rickety handrail bolted to the rock face. She concentrated on her feet and tried not to look down to the beach. The steps twisted and turned all ways as the original creators of them had sought out the best route down. Behind her Damian was counting them off aloud. Going down, thought Emma, was bad enough. Climbing back up again would be worse. After that, they had a long bicycle ride home. Perhaps she oughtn't to have given in to Damian's wish so easily.

She edged round a curve in the rock face and stopped. Damian cannoned into her and yelped. 'What's up?'

'The handrail's loose. Look, all the brackets have been pulled away. We ought to go back, ride into town and report it.'

'Oh, come on, Em! We're nearly at the bottom. I've counted a hundred and three!' he pleaded. 'Just put your hand on the cliff face to steady yourself. It'll be okay. Think of all those old smugglers running up and down here with barrels of brandy!'

'I told you, I don't believe they ever did!'

Yet it wasn't so easy to dismiss the old tale out here, clinging to the cliff face. It was a deserted spot, ideal for a bit of mischief-making if you were so inclined. The noise of the breakers rolling into the pebble beach filled her ears. Sea-birds swooped shrieking in front of their faces. Every so often, a trickle of red earth ran down the cliff as constant erosion wrought by wind and weather took its toll. She felt horribly insecure without the help of the handrail.

Emma tried to control her imagination. The last steps curved round the rock so that she couldn't see the foot of them. But there could only be a couple more. She had just to round the last bend and – Emma stopped again, her eye caught by a splash of red and white.

At the foot of the Stair, propped against the cliff face, sat Mrs Pugh.

So she had climbed down here after all! But there was something odd about the way she was sitting, slumped over, head turned to one side and drooping, legs splayed out inelegantly before her, arms loose.

'Stay where you are, Damian!' Emma called sharply, realising that at any moment he, too, would round the rock. She could hear his protests as she jumped recklessly down the last steps and scrambled over the stones to the seated figure.

It was Mrs Pugh all right, still wearing that garish dress with the red poppies and the strappy high-heeled sandals. But she no longer had anything to say or any questions to ask.

Behind Emma, Damian had grown impatient at the delay. Ignoring her order, he had scrambled down to the beach.

'Stay there!' Emma shouted at him again, but too late. He had joined her and was staring down at the figure in the red and white dress.

'It's her!' he whispered. 'Is she all right, Em?'

'No.' To her own ears, Emma's voice sounded thick and distorted. 'Don't touch her, Damian!' He had stooped over the seated woman. 'She's . . . she's had an accident. She must have slipped, fallen . . .' Emma glanced back at the stone steps and the unsecured handrail.

'Is she badly hurt?' Damian sounded much younger than his thirteen years.

Emma crouched and peered into the remembered, round, parrot face. A trickle of blood ran down it from one ear. 'Yes, I'm afraid so.'

Although clearly that wasn't the exact description of the situation.

Mrs Pugh was dead.

The police provided tea and sympathy. A police sergeant, a smiling young woman of Emma's age with a soft West Country accent, took their statements.

'Those steps will have to be closed off until that handrail's properly repaired!' she said. 'Terrible to think of a tourist taking a fall like that. She was wearing the wrong shoes, of course.' She shook her head. 'Strappy sandals with high heels to go clambering down the Smugglers' Stair! You won't believe what people do. You need proper walking shoes up on that cliff path, let alone to climb down the steps. She shouldn't have tried climbing down there alone, neither. It's always best to have a companion on that sort of expedition!'

In Emma's mind's eye she saw the dumpy, brightly swathed figure of Mrs Pugh on the cliff path, turning her head as if to talk to someone. Had that just been imagination? Emma opened her mouth but before she could speak, the sergeant was offering a lift home.

'You've both had a very nasty shock. We'll get you home, and your bikes. You don't want to let this spoil your holiday, now!'

Emma glanced at Damian who sat pale and uncharacteristically silent. It wasn't a good idea to prolong their stay at the station. She had nothing by way of hard facts to tell the sergeant, anyway, only an impression.

'Thank you,' she said aloud. 'Come on, Damian.'

They stepped out into the corridor and as they did, a door further down opened and a man came out, holding a sheaf of papers. There was no mistaking that stocky build and the look of scowling concentration with which he fixed the papers in his hand and, at the bus station, had scrutinised his crossword puzzle.

Emma gripped the sergeant's sleeve and hissed, 'Who's that?'

'Detective Inspector King!' she replied, surprised.

He caught his name and looked up. For a moment he and Emma stared at one another and then he raised his eyebrows and came towards them.

'Miss Durrant? Damian? What brings you down here? Or is it

research?' He grinned at Emma. 'Checking on police procedures? We're always willing to help an author out, you know!'

'No,' said Emma coldly. 'We came to report an accident.'

'To one of you?' Concern replaced the amusement in his eyes.

'No, actually to the woman Damian travelled with. You remember her? She wore—'

'Mrs Pugh!' He not only remembered, he sounded shocked and his voice, when he next spoke, was sharp. 'What kind of accident?' His gaze travelled past her to fix the sergeant questioningly.

'At the Smugglers' Stair,' Emma said before the sergeant could speak. 'The poor woman's dead. We've just made our statements—'

Inspector King looked thunderstruck. Then he turned on the sergeant again. 'Let me see that report!'

'Yes, sir!' she said smartly and they both disappeared into the office Emma and Damian had just left.

'That man has absolutely no manners!' Emma fumed to Damian.

He might have heard her because his head reappeared briefly round the door. 'Goodbye for now, Miss Durrant! I'll be in touch!'

'Oh, great!' muttered Emma as she and Damian made their way out of the police station.

That evening the cottage felt chilly. Emma, realising that they were probably both in shock, switched on the convector heater and they sat by it, brooding.

Eventually Damian said, 'I didn't like her but it's awful to think of her slipping on the steps like that. You feel guilty when something unpleasant happens to someone you've been rude about, don't you? I feel as though I sort of wished it on her.'

'Nonsense, Damian!' Emma said sturdily.

'You're keeping jolly quiet, though!' he retorted. 'What are you thinking?'

'Well, if you must know, I'm wondering about Mrs Pugh being alone on that path. I had the impression someone was with her. What about you? Did you see anyone else?'

He shook his head. 'She looked all alone to me.'

'She just didn't seem the sort of person who would go walking on that deserted path by herself. She was gregarious. She button-holed you on the coach, and at the bus station she came over and insisted on talking to me and that man.'

'Detective Inspector King!' supplied Damian helpfully.

'All right – Inspector King! And what about that cousin who came to meet her? Where was she? It feels all wrong, Damian.' She sighed and at the same moment, the phone rang.

'Emma? It's Matt King. I said I'd be in touch, you remember? How are you both? Not too shaken up, I hope.'

'I'm not too bad. Damian's a bit quiet.'

'I thought I'd drive over and see you. Is that all right? I don't want to make a nuisance of myself.'

Emma hesitated. She didn't feel like receiving a visitor, but didn't want to sound rude. He was probably trying to help, perhaps to make up for his former tactlessness about her books. 'Yes, do come,' she said. 'It might help Damian.'

He arrived twenty minutes later and they sat around with mugs of coffee and discussed the accident.

'Talking about things helps,' he said. 'Bottling up shock is the worst thing you can do.'

Emma reflected that the presence of a real-life detective inspector was certainly having a beneficial effect on Damian, who had bucked up considerably and was showing great interest in the police investigation of the accident. In fact he was getting a little too involved and talkative.

'Em thinks,' he informed the visitor, 'that Mrs Pugh wasn't on her own. There was someone on the path with her when we saw her.'

Matt turned curious eyes on Emma, who flushed.

'It was just an impression. I didn't see anyone else. But she was turning her head as if to talk to someone.'

'How about you, Damian, did you get that impression?' Matt turned to the boy.

'Not really. I wasn't looking for that sort of detail. I just saw Mrs Pugh and thought, oh no! I've been telling Em that I feel guilty about her now.'

'Why is that?' Matt's eyebrows twitched.

'Because I feel as if I wished her bad luck. I joked to Em about someone murdering Mrs Pugh. I was rude about her because I didn't like her and I can't even say something nice about her now she's dead. You're supposed to say nice things about the departed, aren't you?'

'Not in my line of work,' said Matt ruefully. 'We generally find out all the skeletons in the cupboard.'

'Em and I didn't push her down the steps or anything!' pursued Damian disconcertingly. Faced with startled protests from the other two, he was unrepentant. 'Detectives are suspicious about things like that, aren't they? When people apparently pitch themselves downstairs? You write mysteries, Em, you ought to know that!'

'This isn't one of my books, Damian! And yet—' she turned to Matt. 'It doesn't feel right. The more I think about it, the more

I'm convinced that woman would never have gone for a country walk alone. And as for climbing down all those steps, knowing she'd have to climb up again . . . She wasn't the type for it!'

'She didn't have the shoes for it!' he reminded her. 'Believe me, Emma, we get tourists doing the craziest things! According to the relative she was visiting, she set out alone. Unless she met another walker, there probably wasn't anyone with her. You were some distance away, after all, Emma. Did you see anyone else at all up there?'

'No,' Emma confessed. Then an image flashed into her mind. 'There was a boat!' she exclaimed. 'You remember, Damian? There was a boat just offshore, fishing or something. Anyone on that boat looking towards the coast would see the cliff face and the Smugglers' Stair and anyone walking on the clifftop! You'd spot Mrs Pugh a mile off in that poppy dress! If you find the person in that boat, Matt –' she turned excitedly to him, 'you might have another witness!'

'No one's come in to report seeing anyone fall,' he pointed out.

'Perhaps they didn't see the fall. But they might have seen her talking to a companion, or just walking along with one.'

He was looking doubtful. 'We'll check it out. The local press will report the affair tomorrow and we might get a phone call, but I'm not optimistic. I think you'll find the sandals are the villains in this mystery, Emma. This isn't one of your books, as you say.' He leaned back, stretching out his legs. 'Don't you find it warm?'

'Damian and I were cold.'

For once he looked mildly embarrassed. 'I should have thought of that. Try not to worry about it. It was a sad accident, that's all.'

He smiled at her. It made crow's feet crinkle round his eyes, softening the official brusqueness of his manner. Emma turned her gaze away, fidgeted on her chair and muttered, 'We'll be all right.'

'Had supper?' was his practical question.

'I forgot!' Emma was quite dismayed. 'Oh Damian, I'm sorry, are you famished?'

'Yes!' said Damian simply.

'Well, then,' said Inspector King, getting to his feet and setting off purposefully for the kitchen. 'I'll cook up something! I'm not a cordon bleu chef but I can manage bacon and eggs.'

'Em's a veggie!' called Damian.

'A what?' Matt turned, startled.

'I'm a vegetarian!' Emma found herself sounding defensive. 'Look, you cook the bacon and eggs for yourself and Damian. I'll make myself an omelette.'

'I can make omelettes,' he said.

'But I don't want it fried in bacon fat! I'll do it.' Her voice rose in protest.

'Aha!' he said with a grin. 'You're feeling better!'

'We're going to put this behind us!' said Emma to Damian at breakfast the next morning. 'How did you sleep, by the way?'

'Like a log,' he confessed.

'Good. Well, I'm going to settle down and do some serious work today. What will you do?'

Damian was shaking the cornflakes packet and peering into it, trying to locate the free gift. 'Oh, I'll take the bike out again.'

'Watch out for traffic on these narrow lanes. Lorries sometimes use them. Even cars are a tight squeeze.'

'I thought I'd cut across country. I'll make a couple of

sandwiches, or take an apple with me, like we did yesterday, and come back at teatime. Then you can get on with your book.'

He set off and Emma sat down to work. But writing about fictional violent death, when only yesterday she had witnessed a real death, was not easy. Mrs Pugh lurked at the back of her mind. Looking out of the front window and seeing the red roses bobbing recalled the red poppy dress. It was as if Mrs Pugh herself stood outside and signalled to Emma through the panes, smiling ingratiatingly, her sharp little eyes asking questions. When the phone rang, Emma was quite pleased to have an excuse to leave her chair and answer it.

'Emma? Matt. Just calling to see how you are this morning. Hope I'm not interrupting a moment of inspiration.'

'No inspiration. My mind's log jammed. We're fine. Damian's gone off for the day on a bike. Thanks for coming round yesterday. Matt –' Emma hesitated. 'You haven't forgotten about the boat? The one I saw from the cliff? The more I think about it, the more sure I am that we – you – could have a witness!'

'Oh, yes, the boat . . .' he said vaguely. 'I think I told someone about that. But don't let your imagination run away with you on this one, Emma. Keep it for the books, eh?'

'Listen, you don't have to sound so patronising!' Emma waxed indignant again. 'I know you're the real detective and all my sleuths exist on paper, but I am entitled to an opinion. What's more, Damian and I are the only witnesses you've got so far!'

'We are aware of that.' For a moment his voice sounded grim. Then he went on briskly, 'You'll have to come to the inquest. It's on Friday, by the way, at ten. I'll come and collect you both. Nothing to worry about, just tell your story – I mean,' he amended, 'just tell the coroner what you actually saw, not what you think you might have seen, right?'

'I shall answer any questions he asks me!' Emma informed him crisply.

'Good, that's the ticket. Well, keep up the good work, Emma!' He rang off.

The last request was impossible. Emma worked on in a desultory manner before finally screwing up her efforts and casting them into the wastepaper basket. She went out to the kitchen and took her mind off things by making a pot of vegetable soup, a courgette quiche and a tray of Melting Moments.

When Damian came home at four o'clock, Emma was sitting in a flour-dusty apron on a kitchen stool, drinking tea.

'Smells nice in here!' said Damian appreciatively, putting his head round the door and eyeing the Melting Moments cooling on a rack.

She pushed the rack towards him. 'Help yourself. Tea in the pot. Get very far?'

He fidgeted about in the doorway and gave a furtive smile. 'I went back to the Smugglers' Stair.'

'Oh?' Emma put down her mug. 'Was that a good idea today? We were going to put this behind us. Besides, I thought they were going to rope it off to stop the public going down.'

'They have.' Damian came in, took a Melting Moment and bit into it. 'They put a notice up,' he said indistinctly. 'But I climbed over it. Hold on!' He saw protest on Emma's face. 'It was quite safe. I've got proper shoes. The police think Mrs Pugh slipped because of her sandals, don't they? That woman police sergeant went on and on about the need to wear sensible shoes for exploring.'

'Yes, and I've been thinking it over. The police are probably right. I dare say the silly woman was just the sort of person who would go walking all alone up there in high heels! That's what the coroner will find. Accident. You and I have to pitch up at the coroner's court on Friday, by the way.'

Damian was looking smug. 'Do we? Well, then it's a good thing I did ignore the notice and go down to the beach, because I found something really interesting!'

He got off his stool and disappeared outside. A few moments later he was back, his hands held behind his back. 'I went beach-combing. The tide was out and I was looking for anything interesting by way of flotsam and jetsam. But first I found one of these . . .'

Damian, showing a fine sense of showmanship, took one hand from behind his back and held up a dripping object. 'After a search along the whole length of the beach, I was lucky enough to find the other one, washed up behind a rock quite separately from the first one, so it was just chance. What do you think?' He brought out the second object and held it up beside the first.

'I don't know what to think,' Emma said weakly.

He was holding up a sea-sodden, seaweed-draped but still quite intact pair of women's walking shoes.

Part Two

'A pair of shoes,' said Inspector King, reaching out and tipping one over with a fastidious finger. A small dead crab fell out of it.

The shoes, still damp the following morning and in addition by now distinctly smelly, lay on a sheet of newspaper on his desk. Emma, Damian and Matt King stood round it looking down at them.

'From the beach where Mrs Pugh died. A woman's walking shoes!' Emma emphasised the last words impatiently.

'Yes, indeed,' he agreed, apparently indifferent to any significance. 'As you say, from the beach at the foot of the Smugglers' Stair. A flight of steps, my lad, which is roped off, access strictly forbidden by a clearly visible police notice!' He turned to Damian.

Damian reddened and shuffled. 'I know, but I was curious. It wasn't dangerous for me.'

'The late Mrs Pugh thought it wasn't dangerous for her! I've got one body found at the bottom of the steps, I can do without another.'

'Sorry, sir!' said Damian contritely.

'Look!' Emma interrupted. 'Damian knows he shouldn't have ignored the rope and notice. I've already grumbled. But he did find the shoes! Don't you see what this means?'

'No,' said Matt. 'But I was forgetting. You write detective stories!

181

These shoes are a clue, is that it? You think, perhaps, they might have belonged to Mrs Pugh?'

Emma almost hissed with exasperation. 'Of course I do!'

'But she was wearing her shoes when you found her,' he pointed out with aggravating calm.

'She was wearing high-heeled sandals! Everyone is saying how stupid she was to try and climb down the Smugglers' Stair in high heels. But perhaps she took along her walking shoes for that.'

'So why wasn't she wearing them?'

'I don't know!' Emma fairly shouted.

'Let's all sit down, shall we?' Matt set the example, seating himself behind his desk and placing his palms flat on it, one either side of the shoes. 'You are asking me, Emma, to accept that Mrs Pugh went out with two pairs of shoes?'

'Why not? I frequently do. Lots of women do. If I'm going to a party, I often go in flatties, especially if I'm driving, and take my high heels. Or vice versa, I go visiting in heels and take along flat shoes in case someone suggests a walk.'

'Yes, yes!' He held up his hands to stem her words. 'But Emma, these shoes weren't on Mrs Pugh's feet, they weren't even in a bag near her body or anywhere on the beach near where she was found! To me that suggests they belonged to someone else who didn't want them and threw them away. I prefer people not to throw their rubbish in the sea, but this person did. The tide washed them up where Damian found them.'

'They're new! Oh, for goodness' sake, Matt!' Emma seized the shoes and turned them over. 'Look at the soles and heels! Hardly any wear. They're soaked, full of seaweed and grit, but they're still new. Someone bought these to come on holiday.'

'And foolishly left them near the waterline. Any summer visitor, almost anywhere along the bay, could have done that. We have no reason to suppose they were Mrs Pugh's!'

'What about that cousin of hers?' Emma challenged. 'She could identify them.'

'Mrs Lampeter? Poor woman. She's very upset. She had the unfortunate task of identifying Mrs Pugh's body. I hardly think, Emma, I can push these unsavoury objects under her nose!' His voice rose and over-rode her attempted interruption. 'Especially as Mrs Pugh was wearing her sandals when she slipped and fell! If she had brought along walking shoes, why didn't she put them on before attempting to climb down to the beach?'

'Perhaps,' Emma said tautly, 'she did!'

There was a silence. A large bluebottle buzzed above the shoes.

Matt waved it away with an irritated hand. It flew up to the window and beat itself against the panes.

'Okay! What happened? She fell down the steps, fracturing her skull, but thoughtfully changed her shoes and lobbed the flat ones into the briny before dying! Come on, Emma, even if for some totally unimaginable reason she had wanted to do that, it would have been physically impossible. Even you must see that!'

'Then someone else did it for her!' Emma said.

This time the silence lasted longer. Damian looked nervously at the inspector.

'Why?' Matt asked softly.

'Because they wanted it to look like an accident, that she tripped because of her sandals and the loose rail, which whoever it was had deliberated damaged on a previous visit – or pulled loose after the event! Then, while she lay dead or dying, the same person took off her shoes and buckled on the sandals, throwing the shoes into the sea. He or she didn't think the sea would wash them straight back.'

'Who?' Matt's voice hadn't changed.

'The person who was with her. I'm sure someone was, Matt, although I didn't actually see—'

'Why?' he asked again, not allowing her to finish.

This time even Emma was stumped. 'I don't know.'

'Neither do I.' He leaned forward. 'Don't you think this is all rather a wild story? How about you, Damian? Do you go along with this theory of your aunt's?'

Damian hesitated and cast Emma an apologetic glance. 'I suppose not really, but, well, people do get murdered.'

'And that's what we're talking about, isn't it? Murder?' Matt's eyes turned back to Emma and no longer expressed friendly tolerance. 'For crying out loud, Emma! What do you think murder is? An entertainment for a dull day, like one of your books? Don't you think that at the very least, you're being highly irresponsible? You're making accusations for which you haven't a shred of evidence. No! I don't count a pair of ownerless, soggy shoes! You're putting ideas in that boy's head – sorry, Damian, but I was thirteen once and wanted life to be an adventure. Sadly, there's nearly always a rational, if disappointing, explanation for things. Mrs Pugh fell because she tried to climb down a well-worn flight of cliff steps in unsuitable footwear, all alone, when part of the handrail was loose.'

'That's what you intend to tell the coroner?' Emma demanded.

'Of course it is! What do you want me to say? I can't hold up a pair of old – all right, new! – shoes and assert in the face of the evidence that I suspect foul play! Can you imagine the coroner saying, "Oh yes, inspector! Unlawful killing, not a doubt! Inquest adjourned while you complete your enquiries."'

'I don't think it's funny!' Emma said coldly.

'Neither do I!' There was an edge of steel in his voice which she hadn't heard before and couldn't ignore. The bluebottle buzzed. Matt whirled and slapped at it. It fell off the window-pane and lay by the shoes, waving its legs and making whirring noises.

Emma, too, accepted temporary defeat. 'Right! Damian and I won't bother you any further! We'll take these—' She reached out a hand.

'No—' Matt scooped up newspaper and shoes in a single skilful movement and transferred the bundle to a wire tray. 'I'll take care of those. I don't want you running around the whole area asking every Tom, Dick and Harry if they recognise them!'

'You don't want me going to ask Mrs Lampeter if she recognises them!' Emma challenged, tossing back her long hair.

'Fair enough. I don't. Mrs Lampeter is distressed enough.'

'I would do it tactfully!'

'Emma!' Matt said crisply. 'You won't do it at all!'

Damian muttered a warning, 'Em! Please!'

Emma simmered. 'What about the boat? Have you at least enquired about that?'

'Thank you. I passed your information on. It's being dealt with.' He gave a forced smile. 'We appreciate all your help, Emma. But when it comes to sinister plots, just keep it for your books, okay?'

* * *

'He was hopping mad, Emma,' said Damian when they got outside.

'He was? What do you think I am? No wonder there are so many unsolved crimes!'

'I don't know . . .' He sounded unhappy. 'It's all a bit far-fetched when you think about it. Why should anyone want to bump off Mrs Pugh? I mean, seriously! I know she wasn't exactly likeable and asked questions all the time—'

'Yes!' Emma stopped abruptly. 'And I'm going to ask a few!'

'Look, Em, we ought to leave it alone—'

'I shall take full responsibility. Perhaps you'd better go back to the cottage.'

'Where are we going?' Damian clearly had no intention of being left out, whatever his misgivings.

'Down to the seafront. There's a wooden hut there where fishing boats can be hired. I'll just enquire. It won't do any harm.'

It was lunchtime and the seafront more or less deserted in the sunshine. No one was in the hut, but a small motorboat was secured alongside a wooden jetty. Crouching in it was a man tinkering with the engine. He was wearing a sleeveless T-shirt and his strongly muscled arms were tanned to a walnut hue.

'Excuse me!' Emma called as she and Damian edged cautiously along the jetty.

The man straightened up, the little boat rocking precariously, and raised his eyes to their enquiring faces. He had thick, curling black hair and beads of perspiration ran down the wind-and-weather-tanned skin of his face. His jeans were liberally smeared with paint and Emma couldn't help thinking he looked more than a little disreputable.

'Hullo, there,' he said, wiping his hands on an oil-smeared rag. 'What do you two want?'

'To enquire about the fishing,' Damian said, before Emma could. 'Are you in charge?'

He transferred his gaze from Emma with some reluctance. 'I am that. Luke Pardoe. Just you stay there.'

He threw down the rag and rubbed his forearm over his sweating brow. As he began to clamber onto the jetty, Emma and Damian beat an automatic retreat to the shore. He joined them by the hut. He was even larger than he'd looked down in the boat, towering over them both.

'When do you want to go out? All day or half day?'

'We're not sure,' Emma said nervously. 'We just came to enquire how much it cost.'

He jerked a grimy thumb at a wooden board nailed to the hut on which was written a list of tariffs.

'I haven't got a rod or anything,' Damian explained.

'Can provide tackle. Says so, up there.'

Emma made an effort to take the conversation in hand. 'You must get a lot of visitors wanting to go out.'

'Fair few. Not all as pretty as you.'

She ignored this gallantry and the twinkle in his eyes which accompanied it. 'Damian and I were up on the cliffs the other day and saw people fishing from a boat. Perhaps it was even one of your boats. We thought what fun it looked and it gave us the idea.'

'Oh, is that so?' The dark eyes looked her up and down shrewdly.

'You must get, er, a marvellous view of the coastline from out there at sea. I expect you can see the whole of the Smugglers' Stair and everything?'

He stooped over her. Emma involuntarily took a step back, unnerved by the proximity of those gleaming dark eyes and the mixed smell of paint, oil, sweat and sea.

'Now what,' Luke Pardoe asked her softly, 'do you really want to know, eh? Or have you just come to pass the time of day? Not that I mind! I like a bit of company, the right company!'

'She came to ask about the fishing!' Damian said fiercely. He moved protectively between Emma and Pardoe.

'Oh, she's fishing well enough! Fishing for information and she's not the only one! Right curious lot we've got round here! I've never been so popular as these last few days!'

'Who else has been asking?' Emma burst out before she could stop herself.

He grinned at her, white teeth flashing in his sunburned face. 'Ah, that'd be telling, wouldn't it?' He turned to Damian. 'All right, lad, you come back when your sister's made her mind up and I'll take you out! Just at the moment, though, I'm busy.'

He turned and redescended to the boat. There was a clang of metal against metal as if he'd dropped a spanner and they heard him swear.

'He's suspicious,' whispered Damian. 'He won't tell us anything.'

'I wish I knew who else had been asking.' Emma sighed.

'He thought you were my sister.'

'I don't mind that. Inspector King thought I was your mother!'

'Wish you were!' said Damian abruptly. He turned scarlet and walked quickly away.

The evening before the inquest Inspector King telephoned. Damian took the call and came to pass on the message.

'He's sorry he can't come and fetch us tomorrow morning, after all. We'll have to make our own way to the inquest.'

Emma rested her forearms on the typewriter. 'Have you thought what you're going to say to the coroner?'

'I'm just going to say I saw her from a distance and then at the bottom of the steps. I don't think we ought to mention the shoes. The inspector wouldn't like it and get mad at us again.'

She had to admit he was right.

The inquest took place in a small room provided with uncomfortable wooden chairs. Emma looked eagerly for Mrs Lampeter.

She recognised Mrs Pugh's cousin at once, even though she had only glimpsed her at the bus station. Mrs Lampeter was in mourning, an unseasonably warm dark coat. Though upset, her voice was surprisingly clear and low pitched. When Emma closed her eyes, she could easily have imagined she listened to a very young man.

Mrs Lampeter gave in evidence that her cousin Felicity Pugh had gone out for a walk on the first morning of her holiday, promising to be back in time for lunch.

'I understand,' said the coroner, 'there is some question of unsuitable footwear. Can you tell us what kind of shoes Mrs Pugh was wearing?'

'Sandals!' said Mrs Lampeter. She delved into a pocket of the dark coat and produced a crumpled hankerchief. 'I told her to be careful! I said those high heels wouldn't do!' She dabbed at her nose. 'Poor Felicity! I keep thinking about it! If only I'd gone with her! But I was busy making us a special lunch, because it was the first day of her visit, you understand.'

189

Emma and Damian both said their pieces as agreed. A doctor gave cause of death as fracture of the skull. A young man from the local council said that the handrail had been inspected at the beginning of the season and had been in good condition then.

'The police report states that the bottom section had been pulled away from the rock,' the coroner said, consulting his notes.

'We can't be responsible for vandals,' said the man from the council in an aggrieved tone. 'We do inspect at regular intervals and report all signs of vandalism to the police!' He glared at Matt.

The coroner gave his opinion as accidental death. He expressed his condolences to Mrs Lampeter and said that in the circumstances no blame could be attached to the council. He hoped the police were trying to find the vandals.

'Come on!' Emma grabbed Damian's arm as the court rose. She set off in hot pursuit of Mrs Lampeter and caught up with her just outside.

'Mrs Lampeter!'

The woman in the dark coat turned and peered uncertainly at them.

'I hope you don't mind!' Emma panted. 'I – we – just wanted to say that we're very sorry about your cousin.'

'Oh yes, you found her. Such a shock.' Mrs Lampeter's mild blue eyes turned to Damian. 'And you're the young man Felicity met on the bus! She told me. It was nice of you to keep her company.'

Damian reddened in embarrassment and looked down at his feet.

'It's been such an unpleasant start to your holiday,' Mrs Lampeter continued to him. 'I do feel I ought to try and make it up to you. I'm sure Felicity would have wished it. Why don't you both come to tea? Monday? Would that be all right?'

Emma, from the corner of her eye seeing Matt King approach, said quickly, 'How kind of you! We'd love to come!'

'Well, Emma,' said Matt, coming up as Mrs Lampeter walked away. 'I hope that wasn't too much of an ordeal.'

'Not at all. I hope,' said Emma, 'that you manage to find the vandals who damaged the handrail!'

'That's not my department. I'm sure someone's looking into it.'

'That man from the council . . .' Damian was scowling in thought. 'He was dead keen to blame vandals for pulling out the handrail, wasn't he? I know it isn't your department, as you say, but do you think vandals did it, inspector?'

'I go by facts, Damian. When enquiries have been made, we'll know.'

'I thought,' said Damian, fixing him with a stern eye, 'that detectives had hunches.'

'Only in your aunt's books!'

'Oh, we're back to knocking my books,' Emma put in sweetly. 'There's a surprise!'

'I am not—' The inspector bit back his reply. 'I just came over to have a word with you. I saw you were talking to Mrs Lampeter.'

'Damian and I,' Emma said coldly, 'were expressing our condolences. I take it we don't need permission from the police in order to do that?'

'Of course not,' Matt King said mildly. 'If that's all you were doing.'

Emma chose not to answer and before her stony stare, even

191

Inspector King had the grace to look a little abashed. Damian came to the rescue of both.

'I've been thinking, I wouldn't mind being in the police, doing your job. Either that or an investigative journalist.'

'Just so long as you remember that we have to go by the rules and the journalists can bend them!' Matt turned to Emma and hesitated. 'Actually, the real reason for coming over to speak to you was that I was wondering if you had time for a spot of lunch?'

'It's kind of you,' Emma said. 'But being vegetarian—'

'I know a hotel which does an excellent salad bar.' He smiled disarmingly.

The hotel was an Edwardian building with a spacious restaurant which, besides regular lunches, offered a wonderful serve-yourself cold table against a backdrop of gilded ornamental plaster and starched linen. There was a restful murmur of voices, tinkle of glass and discreet clatter of china. Through long, velvet-draped windows a beautiful view of the sea could be seen.

'This is very nice,' Emma said with genuine pleasure. 'Rather a change to the cottage! Are you going to eat all that, Damian?'

'Yes,' said Damian simply, settling down to his heaped plate.

'Growing lad,' said Inspector King. 'Healthy appetite! I want to apologise for not driving you to the inquest as I promised. I was – held up on the telephone, long distance.' He poured Emma a glass of white wine.

'That's all right. We splashed out and called a taxi to take us down and then we'll cycle back.'

Damian looked wistfully at the wine, but resignedly picked up the Coca-Cola with which he'd been provided.

'And I didn't mean to suggest, back there, that you would be so tactless as to question Mrs Lampeter about her cousin right after the inquest! I thought she was bearing up well.'

'She seemed very pleasant,' Emma said warily, with a warning glance at Damian. There was no reason to tell Matt King about the invitation they'd received to tea. But Damian was eating his way steadily through his plateful and not contributing to any conversation.

'Yes,' Matt agreed. 'She's a very nice lady and quite a well-known personality locally. She does a great deal of charity work.'

'I'm still surprised she didn't persuade Mrs Pugh to get some proper shoes.'

'Ah, the shoes,' Matt murmured. 'I'm glad you didn't mention those to the coroner, Emma.'

'I did my duty,' said Emma virtuously. 'I gave them to the police.'

'Yes, you did. There is one other little thing . . .'

Emma raised her eyebrows over the rim of her wine glass and fixed her expressive grey eyes on Matt King's face. He turned slightly pink.

'Luke Pardoe, who runs the fishing concession . . .'

'I don't believe it!' She put down her glass. 'How do you know—'

'Never mind that! Strictly between us, Emma, you ought to be careful there. Oh, Pardoe's a fine fisherman and handles a boat better than anyone I know. But he's, well, a rough diamond, shall we say?'

'He fancied Emma!' said Damian indistinctly through a mouthful of ham.

'Oh, did he?' Matt sounded sharp. 'What did he say?'

'He didn't say anything!' Emma retorted, glaring at her nephew. 'Don't talk nonsense, Damian!'

'I think you should steer clear of Pardoe, Emma!' Matt said a little more vehemently than might have been expected. 'Just a word of friendly advice!'

'I think he's jealous!' shouted Damian into the breeze as they cycled home.

'Who is? Matt King? Honestly, Damian! What rubbish!'

'He went all red when you looked at him!'

'He's probably got a guilty conscience! How did he know we talked to Pardoe?'

Mrs Lampeter lived in a large detached house, with a well-kept garden, in a secluded road of such houses a quarter of a mile from the seafront. There were double garages aplenty here and every sign of prosperity. Emma and Damian wheeled their elderly bicycles up the raked gravel drive on Monday afternoon and propped them self-consciously against the tiled porch.

'I'm so glad you could come,' said Mrs Lampeter. 'Please call me Rose. Now, Damian, I haven't forgotten what healthy appetites boys of your age have! I remember when my son, Edward, was thirteen. My goodness, how time flies!'

She went to a table and picked up a photograph in a silver frame. 'This is my son when he was about your age, and this—' She put down the frame and picked up another. It held a studio portrait of a good-looking man with brushed back hair and thin features like his mother's. 'This is Edward now! Of course, to me he hasn't changed so much from when he was a boy. But then, mothers always say that, don't they? I expect your mother, Damian, embarrasses you by saying how like your baby pictures you are!' She smiled kindly at him.

'I shouldn't think so,' said Damian stonily. 'She's got her work to talk about. If she's got any of my baby pictures they'll be in a box somewhere in England. She and my father are in Africa working at a refugee camp. Conditions are pretty primitive and they only have room for essentials, no personal stuff.'

Mrs Lampeter wheeled in tea on a trolley. In her comfortable drawing room, against the background of a softly ticking grandfather clock, Damian tucked into a variety of sandwiches and cake. Emma studied Rose Lampeter who wore, as she had at the bus station, twill slacks, today teamed with a cotton shirt.

Mrs Lampeter noticed her interest but misinterpreted it. 'One doesn't wear mourning nowadays except for funerals and, of course, the inquest. I can't help feeling it's a pity somehow.'

'What's a pity,' said Emma, 'is that Mrs Pugh wasn't dressed more like you for her walk! Didn't she bring any flat shoes?'

'No. I particularly told her to buy herself a pair before she came. But Felicity could be very obstinate. I suppose I shouldn't say it, but she was a dressy sort of person. She liked bright colours and pretty things. I don't think she saw herself in outdoor wear. It was all the more tragic because she hadn't been to see me for at least two years but we wrote regularly. When one reaches my age, one has so few relatives left. I shall miss Felicity. However, everyone has been so kind. Matthew King has been very helpful. I knew his mother, you know, before she went to live in Spain.'

Emma's teacup rattled in its saucer. 'She lives in Spain?'

'For the last six or seven years. She had very bad arthritis and wanted a drier climate. The sea air didn't suit her. She can't travel much now. I believe Matthew goes out to Spain to visit her every year.'

'Right!' muttered Emma to herself as she and Damian began their long ride home.

'Em—' Damian called, frowning in thought.

'Hold on, Damian. There's something I'm trying to work out!'

'But Em—'

'Later!'

They had reached the town centre. Emma stopped and turned to Damian, riding behind her. 'Look, can you go on ahead to the cottage? I – just want to call in and see someone about something.'

'Okay,' he said. 'I want to write a letter, anyway.'

'Emma?' said Matt King, rising in surprise to greet her.

'I won't keep you long!' Emma said, seating herself on the other side of his desk. 'I think you haven't been quite frank with me, Inspector King! Moreover, I think you have made use of me!'

He looked at her warily. 'What notion have you taken into your head now?'

'Just something I've worked out. Damian and I have just had tea with Rose Lampeter. She told me your mother lives in Spain and never comes back to England.'

'I see . . .' Matt leaned back and folded his arms truculently. 'Go on.'

'The day we met at the bus station, you told me that you had just seen your mother off on a bus. But if that were so, why were

196

you still hanging about? Only she hadn't left on a bus, had she? Because she's in Spain. So why were you there at all? Why were you waiting at that particular bus halt? Whom were you waiting for, Matt?' She gazed at him interrogatively.

'You tell me,' he said. 'Since you've worked it out, you say.'

'I will. The bus came in. Several people got off but only Damian and Mrs Pugh came to speak to us. Mrs Pugh then went off with Mrs Lampeter. You then kindly offered to drive us home, although we refused and took a taxi. But that you offered meant you no longer needed to stay there. That means whoever you wanted to see either wasn't on the bus, after all, or—' She leaned forward and a lock of brown hair fell inconveniently over her face. She swept it back behind her ear. 'Or you had already seen her!'

'*Her*, Emma?' Matt asked quietly.

'Yes. I was waiting to meet Damian. But you, I think, were waiting for Mrs Pugh! She didn't know you but you knew her somehow and I'd very much like to know about it! In fact, I think you owe me an explanation. You deliberately attached yourself to me at the bus stop as cover. She might have noticed a single man standing around staring at her. But not a couple, one of whom at least had a bona fide reason for being there! So, Matthew King, are you going to tell me?'

Part Three

'No, Emma,' said Matthew King. 'I am not going to tell you why I was waiting at the bus station.'

'Why not?' Emma's hair chose that moment to fall over her face. She scraped it back with both hands and glared at him from a frame of tangled brown locks.

Inspector King studied her flushed face and sparkling eyes thoughtfully for a moment and then sighed. 'Because, frankly, it's none of your business.'

'None—' Emma gurgled in fury. 'You deliberately made use of me! I'm entitled to know!'

'I don't admit I did anything of the sort. You're letting that writer's imagination of yours run away with you again. Moreover, I'm sorry, but, you know, you aren't entitled to know anything! This is police business.'

Emma rose to her feet, aware that her windswept appearance hindered any display of dignity. 'Right! If that's your attitude then I'll leave! I thought the police wanted to encourage cooperation from the public. But if this is how you do it, just don't expect me to come to you again with any information!'

As she marched out she heard him call, 'Emma, wait a moment!' But she ignored him.

Emma pedalled home at a fine pace. She hauled the bike up

the steep hill out of town, muttering her opinion of Inspector King, rode with hair streaming in the wind through Sidford and Sidbury, and eventually fell panting and exhausted through the cottage door, her shirt clinging to her body with perspiration.

Damian was composedly frying sausages for his supper. 'Your face is red!' he observed, glancing across from the stove.

Emma growled and went upstairs to run a bath. When she came down, freshened and calmed, Damian was watching television. She made herself a peanut-butter sandwich and joined him on the sofa.

'Sorry I left you to come home alone,' she apologised. 'I called by the police station to see Inspector King, but I needn't have bothered!'

'I had a letter to write, I told you. I posted it at the bottom of the lane and met Mrs Collins there. She said to come up to the farm any time I was at a loose end. I thought I might do that, if you don't mind.' He glanced sideways at her.

'Of course I don't mind, Damian. It's your holiday and you must do whatever you want. I'm sorry I dragged you along with me on a wild goose chase, seeking out Pardoe and involving you in my botched attempts at detection.' She sighed. 'Only, even if I haven't achieved much, I still don't think it's all just my imagination, no matter what Matt King says! He knows I'm right! He's just refusing to tell me what's going on. It's infuriating and it's unfair. But it isn't anything you should worry about, Damian.'

The news had started and was showing pictures of a feeding station in Africa. Damian leaned forward intently. The pictures vanished and were replaced by a home-based news item. Damian relaxed.

'Did you think you might catch a glimpse of your parents?'

Emma asked sympathetically. 'I always scrutinise those scenes in case I see Bridget.'

'I did see Mum once, just briefly, weighing a baby.' Damian's voice was curiously toneless.

'You miss your parents, don't you?' Emma bit into her sandwich.

Damian didn't reply directly. Instead he said, 'When I was very small they could take me with them overseas. It was fun. I remember playing around in the dust with other children and messing about in the water by the riverbanks. It was when I got big enough to go to school they had to leave me behind.'

Emma laid aside the rest of the sandwich. 'I remember. You were what, six or seven when you first went to boarding school?'

He nodded and she went on, 'That was tough, on you and your parents.'

'Yes.' Damian hesitated and then began to speak slowly, picking out his words with great care and deliberation. He clearly wanted to explain something which mattered a great deal to him, and he was trying to sort it out in his own mind as well as explain it to her.

'I told you and Inspector King that I have confused feelings about Mrs Pugh, because I couldn't say anything nice about her after she had that – accident. I have confused feelings about Mum and Dad, too. I'm ashamed of it. I wish I didn't.'

'No one should ever be ashamed of their feelings, Damian!' Emma said earnestly.

He ignored this and continued, 'You see, I do love my parents. I do understand that their work is important, life saving, and they run into all kinds of dangers. I admire them. They're really great. Only – only I can't help wishing they had managed to find just a bit more time for me over the years. I wish I just saw them more often. They do write when they can. I feel selfish when I start thinking like this, because what they do is more important than I am. The people they help need aid so desperately – but I can't help it. It's as if they have time for everyone else in the world but me. I expect you think that sounds miserable and self-centred.'

'I don't think anything of the sort! I do understand why you feel that way, and it's quite natural, but I know Bridget and your father are thinking of you all the time, even when they're so busy. They do worry about you too, Damian.'

'I know that. But they don't need an extra worry, do they? Not when they've got so many. Sometimes I think their lives would have been much simpler if they hadn't got me.'

'No, Damian!' Emma, shocked, took his arm. 'Your parents think the world of you! Just think how much it means to them when their work gets them down, to be able to think about you and know that they have got something, someone else, in their lives. You're so important to them. Oh, I know I'm right and I do wish I could explain it better!' She gestured in despair.

'It's okay, Em. Thanks, anyway, and thanks for having me here this holiday and for all the times you come to school and take me out to tea at weekends.'

Damian sat up straight before she could reply to this, plainly dismissing the subject. 'What'll you do tomorrow? Work on your book?' he asked briskly.

'I should, but I can't, not with this Mrs Pugh business unsolved. It just fills my mind and I can't think of anything else. Besides, Matt King needn't think I'm just going to be dismissed like that! Now, I don't really want to bother you any more, Damian, but would you mind taking me back to the beach at the foot of the Smugglers' Stair and showing me just where you found those shoes?'

'You know,' her nephew warned her, 'the inspector isn't going to like it. He wants you to leave it alone.'

'Inspector King,' said Emma grimly, 'plays his cards very close to his chest. Fair enough. I can play by those rules too. I'll do my own investigating from now on without any consultations with him! After all, he has no one to blame but himself! I offered him all my information and he wouldn't give me a scrap in return! But it all confirms what I've thought from the moment we found poor Mrs Pugh. There's something fishy about the whole thing. I'm going to find out what, and our – I mean, my – investigations have to start with the shoes you found on the beach!'

Damian gave her a sideways glance. 'You are still sure they were her shoes, then? Mrs Lampeter told the inquest that Mrs Pugh had refused to buy any flat shoes.'

'I know she did,' returned Emma. 'But I think Mrs Lampeter lied.'

There was a stiff breeze blowing the next morning at the Smugglers' Stair. The steps were still roped off but the police notice had fallen over face down. Thus, Emma pointed out, they could honestly say they hadn't read it. They climbed over the flimsy barrier and made their way down to the beach unaided because the damaged hand-rail had been removed altogether, even the brackets in the cliff wall. Presumably the council meant to replace it entirely.

The waves rolled in from a choppy sea, following rapidly upon one another and flicking spray into the air. The seabirds were clinging to the shoreline. 'That means bad weather out at sea,' said Emma, dredging up an item of folklore from distant memory.

'Someone has taken a boat out, even so.' Damian pointed. 'He must be good at handling it. He's brought it round here.'

Drawn up on the pebbles at the far end of the beach was a small motorboat with a tiny, white-painted cabin. There was no sign of anyone near it. Emma glanced up at the red wall of rock and the grassy rim of the cliff behind which ran the path. There was no one up there, etched against the skyline.

Damian, with a straightforward boy's curiosity, had already scrambled across the pebbles and rocks to the beached boat and was prowling round it. He had taken off his trainers and, after tying the laces together, hung them round his neck. He didn't seem to notice the pebbles cutting into his bare feet.

As she made her way towards him, he called out, 'You know, Em, this is Luke Pardoe's boat!' He splashed through the shallow water in which the stern rested.

'They all look the same to me,' said Emma doubtfully. Her heart sank. She didn't really want to come face to face with Pardoe out here in this lonely spot, even with Damian as witness. She glanced nervously over her shoulder.

'It's definitely Pardoe's! I remember that scraped mark on the cabin paintwork, by the porthole there, and the name, *Lucy*.'

'You're more observant than I am,' she admitted, downcast. So much for Emma Durrant, the great detective. She couldn't even recognise Pardoe's boat! She frowned. 'So where is he? Hey!' Her voice rose in a squeak of alarm. 'He mightn't like you doing that!'

Damian had climbed into the boat and was investigating the

cabin. Now he reappeared. 'There's a dirty old denim jacket in there and an open bag of tools. Oh, and some binoculars. I wonder where he is.' He looked up and down the beach and then pointed towards the cliff. 'Perhaps he's in there?'

He was indicating the dark mouth of the Smugglers' Cave. Emma had been inside it once, over a year ago on a previous visit. She remembered it as a fairly shallow cavern worn out of the rock in ages past by pounding sea. The opening was about eight feet across and she couldn't, from here, see anyone inside it. She wondered whether the old tales were true and contraband landed here had been stored inside it before being laboriously carried up the cliff stair.

'Let's go and explore it anyway,' said Damian, reading her mind. 'It doesn't look as if he's in there, but it might be interesting.'

They approached the cave, Damian with great enthusiasm and Emma with feelings of dread she couldn't explain.

'Empty!' said Damian at last, disappointed. He didn't say quite what he'd hoped to find and his voice echoed off the rocky sides, emphasising his announcement.

Emma relaxed. 'You can't expect to find clues like Mrs Pugh's shoes every time, Damian!'

But it hadn't been anything as mundane as a pair of shoes she'd feared encountering. Matt King, she thought ruefully, would say she had been letting her imagination run riot again! Just what had she expected, after all? On the other hand, where was Pardoe? Had he climbed the Stair to the cliff above? Was he even now watching the beach from up there and had seen them looking at his boat?

She glanced over her shoulder at the open entrance, more than half-expecting to see Luke's disreputable figure standing there in paint-stained jeans, grinning at her. But only the abandoned beached boat could be seen, rocking slightly as the waves lapped at the stern.

An uncomfortable crawling sensation ran up her spine. The cave smelled of damp stone and rotting vegetation. She wanted to get out of there. Despite the nearness of open air, she was experiencing a sense of claustrophobia, almost of panic.

'Come on, Damian, let's get out of here! It gives me the heebie-jeebies!'

Damian, suffering no such inhibitions, had made his way to the gloomy far recesses of the cave. 'There's a sort of tunnel here, Em! It's only a couple of feet high, but I could crawl in easily. Hold on, I'll see how far it goes.' The last words sounded muffled, indicating that Damian was already investigating the hole in the rock.

'Wait!' she called anxiously, starting towards the back of the cave. 'It mightn't be safe!'

Damian didn't answer.

Oh no! she thought. *He's got himself stuck!* Emma stumbled over the stony floor and was rewarded with the sight of Damian's bare feet. The rest of him was swallowed up by the rock wall of the tunnel. 'Are you okay?' she called.

'Ye— es . . .' He didn't sound too sure.

'Do be careful!' she urged.

Without warning, he suddenly emerged backwards on hands and knees and, still in that position, looked up at her, his eyes wild and his mouth open but speechless.

'What is it?' Emma whispered. She dropped onto her knees and made to peer into the tunnel. Her eyes had difficulty adjusting to the poor light and she couldn't really make out anything, except some sort of obstruction which filled the narrow space.

Damian put out his hand to pull her back. 'No, don't look, Em!'

Something in his voice caused her to turn her head sharply towards him. 'What is it?' The nameless dread returned, seizing her heart and stomach in a vice-like grip. More than anything else, she wanted to get up and run out of this horrible cave.

Damian swallowed. 'He's in there!' he said hoarsely.

'He?' Instinct caused her heart to sink again and she knew whom he meant. 'Pardoe?' She glanced hesitantly at the small aperture. 'Are you sure? There isn't room for him. He's a big chap.'

'There's room for him the way he is,' said Damian shakily. 'He's lying flat. Someone's bashed his head in and shoved him in there!'

Emma and Damian sat on the rocks and watched the police seal off the cave. The tide had gone out and Pardoe's boat was now high and dry. A seagull perched on the cabin roof. After a while Matt came across the pebbles to join them.

'You're making a habit of finding bodies, Miss Durrant!'

'I found him,' Damian said quietly.

'Yes, you did, didn't you?' Matt reached out and ruffled the boy's hair. 'Bad luck. A word with you, Emma, if I may? Damian, if you go up to the cliff path, you'll find someone with a Thermos. Get them to give you a cup of hot tea.'

Damian nodded, took his trainers from around his neck and pulled them on to his feet. He got up and wandered away across the pebbles.

Matt took the place vacated by the boy and together they watched Damian as he began to climb the Smugglers' Stair.

'What were you doing out here, Emma?' Matt asked quietly.

'Looking for clues,' Emma said. 'It sounds foolish. I suppose it was. But I want to know the truth about Mrs Pugh and you made me so cross.'

'Yes, I did. I'm sorry about that.' Matt paused. 'Look, Emma, I can't tell you all the whys and wherefores of this because it's official, do you understand? As soon as I can, I will tell you. I promise—'

There was a shout. One of the men searching the beach was gesturing towards them. Matt got up with a murmured excuse and made his way to the spot. Emma watched apprehensively as they stooped over something lying by the water's edge. She saw Matt reach down and lift it gingerly with his fingertips. It looked, from where she sat, like a piece of metal, possibly a spanner. Luke Pardoe, when they'd met him by the fishing concession hut, had been working with a spanner in his boat.

The breeze seemed to grow chillier and she shivered. Hugging herself for warmth, she watched as the object was carefully transferred to a small bag and sealed up. Matt came back.

'Is that – it?' she asked bleakly. 'The murder weapon?'

'Possibly.' He took his seat by her again. 'Emma, I hope I can talk about it to you soon. In the meantime, I want you to take great care of yourself and the boy. I am very serious about this. I know you like to make up your own mind about things, but please, this time, take my advice. Keep all doors locked and windows shut. That cottage is pretty isolated.'

'The Collinses are only just up the lane, at the farm.'

'Yes. If it weren't for that, I'd suggest you moved down to a bed and breakfast in town. In fact, I'd like you to consider doing that anyway. If you decide to stay at the cottage, and you get worried about anything at any time of day or night, just pick up the phone and ring the police and we'll be out there straight away.'

She turned her head to look him full in the face. He wasn't, she thought, a good-looking man, not conventionally so, but he looked a resolute, practical sort of person and he inspired her with confidence just now, despite all her previous misgivings about his attitude.

'Are we in danger?' she asked him. 'Why, Matt?'

He leaned forward. 'Emma, we don't know that Mrs Pugh's death was anything but an accident. But Pardoe's death, and the attempt to hide his body, make a case of murder. He hasn't been dead very long. When you and Damian arrived, the killer could only just have left the scene. Whoever it was must have been up there on the cliff path and probably saw you both, down here, looking at Pardoe's boat, going into the cave. Perhaps you saw more than that. Perhaps you also glimpsed the killer.'

'We didn't! We saw no one!' she protested. 'We looked around for Pardoe and there wasn't a soul! All we saw were seagulls!'

The breeze caught at her hair and wrapped it over her mouth and chin. Matt King stretched out his hand and gently picked the tangled wisps free.

'You know that,' he said. 'But does the killer?'

The next morning Mrs Collins appeared at the door and asked, 'Jim says, does the young lad want to come up to the farm and lend a hand? 'Twill take his mind off things and we could do with an extra pair of hands today.'

'Yes, please!' exclaimed Damian, scrambling up from the breakfast table.

'You'll have to work, mind!' said Mrs Collins, winking at Emma.

'Of course I'll work! I don't mind!' he insisted.

'Thanks,' said Emma, as Damian went to change into his oldest clothes. 'He seems to be bearing up, but he does need something to occupy him.'

'Terrible business, that murder,' said Mrs Collins, taking Damian's vacated chair and folding her plump forearms on the table. She shook her head. 'Not that I'm surprised Luke Pardoe met a bad end. He was always unreliable, as you might say, and not fussy about the company he kept. Thought himself a bit of a fine fellow, too, with the girls and such, and always watching out for a way to make a pound or two. Folk round here all knew about him.'

'Do you know of a Mrs Lampeter?' Emma asked on impulse.

'Oh yes!' Mrs Collins brightened. 'A very nice lady, a great one for organising fetes and such. I've always thought she must be lonely in that big house, since her son left. He's a very successful businessman up in London. She's very proud of him and he does remember his mother and come down and visit from time to time, though of course he's a sight too busy to come often.'

Damian came clattering down the narrow spiral staircase.

'I'll feed him, don't you worry!' said Mrs Collins. 'You have a day to yourself, m'dear!'

In theory she ought to be glad of a day to herself because a pile of blank sheets of paper alone represented the next great work of mystery fiction by E. Durrant.

Emma sat down at the typewriter, filled with determination. Mindful of Matt's advice, she had first taken the precaution of

209

locking the back and front doors. Damian was at the farm. The telephone was at hand if needed. Nothing to impede creation.

She did manage to work on until lunchtime. Reasonably pleased with her progress, she went out into the kitchen and made herself lunch. But then she got to thinking about recent events again.

Whatever Matt King said, he must know that Luke Pardoe's death at the beach where Mrs Pugh had died, was altogether too much of a coincidence. All right, thought Emma, so stranger things did happen! But even though Matt wouldn't admit it to her, she was fairly sure he had accepted that Mrs Pugh's death needed looking into again. She wondered what he had done with the shoes Damian had found on the beach. And Pardoe? He'd warned her off Pardoe after the inquest. But he hadn't explained how he knew she'd been talking with the fisherman. The only explanation was that he'd been watching Pardoe.

'So,' said Emma aloud, 'if Matt was at the bus station to look out for Mrs Pugh as I believe he was, and if he has been watching Pardoe, then I can assume that somehow, Mrs Pugh and Luke Pardoe are connected – even without both having been found dead at the same beach, and both by Damian and me!'

She tried to imagine Mrs Pugh, heavily lipsticked and powdered in her tight bright dress and high heels, hobnobbing with Luke Pardoe in his scruffy jeans and sleeveless T-shirt. It seemed unlikely. It was impossible to think of anything they could have had in common. Or what on earth could Mrs Pugh have been doing that was in any way remotely criminal or likely to interest the police? Pardoe had been a bad lot by all accounts. Mrs Pugh had not been a likeable person, but a crook? Surely not.

Try it another way. Why had Pardoe gone to the beach? Not to fish. To meet someone then?

There was a tapping on glass. Emma glanced uneasily at the window but it was only a spray of rosebush.

So what about Mrs Pugh? Not someone Emma could imagine volunteering to climb down so many steps to a rocky beach. Had she gone there to meet someone? Had Emma been right after all in thinking she saw Mrs Pugh talking to an unseen companion? Had she and Pardoe gone to meet the same person?

In Emma's kitchen, a shadowy form seemed to hover, someone never seen but who must have been there on both occasions. The killer.

'Writer's imagination again!' she admonished herself. She needed some fresh air. Normally she would have taken her bicycle or just walked along the lonely lanes. But after Matt's warning she didn't feel like doing so alone. Damian was busy at the farm and it wouldn't be fair to call him away. The alternative was to go down into the town and stroll along the promenade. There would be plenty of people there and absolutely no danger.

Emma washed up her lunch things, changed into a more respectable pair of cord slacks and a clean shirt, tied up her hair and, lugging her bicycle from the shed, set off down the hill.

She parked the bicycle in the car park of a supermarket, chaining it carefully to a convenient metal pole. Anyone would have to be pretty desperate to pinch this bike, but she depended on it and better safe than sorry! Emma set off to walk briskly along the seafront.

The town seemed extra busy today as she traversed its narrow streets on her way to the shore. As she neared the pedestrian shopping precinct she saw why. There was a sort of fair or craft market taking place. People clustered round a variety of stalls set out in the traffic-free paved area.

Diverted from her original goal, Emma made an automatic beeline for a stall selling second-hand books. One box contained a pile of ancient hardback copies which looked very much as if they had come from a house clearance. She began to pick them over curiously. Here, on brown-edged sheets smelling of dust and damp, were lurid tales of romantic adventure and incredible derring-do. Frail heroines were kidnapped by desert sheiks. Sinister bearded spies imprisoned the hero in impossible situations from which he always easily escaped. There were well-thumbed cook-books full of war-time recipes and any number of those practical advice manuals beloved of a former generation. Amongst them all, Emma came across a book of children's rhymes. Riffling through it, the word 'stair' caught her eye.

After her adventures at the Smugglers' Stair, the coincidence struck her and she began to read.

> As I was coming down the stair,
> I met a man who wasn't there.
> He wasn't there again today.
> I wish, I wish he'd go away!

Emma shivered. The little scrap of nonsense verse suddenly seemed sinister, as though this yellowed little book with its musty smell must hold a message for her. But what? She forced herself to read it again. What was it trying to tell her? A man who wasn't there. A killer on the Stair. That rhymed, too, and it echoed her earlier conjectures uncannily.

'Miss Durrant?'

Emma squeaked and jumped, dropping the book. She whirled round.

Standing beside her was a tall, thin-faced man, handsome in a rather old-fashioned way. In his light jacket and linen hat, he looked rather out of place amongst today's holidaymakers with their bright, casual clothing. Nevertheless, something about him seemed vaguely familiar though she couldn't quite place him. She frowned.

'I'm so sorry,' he apologised, seeing her bewilderment.

He removed the hat and held it to his chest in a gesture which increased the old-fashioned effect. Yet he wasn't old. His hair, now that it wasn't crowned by the hat, could be seen to be thick and wavy and Emma reduced her estimate of his age from early forties to late thirties. The feeling that she ought to know him grew stronger but, for the life of her, she couldn't put a name to him or remember where she'd seen him before.

'I didn't mean to startle you. Of course, you don't know who I am! Please excuse my speaking to you but my mother pointed you out earlier,' he was saying.

'M-mother?' Emma stammered.

'Yes, she's just gone into that shop over there.' He gestured with the panama towards a draper's. 'I thought I'd just come over and introduce myself while I waited for her.' He smiled. 'My name is Edward Lampeter.'

Part Four

'This is very pleasant,' Edward Lampeter said.

The three of them sat in the café to which Edward had insisted on conducting Emma and his mother in order to buy them a real Devon cream tea.

Emma wasn't averse to the cream tea, nor at having another chance to quiz Rose Lampeter, but the unexpected arrival of Edward on the scene put a whole new complexion on matters. She couldn't help feeling she'd been wrong footed and, in this cheerful little café, she felt somehow trapped.

'A pity,' observed Edward now, 'that your nephew isn't with us! Where is he today?' He smiled genially at Emma across the tea things.

'Damian's helping my neighbour, Mr Collins, on the farm.' Emma concentrated as she spoke on spreading a spoonful of clotted cream over her scone.

'Poor Felicity took a great fancy to that boy!' said Rose Lampeter. She picked up the teapot and poured tea for them all. Her hand shook slightly.

Emma wondered whether it was the thought of the late Felicity Pugh which caused it to tremble. Rose was definitely ill at ease and Emma couldn't decide whether she was distressed or simply nervous. That she was still upset would be understandable. But there was something more than grief in the timid glances Rose kept giving her son. It was as if she sought his approval before speaking.

Edward, on the other hand, was completely at ease. 'It's rather nice to think Felicity and young Damian hit it off so well. The generation gap couldn't have been so wide after all! A little surprising, that, don't you think, Miss Durrant?'

'I don't know,' said Emma cautiously, adding, 'please call me Emma.'

'I wonder what they talked about.' Edward leaned back in his chair to signal to the waitress for more hot water.

'About holidays and Damian's school, I expect.' Emma tried to sound nonchalant but she had the strong impression this answer wouldn't satisfy Edward.

'Do country holidays hold the same attraction for boys nowadays?' Edward mused. 'Perhaps rather dull for them. They all seem to be computer buffs, don't they? It's a technological age. Do you write your books on a word processor, Emma?'

'In London, yes. But down here I've only got a typewriter.'

'That must be a bit of a disappointment for the young man.' Edward's eyes gleamed disconcertingly as they fixed her.

'No, I don't think so!' Emma knew she sounded nettled. 'I don't know that Damian is mad about computer games or anything to do with computers. He hasn't said so. He likes to be outdoors. He was very keen to go up to the farm today.'

'My generation,' Rose blurted, 'managed very well without computers! Edward was always very quick to learn anything, but to my mind they seem to make life so complicated—' She broke off and cast her son another hunted look.

'Well, all technology is a good servant and a bad master,' Edward said placidly. 'Don't you agree, Emma?'

'Now what was all that about?' thought Emma as she cycled furiously homeward. 'What on earth did they want to know? They were fishing for some information or other, or Edward was.'

As she puzzled about it, struggling to push the bike up the steep hill, it crossed her mind that perhaps Inspector King might be interested in her meeting with the Lampeters. But she quickly dismissed this idea. She'd told Matt she wouldn't confide in him again and nor would she! A pang of guilt accompanied this stern resolve, but she dismissed that also.

Damian came home about an hour after Emma reached the cottage. His face was scarlet beneath the dust and he looked exhausted but happy.

'You've caught the sun!' she told him with some concern.

'I've had a really mega day!' said Damian. 'I think I'll go in for farming, not be a police detective.'

Mega? Perhaps Damian was a computer addict, after all. 'What about supper?' Emma asked.

'Mrs Collins fed me so well I really couldn't eat much tonight, Em. She'd made a huge meat and potato pie and apple crumble. She put gigantic helpings on my plate and Mr Collins said, "You eat all that up, my lad! A man can't do a day's work on a sandwich!"'

Damian managed a fair imitation of the farmer's Devon burr, but there was a note of pride in his own voice at having been counted amongst the men.

'I don't want much, either. I had a cream tea in Sidmouth.' Emma paused and then told him about her meeting with the Lampeters.

Damian's reaction was quite unexpected. 'Edward Lampeter? You've been talking to him? Gosh, Em, you've got to be careful!'

He looked and sounded so agitated that Emma stared at him in surprise. 'Damian? What on earth is the matter? What do you know about Edward? You've never met him.'

Damian shuffled about and looked down at the stone-flagged kitchen floor. 'Look, Em, I'd better tell you. I thought I'd do a bit of sleuthing, too, to help you. Only, I didn't want to say anything too soon, in case it came to nothing.'

'What's all this about, Damian?' Emma sat on a stool and pointed at another. 'Sit down there and tell me just what you've been up to!'

Damian sat. 'You see, when Mrs Lampeter talked to us about her son, Edward, I knew I'd heard that name before. Then she showed us photos of him both as a boy and a recent picture. Well, at school we have a boy called Jason Carter. Jason's father had some sort of business deal with someone called Edward Lampeter and it went wrong. Jason told us that this man Lampeter was a real crook, only his father hadn't known that when he started out with him. Jason's father nearly got into a lot of trouble because of his dealings with Lampeter and he also lost a lot of money! Lampeter got away scot free and Jason's dad nearly went to gaol! Luckily he had a jolly good lawyer who got him off! It was in the newspapers, pictures and all. Jason showed us. The man in the news picture with Jason's father – well, I was sure it was the same one as in Mrs Lampeter's photo frame!'

'I see.' Emma twisted a strand of long hair in her fingers thoughtfully. 'So what did you do?'

'I wrote to Jason, that letter I told you I posted the other day. I asked him to phone me. I said I thought we'd come across Edward's trail down here.' Damian looked a little ashamed. 'I should have told you, Em, but honestly, I thought perhaps I was making too much of it and it'd all come to nothing. Jason hasn't rung. He must have the letter by now, if he's home. He might have gone away somewhere with his family for the holidays.'

Emma mulled it over. 'I must confess, I didn't like Edward much, though I don't know why. I felt I was being manipulated. He asked odd questions. Not odd enough to be really peculiar, but just unexpected. He talked about computers and he wanted to know what you and Mrs Pugh had talked about on the bus. Damian, she didn't talk about computers, did she? It sounds crazy. It wouldn't be her sort of subject at all.'

Damian's eyes had opened wide. 'But she did, Em!'

He jumped off the stool. 'I told you she kept asking questions. Well, at one point, she started on about computers. What exactly were floppy disks, what did they look like? She'd never seen one. How much information could be stored on one disk? I told her they were plastic things about so square – ' Damian made a shape with his hands. 'But the actual disk was circular and hidden in the middle. There was a paperback novel sticking out of her bag, so I used that as an example and explained the text of that whole book could be stored on one disk. She said, "Fancy that!"' Damian grimaced.

'Right . . .' said Emma, restoring the strand of hair to its place behind her ear. 'We're getting somewhere. I just don't know where. The difficult thing is deciding what to do next.'

But at that moment the telephone rang.

The voice at the other end was youthful. 'Can I speak to Damian, please? This is Jason.'

Emma clapped her hand over the mouthpiece. 'It's your pal – Jason!' she hissed.

'Gimme that!' said Damian inelegantly, grabbing it from her. 'Sorry—!' he added belatedly.

But Emma wasn't worried about manners. She was hopping up and down, urging him to take the call.

After a short time during which Damian irritatingly kept saying, 'Yes, yes . . .' and 'No, I don't think so . . .' he handed her the phone.

'Jason says his father would like to speak to you if he may.'

Emma took the receiver nervously. 'Hullo? Emma Durrant here.'

'Andrew Carter,' said an authoritative male voice. 'I understand from my son that you've had some dealings with Edward Lampeter.'

'Yes, but it could be a different man of the same name, not the one you know,' Emma said cautiously.

'I have reason to think it might be the same one. I wonder, Miss Durrant, if it's possible for you to come up to London, to my office? I hesitate to ask you to give up an entire day because I know you're a busy writer. But I think it might be very useful to meet.'

'Er, yes!' Emma thought quickly. 'I can get the train from Honiton. I can come tomorrow!' Eagerness touched her voice.

'Very well. If you could call at my office around twelve? We could talk and then perhaps you'll allow me to buy you lunch.'

219

'Thank you, I'll be there. Oh—' The inevitable corollary to any invitation to eat. 'I'm a vegetarian.'

'Indeed?' Carter sounded pleasantly surprised. 'So am I!'

'That's the one, then!' said Emma a little later, after consulting the train timetable. 'It's a three-hour journey by rail, however I do it, from Honiton or Axminster. I'll phone tonight to arrange for a taxi to collect me at the crack of dawn tomorrow and take me to Honiton in time for the breakfast-time train. It'll get me to Waterloo shortly before twelve. That leaves you on your own all day, Damian.'

'No problem!' said Damian cheerfully. 'I'll go up to the farm.'

'Hm, I wonder if Mrs Collins would let you sleep over there tomorrow night? I should get back, but if for any reason I were held up and had to stay the night in London, I'd be happier knowing you were at the farm.'

'I know!' She held up a hand to forestall the outraged protest on Damian's face. 'I know you can manage fine by yourself here. But in the circumstances, I'd prefer it, okay? You can take a sleeping bag so that Mrs Collins hasn't to make up a bed specially.'

Mrs Collins, when phoned, pronounced herself delighted to give Damian a bed for the night in question. Damian, torn between desire to sleep at the farm and a wish to make it clear he wasn't a helpless child, agreed with quite good grace.

'That's that, then!' said Emma. 'Just think, Damian, by this time tomorrow, we might have all the answers to our mystery!'

During the long rail journey up to London, Emma turned over every fact she knew. When she reached Waterloo, she rushed to grab a taxi and made it to Andrew Carter's office shortly after twelve.

Jason's father was a tall, spare, fair-haired man with sharp grey eyes and an affable manner. Emma liked him on sight.

'I do appreciate that you've taken so much trouble to come!' he said as he shook her hand in greeting. 'I hope it's going to prove worth your while!'

Emma, puce with excitement and the dash across London, nodded vigorously. 'I'm sure it will! Believe me, I really want to know about Edward!'

He smiled at her but his grey eyes were serious. 'Ah yes. Actually, there is someone who can tell you a lot more than I can! He'll be here shortly.' Andrew glanced at his watch. 'How about a cup of coffee to restore you after your journey? I've booked a table for half past one for lunch. A little late, perhaps, but we ought to talk first here, I think. It's rather more private than in a restaurant.'

There was a buzz from his desk. 'Yes? Good. Send him in, would you?' Andrew straightened up. 'Excuse me one moment, Emma.'

He went to the door as it began to open to greet the new arrival. Then he turned back to Emma. 'This is Superintendent Page of the Metropolitan drugs squad.'

'How do you do!' gasped Emma, startled.

Superintendent Page bore a remarkable resemblance to a bulldog, having broad shoulders, a round face with squashed features, and sandy hair. He grasped her hand in a massive paw.

'Hullo there, Miss Durrant! I'm a great admirer of your books! Of course, they're not—'

'I know!' said Emma resignedly. 'They're not like real life. They're not meant to be. They're fiction!'

'That's why I read 'em!' said Superintendent Page cheerfully. 'I get enough real-life crime, thanks! What I like about your books, is that the hero always nails the villain at the end. Wish I did!'

Andrew's secretary arrived bearing the coffee. When she'd departed again, Andrew said, 'Which brings us nicely to Edward Lampeter, I think!'

Superintendent Page's battered features creased up in a grin. 'You start, Miss Durrant! Let's hear your tale! Begin at the beginning, if you don't mind. You'd be amazed how many people don't. They start halfway through and keep going back and forth. But you're a professional writer, you won't do that.'

'The beginning?' said Emma thoughtfully. 'Well, the start of it all was when I went to meet my nephew . . .'

They listened to her in silence. When she'd finished, the superintendent stirred on his chair and reached across to put his empty coffee cup on the desk.

'Right! Well, Miss Durrant, I think the time has come to take you into our confidence.'

'That'll be a change!' muttered Emma, with thoughts of Matt King.

She hadn't really intended Page to hear her, but he had and grinned broadly again. 'Now, don't go blaming Inspector King! He couldn't confide in you. He hadn't been given the required authority to do so! Besides, your dealings with Matt King took place before your meeting with Lampeter. That did change things.

'Let me tell you about Edward. We have reason to believe that money from the supply of certain illegal substances is being "laundered", in the popular phrase, through the books of quite bona fide companies of which Edward is a director. To cut a long story short, we raided Edward's offices but failed to lay our hands on any evidence of the dealings in question. The records we found dealt only with legitimate business. We know there is a second set of records, probably on disk, but we can't lay our hands on it.

'This brings us to Mrs Felicity Pugh!' Page sighed. 'You know, we all underestimated that lady! Fatally so, I'm afraid. A couple of years ago, in a quite separate business deal, Edward invested some money belonging to his mother's cousin in one of his enterprises. It failed and Mrs Pugh lost her money. She was furious. There was a family row and she vowed never to speak to her cousin Rose Lampeter or Edward again. She also complained to the police, but although the fraud office investigated, it couldn't find any evidence of crime. So that seemed to be that.

'However, when we failed to find what we sought in our raid on Edward's offices, we were, quite frankly, left with egg on our faces. We had to go back to square one, start again. We studied Edward's file and we came across Mrs Pugh and her two-year-old complaint against him. Someone was sent to talk to her again. She told us something which really interested us. Her cousin Rose Lampeter had been in touch. Rose wanted to patch up the quarrel and had invited Felicity to stay with her in Sidmouth.

'Felicity no longer felt angry towards Rose, although she still hadn't forgiven Edward! She had decided to accept the invitation. She was asked by us if she would just keep her eyes and ears open whilst staying with her cousin. We didn't ask her to do any sleuthing!' Page's voice became insistent. 'We just asked her to be observant and tell us if she heard or noticed anything unusual which Rose said or did with regard to Edward. Edward, we knew, had visited his mother several times of late. Rather more frequently than he had been in the habit of doing. We wondered if he was just a very dutiful son, or if he had some ulterior motive in going down to the coast so often.'

'Mrs Pugh was observant, all right!' said Emma. 'And telling her not to sleuth was like telling a bloodhound not to follow a trail! She liked to ask questions, too. Asked them all the time. Sorry, didn't mean to interrupt.'

Page pulled a wry expression. 'But you're quite right! As we now know. That's why I said we all underestimated Mrs Pugh. Not only her curiosity and persistence, but also her intelligence. I don't mean she was a particularly clever woman. If she had been, she'd have been more discreet. But she was sharp enough in lots of ways. She'd realised the sort of thing we were looking for. That's clear from the questions she asked your nephew about computer disks. Now, what we don't know is whether she found any such things, or learned where they were kept. From the suspicious manner of her death, it looks as though she did.

'We want you to be very careful from now on, Miss Durrant. Don't avoid the Lampeters, but do remember what happened to Mrs Pugh. If you meet them again, report every word either of them says to Inspector King. He knows, by the way, that you're meeting with me here today.'

'Oh,' said Emma glumly. 'Does he?'

Emma parted from Andrew Carter, after a very pleasant lunch, in mid-afternoon. She didn't really want to stay overnight in

London. She had loaned her flat and word processor to an impecunious writer friend who was intent on the 'great novel'. If she turned up there, she would probably disturb the creative flow. Damian, of course, would be staying at the farm tonight. But she would go back to Devon anyway. She needed the time alone to think.

It was evening before she reached the cottage and it looked very isolated indeed as she got out of the taxi and put her key in the lock. The silence all around was oppressive. Every little creak of the woodwork made her jump out of her skin. She wished Damian were there, but she didn't want to go up to the farm and bring him back after the arrangement they'd made. She put on the kettle, drew the curtains and switched on the convector heater.

The ring of the telephone split the silence like an air-raid siren.

For some reason, Emma was convinced the caller would prove to be Edward Lampeter. Perhaps he knew she'd gone to London? She picked up the receiver and babbled, 'Yes? Who is it?'

'Matt King. Emma? Are you okay?' He sounded anxious.

'Oh yes! Oh Matt, I'm glad it's you!' she burst out. 'I'm fine. I just got back from London. Matt, I'm sorry I was so cross . . .'

'Stay put!' he ordered 'I'm coming over there.'

He arrived twenty minutes later, by which time Emma had pulled herself together, and also changed her dress and brushed her hair.

It was dark outside when she looked out at the sound of Matt's car. She opened the door to him and they smiled awkwardly at one another.

'Come in!' she invited him after what seemed undue delay.

'Not disturbing you?'

'No, not at all. Damian's sleeping over at the farm.'

'I was wondering how you'd got on in London. How did you find Page?'

'Rather sweet. Oh, Matt!' Emma spread out her hands in apology. 'I'm sorry I didn't come and tell you I'd met Edward. I did think about it, and then decided against it.'

Matt took one of her outstretched hands. 'My fault. I was tactless the last time we met, to put it mildly! I could have tried to explain my situation. Friends?'

'Friends!' she said firmly.

Matt seemed to realise he was holding her hand and dropped it abruptly. 'Look here, Emma. I don't like you being here all on your own tonight. Can't you go up to the farm as well?'

'I'm all right. I can't bother Mrs Collins for a second bed.'

'Well, how about taking a room in a bed and breakfast overnight? There are plenty of local places.'

'Honestly, Matt, I'll be fine!'

Actually, she wasn't at all sure she'd be so confident once he'd left.

'I'm responsible for you!' he said. 'You're an important witness. As the officer in charge of the case down here, I'm recommending you move yourself to other accommodation tonight!'

That did it. The pompousness with which this instruction was delivered destroyed Emma's new feeling of goodwill towards him. It wasn't as if he'd said he was worried on his own account about her . . . Not that she expected him to say that, of course! All the same . . .

'I shall stay here at the cottage!' she said aloofly. 'I shall be quite all right, thank you, Inspector King!'

They locked eye contact and he saw that she meant what she said.

'All right, Emma!' He sighed and glanced round. 'Then I'll stay too and—'

'You'll what?' squeaked Emma, outraged.

'And sleep in the armchair, all right? I can't organise any other protection for you at this late hour. Otherwise I'd get a woman officer up here. It's either that or you go to a bed and breakfast!'

'I see!' snapped Emma. 'You mean to manoeuvre me into going into a rented room for the night! Well, I won't. Sleep in the chair if you want to! You'll get a crick in your back!'

'Nonsense!' he said aggravatingly. 'It looks perfectly comfortable!'

As she fetched him a pillow and a blanket, Emma did relent so far as to say, 'There is Damian's room.'

'Thank you! I shall be fine here!' He was being obstinate too. They were two of a kind.

It would have been considerate of Emma to have expended more sympathy on her guest's discomfort, but as soon as her own head hit the pillow she was fast asleep. The long day and the journey to and from London had taken its toll.

She was awoken by a tap on her bedroom door and a male voice calling, 'I've brought you a cup of tea!'

Emma opened her eyes. The sun was streaming through the window. She sat up. 'Thank you!'

'I've put it on the floor outside your door. Don't knock it over!'

He would have to add that bit of needless instruction, wouldn't he!

Emma swung her legs out of bed, pulled on her dressing gown and went to fetch the mug of tea. She sat on the low windowsill gazing out at the lane, sipping the hot brew and planning breakfast.

But only a minute or two later, the cottage door slammed and Matt appeared on the path below. He glanced up at the window, saw her, waved a hand in laconic farewell, got into his car and drove off.

Emma glanced at her alarm clock. It was a quarter past eight. He had, of course, to be at work on time. The vision of the cosy little breakfast party broke into fragments.

'Oh, Matt King!' Emma said crossly aloud. 'Just when things start to go right, why do you always spoil them?'

Emma breakfasted in solitary splendour. She supposed Damian was being fed a gigantic farm breakfast by Mrs Collins so she wasn't surprised that he hadn't come home early. However, she confidently expected him by lunchtime.

But lunchtime came without any sign of Damian. He must have got involved at the farm and was enjoying himself. Still, he ought to have picked up the phone and told her.

Emma's morning hadn't been a success. She'd tried to write, but it had been hopeless. She'd spent the entire time puzzling about Mrs Pugh when she wasn't, for some inexplicable reason, thinking about Inspector King.

Two o'clock came and she decided what she needed was fresh air. She'd walk up to the farm and see what Damian was about. Emma pulled on gumboots as a precaution and set off up the lane.

The tyre tracks of Matt's car were visible outside the gate in the dust. There was also another set of tracks. Emma frowned. Around eleven, when she'd been drinking her coffee, it had seemed to her she'd heard a car. But it hadn't stopped outside so she'd not bothered to look out. Occasionally summer visitors took a wrong turning and drove up the lane thinking it soon joined a proper road. Instead they found themselves driving over a pot-holed single-track surface into the blue beyond and turned back.

It was a lovely morning. Birds rustled in the hedgerow and the sheep baa-ed sociably at her as she passed. Mrs Collins was taking down her dry morning washing from the line.

'Good afternoon!' called Emma. 'Thanks for putting up Damian last night!'

Mrs Collins removed a wooden peg from her mouth. 'Pleasure, m'dear! How did you get on in London, then?'

'Fine. Er, where is Damian?'

Mrs Collins stared at her blankly. 'I don't know, m'dear. He went off home this morning, around eleven it was. He gave me a hand collecting the free-range eggs, and then he said you'd be expecting to see him, so off he went.' Mrs Collins started forward in dismay. 'Why, Emma! Whatever is wrong? You've turned as white as a sheet!'

'You – you are sure he isn't with Mr Collins somewhere on the farm?' Emma whispered.

'No, dear. My husband's gone into Sidmouth.'

Emma turned and raced back down the lane. Indoors, she grabbed the phone and, with a trembling finger, punched out the number Matt had left for her.

229

As soon as she heard him speak, she burst out, 'Matt! You've got to come quickly! It's Damian!'

'Take it easy, Emma!' came his voice, calming her considerably by its unflappable competence. 'What's Damian done?'

'Nothing! I don't know! He's gone! He didn't come back from the farm this morning. I've just gone up there to look for him and Mrs Collins said he left at eleven to walk down to the cottage. Something's happened to him, I know it! He's a very reliable boy. He wouldn't just go off and not leave a message. I'm responsible for him! Bridget trusts me! I should have checked earlier and not left it until this afternoon. It's all my fault! I heard a car around eleven but I didn't think anything of it – oh, Matt, he's been kidnapped, I'm sure of it!'

Part Five

'I agree it's a possibility. But before we leap to the conclusion that Damian's been kidnapped,' Matt King said reasonably, 'let's remember we're talking about an adventurous thirteen-year-old boy—'

'Let's remember,' Emma interrupted heatedly, 'that we're really talking about Edward Lampeter! Can't you see what's happened? Edward wants to know exactly what Mrs Pugh said to Damian on that coach journey! He quizzed me and found I couldn't tell him. So he's grabbed Damian and is interrogating him! Damian must be terrified! We've got to find and rescue him! Do something, Matt! You're a police inspector!'

They stood facing one another in the middle of the cottage's tiny living room, to which Matt had been summoned by Emma's incoherent phone call. His promptitude in arriving within fifteen minutes was commendable. But now he was here, he wasn't responding in the way Emma had expected. He stood there, his head perilously brushing the exposed blackened oak beams of the ceiling, with that truculent look on his face which she'd come to recognise as meaning he thought she was letting her imagination run riot.

'Even you,' she said crossly, 'can't say I'm getting carried away over this! This hasn't happened in a book, mine or anyone else's, it's happened for real, to us! Me and Damian!'

Meeting her glare, Matt pointed out, 'If Edward wants to talk to Damian, why doesn't he just get his mother, Rose, to invite the pair of you to tea again? Then he could chat away to Damian about anything, including Mrs Pugh. Emma, I realise that Damian's normally reliable. But no one's perfect, and certainly no thirteen-year-old boy is! He could turn up around teatime, full of apologies, having become so engrossed in something he just forgot the time!'

He could hardly have expected this piece of logic to be well received.

Emma hissed, 'Rubbish! He doesn't do that sort of thing! He's got a wristwatch and knows, in the present circumstances, I'd be going scatty!'

'It would help if you calmed down!' Matt moved back prudently as the light of battle glowed in his companion's eyes. 'All right, have you checked whether he's got his bike with him?'

'He hasn't! And how far could he get on foot?' yelled Emma, furious and despairing.

'I'd say, quite a long way. When I was his age—'

'We're not talking about you! We're talking about my nephew!'

Emma's rage suddenly turned to utter dejection. She collapsed into the nearest armchair – which happened to be the one in which Matt had spent the previous night.

'You just don't understand!' Resting her elbows on her knees, she buried her face in her hands and her long hair fell forward veiling her upper body. 'My sister trusted me to look after him! I've let her and her husband down, quite apart from failing poor Damian! I got him into all this, me and my wanting to be a detective! Now I feel absolutely useless! I can't help Damian, I can't do anything! All I can do is scribble my books, and even those, according to you, are hopelessly inaccurate!'

Matt sighed and crossed the room. He balanced on his heels in front of her, brushed back the tangled hair and gently pulled her hands from her face.

'Emma, listen to me! Don't crack up now. It won't help and it's not like you at all! Where's that fighting spirit? I know about your sister and her medical work overseas. She's a fine woman. But we're not all of us cut out to be heroes! You do what you do best and very well, too! I find it hard to write a coherent police report and couldn't start to write book! Damian obviously thinks you're the bees' knees and I know that youngsters that age are very critical of adults and don't bestow their approval lightly!'

'So if you're right, why's he gone off without telling me?' mumbled Emma.

'And I also think you're rather special!' said Matt unexpectedly, ignoring the interruption.

That jolted Emma out of her fog of despair. 'Matt?' She stared at him.

He flushed brick red, stood up and went on hurriedly, 'Okay, I'll set a search in motion. You stay here in case he comes home or contacts you. If he does, let me know at once!'

With that, he fairly bolted out of the cottage. Emma went to the bathroom to wash her face. She peered into the mirror. A wild countenance, with blotched complexion, swollen eyes and a frame of dishevelled locks, stared back at her. Matt was right. It didn't help anyone, neither Damian nor herself – and certainly not the police – to lose all power of rational thought. And what on earth did she look like?

'Now then, Emma!' she told the reflection firmly. 'This is no time for a fit of the vapours! Pull yourself together!'

Either this admonition or Matt's lecture worked. She went to the kitchen and made a mug of coffee. As she sipped it, she set herself to think.

No matter how cautiously Matt King might express himself, she was sure he believed, as she did, that there was a strong possibility Edward Lampeter had abducted Damian. He might have waited by the farm entrance for the boy to leave that morning and offered him a lift down the lane. Damian wouldn't have trusted Edward, but he might have thought it was an opportunity to play detective and, on impulse, decided to take the risk. This was the most likely scenario.

So, what would she do were she in Edward's shoes? She'd hide her prisoner somewhere. But not at his mother's house. That would be far too obvious. Either the police or Emma could turn up at any time. Somewhere else.

The discordant peal of the telephone broke into her thoughts and sent her scurrying to the receiver. 'Damian?'

'Hullo, m'dear!' Mr Collins's familiar voice boomed down the line. He had little faith in the ability of wires to carry sound and believed in helping things along by shouting.

'Oh,' said Emma. 'I thought it might be Damian.'

'I'm ringing about the boy!' bawled Mr Collins. 'I just come from town! Phone was going and I picked 'un up. Boy says, he tried to give you a call but your telephone is out of order. Couldn't get through, he reckons. Anyhow, he wants you to meet him, urgent. Over on the cliffs at the top of the old Smugglers' Stair. Made me promise to tell you straight off. Says, don't hang about and get over there sharpish!'

234

'Is he all right? How did he sound?' Emma asked anxiously.

'I don't like these gadgets!' thundered Mr Collins. 'Never pick 'em up if my wife's around. Voices all sound the same to me over the phone, miles away and squeaky.'

Emma put down the phone, torn between relief and an upsurge of anger. What on earth was Damian playing at? If he'd meant to go to the clifftop, why hadn't he told her first?

Well, she'd find all that out in due course. Damian's message had asked her to hurry. She ran out of the cottage, mounted her bicycle and set out, head down and feet going like pistons, for the headland.

It wasn't until she was nearly there that she remembered Matt had asked her to tell him the moment Damian got in touch, and that she'd forgotten to do so.

The clifftop appeared completely deserted when Emma finally arrived, breathless and hot. She almost fell off the bicycle, propped it under the hedge and peered anxiously down the path in both directions.

Not a soul. 'Damian!' The wind caught her voice and tossed it away, out to sea, to be lost amongst the shrill cries of the seabirds.

'Damian, it's Emma! Where are you?' She moved cautiously to the edge and looked over. The beach below was deserted, white breakers rolling over the shingle.

There was a rustle in the hedge. Emma whirled around. 'Damian—?' She broke off in horror. 'You!'

'Good afternoon, Emma!' said Edward Lampeter politely. 'Such a lovely day, don't you think? I appreciate your having come so quickly.'

'How – where's Damian?' She started forward but was stopped by his expression. 'How did you force him to make that telephone call?'

'I didn't, my dear. I managed to persuade my mother to make it. Her voice, over the line, sounds not unlike a boy's. It wouldn't have fooled you, of course. I had her telephone the farm. They don't know the boy's voice so well and anyway, they'd only be concerned to pass on the message. They obviously did so.'

In the ensuing silence, Emma's heart seemed to thump so loudly, she fancied she could hear it and that Edward could also. He was smiling at her, still quite at ease but with eyes as hard as the pebbles on the beach below.

'You killed Mrs Pugh!' she said bleakly.

Edward looked surprised. 'Certainly not! That was an accident.'

He saw the disbelief on her face. 'Yes, really! Felicity was a most irritating woman and always keen to poke her nose into other people's business. In this case, into mine! She came across some – some property of mine which I'd left at my mother's house for safekeeping. During a walk with my mother along the clifftop here, she was so imprudent as to let my mother know she'd found – it.'

'You mean the disks,' Emma shouted into the wind. If she could keep him talking, all time was precious. Someone, anyone, might come along the cliff path from the town. 'The disks with the financial record of your criminal dealings!'

'You *are* well informed!' Edward said coldly and Emma realised that in her rashness, she had made matters far worse for herself. There was no way now he would let her walk away from this clifftop. But for the moment, he was still talking.

'My mother and Felicity quarrelled about it, just about here . . .'

Edward indicated the top of the Smugglers' Stair. The police notice had gone. Probably someone had thrown it over the hedge.

'In the course of it, Mother gave Felicity a push – in anger, without the intention of doing real harm. But Felicity fell. The handrail was loose and she was unable to save herself.'

'The shoes?' Emma asked tightly.

'Oh yes. Mother was afraid of the police asking questions. Felicity, who never dressed sensibly for any occasion to my knowledge, had walked out from town as far as the path in her sandals, carrying flat shoes with her. She'd changed into those for the walk along the path. Mother simply changed the shoes back for sandals, hoping people would think Felicity's high heels, together with the rail, which Mother loosened even more for added effect, had caused the accident. And so everyone would have thought, my dear, if it hadn't been for you.' Edward's eyes rested on Emma's face and his voice grew spiteful.

'Only me? What about Luke Pardoe?' Emma managed to ask, though her throat was suddenly very dry.

'The wretched Pardoe? A worthless type and remarkably stupid. He was fishing out there that day.' Edward gestured towards the sea. 'He saw Mother push Felicity and he also saw her wrench at the handrail. He tried to blackmail her, at which point she panicked and called me to come down and sort things out.'

'And you persuaded Luke Pardoe to meet you on the beach down there, just as you tricked me into coming here,' Emma said dully. 'I should have thought about that.'

'Yes,' Edward agreed. 'I had thought Pardoe might be bought

off but I decided, after talking with him, that it was too risky. He was not, you see, reliable and it's never a good idea to put oneself in the power of a blackmailer. But even then, Miss Durrant, you caused me a problem. I had intended to take the body out to sea and push it over the side, to make it look as if Pardoe had fallen from his boat and drowned. But before I could do so, you and the boy arrived on the clifftop and began to clamber down the steps. I just had time to drag Pardoe's body into the cave, hoping that you wouldn't spot it.'

Edward sounded quite exasperated as he added, 'But you did! Really, Miss Durrant, you have caused me endless difficulties!'

'Then you were watching us,' Emma muttered. 'I felt as though eyes were on us. Where were you?'

Edward smiled slightly and indicated the headland jutting out beyond the cave below. 'Only a few yards away, just around the corner. You might easily have come across me if you hadn't been diverted into the cave. While you went to summon the police, I was able to make my escape.'

Emma raised her head and whispered, 'And Damian? Where is he? Have you hurt him?' So anxious was she that she forgot her fear and started towards Lampeter.

He too was moving, towards her. 'I really am very sorry, Emma. But I'm afraid there has to be another accident . . . They really should have sealed off these steps properly.'

He reached out towards her. Emma gave a cry and stepped back, then turned and tried to run. But her foot slipped and she fell full length. Edward stooped over her. She tried to roll aside, forgetting how close they both were to the edge.

Suddenly, beneath her there was nothing. Emma's hands

grasped at air as she slithered over the edge of the cliff and began to slide helplessly down it towards the stony beach, far, far below.

She scrabbled desperately with both hands at the cliff face, seeking anything which would arrest her fall. Miraculously, her fingers encountered a tiny sapling which had sprung, in defiance of gravity or lack of soil, out of a fissure in the rock. At the same time, her toes caught in a wide crack forming a tiny ledge. Her descent was halted.

But her situation was little better. The sapling bowed beneath her weight and the crack in which her toes had gained purchase was too shallow to support her heels as well. Unable to relax, her legs began to ache with the strain, while her arms felt as if they were being pulled out of their sockets. Emma pressed herself against the cliff, feeling the stiff breeze chill the sweat which drenched her body.

Twisting her neck, she looked up to see how far she was from the top. Not so very far but too far to reach without help. To her dismay, she saw Edward Lampeter's face peering down at her over the edge, a look of savage determination in his eyes. He, alas, seemed all too near for comfort. She felt utterly at his mercy. Had she been able to climb up, he would be awaiting her. Had she been capable of finding her way safely down, Edward would have reached the beach before her by way of the Smugglers' Stair and would be waiting for her there.

But she was capable of neither and, with indescribable dread, saw Edward reach down towards the sapling with the obvious intent of shaking it to loosen her grip.

Then, without warning, his face vanished. At the same time

Emma became aware of shouting voices and the thud of feet running along the cliff path above.

'Emma!' yelled a hoarse, worried voice above her head.

She looked up again and saw that, incredibly, Matt's face had replaced Edward's. Emma's heart soared. Thank God! Although she was still marooned in her fragile situation against the cliff, help was at hand.

But had it come in time? Emma's aching limbs couldn't hold out much longer. Blood pounded in her ears. Beneath her was that terrifying and potentially fatal drop to the rocks below. She knew she mustn't look down, yet felt an almost irresistible urge to do so.

Matt was stretching down his arm. 'Emma, can you reach up one hand and grasp mine?'

To take one hand from the sapling, when her feet rested on such a precarious support, took a great deal of courage. Emma managed it somehow, she was never sure afterwards how. Her sweating palm was caught fast in Matt's sure grip.

'Okay, take it easy. Just do exactly as I say. To your left there's a ledge, a little higher than your feet are at present. Don't look down! Just take my word for it. Can you feel for it with your left foot?'

She obeyed and found the ledge. Gripping his hand, Emma managed to move up to this higher position.

'Well done! Now, the same thing, but to your right . . .'

In this way, following his instructions and clinging to his hand, Emma slowly crawled up the cliff face and was hauled, panting, over the grassy edge and onto the path.

At first she clung to Matt, the world swirling disconcertingly around her. She felt quite sick. Then her stomach settled and her vision steadied. She looked up and saw his face looking anxiously down at her.

'I'm – all right . . .' she managed to whisper. 'Oh, Matt, I was never so pleased to see anyone in my life! He was going to make sure I fell! Where – where is he?' Even now she was safe, she couldn't keep the fear from her voice at the mention of Lampeter.

'It's okay,' Matt said soothingly, hugging her shoulders. 'He can't hurt you. He's over there!' He jerked his head towards the cliff path behind him.

She looked past him. Edward Lampeter, sullen but helpless, was being frog-marched along the path, held securely between two police officers. As if he sensed Emma's eyes on him, he turned his head and looked back and for a moment their eyes met. Then Edward turned his head away. Emma shivered and gripped Matt's hand for reassurance.

But then she saw, in the distance, another figure, that of a woman, hurrying along the path towards them from the direction of the town. She looked familiar.

'Matt . . .' Emma gasped. 'Rose Lampeter . . .' She raised a trembling hand to point.

'She's the reason we're here!' Matt said. 'Her son persuaded her to make the phone call to the farm, but afterwards, when he'd left the house, she called us. She realised it had all gone too far and, devoted to Edward though she is, she knew he had to be stopped.'

Emma clutched at the inspector's sleeve. 'Matt! Where's Damian? We've got to find him! Ask Lampeter where he is!'

Before he could answer, Emma had scrambled to her feet and

run after the police officers and their prisoner, reaching them just as Rose Lampeter came stumbling up.

'Oh, Miss Durrant, are you all right? I was so afraid I'd be too late!' she panted.

She turned to Matt, who had followed Emma, and held out her hands imploringly. 'Inspector King, you must understand! Edward was trying to protect me! Everything he did was done for that reason! If only I'd come to you at the beginning, when I pushed poor Felicity down the steps! I didn't mean it, of course – she just made me so angry! Snooping about my house like that, the very first evening of her visit! And finding Edward's things and searching through them! It – it was so disloyal of her! I know she was angry with poor Edward because of that money she lost. But that wasn't his fault!'

Lampeter had been listening to his mother's speech impassively.

'Where's Damian?' Emma shouted, turning on him, her voice cracking.

Rose stared at her, then at her son. 'Edward? The boy? Where's the boy?'

'He's all right!' Lampeter said sourly. 'He's down there . . .' He nodded towards the beach below. 'In the cave.'

'Emma!' Matt called sharply. 'Mind out!'

But Emma had raced to the Smuggler's Stair and was plunging recklessly down the narrow steps. She reached the beach, stumbled across the shingle and through the dark open mouth of the cave.

Damian was lying on the sandy floor at the back of the cave, his ankles and wrists tied and a handkerchief bound over his mouth.

Emma's fingers wrestled with the knots, as protesting and inarticulate noises came from the prisoner.

'Here, let me!' Matt exclaimed, arriving in the cave and dropping to his knees beside her.

No doubt he'd had a fright, but when Matt had untied his limbs and removed the gag from his mouth, Damian seemed more embarrassed than anything else.

He sat on the floor, his scarlet face a study in frustration and rage, rubbing his wrists and looking from one to the other of them. 'Hullo, Em . . . Inspector!' he said awkwardly.

'Are you all right?' Emma demanded, grasping his arms.

'Yes, let go, Em! Honestly, I feel such a fool! I just let him kidnap me! Did everything he suggested and wham! Here I was, trussed up like a blooming chicken!'

'It doesn't matter, you're safe!' Emma gave him a hug.

'Have you got Lampeter?' he asked anxiously, disengaging himself politely but firmly from her embrace.

'Yes, yes. The police have taken him away!'

'Just wish I'd seen that!' muttered Damian vengefully. 'Still, I'm glad you're okay, Em. I was worried about you after he left me here. How did you find me?'

'Er – I'll tell you the details later,' Emma prevaricated. 'But Mrs Lampeter went to the police, which is why they turned up here – fortunately!' she added.

She and Damian both looked up towards Matt King who sat on a nearby boulder, his forearms resting on his knees, watching them.

'Still want to be a policeman, Damian?' Matt asked.

'Not sure,' said Damian. 'Oh, not because of the danger!' His voice rose indignantly, lest any thought of faint-heartedness be presumed to be behind his doubt. 'But because I've been thinking about farming as a career. But on the other hand,' his voice grew meditative, 'I bet you don't get nearly as much excitement farming.'

The inspector gave a snort. 'Thought you'd have had enough excitement to last you the rest of your life!'

'Can you walk?' Emma asked Damian.

He struggled to his feet and shook off her supporting arm. 'Of course I can!'

'Let him go!' advised Matt, as Damian made his way, a little unsteadily, out of the cave. 'He's shaken up but he isn't hurt – except in his self-regard. When you're thirteen, dignity is all important.'

'I know. He doesn't want a mere woman fussing over him!' Emma pulled a wry face.

'You're not a mere woman!' Inspector King said.

Emma looked up at him. They were alone together now in the Smugglers' Cave. It seemed very quiet, the only noise the muffled sound of the breakers beyond the cave entrance.

'I haven't thanked you,' she said. 'For getting me off the cliff. And I'm sorry I forgot to phone you, after Mr Collins rang.'

'All's well that end's well.' Matt paused. 'That is to say, there is just one thing – just to make it all end as I think it should.'

'What's that?' Emma frowned and pushed back her hair.

'Why, this of course.' He stooped and kissed her.

'Oh,' said Emma, when she was able. 'Yes, of course . . .'

The summer holiday came to an end. The new book had actually been completed, too. The draft lay in manuscript on the desk, a satisfactorily thick pile of papers.

'And even if I do say so myself,' said its author modestly, 'I'm quite pleased with it! Although, one oughtn't ever to say that, Damian. It probably means my editor will hate it.'

'It read all right to me,' said Damian loyally.

The time had come for him to return to school. His bag was packed and he'd been crammed reluctantly back into his flannels and tweed jacket.

Apart from that, he looked a completely different boy to the one who had got off the coach, with Mrs Pugh close behind him, some six weeks before. His face and hands were tanned brown and his hair bleached by the sun. He seemed to have grown at least another inch and put on weight. The tweed jacket would urgently have to be replaced.

'I'll get on to the school outfitters!' said his aunt, tugging the lapels together across his chest. 'This one won't last out another term! Not at the rate you're growing!'

'I had a letter from Mum this morning,' Damian told her.

'I saw the stamp. Everything all right?'

'Yes. We'll see them soon. They're coming home soon for some leave. In about three weeks' time.'

'That is good news! But in that case, we'll definitely have to get you a new jacket before Bridget arrives. She can't see you in that one!'

Damian sat on the window-seat and turned his head to look out at the lane. The roses were over in the flower bed by the front door and had dropped red and white petals like confetti on the path.

'You remember what we talked about, Em? You know, when I said I felt a bit left out of things with regard to Mum and Dad?'

He turned his head back and met her eyes. 'I feel better about it all now.'

'Good,' said Emma, not sure what to say. 'I am glad, Damian.'

'I've sort of got things sorted out in my mind.'

'You're growing up,' she said. 'It's always a difficult time. I remember!' She paused. 'I've got things sorted out in my mind, too, things which worried me.'

'You helped me sort them out, Em. Thanks for listening and saying all the right things.'

'Not at all. Always happy to lend an ear!' Emma thought about it. 'Matt helped me with my problem.'

'Oh, yes?' Damian grinned.

Fortunately, Matt's car drew up outside at that moment. Emma opened the door as he came striding up the path. He smiled broadly when he saw her and as he bent his head to come through the door, she put her arms round his neck to give him a welcoming embrace. Damian watched them with interest.

Matt saw him and raised his head. 'Oy, you ready? We've got plenty of time but I suppose we ought to get down to the bus station!'

'I'm ready,' said Damian, adding wistfully, 'wish the holidays weren't over!'

'Till next year, eh?' Matt ruffled the boy's hair.

'You are going to take the cottage again, aren't you, Em?' Damian demanded.

Matt met her gaze. 'Are you, Emma?' he asked quietly.

'Yes, of course! I mean, I might stay on anyway . . .'

'I was hoping that,' he said.

Damian sighed at the sight of his aunt and the inspector gazing at one another in what he obviously thought an undignified manner. His own mind, however, was still running on the previous few weeks.

'It was a really great holiday!' he said enthusiastically. 'Catching crooks and everything!'

'I don't know that we can promise that next year! I rather hope not!' Matt teased him.

'I don't know . . .' said Emma dreamily. 'It was exciting . . .'

'Emma?' exclaimed Inspector King, startled, a look of horror crossing his face. 'No, please! Not again! Just keep it for the books in future!'

The Watcher

I had been awoken by the dull boom of the foghorn and scrambled from my bunk to the porthole. It showed me nothing but a curtain of pale grey mist. I was aware the ship had stopped. There was movement as she rose and fell on the swell of the waves but the throb of the engines beneath my feet had ceased. I snatched up my wristwatch from the bedside cabinet and dressed hurriedly, pulling on a thick sweater.

The young stewardess was outside the cabin door. The horn sounded again, drowning our exchange of morning greetings. As its echo died away, she said, 'We've stopped because of fishing boats out there. We'll be a little late docking at Lisbon.'

The news didn't bother me. If there is one thing I have, it is time. On my way to the dining room for breakfast I encountered one of the ship's officers and asked where, exactly, we were located. He replied that we were off Cabo da Roca, that rocky outcrop on the Portuguese coast where Europe first puts a toe into the Atlantic.

I know this stretch of coastline well. Its sudden fogs are notorious. The sea here is treacherous. It dashes itself on the rocks and sandy beaches, its seething challenge taken up by daredevil young surfers.

I have been involved with the sea all my life. My name is van

Leeuwen. Sometimes I say jokingly that I am a Dutchman, but in reality I am an Englishman, born and bred. My ancestor, Cornelius van Leeuwen, came from Holland to England in 1688 in the entourage of William of Orange.

William landed with an army in the name of the Protestant cause and of his wife, Mary, to seize the throne of his Catholic father-in-law, James II. The English disliked James and welcomed William for the sake of his wife. They had badly underestimated the man. In taking the English crown for Mary, William also took it for himself, and the pair reigned jointly. After Mary's death, William continued to reign alone.

By now the English disliked him as much as they'd disliked James: but William was more difficult to dislodge and he wasn't a man who forgave his enemies.

One concession had been wrung from him. His Dutch soldiers had been sent home to the Netherlands. My ancestor, Cornelius, remained in London, however, because he had shrewdly married an Englishwoman, a plain lady with a decent fortune.

My family later became prosperous merchant shipowners. So, you see, although I have never been a sailor, the sea is, so to speak, in my blood. We made our money by it.

I had been retired from business for some years. My wife was dead. I had no family. I travelled a great deal, preferably on cruise ships. The ship on which I found myself on that particular trip was small as cruise ships go. She had just been completely refitted in a Scandinavian yard. The purpose of the refit was that she should take cruise passengers around the Mediterranean. But her first voyage in her new livery had, of course, to be from Scandinavia. This first sailing would terminate at Rome's seaport of Civitavecchia. The passengers she had taken aboard in the North would disembark and return home by air. New passengers would board her and she would take these on a leisurely cruise around the Mediterranean and up the Adriatic coast. I, having the time, had paid to participate in both cruises. Instead of disembarking at Civitavecchia I would stay aboard and greet a new set of sailing companions.

I eat little in the morning, two cups of good coffee, a bread roll and a little jam. Leaving the dining room, I felt in my pocket for my cigarettes. I am not a heavy smoker but I like a cigarette after a meal. Smoking anywhere inside the ship wasn't allowed. Modern sensibilities were against it. But old habits are hard to break. Despite the inclement weather, I was forced to quit the warmth of the reception area for the fog-shrouded deck.

To my right, I knew, there was a companionway up to an upper deck. To my left another led down to the deck below. I had no wish to fall down those steps and break my neck. It is easily done. I know that. The fog closed in on me, a silent world. The fine wet sea mist trailed icy fingers across my cheek and impudently fingered the back of my neck. I lit my cigarette and threw the spent match away from me to fly over the invisible rail into the sea. For safety's sake I remained by the door into the reception area.

That is when he spoke.

'Good morning, Mr van Leeuwen.'

The voice was low, male, and unfamiliar. It had no particular accent. The speaker might have been an Englishman or someone who spoke good English. I could make out nothing of him but he must be standing over there to my left at the head of the companionway down to the lower deck. Perhaps he was surer of himself than I was, or perhaps he did not have my experience of such things.

I replied civilly, 'Good morning.' I thought that probably, like me, he had been forced out here for a smoke. I tried to make out the red glow of a cigarette in the swirling fog but was unable to do so. I added, 'The sun will soon burn off this fog and we'll be underway again.'

'No doubt,' he said carelessly.

I had expected that he would identify himself. He must know I couldn't see him. He, of course, had seen me through the glass door as I'd crossed reception and stepped out on deck. I felt irritated and at a disadvantage.

It was as if he could read my mind. 'You are unable to identify me, Mr van Leeuwen.' The wretched fellow sounded amused.

'Certainly I don't recognise your voice!' I replied testily. I am too old for playing silly guessing games.

'Don't you?' he said. 'But we have sailed together before, Mr van Leeuwen. We are old shipmates, you might say.'

I rapidly reviewed the faces of my fellow passengers. None appeared familiar. A crew member? A waiter? A steward? Surely none of these would treat me with such off-hand familiarity?

'I've sailed on a good many ships in my time,' I said. 'On which ship were you a fellow passenger?'

'On this one.' He chuckled. 'But she was then named the *Berenice*. Don't you remember the *Berenice*?'

I felt an unpleasant tightening in my chest that had nothing to do with the cold. The *Berenice*. The one ship I'd never forget. The voyage I'd never forget. But what did he mean by saying this ship was the old *Berenice*? As far as I knew, she was no longer in service.

'You're talking nonsense!' I said curtly. 'This ship is a new one. It's her first sailing.'

'Not a new ship,' he corrected me patiently. He still sounded amused. 'New name, new paint and furnishings, but an old lady tricked out like a young girl. It's not surprising you didn't recognise her.'

He had sown doubt in my mind. Had there been something familiar about this ship when I'd boarded her? If so, I'd put it down to my long acquaintance with similar ships. 'I think you must be mistaken,' I said. 'Won't you come nearer and show yourself? Or tell me your name?'

His only reply was a sort of grunt.

I had been growing steadily colder. My cigarette had burned down. I threw it away from me, after the match, over the rail. For two pins I'd have thrown it right at my unseen companion with his misplaced sense of humour.

'If you knew me then,' I continued, my voice colder than the fog, 'you must know that voyage has sad memories for me.'

He laughed then, yes, laughed! I heard him distinctly.

I took a step towards him, heedless of danger, but he was quicker. My ear caught a movement in the thick white blanket of fog, a shoe scraped against the deck. I heard his footsteps, tap-tap-tap, on the stairs as he scurried away down the companionway to the lower deck. To follow him was impossible. He had gone. I had lost him.

But this was still a ship at sea. He was still aboard somewhere. I had only to seek him out. Or he would seek me out. Oh yes, he would seek me out again. By that mocking laughter he had let me know that he shared my secret. He knew the truth of what had happened all those years ago aboard the *Berenice*. For some reason he had done nothing about it until now. But seeing my name on the passenger list, he had decided to make his move at last. I understood his game. You see, I am a rich man. If you know a rich man's secret, you can make a good profit for yourself.

My hand scrabbled for the door catch behind me. I pulled it open and escaped back into the blessed warmth and clarity of the reception area.

'Why, Mr van Leeuwen!' exclaimed the girl there. 'You stayed out there too long. You must be chilled to the bone. You're as white as a sheet.'

I mumbled some reply and went back to the dining room where I was able to get myself another two cups of good strong hot coffee. It restored my circulation, my spirits and my brain to working order. A businessman is a man of action. I would not be made a fool of. I would not be teased and tormented. I would never let myself remain in the hands of someone I was sure intended blackmail. He would pay for his impertinence.

Like old William of Orange, I didn't forgive those who offended me.

From the moment the fog lifted and we got underway again my entire effort was dedicated to identifying my enemy. I did not even notice one of my favourite sights on entering the port of Lisbon: the Tower of Belem. When the Portuguese explorers set sail in their tiny wooden caravels, they had as their last sight of their homeland that squat square tower. If they were lucky enough to return safely after their perilous voyages, what joy must have filled their hearts when the lookout sang from his high perch that he could see on the horizon the familiar sight, gleaming white in the sunshine.

There was no joy in my heart: nothing was there but vengeance. But for this I had to establish facts and the first was whether this ship was, as he'd told me, the former *Berenice*.

I made my way to the bridge and fell into conversation with the captain. I remarked how well the ship had been refitted. He was pleased to tell me no expense had been spared. The modern cruise ship had to offer every comfort and amenity, even a small ship like this one.

I preferred small ships, I told him. I had never been tempted to take a cruise on one of those huge floating hotels. How old, I asked him, was our ship?

About thirty years old, he told me. Old enough. My heart sank but I carried on with my planned questioning. No doubt, I said, the ship had been renamed for her new owners? Yes, he replied and told me her previous name. It was unfamiliar. My heart rose again. Had she ever, I asked casually, been called the *Berenice*? He shook his head. Not to his knowledge. Changing a ship's name was common these days. Each change of ownership, each change of use, saw a newly painted name on her bows. In the old days of sailing ships it had been considered unlucky to change a ship's name. Sailors then were superstitious. They knew that ships with a dubious history were sometimes renamed in an attempt to escape their past.

Escape the past was what I had assumed, until now, I had done.

But I left the captain feeling much happier. It seemed unlikely that the ship really was the old *Berenice*. Telling me so had been part of my enemy's plan to unsettle me and make me amenable to his will. Nevertheless I examined the ship from stem to stern until I was certain in my mind she had never been the *Berenice*. It was a small triumph. I had caught him out. Yet he had certainly been aboard the *Berenice* twenty years before, and he knew the truth of what had happened that evening.

We had been taking a Mediterranean cruise, my wife and I. The *Berenice* had called at Corfu and turned towards the Dalmatian coast. In doing so we found ourselves sailing into a strong wind which caught the ship on the quarter. The *Berenice* began to pitch and roll violently. In the dining room, glasses and cutlery had to be removed from the tables before they crashed to the deck. Many passengers, turning green, retired to their cabins. My wife and I were amongst the few who made it into dinner. This was not because we felt much like eating but because to sit at table was preferable to sitting in our cabin or in a near-empty lounge with only ourselves for company.

We had long had nothing to say to one another. Even at dinner we spoke only to the waiter. I did ask my wife as we rose to our feet whether she wanted a drink at the bar. She replied briefly that she did not. It struck me that she seemed more than usually silent and resentful. She was probably feeling seasick.

When we were first married we had been reasonably happy. It had not been a marriage founded on passion. Neither of us pretended that. But marriages founded on respect and companionship often outlast marriages founded upon lust. We told ourselves we had every hope of contentment.

For my own part, I married my wife for her money. My business had been in some difficulties. My financial reputation had suffered. Like my ancestor, old Cornelius, I looked around for a plain but wealthy woman to solve my problems. Like Cornelius, I found one.

Her family was descended from a long line of country squires. They held no title but they owned a huge, uncomfortable, draughty country house and land, including two farms. They had invested wisely, spent frugally, and were thus both rich and well connected. My wife was thirty years old when I married her. Her father had just died and her mother was an ageing despotic former beauty who treated her daughter abominably.

So the marriage suited us both. As soon as it was known I had 'married money', confidence in my business returned. My wife gained a ring on her finger and freedom from that dragon known as Mummy. She was content to invest the money she had already inherited from her father in my business. For the rest of it we should have to wait until the dragon died. This my mother-in-law obligingly did only a year later. She choked on a fishbone while dining alone in that mausoleum of a country house.

The funeral was attended by local gentry and reported in the quality newspapers. The house, farms, the rest of the land and every penny of the money was now my wife's outright. It really seemed as though the sun shone upon our union.

Unfortunately this filled my wife's head with a new idea. We should have children, someone to inherit when 'we were gone'. My own idea had been to immortalise my name in a charitable foundation after my death. But my wife, as I explained, came of a very old family. For her, voluntary extinction of a bloodline was unthinkable. I gave way to her wishes. She held the purse strings and I was beginning to realise she was well aware of this.

'Very well,' I said, 'we shall have children.'

But children did not arrive, not even one child. My wife went from doctor to doctor, specialist to specialist, underwent every kind of treatment to no avail. Our private life consisted of keeping charts and taking temperatures.

One day I lost patience. I told her enough was enough. She must resign herself to the inevitable. She – we – would always be childless. She never forgave me those words.

Things got worse. We kept up a civilised front but there was nothing behind it. My wife was still only thirty-nine. I noticed she had begun to look at me speculatively.

I had no intention of being traded in like an old car. Besides, the business could not have stood the withdrawal of so much capital. Divorce, as far as I was concerned, was out of the question.

I was going to have to do something to mend fences. I saw the cruise on the *Berenice* advertised. I persuaded my wife the holiday would do us both good. We could talk things over. She agreed reluctantly.

We didn't talk things over and, if anything, the relationship grew worse once we were shut up in a small ship. The more I tried to engineer a rapprochement, the more she became stonily indifferent. By the evening the *Berenice* ran into bad weather, I had realised my plan wasn't going to work. I'd have to think of something else.

We left the almost empty dining room and despite the pitching of the ship, I went out on deck for my customary cigarette. To my surprise, a few minutes later, she followed me.

'Go inside!' I shouted at her above the wind. I could see how unsteady she was on her feet and how she clung to a handrail.

'I've reached a decision!' she shouted back.

It was ludicrous. Here we were, being tossed about on the ocean, hanging on for dear life, and she'd chosen this moment to discuss things!

'For goodness' sake!' I exclaimed. 'Tell me what it is later. I'll be inside in five minutes when I've finished my cigarette. I'll see you in the cabin.'

'NO!' she yelled. 'I want to tell you now!' The wind snatched the words from her and hurled them into the air.

I realised what had happened. She had worked herself up to this moment. She was going to tell me she wanted a divorce, and from her viewpoint the present time wasn't such a bad one. If she told me in the cabin, we'd argue. Out here, the wind whipping at our hair and clothing and the deck turning into a ski slope beneath our feet, we were in no position to enter into any argument. It was all we could do to stay upright. She meant to give me my marching orders and then retire inside before I had a chance to reply. By the time I got back down to the cabin after her, it would be too late. I would have lost all initiative. I would be left to repeat useless arguments and undignified pleadings. She need say no more.

At that moment the *Berenice* lurched violently. My wife lost her grip and stumbled towards me. Automatically I grabbed her arm to save her. We teetered for a moment in an enforced embrace. She shouted at me to release her. I shouted back that she was a fool. She would fall.

Then it came to me, there in the middle of the confusion: a moment of absolute clarity, the answer to the situation. In our struggle we had moved to the top of the companionway leading down to the deck below.

'Go on, then!' I shouted. 'You want to be free of me. I want to be free of you!' I threw her from me with all the force at my disposal.

Her shriek was lost in the roar of the waves and gale. She stumbled backwards and flailed about her. But on the stairway there was nowhere for her foot to find a hold. She grabbed at the handrail but her own weight, as she fell, tore it from her grasp. Down she went headlong, tumbling and twisting, to land with a horrid thump on the deck below.

She lay still. I made my way down to her prudently. I didn't want us to be a pair of casualties! Her eyes were open. I thought for one moment that she was still alive. I reached out my hands to her neck to press on the carotid arteries, just to make sure. But even as I did so, I saw her eyes glaze. It was not necessary to do any more. I had done enough.

Everyone was very kind to me. My wife's body was put ashore at Split. The British vice consul helped me arrange to send the coffin back to England. The funeral was held at the same country church which had seen her parents' obsequies. I invited selected mourners back to the draughty house for cold ham and salad. I served champagne.

'To celebrate my dear wife's life,' I told them as I raised my glass. 'To her memory!'

'To her memory!' cried all the old colonels and horse-faced women.

Even our member of parliament was there. My wife had been a contributor to party funds. He was clearly worried I wouldn't do the same.

I told him not to worry. I would honour all my late wife's commitments. He thanked me effusively before he realised it sounded in bad taste.

Of course, I didn't give them anything.

All this was in the past and I had believed would remain there. I had been sure no one had seen me push my wife. No one had seen me stretch out my hand to her neck as she lay prostrate. Now I knew there had been a witness.

I became obsessed with finding him before our ship reached Civitavecchia. I knew I was the only passenger remaining aboard for the Mediterranean trip after that. I scrutinised every face. I listened to every voice. I fully expected him to speak or that I would receive a note pushed beneath the cabin door. But there was nothing, no contact. I couldn't find him.

My anger had built up into intolerable pressure. I'd become a modern-day Flying Dutchman! Pursued by the past I was a prisoner on this ship and my nemesis was here with me. But where? Who was he? Where did he hide himself? How long did he mean to play this game of hide and seek? He was taking on the character of a sea wraith. But I am not superstitious. I am a businessman. I deal in reality. He was flesh and blood and could make mistakes. He had made one in telling me this ship had formerly been the *Berenice*. I had already established that wasn't true. He would make another mistake and then I would have him!

We reached Civitavecchia. The new passengers came aboard,

happy and enthusiastic. I greeted them tersely and avoided them. They soon avoided me. I now decided my tormentor was one of the crew. I concentrated on stewards and dining-room staff. Most of them were too young to have been employed on the *Berenice* twenty years earlier. The same was true of the ship's officers. So was the man I sought toiling in the ship's engine room? Cooking my meals in the galley? Meals I could not eat. My rage took away all appetite and with it was growing my frustration. He was playing me as an angler plays a fish on a line.

We made a slow progress down the long coast of Italy, calling at different ports. I sought him in Naples and in Capri. I peered down narrow streets and searched in ornate churches. My eyes scoured the hillsides of Sicily for him. With each day that passed, my failure to find him ate at me like a cancer. Each night I dreamed of him, knowing it was possible he would contact me the following day. Time was running out for him, too.

We reached the Gulf of Taranto and early one fine balmy evening the ship found herself anchored at the small ancient town of Gallipoli.

I walked ashore alone and began to wander the narrow streets, reviewing everything in my mind. See here, I reasoned, in the turmoil of the storm how could he swear I had acted deliberately aboard the *Berenice*? If he had been really sure of what he had seen, he would have alerted the captain at the time. Instead of sympathy, I would have found myself confined to my cabin until we reached Split. There I would have been handed over to the local police. My persecutor had his suspicions, but he had no proof. When he confronted me, I would laugh in his face, just as he had laughed at me.

It was with a brisker step I began to explore the town, actually forgetting my troubles and beginning to take some interest in my surroundings. Gallipoli is a place of quiet streets between high baroque buildings, coloured gold and pale yellow in the evening sunshine. Women sat on wooden kitchen chairs before their doors and gossiped. They were all alike to my eye, stocky in build, wearing black or dark dresses. Good, pious, hard-working mothers and grandmothers.

As for their sons and grandsons, they were celebrating Gallipoli's win in some football match. Exuberant young men toured the streets, too narrow for cars, on motorcycles. They wore red shirts and the pillion passengers brandished red silk flags. It gave them the appearance of wild revolutionaries but red was, I supposed, the colour of the home team. I smiled indulgently at them as they wove their way past, shouting news of their victory up at windows where the inhabitants might not yet have heard about it.

It was then, as I stood at a street corner feeling almost happy for the first time since the day of the fog, that he chose to speak to me again.

He, too, had been watching the celebrating football fans. 'Well, Mr van Leeuwen,' he said, 'what it is to be young, eh? Young and conscience clear.'

I whirled round but just at that moment a gang of the young-sters ran past me round the corner and disappeared up the street. In the flurry of bodies, he was lost. I hesitated. What to do? I decided I would go back to the ship and wait. He, too, would have to return. I would stand at the foot of the gangplank. There was no other way to get aboard. I would scrutinise each face and, this time, in some way, he would betray himself.

I set off. The gossiping women watched me go past. I bid them '*buona sera*' and they politely returned my greeting. I felt them watch me as I proceeded. They were curious to a point. They knew I had come from some moored cruise vessel. They would speculate as to why I was alone, perhaps. But I was a foreigner and they found their world in these narrow streets and in family affairs.

I'm not sure at what point I realised he was following me. I had heard nothing but I became aware of an itching feeling between my shoulder blades. I whirled round but saw only the gossiping women. But some doors had no female guardians, although they stood open letting light and air into those dark, cluttered, but proudly tidy homes. This was a community of neighbours, of trust. He could have darted into any of those untenanted doorways. I did not want to attract the attention of the women by peering in and, unfortunately, I knew no more Italian than the words of greeting I had spoken to them, so I couldn't ask them if they'd seen anyone.

He was definitely behind me but he was clever. I gave him that. Just occasionally I heard the echo of a footfall but he was never there when I turned. I had almost reached the waterfront. I began to hurry. Somehow, I felt that once I could see the sea, I would shake off this stealthy pursuit. He would have to come out into the comparative open, leaving the protection of the narrow streets, the open doors, the red-shirted crowd of happy football fans. The women and the youths were watching me more closely now. The youngsters had even forgotten their victory. The women were whispering whereas before they'd spoken loudly. The fans had stopped celebrating, their youthful attention now attracted by a new and strange sight – that of me, running now, running towards the harbour and the safety, as it now seemed, of the ship.

Then I heard him again. 'Don't run so fast, Mr van Leeuwen! We're not young men any more, you and I! We can't keep this pace up!'

I stopped and turned and saw him at last.

He was indeed an elderly man, short, balding and out of breath. 'Wait, please!' he panted. He held out his hand to me. He was holding something.

I leapt at him. I grabbed him by the neck and he fell beneath the weight of my onslaught to the pavement. I cracked his head upon the stones, raised it and cracked it down again. I felt, rather than heard, the skull split like an eggshell. I couldn't stop. I kept lifting his head, and cracking it down again. I was in another fog, this one a fog of fury, exasperation, revenge and fear.

Hands seized my shoulders and pulled me away from my victim. The fog cleared. I saw lying at my feet an elderly Italian, blood running from his head, his eyes open but glazing already in death. Nearby on the pavement lay my wallet.

I understood then what had happened. He was not my persecutor. I had dropped my wallet as I hurried and the poor old chap had picked it up and run after me with it. Not only was he not my persecutor, my persecutor had never existed outside my own head. In that sense he had travelled with me for twenty years. But I had stilled his voice or refused to listen when he had whispered to me. Something – perhaps a similarity of our ship to the old *Berenice* – had triggered his escape from my subconscious. I won't call it my conscience because I don't believe I have a conscience, not in the religious or moral sense. Rather, I had an awareness, which I had suppressed, that a deed like murder cannot be hidden for ever. The truth would come out.

When I had boarded the ship at the beginning of our cruise, the demon within me had been let loose. In the fog, alone on the viewing platform, he had spoken to me. I had heard him and listened to him at last. Even when I had established that our present ship was not the old *Berenice*, it was still too late to silence him. Once he had crawled out into the light of my awareness, he could not be thrust back into the darkness. Like the genie in the Eastern fairy tale, he could not be returned to his bottle.

I looked around me. I was surrounded by a silent circle. Two of the football fans held me tightly by my arms. One knelt by the dead man. Some of the gossiping women had left their wooden chairs and stood nearby, their lips moving in silent prayer, their broad work-worn hands clasped, their eyes cast down and fixed on the body. The young men watched me with hostile dark eyes. One of them spoke into a mobile phone. He was calling the police. Another approached with his club flag and draped the scarlet silk over the old man's lifeless form, covering it from our gaze.

'I'm sorry,' I said. 'It was a mistake.'

I don't know if they understood me. They gave no sign. But I spoke the truth. I was sorry for the death of this old man who had only intended to do me a good turn and give me back the wallet I'd dropped. I am a rich man and he had been a poor one.

I would not have missed the money. But he had been an honest man, and I?

For the first time the mental fog had cleared and I saw everything I had ever done with crystal clarity.

'You do not need to hold me so tightly,' I said to the young men who held me captive. 'I'm not going to run away.' I allowed myself a smile. 'I have nowhere, now, to go,' I said. But they didn't understand me.

Murder on the Menu

'I've put you down for the savouries,' said Clarissa Hooper. She smiled in her bright encouraging way.

Daisy wiped her hands nervously with a rag, smearing the paint more freely. She wondered why, when Clarissa smiled, the smile never reached her eyes. Clarissa's large, protruberant, pale blue eyes were as blank as a dead fish's.

Daisy said, 'I'm afraid I'm not much of a cook.'

'Nonsense!' retorted Clarissa, as Daisy had known she would. 'You can throw together something, can't you? Anybody can.'

Daisy said, 'I can't,' as firmly as she could, but it was useless. Clarissa merely gave a jolly laugh as though Daisy had made a joke. An idea struck her. She needn't actually make the savouries, whatever they might be. She could buy some in the nearest bakery. What difference would it make?

As if she could read Daisy's mind, Clarissa continued, 'The important thing is that everything should be home-made. Elderly people enjoy home-made food. Last year some people brought baker's goods and we don't want a repeat of that! We want this party to be a success!'

The 'we' irritated Daisy. She also wanted the party for the village old folk to be a success, but by 'we' she suspected Clarissa meant 'I'. Clarissa used 'we' as royal personages do, to indicate

267

both the person and the majestic office. Clarissa, as chairwoman of the village Women's Institute, behaved very much like the all-powerful ruler of a pocket principality. To argue with her was not only useless, it was made to feel like treason.

Reluctantly Daisy asked, 'What sort of savoury?'

'Good question.' Clarissa nodded approvingly. 'We don't want everyone bringing the same thing. That's why I've made a list. Mrs Forbes is in charge of sandwiches. There are three of you making savouries. One person is bringing cheese straws and another is bringing mushroom vol-au-vents. So I leave it up to you. Perhaps something in the pastry line?'

'Pastry!' gasped the horrified Daisy, but Clarissa was already gathering up her various belongings.

'I must be on my way. I've got to call on the vicar before I go home and I've told the girl to have my lunch ready at one sharp.'

Despite these words, Clarissa didn't go, but fidgeted with her capacious bag, eyeing Daisy thoughtfully all the while. 'You don't have any family, do you, dear?' she asked unexpectedly.

To this rather impertinent question, Daisy replied that she had an aged uncle who lived by the seaside.

'Then you'll have expectations,' said Clarissa, even more rudely, thought Daisy. What business was it of Clarissa's? Nor had Daisy any expectations of curmudgeonly Uncle Frederick. He had twice informed her that she wasn't to build up her hopes on his account! He was, in addition, in robust good health despite being well into his eighties.

But she'd mistaken Clarissa's interest. 'I have a nephew,' Daisy's visitor began and then hesitated unhappily. Lack of confidence was unlike Clarissa. Daisy realised the woman wanted to talk something over but didn't know how to begin.

'Yes?' Daisy encouraged.

'I've helped him many times in the past for my poor late sister's sake,' Clarissa rushed into speech. 'But in the end I had to put my foot down. I wrote and told him it was time he stood on his own two feet.'

'Where does he live?' asked Daisy, though she didn't really care.

'In London, where he works for an insurance firm. Naturally, he knows that when I die, he'll have everything, but until then he's got to live on his salary. I've told him so.'

Clarissa recalled the reason she was there. 'So you'll see to the savouries? I'll call by tomorrow and collect them. Two dozen individual servings will do!'

'*Two dozen* . . .' But Clarissa had swept out, cutting short Daisy's outraged squeak. Through the window, Daisy saw her mount her bicycle and pedal away to bully the vicar, a mild-mannered man known to be in awe of Mrs Hooper.

Daisy sat down with a bump on the nearest chair. She couldn't remember the last time she had made pastry. She didn't think it was a very good idea to start now. The elderly – for whom these delights were intended – probably had false teeth. False teeth gummed up with Daisy's pastry. She could imagine the scene. The village elderly were vociferous in complaint if things weren't to their pleasing at their annual summer garden party, held in a paddock adjacent to the back of Clarissa's property. Daisy wasn't in the first flush of youth herself any more, but that didn't necessarily make her sympathetic to the village old folk who were never so happy, she'd found, as when finding fault.

She realised the paint had dried on her hands. The painting on which she'd been working when Clarissa had arrived stood in its half-finished state on the easel. Daisy sighed. Clarissa never bothered to ask if you were busy. She always barged in and started talking, oblivious to how inconvenient it might be. Daisy glanced at the clock. It was ten minutes to twelve. Clarissa had arrived at eleven and harangued Daisy for fifty minutes. The morning was completely ruined. It was impossible to restart work now. Daisy went to wash her hands and hunt for a cookery book.

The kitchen was occupied by Mavis Potter who was about to put on her coat and sneak off early. Being as impecunious as only an artist can be, Daisy couldn't afford proper domestic help. She was reduced to employing Mavis, mornings only. Mavis was fifteen, a slapdash worker, inclined to cut corners. But she was prepared to work for very little wages.

'I'm all done, mum!' announced Mavis perkily. In readiness for the walk home she had applied scarlet lipstick unevenly to her mouth.

Daisy wondered whether she ought to say anything about the lipstick, which she didn't think was really suitable for a fifteen-year-old. Moreover she doubted Mavis was 'all done'. Mavis's work was invariably half-done. But after Clarissa's visit, she couldn't be bothered to argue with the daily help. So she said, 'Very well, Mavis.'

Mavis clattered noisily away.

As it was almost lunchtime, Daisy made herself a sandwich and took it and the cookery book into the garden to enjoy the sun. Rose Cottage was on the outskirts of the village and Daisy had leased it from an old lady, a well-known and respected village resident, who had retired to the Caribbean for her health. The pretty cottage garden faced the road and people passing by frequently stopped to admire it and to chat over the hedge.

Daisy settled down in the shade of an apple tree. She took a bite from her sandwich and gazed dismally at the closed book. It was all very well for Mrs Forbes to promise sandwiches. Mrs Forbes' maid would prepare them. Daisy suspected that the providers of the cheese straws and mushroom vol-au-vents would have similar help. There was no question of asking Mavis to cook anything. Daisy would have to do her best. On impulse she flipped open the book, resolved to try to make whatever was on the page at which it opened. If it was a disaster, and it was almost certain to be that, she'd have to buy from the bakery after all and explain to Clarissa. It would be humiliating but unavoidable.

Pigs In Blankets was the wording at the head of the page. The name appealed to Daisy who read on to find out what these delicacies might be. They were, it appeared, sausages wrapped in bacon. Pigs in blankets it would have to be.

A metallic rattling attracted Daisy's attention. She looked up and saw Clarissa bicycle past coming from the direction of the vicarage. The rattle was caused by a loose mudguard on the bicycle's rear wheel. No doubt she was on her way home to lunch prepared by her excellent cook. Clarissa waved cheerily at Daisy who waved back, feeling guilty. She got up and went back to her kitchen. The clock on the wall there told her it was twelve thirty. She knew she had bacon but she hadn't any sausages. The kitchen clock now informed her it was twenty minutes to one. It was Wednesday, which was half-day closing, and the village butcher's shop would pull down its shutters at one for the rest of the day. There was no time to lose. Her abundant greying hair, which she'd pinned up that morning, was falling down again but she had no time to tidy it. Daisy pulled on a wide-brimmed raffia sunhat and hastened out.

Closing the garden gate carefully against stray dogs, she strode along, placing her feet in their sensible flat sandals squarely on the ground, her long skirt flapping at her ankles. The butcher's was at the far end of the already deserted main street. Everyone was at table. Daisy passed Clarissa's rather nice white-washed Georgian house and reflected with resentment that Clarissa would be within, settling down peacefully to her lunch oblivious of any upset she'd caused to anyone else.

Daisy arrived, panting, at the butcher's to find he'd just that moment shut the door and hung the 'closed' notice in it. She peered through the glass and tapped urgently. The butcher came to the door to point majestically at the notice, but seeing who it was, opened up the door again. He liked the artist lady who'd taken Rose Cottage.

'I only want two pounds of small sausages!' apologised Daisy.

'Two pounds of sausages it is!' said the butcher.

Perspiring freely in the hot midday sunshine, Daisy set off home again, carrying the wrapped sausages. Halfway down the main street her progress was halted by a shrill scream.

It came from the house to her left, the white-washed Georgian house which belonged to Clarissa. As she stood before it, wondering what she should do, the door flew open and a maid rushed out into the street. Seeing Daisy, she made for her and grabbed her arm.

'Oh, miss! You've got to come. Madam's dead!'

'Pull yourself together,' said Daisy automatically, trying to detach the girl's grip. Clarissa got through maids at a great rate. Mostly they only stayed a month or two before they decided they'd rather work elsewhere. This girl, Daisy saw, was yet another new one. She wondered whether she was given to imagining things.

'Mrs Hooper can't be dead,' Daisy said reassuringly. 'I saw her only half an hour ago.'

'Oh, she is, she is and it's horrible!' wailed the maid, clinging even more tightly.

Much against her will Daisy allowed herself to be dragged into the house. As they went, the maid gave an incoherent account of what had happened.

'It's Cook's day off so I had to prepare madam's lunch – just a salad and a rice pudding. I got it all ready but I hadn't heard her come home, so I went along to the dining room to see if she was there. When I opened the door, I saw her lying there – like that!'

They had reached the door of the dining room. The maid stopped short and pointed at something unseen on the further side of the door.

'I can't go back in that room, I swear I can't!' Tears trickled down her face.

Daisy had perforce to enter alone. It was a small but pretty room from which French windows opened onto the garden. A single place was neatly laid at the well-polished dining table. The chair before it, however, lay upturned on the floor. Beside it sprawled Clarissa, on her back, one hand clutching at her throat around which was a tightly pulled cord. Her pale eyes bulged even more than they had in life and her tongue protruded between her open lips. That she was dead there was no doubt.

The maid was still hovering outside in the hallway. Daisy returned to her, taking care to disturb nothing on the way.

At least the girl had calmed down now that there was someone else to take responsibility. She was dry eyed and her expression was more inquisitive than horrified. Daisy was relieved. An hysterical maid on top of everything else was something she could do without. She eyed the girl, a pretty young woman with glossy brown hair. In her black uniform dress and white apron and cap she looked, Daisy thought ruefully, as unlike Mavis Potter as could be imagined. She certainly looked reliable enough to be sent with a message.

'You must go and fetch Constable Wilkes,' Daisy said firmly to her. 'And also Dr Partridge.'

The maid's bright gaze widened. Her mouth opened and she put her hand to it in dismay. 'Is madam alive then?' she gasped. 'I never would've left her if I'd thought—'

'No, I'm afraid Mrs Hooper is dead. But the constable will want a doctor's opinion. Go along now and whatever you do, don't gossip to anyone on the way!'

'No, miss!' said the maid huffily and hurried off.

Left with the body, Daisy was uncertain what to do. On the principle that it would be best to do nothing, she went outside the house again and looked up and down the street. Not a soul except for the distant figure of the maid, hurrying towards the police house. Poor Constable Wilkes would be sitting down to his midday meal, nicely cooked by Mrs Wilkes. The news that he had to get up straight away and go out, wouldn't be welcome.

A thought struck Daisy. She walked down the path at the side of the house and came out into the back garden. Clarissa's bicycle was propped against the garden shed in which she probably kept it. The garden was mostly laid to lawn and beyond it stretched the grassy paddock which would see the old folks' revels. Daisy frowned. She returned to the house and, this time, found her way to the kitchen. It was immaculately clean and tidy, crisp gingham curtains at the open window moving slightly in the warm draught. Clarissa's lunch, which she would now never eat, stood ready. It made a pathetic sight, the ham salad on a tray and the rice pudding – rather lumpy with a burnt skin – being kept warm in a bain-marie. Daisy looked out of the kitchen window. It gave onto a small paved area and beyond that was a high privet hedge so that it was shielded from the back garden itself.

Much stamping of feet from the front of the house announced that at least one of the two people she'd sent for had arrived. Daisy hastened back to the dining room.

Constable Wilkes, a portly figure with half his tunic buttons undone indicating the haste with which he'd left home, was stooped over the prostrate Clarissa. His red face creased in dismay, he was repeating, 'Well, I never . . . Well, I never . . .'

He straightened up and took out his notebook and pencil but then appeared at a loss to know what to write in it. Fortunately, Dr Partridge arrived at that point. He too had been called from his lunch, as shown by the napkin still tucked into his waistcoat. Hot on his heels came the breathless maid with an air of triumph about her now that she'd successfully completed her mission.

'I got them both, miss!' she announced to Daisy.

Partridge knelt briefly by the body. Then he scrambled to his feet and addressed himself to Constable Wilkes. 'You'll have to get hold of Inspector Morris in town. This is clearly murder.'

'Murder!' screeched the maid, relapsing into her earlier panic. 'I'm not staying in this house another minute!'

Once news of Mrs Hooper's death got around, the village was in turmoil. Who could have done it? She hadn't been a popular lady, it was true. 'But you don't go murdering someone because she likes giving orders, do you?' asked Mrs Potter, mother of Mavis. General opinion agreed with this. Nor could the one obvious suspect, Mrs Hooper's wayward nephew Gerald, be blamed. The police established immediately that he was at work in the London office of the company which employed him for the whole of that day. In fact, he had not even taken a lunchbreak because of business involving an important new client. Everyone working at the firm had seen and spoken to him constantly throughout the day.

The police came and went. The case remained unsolved. Rumour had it the police believed the murderer had entered the dining room through the French windows. Possibly he was a thief intent on making off with the silverware. He had escaped the same way, running through the back garden and across the paddock beyond unobserved. The maid's view from the kitchen had been barred by a privet hedge.

The body was released for burial and Gerald Horton, the nephew, attended the funeral looking distressed. He kept his handsome face bowed in sorrow and respect and made quite an impression. Mavis Potter, completely bowled over, declared he looked just like Ronald Coleman.

This caused Daisy to become quite cross and declare, 'Don't be silly, Mavis, and by the way, I don't think your mother would approve of your spending money on lipstick.'

Gerald hurried away immediately after the funeral, much to Mavis's regret. Shortly after that, a For Sale notice went up at Clarissa's Georgian house. Mr Horton had no wish to keep it on and everyone said they could understand that.

Daisy had been interviewed by the police early in the investigation and given her account of having been called to the body by the maid. They'd written it all down and, since then, hadn't bothered her again. Daisy had waited, with the rest of the village, for an arrest to be made, as sooner or later everyone believed it must be. When no arrest was made, the atmosphere in the village became tense.

'Mother says we've got a murdering madman amongst us!' Mavis told Daisy with some relish.

Daisy put on her raffia sunhat once more and walked down the main street. She stood before Clarissa's house, with its For Sale notice, for a few minutes in silent tribute, then caught the bus into town. There she went to the police station and asked to speak to Inspector Morris.

'Well now, Miss Winslow,' said Inspector Morris politely. 'What can we do for you?'

He smiled at his visitor. He remembered speaking to her just after the murder. She was dressed now, as she had been then, in a way Morris categorised as 'bohemian'. She wore a long skirt, a velvet waistcoat and a raffia sunhat from beneath which peeped untidy greying curls. She was hung about with a great many bead necklaces and bangles which had a home-made look to them. 'Arts and crafts,' thought Inspector Morris dismissively. He didn't know why she was here but it was probably to waste his time. She had doubtless enjoyed the attention she'd got after the murder and was seeking more of the same.

Daisy folded her hands in her lap and took a deep breath. 'May I ask if you are any further on in your enquiries into Mrs Hooper's death?'

Morris looked distinctly put out at this forthright approach. 'These things take time,' he retorted testily.

Daisy's courage almost failed her at that point but she swallowed and went on, 'I should perhaps have come sooner but I thought, you see, that you'd have solved it by now. In any case, you wouldn't be interested in *my* ideas. But as you haven't, haven't *yet*—' Daisy tactfully amended her words, seeing an alarming reddening of the inspector's complexion. 'Not yet arrested anyone, I decided I must come and tell you what's been on my mind. I've thought and thought about this since poor Clarissa Hooper died. Indeed, my brain's been buzzing with nothing else. And now I think – I think I know how it was done.'

'We know how it was done,' said the inspector who'd been listening with growing impatience, his worst suspicions about the visitor confirmed. 'With a length of picture cord, could've been bought anywhere.'

'No, I mean, I know how they did it, Clarissa's murderers.'

'Oh, two of them?' asked the inspector in a dry way. He glanced at his wristwatch. 'I'm sure you have a very interesting theory, Miss Winslow, but—'

'There had to be two of them,' said Daisy, ignoring his signs of restlessness in her eagerness to explain, 'in order for Gerald Horton to have an alibi. He is, you see, the only person with a motive and bound to be suspected. Clarissa Hooper had left him everything in her will. She told me so the morning of her death. She had been giving him money, but she'd recently refused to give him any more. He's a rakish young man and gave her a lot of cause for concern. I dare say he owes a great deal and was desperate when she told him she'd give him no more.'

'So who was his accomplice?' asked the inspector. His tone was still patronising but the look in his eyes had grown shrewder.

'Oh, that girl, that maid person. It's a terrible thing to think that a young woman could commit murder but she's probably madly in love with Gerald. He's a good-looking young man and anyone who could persuade Clarissa Hooper to give him money over a period of some years must have a silver tongue. Introducing her into the house wasn't difficult. Clarissa was forever changing maids. All they had to do was wait until she was looking for yet another and Gerald sent along his young woman.'

Morris drummed his fingers on his desk. 'As a matter of fact, we've lost trace of that maid. She must have taken a new post. We're trying all the agencies which supply domestic staff.' He leaned back in his chair. 'But surely, if you're right, Horton and his ladyfriend would be taking a great risk planning to murder Mrs Hooper in the middle of the day when anyone might come by and see them?'

'Not really. You see, it was lunchtime, the one time of day when *nobody would come by*. Mid-morning or mid-afternoon would have been quite a different proposition. People would be moving about. For example, Clarissa was organising the old folks' party. She came to see me at eleven that morning to discuss it. She asked me to make some pigs in blankets.'

'Some what?' asked Inspector Morris, looking alarmed.

'They're sausages wrapped in bacon. Actually, she didn't specifically ask for pigs in blankets. She asked for savouries, but I decided on pigs in blankets. She left my cottage at ten minutes to twelve to go to the vicarage.'

'She did go there,' said Morris. 'The vicar confirms it.'

'That's right. I saw her myself. She bicycled past my cottage at half past twelve on her way back home. Clarissa was a stickler for doing everything in an orderly way. She told me she'd ordered her lunch for one o'clock so I knew that's where she was going.

'I was in a panic because I'm not a very good cook and I hadn't any sausages. Also it was Wednesday, half-day closing. But one didn't refuse Clarissa,' Daisy said ruefully. 'I put on my hat and rushed to the butcher's. It was twenty minutes to one when I left my cottage. There was no one about. It was lunchtime, you see. I passed Clarissa's house. It was all quiet. It didn't surprise me because, on her bicycle, she'd have got there long before me. I calculate it would have taken her less than five minutes to reach her house after passing my garden. So she got home at twenty-five minutes to one and that gave her murderer plenty of time. Remember, Clarissa ate at one sharp. It was the cook's day off. Only the maid was in the house, by her own admission.

'At one o'clock I had reached the butcher's. He'd just closed but kindly opened up again to sell me the sausages. I saw, as I left the butcher's, that his clock read ten past one. I was very grateful to him for staying open an extra ten minutes, just for me. I was passing Clarissa's house when the maid rushed out. You know that bit.'

Daisy frowned. 'I suppose, with the shock of finding her like that, I didn't really think beyond sending the girl for Constable Wilkes and Dr Partridge. But afterwards, I got to thinking that one or two things were odd.

'To begin with, the girl had said she hadn't heard Clarissa return. Now, she might not have seen Clarissa because of that privet hedge outside the kitchen window. But she would have heard her bicycle as Clarissa pushed it down the garden because it makes a frightful rattle and the kitchen windows were open. I'd heard it myself earlier and I saw the bicycle leaning against the garden shed while I was waiting for the constable to arrive. The girl had prepared the lunch so that everything would look right. She took great care to tell me, as she was taking me into the house, that the lunch consisted of salad and rice pudding. Sure enough, I saw ham salad and a rice pudding in the kitchen. I sent the girl for help, as I told you, and that's when the second funny thing happened. The girl had calmed down very quickly – a bit too quickly, to my mind! But when I asked that Dr Partridge be summoned, she looked really dismayed and asked whether madam was still alive? She was afraid, you see, that I'd detected signs of life in poor Clarissa. When I explained it was because I thought a doctor's opinion would be needed –' Here Daisy paused and gave the inspector a nervous smile.

'Quite right,' said Morris. 'Very clear thinking on your part.'

'Thank you. Well, when the girl realised that was why I wanted Partridge there, she relaxed again and went off in very good spirits indeed! So cold blooded—' Daisy stopped and the inspector waited courteously for her to begin again. 'Then I thought of the third odd thing and really, it's the oddest of all. If Clarissa had asked for lunch at one, she would have expected to see it arrive at one on the dot. Yet when the maid ran out into the street, claiming to have just found her mistress dead, it was well gone ten past one. If the lunch had been ten minutes late in arriving, Clarissa would have been along to the kitchen to find out why!

'So what I believe happened was this. Gerald and the girl had waited for the cook's day off. Gerald made sure to be working in his office all day in full view of everyone. The girl heard Clarissa's bicycle rattle past the house on its way to the shed and got ready for her part in it. Just on one, she went to the dining room. Clarissa was at table, expecting her lunch. I saw from the position of the furniture that she'd been sitting with her back to the door. Hearing the door open, Clarissa would've assumed it was the salad arriving. Instead it was that awful girl – with a length of picture cord. It must have been so easy, Clarissa so unsuspecting . . .'

'Would you like some water?' asked the inspector, as Daisy had turned very pale and broken off her narrative.

'After. Let me finish. I'm almost there. Once she was satisfied Clarissa was dead – it must have been a quick death, for that I'm grateful for Clarissa's sake – the girl opened the French windows to suggest how the killer had got in. After that she ran into the street screaming and grabbed the first person to come along. It happened to be me. Had no one been there, she'd have stood there screaming until someone came out to see what was going on. It was so simple.'

Morris heaved a sigh. 'It all makes sense, I agree. Between you and me we haven't dismissed Gerald Horton's involvement just because he has an alibi. You're right and he does owe a lot of money. He's a gambler and a very bad one. No doubt someone is pressing him for payment. But we need to find that girl, that maid, if we're to make it stick. As I told you, we're trying all the domestic agencies—'

'Oh no,' said Daisy quickly. 'Not those. Try the theatrical agencies. I'm sure she's an actress. Such a pretty girl and able to vary her emotions at the drop of a hat, even produce tears!

'Besides,' she went on confidentially, 'I saw that rice pudding! It was clearly made by someone who'd never cooked such a thing in her life! It looked nearly as bad as something I might make, but then, I have no pretensions to any domestic skills. I tried to tell Clarissa so when she asked me to make the savouries but she wouldn't listen. But such a professional-looking maid as that girl appeared to be should have been able to manage plain cooking.'

'It's not something I'd have noticed,' admitted the inspector.

'So she was no professional maid! I understand actors leave their details and photographs with agencies. I don't mind how many photographs I have to look at. I'm sure I can identify that girl.'

And so it turned out. The girl proved to be a largely unsuccessful actress and – as Daisy had guessed – very much under the sway of Gerald Horton. But not so much that she was prepared to face a charge of murder alone. She confessed everything.

Clarissa Hooper's house stood empty for a long time as no one local fancied living in it. Eventually a couple from outside the area bought it.

While all this was going on, the old folks' party took place, though its location was moved to the vicarage garden. It was very successful. But somehow, Daisy never got round to making the pigs in blankets.

One Bad Turn

Arthur Hooper came downstairs tying the strings of his spotless white apron as he went. Opening up the shop always filled him with deep-seated pleasure. Outside on glazed tiles above the shop window it read 'Hooper and Son. High-Class Provisions'. Of this duo, Arthur was 'and son' – for he was a bachelor, middle aged, balding and contented.

He lit the gaslamps in the shop as it was still not quite light outside. What a cavern of riches they revealed! Fat bacon and pink hams, pork pies oozing grease and jelly, yellow wheels of cheese, tea in bins and coffee beans in sacks, liquorice strings and tiger-nuts, biscuits of every description in glass boxes (and broken ones a penny a bag). All of it Mr Hooper's personal kingdom. He always opened early and often picked up a bit of extra trade thereby. Perhaps a child from a poor family sent to buy twopenny-worth of tea in a twist of paper, or a maid from a better-off one for half a pound of butter sliced from the small mountain of it which kept cool overnight in the cellar.

But as he went to open the front door today the satisfied look faded from his face. Slumped in the doorway was a motionless figure.

'Another of 'em!' said Mr Hooper resignedly.

It wasn't the first homeless wretch he had found asleep in his entry. He wasn't an unkind man and when he discovered such an unfortunate generally roused him with a shake and sometimes gave him a stale pork pie. But this morning his unwanted lodger was a woman, a poor ragged creature, and shake her though he did with increasing briskness, he could not wake her.

'Dead drunk!' said Mr Hooper. He bent and inspected the pale face framed by lank wisps of hair. 'Oh, my Gawd!' Not drunk, just dead. The night had been very cold.

'I can't have her found here!' muttered the grocer. 'Folk are fussy in Camden Town! Who's going to buy a pork pie or a pound of back rashers from a shop what's got a corpse in the doorway?'

He glanced along the street. Next door was a milliner's run by Miss Minchin. She was a lady of uncertain years and temper who wore black bombasine with a gold fobwatch pinned on her bosom and fingerless lace mittens. Mr Hooper did not much care for Miss Minchin. Last summer on a particularly hot day she had marched into his shop – full of customers at the time – and declared she could smell the cheeses out in the street, 'like dead bodies!' she had said.

Mr Hooper was visited by an unholy temptation to mix expediency with revenge – and succumbed. 'I'll give her dead bodies!' He grasped the corpse by the shoulders and dragged it the short distance to Miss Minchin's doorway and propped it there. 'She can have this one!' Then he went back and carefully washed his hands. You had to be clean in the grocery business.

Miss Minchin opened her shop an hour later. He knew the time to the minute because an unearthly screech split the air. Footsteps pattered on the pavement and she appeared distraught. Luckily the shop was empty.

'There's a murdered corpse in my entrance – it's that Ripper about his devilish business again!' she declared and fainted, blocking the door.

Mr Hooper, highly alarmed but more by her words than her swoon, dragged her inside. Her heels scraped two long grooves in the clean sawdust and she was more awkward to handle than the corpse. He draped her against the mahogany counter next to the brass scales, splashed water in her face and went to investigate her claim.

It was still early and cold, but full light now and he could see there was indeed blood on the ragged bodice and tattered shawl of the deceased vagrant. Not the work of the Ripper, obviously, but the all too run-of-the-mill result of a brawl when the pubs turned out the previous night. The blood frightened the grocer. He should have sent for the constable at the start. He'd failed to report a death, tampered with the evidence at the scene of a crime, he'd got himself into terrible trouble! And he was about to get into worse.

Miss Minchin, who had recovered consciousness alone and was now doubly angry, appeared behind him. 'I'm a quality milliner! I can't have murdered bodies in my door! You'll have to help me get rid of it!'

'Why me?' he asked feebly.

'You're a man, aren't you?' demanded his neighbour witheringly. 'You can't expect a delicate female to deal with it! Think of something!'

A rumble of wheels and the clip-clop of hooves heralded the coalman's dray which turned into the street. As one, Mr Hooper and Miss Minchin moved to conceal the body in the doorway.

The coal-dray stopped and the coalman unloaded a sack and bore it into a house opposite. On the other side of the road, unlike the shops, they had no rear access and everything was carried through.

Panic and Miss Minchin's ferocious expression prompted Mr Hooper to a reckless decision. 'Take her feet!' he ordered.

Between them they lugged the body across the road, loaded it on the dray and pulled empty coalsacks over it. In the nick of time, they scurried back before the coalman came out, resumed his seat, whistled to his horse and drove unsuspectingly away.

Mr Hooper wiped his perspiring brow. 'You go home, Miss Minchin, and forget all about this!'

He went home himself and tried in vain to follow his own advice.

The coalman drove to the next street and stopped before the Rose and Crown. Coal for the public house was delivered down a chute into the cellar. The coalman opened up the trapdoor and set about completing his delivery, but when he threw the last sack on the cart he saw, sticking out, a foot . . .

He scrambled up and dragged aside the covering. 'Cripes!' he exclaimed. ''Ow did that get there? I'm not taking the blame fer this!'

He glanced furtively around, hauled the body from the dray and, with a practised hand, sent it plummeting down the coal chute into the cellar. Completely forgetting to reclose the trapdoor, he drove off as fast as the old horse could go.

* * *

Shortly afterwards, the landlord of the Rose and Crown descended with the potman to breach today's casks in the cellar. The larger pavement flaps for admitting barrels were closed but light flooded in through the small trapdoor in the corner above the coal heap.

'You'd better nip up and close that!' said the landlord. 'Before someone falls through!'

'Look!' gasped the potman. 'Someone 'as!'

They edged cautiously towards the body. 'Poor old girl, broke her neck!' gulped the landlord. 'If the brewery hears about this— Listen! You've got to fetch them three dozen pies from old Hooper's. There's an alley behind those shops. We'll put the poor soul in the barrow, cover her over, you wheel her round and dump her in the alley, fetch the pies and come back!'

The potman trudged, trundling his grisly burden, to the alley behind the shops as he was bid. But when he came to tip it out, it occurred to him that it was covered with coaldust and this might lead to its being traced back to the cellar of the Rose and Crown. The door to one of the backyards was ajar. The potman peeped in – yes, a coalshed! He quickly transferred the body to the shed, without bothering to discover behind which shop he was, and beat a hasty retreat much pleased with his deception. Later that morning, PC Collins, on his beat, put his head into Mr Hooper's shop as he regularly did and asked cheerily, 'Morning, Mr H! Everything in order?'

This query was the regular preamble to an invitation to a cup of tea in the back room.

Mr Hooper dropped the packet of sugar he was filling. 'Good – good morning, officer!'

'Chilly today!' observed PC Collins, coming further in and slapping his reddened hands. 'You all right, Mr H? You look a bit pale!'

'Got a cold,' mumbled Mr Hooper, backing away and clasping the sugar packet to his bosom. 'Come on last night.'

'What you need,' said the policeman, 'is a cup of hot tea!'

Mr Hooper pulled himself together. It was only old Collins for his morning cuppa. When he first saw him, he'd almost thought that Minchin female . . . *Act natural!* he ordered himself sternly.

'Quite right, constable!' he agreed in a high-pitched voice. 'Please come through . . .'

PC Collins seated himself in the back room, took off his helmet and unbuttoned his stiff collar while Mr Hooper nervously made tea.

'If you don't mind a personal remark, Mr H – you've got a smear of coaldust on your forehead!'

The tin kettle clattered on the range. Mr Hooper giggled hysterically and rubbed his brow. 'I must finish bagging up – here's your tea! Make yourself at home!' he stammered and bolted back to his shop. He couldn't sit and share a pot of tea under the eye of the policeman. His nerves were all to pieces.

PC Collins finished his tea alone and decided to avail himself of his friend's backyard convenience before setting off again. As he emerged from the whitewashed privy, he saw that the coalshed door was open. Tidily he went to close it – and just chanced to glance in.

Mr Hooper had just finished transforming the loose sugar to a line of neat blue packets when PC Collins appeared in the full majesty of the law.

'There's a dead body in your coalshed, sir!'

'There can't be!' gasped Mr Hooper. 'We got rid of it!'

'Ho!' said the policeman. 'Then I'll have to ask you for an explanation! I observed earlier that you had coaldust on your forehead and you was acting very unlike your usual self!'

'I only wanted to oblige Miss Minchin!' squeaked Mr Hooper, terrifed. 'It was in her doorway. We hid it on the coalcart!'

PC Collins looked perplexed. 'We'll see if the lady confirms that . . .' he decided.

Miss Minchin, immaculate and cool as a cucumber, was artistically arranging a feathered creation on a stand. Appealed to, she stared at them with mild surprise.

'I'm sure I don't know what you're talking about. There was no body in my doorway!'

PC Collins took out his notebook.

'Yes, there was!' yelled Mr Hooper. 'I put it—' He broke off but too late. Miss Minchin gave him a rapier glare of comprehension.

'Listen here!' hissed Mr Hooper desperately. 'He's going to make out I done her in! I know I told you to forget all about it – and I'm sorry for putting it in your doorway – but you can't not back me up NOW!'

'I might remember,' said Miss Minchin in a low serene voice. 'If circumstances were right.'

'Whatdyamean?' croaked Mr Hooper.

She waggled her left hand in its lace mitten under his nose. 'Well, Arthur . . . I've often thought that you being a single gentleman and me a single lady, living next door to each other all these years and both in the business line with a little put by – we ought to think of making it more permanent . . .'

'Marry you?' squawked Mr Hooper. 'I refuse!'

Miss Minchin smiled coyly but with a glacial glint in her eye. She glanced to where PC Collins licked a pencil stub and prepared to record details of a heinous crime encountered in the course of his duties.

'You do have a choice, Arthur . . . But you'll have to make up your mind quickly!'

Troubles Go in Threes

A five-part serial featuring crime writer Emma King

Part One

'It's a pity you set fire to your kitchen, Em,' Damian observed with the candour of fourteen years of age.

'I didn't set fire to it!' his aunt denied vigorously. 'For the umpteenth time, Damian, it was an electrical fault. It's an old house and we had to get the rewiring done. Something got into a muddle before it was finished. Don't ask me how. Matt's sorting it out with the builders.'

All the same, it wasn't an auspicious beginning to a brand new marriage. She and Matt had forgone a honeymoon. They'd spent the money saved on a deposit for the early-Victorian terraced cottage with grand ideas on restoring it. Or she had had grand ideas, Emma thought ruefully. Matt had always been more cautious about the project. But being a CID inspector, he was by nature cautious. She, being a writer of crime fiction, was by nature both artistic and adventurous – or so she had declared to him when describing her plans for the house.

It had all just been beginning to take shape, with Matt more or less won over, when the fire had occurred. It had ruined the recently installed fitted units, the cooker, dishwasher and, for good measure, a large area of the newly tiled floor.

'Never mind!' Emma said resolutely now to Damian. 'We'll be in Pitlochry soon.'

As the Kings had had no honeymoon, the holiday was meant to be special. Nothing was going to spoil it. Not even the memory of the wrecked kitchen! Not even the added nuisance that, at the last minute, Matt had been delayed by work. He'd follow on by train as soon as possible and had insisted they set off without him. He'd even entrusted his brand new car, his pride and joy, to her care. Emma was uncomfortably aware of the Awful Responsibility, but to have undertaken the journey in her own aged vehicle had been out of the question.

Taking Emma's fourteen-year-old nephew along might seem unusual to some. But Emma had cared for Damian in school holidays for some years, despite being a young aunt, still only twenty-eight. His parents worked overseas and he'd been at boarding school from a young age. Matt and Damian got along well and Matt understood Emma's committment to her nephew.

If an objection had arisen it had been from Damian himself, who showed an unexpected lack of enthusiasm for the trip. Emma had been puzzled and frankly hurt, but Matt had supplied the answer.

'He's growing up!' he said. 'Last year he was a kid. Now he's a young man.'

Emma could certainly see changes for herself. Damian had shot up two inches and didn't know what to do with his suddenly acquired height and gangling limbs. His voice was breaking. He was battling against unwelcome spots on the chin. Most of all, as Matt had shrewdly hinted, Damian wanted his freedom.

In one way, boarding school had encouraged him to be

independent. But in another way, being obliged to live by a set of rules had been irksome. All teenagers rebel, she realised. But Damian seemed set to make a point of it. From sunny natured he'd turned alarmingly obstreperous. For the first time, her invitation to come on holiday had been greeted not with a cheer of delight, but a scowl, a shuffling of the feet and a 'What're we going to do when we get there?' His old curiosity and sense of adventure seemed to have quite disappeared. He'd spent almost the entire journey buried in a computer magazine and when not doing that, punching at a hand-held computer game which let out a particularly irritating buzz when points were scored. It was Emma's hope that the thing's batteries went flat before they got to the hotel.

He produced it now and its electronic voice pierced the air.

'I've got to do something!' Damian said plaintively, aware of the despairing glance she gave him.

'There'll be plenty to do in Scotland!' she assured him.

The computer game buzzed in a disgruntled way as if Damian spoke through it.

'Look at the view!' Emma encouraged. 'Isn't it grand?'

The road swirled round, hugging the rising ground to their right. It was a golden evening. The surrounding hillsides, mauve and green, seemed to glow in the slowly setting sun. Ahead of them lay a wonderful time, walking, eating, doing nothing.

'Oh, ye'll tak' the high road . . .' carolled Emma cheerfully.

Damian raised his eyes heavenwards, put away the game, but opened up his computer magazine and, to his aunt's disgust, ignored the scenery to concentrate on that.

* * *

The hotel car park was nearly full. Emma's heart sank a little. Though a competent driver, manoeuvring Matt's car into tight spaces always made her nervous. She peered through the windscreen.

'Perhaps you'd better get out and direct me back, Damian.'

Damian scrambled out and Emma began to reverse cautiously, mindful of his signals.

Without warning there was a horrid clunk and something struck the door on the passenger side. She heard Damian yell 'Oy!' and slammed on the brakes.

She hadn't noticed that a driver had been sitting in the large, powerful car parked to her left. He had opened his door with no regard for Emma manoeuvring alongside him and it had struck the side of Matt's car.

Her heart in her mouth, Emma jumped out. Damian ran up and the three of them converged on the point of impact to survey the damage.

Emma's, that was to say, Matt's car had come off worse with a long scratch on the paintwork.

Emma swung round, her mouth opening in angry accusation. The man towered over her, an impressive even formidable figure. Tall and bulky, he had bushy eyebrows and a heavy jaw in a florid face.

Before she could speak, he demanded, 'Why don't you look what you're doing, young woman?'

She gasped. Not only the sheer injustice of it was breathtaking, but being addressed as 'young woman' in that superior way did nothing to help.

'Me?' she squawked. 'What about you? Didn't you see I was backing in there?'

'You shouldn't have been!' His voice boomed round the car park. 'There isn't room!'

'Yes, there is!' interrupted Damian sturdily. 'I could see clear space either side of Em's car! You weren't paying attention when you opened your door. It's your fault.'

'When I want your opinion, boy, I'll ask for it!' As Damian flushed beetroot, the man turned his attention back to Emma.

But she'd had time to regain her composure. Emma drew herself up to her full five feet four, tossed back her long brown hair, and stared straight up at the angry face glowering down at her.

'As far as I can see, there is no damage to your car. Mine is badly scratched! I'd be grateful for your name and address!'

'Would you, indeed? I've no intention of suffering any inconvenience over such a trivial matter. Buy yourself one of those little tubes of carpaint.'

'Damian,' Emma requested, 'write down his licence number, please.'

'Right!' Damian hunted through his pockets and finally produced a stub of pencil and a shop till receipt. He ostentatiously copied out the offending car's registration, watched with near apoplectic fury by its owner.

'I am Emma King,' said Emma. She'd nearly said 'Emma Durrant', as she wasn't yet used to having gained another surname. 'I'm staying at this hotel. Your refusal to give me your name has been noted.'

'My name is Lawrence Sherwood, staying at the hotel.' An amused look entered his eyes. 'I must say, you have nerve, Mrs King.'

'We've also got a witness!' said Damian.

He indicated a car parked almost opposite across the intervening entrance lane. Someone was sitting in it and appeared to have been watching. But even as Damian pointed, the car started up and drove out with a screech of tyres.

The florid man said sarcastically, 'You mean, you *had* a witness!'

He didn't wait for a reply but turned and strode towards the hotel entrance.

'Matt's car . . .' said Emma dolefully, running her finger along the scratch. 'He'll go crazy. He'll divorce me. It'll be one of the briefest marriages on record.'

'That guy had a bloomin' cheek!' raged Damian. 'It was his fault entirely! Matt will understand.' He didn't sound entirely convinced. 'Troubles go in threes, Mum says. First the kitchen, now this, I wonder what next?' He eyed Emma with a kind of hope.

'Don't depress me any more!' Emma shook a finger at him. 'I'm tired. I need a cup of tea, a bath and a really good dinner!'

The hotel was an old building that had been extended at more than one period. Upstairs it was a rabbit warren of corridors with staircases and fire doors appearing where least expected and a plethora of signs to help bewildered guests.

Damian's room was next to the one assigned to the Kings on a spur corridor off a main one that ran from the lift. In this spur were only three rooms. At the end, fire doors blocked the way. Beyond them, stairs ran both upwards and down to the ground floor. There was a deserted feeling about this nook as if no one outside the occupants of the three rooms used it. With a lift around the corner, there would be little need to make for the staircase except in an emergency.

The first thing Emma did was try to ring Matt to announce their safe arrival. But he was still at work and 'in a meeting'. She put the phone down, both disappointed and relieved. He wasn't going to be happy about the damage to the car. She had been looking forward to Matt joining her at the first opportunity. Now she dreaded it. It wasn't that she'd married a monster. It was that one man and his prized new car had a bond between them which even a new wife found it hard to break.

'Though it wasn't my fault!' she said aloud.

The room had tea-making equipment. Emma filled the electric kettle and began to run the bath, unpacking her clothes while the kettle hissed and water splashed into the tub.

Soaking in the bathtub, she felt stress fade and pleasant thoughts of dinner replace it. She stretched out and wiggled her toes.

There was a loud rat-tat on a door. Emma sat up with a start, spilling water over the side. Who could that be? Not Damian, she was sure, since they'd arranged to meet up at seven to go down to dinner.

She heard a murmur of voices and realised that the sound had come not from her door, but from that of the next room, the one which stood by the fire doors at the head of the stairs.

She supposed that the rooms shared a general layout. On entering hers, the bathroom was to the right and the clothes closet to the left. Thus her bathroom wall backed next door's closet. But that closet must be open and her wall, she now noticed, lacked a patch of tiles. As a result, she could hear quite clearly, especially when the voices next door were raised, apparently in some anger.

Her first instinct was to burst into a few notes of song to let whoever it was know someone was at hand. But then she heard a familiar voice.

'How dare you pester me here?'

Lawrence Sherwood. And even angrier than he'd been earlier in the car park.

Another voice, younger and also male, protested, 'You owe it to me at least to listen!'

'I owe you nothing!' Sherwood's voice dripped sarcasm. 'Isn't it the other way around?'

'I've told you. I won't let you down. If you'd be reasonable . . .'

Sherwood broke in. 'I've been as reasonable as anyone could be expected to be. As for not letting me down, I'll make sure you don't. Now get out!'

There was a brief silence. Emma lay rigid in the cooling water, not daring to splash and call attention to herself. They would guess she'd overheard.

'I won't forget this!' The strange voice cried out with such passion that she felt a spurt of alarm. 'I warn you, Sherwood, you'll be sorry! I won't let you do it! I'll do anything I have to do to stop you!'

A door slammed. Emma waited, straining her ears, but no footsteps hurried past her room. Sherwood's visitor must have gone through the fire doors and down the stairs.

After a moment she heard the faint sound of a television next door. She let out pent-up breath. It was sheer bad luck they'd been given rooms next to Sherwood's. They must be extra careful to keep out of his way.

It would seem she and Damian were not the only ones at odds with Sherwood! The writer in Emma began to speculate about the snippet of overheard quarrel, reworking and dissecting it, wondering if here was a plot for a new novel.

At this point Matt's image materialised in the bathroom steam to warn, 'You don't know what that was about, Emma! A few harsh words spoken in anger are no basis for a reasoned judgement!'

'All right,' said Emma. 'I won't tell anyone about it!' Then she added to the image, 'But you don't have to be so smug!'

In the restaurant, Damian cheered up considerably. 'I hope they've got some vegetarian grub for you, Em, or you'll starve.'

'I did ask when I booked. They assured me that every evening the menu has at least one vegetarian dish. Here we are, spicy Indonesian fried rice with nuts and vegetables. That sounds nice. That's for me!'

'I'll have . . .' Damian's eyes ran lovingly over the menu. 'Either the chicken or the lamb steak. Gosh, this is better than the muck we get at school!'

'Is it that bad?' she asked sympathetically. His well-scrubbed features were topped with damp spikes of hair. Emma reflected that, thankfully, Damian was at least not going through that phase which makes a cult of grubbiness.

He was also an honest youth. 'It's all right provided you like mince.' He put down the menu with an expression of horror that replaced that of anticipation. 'Em! It's that thug who bashed Matt's car!'

'Sherwood?' She tried to glance nonchalantly over her shoulder.

Sherwood was seated alone in a far corner, studying the menu. As she watched, a waiter approached with a tray and set a bottle of mineral water on the table before him. Sherwood acknowledged it with a nod.

That surprised her. She would have put Sherwood down as a fine-wines man. But it seemed he wasn't a drinker.

'Just take no notice, Damian,' she murmured and turned her head back before Sherwood should look across and see her.

It was at that moment that she experienced an odd sensation of being watched.

Emma looked quickly towards the entrance to the dining room. People were arriving in numbers now and there was some jostling. In the small crowd Emma fleetingly caught sight of someone – she thought a slim male figure – turn back, as if he'd changed his mind about dining. It was more of an impression than a clear view. What had taken her eye was the suddenness with which the figure had turned on its heel. The group in the doorway dispersed. A brief glimpse of the corridor beyond showed it to be empty.

'What's up?' asked Damian. 'Is there a problem?'

'Emma!' warned Matt's voice, ever awkward, in her head.

'Only my imagination refusing to take a holiday!' she said.

After a good meal, and the long drive earlier that day, Emma was ready for an early night. Not so Damian. With the resilence of youth, he announced he would go for a walk round the town before turning in.

'Stay in the centre and don't be late back!' she warned him.

'I know!' he returned tetchily and stomped off, offended.

Emma thought crossly that having to call up all her diplomatic skills, just to deal with a fourteen-year-old, was going to be a real pain at this rate. But he was generally a trustworthy boy and sensible. She could only leave it at that.

She took the lift to the first floor. The doors opened silently onto a world in which there was no noise apart from a muffled television. Everyone was still at dinner or in the bar – or perhaps taking an evening constitutional as was Damian. The thick carpet silenced her footsteps as she made her way to her room.

Emma approached the turn into the corridor in which the three adjacent rooms lay. As she did, she heard a loud click.

Almost immediately, as she turned into the spur itself, a warm draught caressed her face. The fire doors that closed the exit at the further end swung awkwardly, creaking in protest. As she watched, the movement slowed and ceased.

Emma walked down the spur towards her room and paused mid-way. The fire doors merely swung back and forth without latching, so the loud click she'd heard had surely been that of a room door closing? But which one? All three occupants had been down in the dining room for the past hour. Damian had now gone out of the hotel and Sherwood, as far as she knew, was still downstairs, finishing his meal.

He might, of course, have left the dining room immediately after her and walked up the staircase. But surely he couldn't have done that faster than her route by lift?

An uneasy tingle ran along her spine. She felt something of the same sensation she'd earlier experienced in the dining room. Someone had been here, moments before her. The impression of another living presence was imprinted on the atmosphere, like a design stamped into wet sand. As she stood there, the feeling was eroding, slipping away, its sharp edges already gone and only a fuzziness left. In a few seconds there'd be nothing, only a memory of swinging fire doors.

Emma pushed open the fire doors and stepped out onto the landing beyond. From below came the faint sounds of a busy hotel. From above, nothing. No one was on either staircase.

Emma went back to her own room, forcing the puzzle out of her mind. She had something more important to do. She picked up the phone and asked for a second time to put through an outside call.

'I was about to ring the hotel!' came Matt's voice down the line. 'Why didn't you let me know you'd arrived? I thought you'd had some sort of mishap!'

'I tried earlier, but they said you were busy. We had a perfect journey!'

Yes, she thought, *until we got here!* But unwelcome news could always wait.

'The weather's beautiful!' chirped Emma. 'And the hotel is excellent!'

Not for nothing was Matt a detective. 'Emma! What are you up to? What's happened?'

'Nothing. I'm just about to make a cuppa and then go to bed.' A sigh. 'I miss you.'

Matt's voice mellowed. 'I know, sweetheart. I'm trying to hurry things along at this end.'

'When will you be joining us?'

'Within the next forty-eight hours. It's almost all clear here.' A pause. 'Emma? You are sure nothing's happened?'

'Not a thing!' said his wife firmly. 'Goodnight, darling!' And she put down the phone before he could ask any more questions.

As soon as she did, the puzzle of the swinging fire doors came back to tease her mind.

'A mystery!' said Emma aloud, picking up a teabag and dropping it into the pot. 'And mysteries are my speciality!'

It was probably imagination and not telepathy, but Matt's voice echoed in her head. 'Emma! Leave it alone!'

'We'll see,' said Emma.

The sun shone brightly through the window to awaken Emma the next morning. She dressed quickly and rapped on Damian's door as she passed.

Despite this, she breakfasted alone. She didn't know what time he'd returned the previous evening, but had no intention of letting him be a lie-abed this holiday. There was, she knew, a tendency amongst teenagers to live by a different clock to everyone else. Left to their own devices, they stayed in bed till noon, and then proceeded to stay up half the night to compensate.

Emma collected a handful of tourist leaflets from reception before rousing Damian by the simple expedient of picking up the phone and making an internal call. He might ignore the knock on the door. But no teenager she'd ever met could resist the telephone.

'Be ready in ten minutes!' she ordered the sleepy voice that answered. Then she replaced the receiver as a wail of 'Em!' echoed down the line.

It wasn't ten minutes, it was more like an hour, but still reasonably early as they set out. Damian had just managed to make the tail end of breakfast.

'How far are we going?' he asked dismally, trailing behind

Emma as she marched briskly down the hill towards the dam and loch.

'To the Fish Ladder. It's for the salmon. A sort of ascending chain of tanks, so they can get past the dam and power station. There's an observation chamber so you can actually watch the fish swim by. We'll start there and then perhaps we can walk right round Loch Faskally. Or we could walk through the woods up to Killicrankie. The Scots ambushed the English there during the first Jacobite rising. I expect you learned about it in history.'

The writer in Emma took over. 'Just imagine, as we climb through the woods, we'll be in the footsteps of the English Redcoats, gripping their muskets and looking all about them, fearful of the men of Atholl, lying in ambush! We'll see the Soldier's Leap, where a fleeing Englishman tried to leap the river across the rocks, rather than fall into the hands of the Highlanders!'

History, it seemed, wasn't taught the way it used to be. Emma had always been fascinated by the conflict of loyalties, the brutality, heroism and heart-rending romance of the Jacobite drama.

Damian murmured, 'I wish I'd brought my game or my mag!'

Exasperated, she snapped, 'You can't walk and read or fiddle with that wretched computer game!'

She saw his mouth set obstinately. Confrontation was no way to deal with a difficult teenager, she realised. Computer games and magazines were of little interest to her, but were genuinely of deep interest to Damian. One ought, so all the theorists opined, to try to share a child's interests. But only a saintly dispostion could put up with that little gadget bleeping and buzzing constantly in the background. As for bringing it on a walk in some of the most beautiful countryside in Britain . . .

305

She tried distraction. 'Look at the lovely scenery! Breathe in the air!' She drew a deep breath. 'Wonderful!' She expelled the breath and peered at him. 'What time did you get back to the hotel last night?'

'Not late!' They locked gazes. 'There were dozens of people still about!' Damian insisted. 'In fact, I nearly got sent flying by a guy who rushed out of the hotel and down the steps, just as I was coming in. He went haring off towards the car park. Not a word of apology!' he added in injured tones.

'Well, what time did you go to bed, then?'

'I got into bed early! Straight away!' A pause. 'I watched a late-night film on the telly. Honestly, Em! I'm supposed to be on holiday! I wasn't expecting to be taken on a cadet corps march!'

'You – will – enjoy – it!' said his aunt through gritted teeth.

After the salmon ladder and observation chamber, both fascinating although they weren't actually able to catch sight of any fish, they set out to walk round Loch Faskally, leaving the climb to Killiecrankie until Matt should be able to come with them.

It was now lunchtime and the sun stood high in the sky, sparkling off the loch's waters. But beneath the trees it was cool, shady, and perhaps because of the time of day, they had this idyllic spot to themselves. They had come provided with an orange each and a packet of oatcakes, so didn't fear hunger. Their situation had at last succeeded in almost winning round Damian. He didn't actually admit to enjoying it, but he stopped grumbling and even came up with an idea for a visit.

'To one of the whisky distilleries. They've got two in Pitlochry.'

'You're too young to drink whisky.'

'It would be interesting to see how it's made,' he said craftily. 'And I've heard they give you a free sample.'

It was teatime when, footsore and weary, they returned to the hotel.

'Oh, for a nice cup of tea!' said Emma.

'There's something going on,' Damian observed.

She followed the direction of his pointing hand. There was a police car parked before the hotel – no, two police cars! The reception desk was deserted. A subdued but tense buzz of conversation came from the office behind. Emma rang the bell.

A flurried receptionist appeared to hand them their keys.

'What's up?' Damian asked her.

She leaned forward. 'Something unfortunate's happened to one of the guests!'

'What sort of unfortunate?' Emma was caught up in Damian's curiosity.

The girl glanced over her shoulder towards the office. 'Poor gentleman,' she said. 'He was out playing golf and he collapsed. I suppose it was his heart. Really sad, don't you think? To die on holiday.'

Someone called her from the office. She made a hurried excuse and disappeared before they could ask further.

'Wonder who it is?' Damian murmured.

'Very sad, whoever.'

Upstairs, as they left the lift, they heard voices and, turning from the main corridor into the spur, found their way barred.

A chambermaid was gesticulating wildly. The hotel manager

307

was standing in the open doorway of Sherwood's room in energetic conversation with someone within.

'Sorry, miss,' said a uniformed policeman. 'But you can't come this way.'

'What am I to do about the towels and linen?' demanded the chambermaid shrilly.

'Oh, leave it for now, Sandra!' snapped the manager. 'No one can go in until the police have finished in there.'

'That's right, miss!' said the policeman to Emma. 'You'll have to go another way round.'

'But we want to go to our rooms!' she objected.

The hotel manager, hearing her voice, turned his head. 'Oh, Mrs King! It's all right, officer. The lady and the young man have the two rooms here.'

A mop of red hair was stuck through the doorway. A young man in a crumpled jacket emerged and fixed Emma with a stern gaze.

'You have the room next to this one?'

'Yes. Is it Mr Sherwood who's died?'

He looked annoyed. 'Where did you hear that? Did you know him at all?'

'He scratched Em's car!' said Damian loudly.

The red-headed man contemplated him. 'Did he, now?'

He turned to Emma. 'I'm Sergeant Miller. Could we have a word?' He glanced at the manager and chambermaid. 'Privately, maybe?'

'We can go in my room!' Damian offered eagerly.

In the quiet of Damian's room, Emma gave details of her own and Damian's identity. Sergeant Miller wrote it all down.

308

'And you're on holiday, then, Mrs King?'

'Yes, I'm between books.' He looked up. 'I'm a writer,' she explained.

Usually this statement met with mild interest. But on the sergeant's face appeared a look of horror.

'You're not a journalist?'

'No, a crime writer. You know, um, murder.'

Sergeant Miller wiped a hand over his freckled face. 'I see. And, er, your husband, is he a writer too?'

'No,' said Emma. 'He's a CID man, like you. An inspector.'

That certainly put the cat amongst the pigeons if it wasn't there already.

Beneath his fiery thatch, Miller's face turned pale. 'Where is he, your husband?'

'In Devon at the moment. He's hoping to join us here very soon.'

Sergeant Miller folded his notebook. 'I'll tell Inspector Loomis.' He sounded apprehensive.

'It's not suspicious, is it?' Damian asked. 'Sherwood's death?'

'Why should it be that?' Miller's voice sharpened.

'People have died on holiday before and it hasn't brought the CID rushing round, taking statements and searching rooms. You were searching his room, weren't you?'

Miller glared at Damian. 'You've an awfully active imagination, laddie! What's this about an incident involving a car?'

They explained. He wrote it down – his notebook was getting quite full by now – and asked, 'Neither of you knows anything about the deceased's personal background?'

They shook their heads in unison.

'Right!' he said, jabbing his pencil at the last page of his notes. 'I must ask you not to gossip about this.'

'I don't gossip!' Emma told him coldly.

'I'm sorry. I used the wrong word. Don't mention this to anyone. Don't discuss it. Nor you, Damian. You're sure there's nothing more you can tell me about Sherwood? You didn't have any other conversation with him? See him with anyone?'

Emma fidgeted, conscious of Matt's invisible presence at her shoulder. She wondered if she ought to mention the overheard quarrel and the impression left by the swinging doors. But she'd seen nothing and the angry words might only mislead. She shook her head.

'Inspector Loomis may want a word with you sometime,' Miller informed them. 'You'll be staying at the hotel a wee while yet?'

'Poor Sherwood,' Emma said after Miller's departure. 'I can't help feeling sorry for him. I dare say he had a medical condition. I noticed he only drank mineral water at dinner.' There was a silence and then she added thoughtfully, 'I suppose it was just routine, the sergeant's questions. But he did seem alarmed that I was a writer and Matt in the CID.'

Damian leaned forward. 'You know, Em, I bet you anything you like that Sherwood was a crook!'

'Why should he be that?' she asked uneasily.

'Because that sergeant nearly went up in the air when he thought you might be a journalist! And why should his Inspector Loomis be so interested?'

'Well, I'm exhausted, what with all the fresh air, exercise and being grilled by Miller. I'm going to take a nap, Damian. Call me later if I don't wake up in time for dinner.'

She threw herself down on the bed and, despite a hundred questions racing round her mind, fell asleep.

She awoke with a start. Shadows had crept over the room. It must be about six o'clock. But it was not a subconscious alarm clock which had roused her but something else.

She sat up on the bed. Outside in the corridor was movement, a bump against the door. Someone fumbled at the handle and then there was the sound of a key turning in the lock. Hinges creaked.

Her heart in her mouth, she called, 'Damian? Is that you?'

'No,' Matt King said, coming into the room and dropping his holdall on the floor, 'it's me! Against all the odds, I got away . . .'

His voice died away and his expression, full of delight at having been able to spring this surprise, changed to puzzled. 'Emma? You look as if you've seen a ghost!'

Emma snapped out of her momentary shock and flung herself at him. Hugging him tightly, she exclaimed, 'Oh, Matt! I'm so pleased to see you!'

No man could be impervious to such a greeting from a pretty young wife. Matt certainly wasn't and responded in like manner.

Nevertheless, some minutes later, he asked, 'Emma! What's going on? Don't try and put me off. I know when you're hiding something! I could tell from your voice over the phone. Just now when I came in, consternation was written all over you! Come on, the truth!'

'I don't know.' She met his quizzical gaze. 'Honestly, Matt. Sergeant Miller wasn't telling.'

'Who's Sergeant Miller?' Into Matt's blue eyes came something very like panic. 'What have you been doing, Em?'

Emma sighed. 'Look, sit down. You must be tired. I'll make us some tea and tell you all about it.'

'You do that,' said Matt. 'Let's hear the worst!'

Emma decided to start at the beginning and that meant the incident in the car park.

'You see, I was backing the car into this narrow space . . .'

The panic in her husband's face increased. 'The car?'

'Yes, it's all right, it's only a little scratch . . .'

'My car!' He leapt up, clutching his dark hair. 'You scratched my car?'

'No! Not me, I didn't do it. Sherwood did.'

'Who is Sherwood?' howled Matt. 'Emma, who are all these people? What on earth has been going on? Can't I leave you alone for five minutes?' Words failed him. He slumped back in the chair. 'Go on!'

'Sherwood damaged your car. He had the room next to this one. But he died today, out on the golf course apparently. But Damian and I think there may have been foul play.'

He was looking sceptical. 'Emma, we've been through this sort of thing before. You know, your imagination—'

'It's not imagination. Sherwood had a quarrel.' Emma told him about the angry words overheard from the bathroom and, for good measure, about the swinging fire doors.

Matt rested his head in his hands. 'I knew it! I knew you'd get into trouble! Honestly, Emma, you seem to attract this sort of disaster. You've only been here twenty-four hours!'

'That's not fair!' she protested indignantly.

Matt growled. 'So this Miller is on the local force?'

'Yes, but I think,' said Emma tentatively, 'that he's going to be replaced by Inspector Loomis.'

Matt said in despair, 'I thought I was going on holiday!'

Inspector Loomis turned up that evening after dinner. He was a dour-looking man with iron-grey hair cut very short and eyes which Emma immediately decided could see through steel panels.

'Ah, I'm pleased to see you've arrived, King!' he said, shaking Matt's hand. 'My sergeant told me you were expected.'

Matt had recovered his composure to some extent. Not entirely, because he'd been out to inspect the damaged door panel on the car. But he managed to return Loomis's greeting affably.

'My wife's told me what happened. There are just a couple of things she perhaps ought to have mentioned to your sergeant.'

'Oh, aye . . .' Inspector Loomis cast a jaundiced glance at Emma. 'Are there now?'

'Emma!' Matt prompted.

Emma repeated her tale of the quarrel and the fire doors. 'I didn't tell the sergeant because I didn't want to mislead anyone.'

'Don't worry your head about that,' said Inspector Loomis. 'We're pretty well able to judge information for what it's worth.'

Matt, seeing that the equivalent of a verbal volcanic eruption was about to explode from Emma, said hastily, 'My wife's told you everything now.'

'Let's hope so!' said the inspector with a meaningful look.

'I have!' said Emma crossly. 'I don't know anything more about Sherwood. But I'd like to!' she added frankly.

'Emma!' muttered her husband.

But unexpectedly, Inspector Loomis was nodding. 'In view of the circumstances, I feel there's need for a certain amount of explanation. Your being in the force yourself, King, means I hope I can rely on your discretion and that of your wife here. And the boy!' he added. 'Not that it's necessary to tell the lad what I'm about to tell you.'

He didn't know Damian! thought Emma.

'The deceased gentleman, Lawrence Sherwood, was a businessman with various interests. All of them are legal, but, shall we say, in areas which sometimes attract a shady sort of interest. He owned a number of gambling clubs and – er – other sorts of clubs.'

Loomis cast a slightly embarrassed look at Emma who was showing close interest.

'Any form?' Matt asked.

Loomis's expression became, if possible, more dour. 'No convictions himself. Kept his hands very clean. Never got caught, at any rate. But he had some very unsavoury acquaintances. It was whispered on the underworld grapevine that he was behind certain incidents. Naturally, when such a man turns up dead, we're interested.'

'No idea yet as to cause of death?' Emma realised Matt was getting curious. Her spirits rose.

'A heart attack, maybe?' Loomis hesitated. 'The pathologist is carrying out tests. It's early days yet.'

'Tests?' Emma seized on the words and also on a certain shiftiness which she fancied she could detect in the inspector's manner. 'Do you think there may be a question of foul play?'

Matt said quickly, 'My wife writes crime fiction. She's apt to look for sinister motives in everything.'

'No, I'm not!' said Emma indignantly. 'It's a fair question. Sherwood wasn't just anyone, the normal sort of visitor.'

'No, indeed he wasn't,' Loomis agreed. He spoiled this by adding, 'Fortunately, Mrs King, we in the police force do not leap to conclusions as quickly as it seems writers of fictional crime do! The tests are merely routine.'

He ignored the sizzling reaction this remark threatened to provoke and turned to Matt. 'I hope I don't need to stress that it is our affair. You, King, are on holiday. This is not, in any case, your patch. Your wife may be hopeful of a lurid case about to break here, but I hope you won't be tempted . . .'

'Of course not!' Matt sounded annoyed. 'It would be highly improper of me!'

'I'm glad you appreciate the fact! As for you, Mrs King!' Loomis's steely gaze fixed on Emma. 'This is not a fictional matter. Leave it to the professionals!'

Matt said sharply, 'My wife understands that!'

'Good.' Loomis rose to his feet. 'I hope you enjoy your holiday, all three of you. Goodnight!'

'That man,' said Emma furiously when Loomis had left, 'makes me want to run out and do everything he's told me not to!'

'As if I don't know how to conduct myself in another force's area!' fumed Matt. 'I have to agree Loomis isn't the most tactful of men!'

He turned to Emma. 'But he's right that it's his affair. I won't interfere and you won't! Just as I told Loomis. I know you fancy sleuthing around but it could be very embarrassing if Loomis found out! Just think about me, will you? And my reputation.'

'Oh, don't be so pompous!' said his loving wife. 'I suppose I can be allowed a normal interest in things, can't I?'

Matt put his arms round her. 'Emma, do you think you could forget crime, real or imaginary, for a while and take a perfectly normal interest in something else – like us?'

That was a much more attractive prospect, and Emma was happy to comply.

Matt was still asleep when Emma awoke the next morning. She leaned over him and called his name softly. He stirred and mumbled but didn't open his eyes.

Emma slipped out of bed and into the shower. Dressing quickly, she let herself out of the room.

Early mornings in hotels tended to be always the same. The sound of many baths being run. Of people scurrying towards the breakfast room. The luggage of those wanting to make an early departure already stacked in the corridor. Chambermaids working with brisk efficiency. She tapped at Damian's door. No reply. Another one who slept in.

'Good morning!'

Emma turned. It was the chambermaid she'd seen before, outside Sherwood's room when the police had been here. Now the girl was pushing along a laundry basket.

'They say I can clear out the poor gentleman's room.' The girl was obviously chatty. She rattled a bunch of keys and unlocked Sherwood's door. 'It gave me a terrible turn to hear about it!'

Emma nonchalantly followed her inside. 'Sandra, isn't it? It gave me a dreadful shock, too. I'd exchanged a few words with him earlier.'

Sandra was suitably sympathetic. 'Were you able to sleep last night? Why don't you ask them to give you a different room, well away from here? I find it bad enough being in here, clearing up. But there you are. Once I've stripped the place and made up the bed with clean linen and all the rest, it will just be a hotel room, like all the others.'

Nodding at this reference to the anonymous nature of hotel rooms, Emma glanced round. 'The police have taken his personal effects?'

'Oh, aye.' The girl rolled the sheets into a bundle and dropped them into the laundry basket. She moved towards the dressing table and the little stand that held the electric kettle and other tea-making facilities and uttered a 'Tsk!' of annoyance.

'What is it?' Emma asked.

The chambermaid turned to her. 'You'd never believe the things people, the guests you know, take. I mean, don't think I'm being personal! Of course *you* wouldn't. But some – you wouldn't think, would you, that anyone would take an ordinary cheap pottery cup and saucer or a tin teapot?' She pointed at the empty tray where these items were conspiciously missing.

Emma stared at it. 'All the teabags and coffee and sugar sachets have gone too.'

'I'm not bothered about those!' The girl shrugged. 'People reckon they've paid for them, and the toiletries from the bathroom, so they take them when they check out. But crockery is different.'

'But Sherwood didn't check out, he—' Emma broke off.

Sandra was still staring moodily at the tray. 'They took one cup and left one. Barmy. Who'd want things like that? I'll have to tell the housekeeper.'

'Emma!' Matt hove into view, radiating suspicion. 'What are you doing in there?'

Emma smiled at the chambermaid and met her husband's eye innocently. 'Just looking. Honestly! There's a single cup, saucer and a teapot missing from Sherwood's room.'

'So what? They're in there somewhere. The girl hasn't looked properly. Come on, breakfast! Damian can join us later when he surfaces. I've knocked on his door.'

Matt gripped his protesting wife by the elbow and marched her down the corridor.

'All right!' she said as she wriggled free. 'You haven't just put me under arrest, you know!'

'Perhaps I should!' he told her. 'At least I'd be sure what you were up to! This isn't our affair. We – me, you, Damian, all three of us – will take no further part in it!'

But Matt was wrong.

Part Two

Unsurprisingly, Damian didn't join them at breakfast. They met him as they returned upstairs, emerging sleepy eyed from his room.

'Congratulations!' said his aunt. 'You've got half an hour! We're going to Aberfeldy today.'

Damian mumbled a reply and set off towards the lift. The hotel's morning cleaning routine was in full swing. Sandra, the chambermaid, appeared and asked, 'I'll clear up in the young man's room now, if that's all right?' She unlocked the door and disappeared inside.

'How is Damian, by the way?' Matt asked, when they regained their own room. 'I didn't get around to asking you yesterday, what with one thing and another.' He grinned and gave a playful tug to the single long braid of hair which hung down her back.

'Damian?' Emma gave an exasperated hiss and jammed her hands in her pockets. 'I just don't understand him. He was always so interested in new places. Yesterday he moaned nearly the whole time because he didn't have that wretched computer game with him.'

Matt laughed and squeezed his wife's shoulders. He looked down at her disconsolate face. The fat plait of light brown hair, her slim form, turquoise T-shirt and jeans gave her the appearance of being hardly more than a schoolgirl herself.

'Listen, love,' he said. 'If the boy doesn't want to come with us, but prefers to go off on his own, let him. He's got his head screwed on the right way and won't come to any harm. Or if he wants to sit in his room and read magazines, why not leave him to it? He won't be happy if we force him to do things he doesn't want to do, and he'll ruin the day for us.'

A tendril of hair escaped and floated before Emma's nose. She pursed her lips and directed a puff of breath towards the errant wisp. Matt chuckled again, stooped and kissed her.

She took her hands from her pockets and locked her arms round his waist. 'You don't mind his being with us?' Her eyes clouded with a momentary doubt.

The laughter lines around her husband's eyes crinkled. 'Do you know, Mrs King, you have a face which mirrors every thought in your head? I swear you'd be no good as a crook and a rotten poker player! But it is one reason I love you.'

Emma tilted her head. 'And the others?'

'Saving them up to tell you later!' He tapped the end of her nose with his finger. 'Of course I don't mind Damian coming along. He's a great chap.'

He was rewarded with a beaming smile. 'I'm so pleased you think that. I've always looked after him in the holidays. Bridget, his mum, knows he's all right because he's with me.'

'He's fine, Em. Just give him space. I remember being that age, persecuted by well-meaning adults!'

'I don't persecute him!' Indignation filled his wife's face, which flushed a rosy pink.

'Well, chivvy him, then!' Matt hastily amended his words. 'It's all right up to a point. But if he wants to spend the morning doing his own thing, let him. That's all I'm saying. After a day on his own, he'll get bored and be only too pleased to join us on our next trip.'

Emma was looking only partly convinced by this proposed strategy. 'Do you know, he really only perked up yesterday and was like his old self, when we found the police in Sherwood's room and Sergeant Miller interviewed us!'

A faint frown puckered Matt's dark eyebrows. 'I don't want Damian to get under Miller's feet, and even less bothering Inspector Loomis.'

'You see? It's not so simple, leaving him to his own devices!' Emma allowed herself a note of triumph. 'Going off for the day and leaving him here, there's no knowing what he might get up to! It's only natural he's interested in what happened to Sherwood. The man was a shady character, as we now know!'

A faraway look entered her eyes. She ran the tip of her tongue over her upper lip.

'Don't do that!' Matt whispered into her ear. 'Not just as we're about to go out for the day! It gives me ideas about abandoning any plans to leave this room!'

Romance, he ruefully discovered, was far from her mind.

'Sorry . . .' she murmured absently. 'Matt, Loomis hinted to us that Sherwood's death could be suspicious. Supposing it turns out to be murder? The more I think about it—'

'Hey!' Matt, alarmed, recognised the signs that Emma's mind had set out along a track from which it would be difficult to deflect it. 'We agreed, you'd leave it alone! This isn't the plot of one of your books! In real life, meddling can have embarrassing if not dangerous results. Remember, curiosity killed the cat!'

'That's rich,' she challenged, 'coming from a policeman.'

'A policeman on holiday! Just keep that in mind, will you? And you're a writer on holiday. Now then, where's that map?'

They were still poring over the roadmap a little later, when a familiar voice was heard protesting in the corridor outside the room.

'Damian's back,' Emma observed. 'But what on earth is the matter?'

Another voice answered Damian's, a woman's. Footsteps retreated rapidly. Emma looked out. Sandra was outside, holding an empty wasterpaper basket.

The chambermaid pulled a comic-apologetic face at Emma. 'I'm sorry, but I seem to have put out the young man's magazine, by mistake. It was in the bin here.' She raised the empty receptacle in demonstration. 'He says he didn't throw it away, so I can only think it slipped off the table and landed in the bin. I wasn't to know. I tipped this bin in the rubbish sack with all the others.'

'Where's Damian gone?' Emma asked.

'To see if he can rescue it.' Sandra hunched her shoulders. 'I'm afraid the bag may have been taken away by now.'

'Don't worry about it,' Emma told her, adding, 'and please excuse Damian. He's going through a difficult phase.'

As if to underline this, Damian reappeared, his face red with despair. 'It's gone! There's no plastic rubbish sack there!'

'It'll be out back in the skip with the others.' Sandra looked concerned.

'Damian!' Emma said firmly. 'It's not that important, is it?'

'Yes, it is! I hadn't—' Damian caught her eye. He bit his lip, turned to Sandra, and mumbled, 'No, it's all right. Sorry, didn't mean to be a nuisance.'

He trailed after Emma to the Kings' room where Matt was folding up the map.

'Cheer up, old chap. We'll stop by a newsagent and buy another copy,' Matt advised.

'Not of that issue, you won't,' said Damian gloomily. 'It's an old one with a special article in it. I borrowed it off a friend at school. I promised I'd take it back next term.'

He slumped into a chair and looked as if his world had ended.

'Your friend will understand. What a fuss!' said his aunt robustly. 'Ow!' This last squawk was caused by Matt's elbow in her ribs.

'Come on!' Matt said to Damian. 'We'll take a look around town, anyway. Emma wants to get some things for a picnic lunch, don't you, love?'

Despite a stiff breeze it promised to be another fine, sunny day. Emma had already discovered a short cut into the centre of town, by a path which led round the back of the hotel. They were passing an untidy corner of the otherwise well-kept gardens, when Damian gave a yelp.

'There it is! Behind that wall!' He pointed.

'What is?' Emma looked bewildered.

'The rubbish skip! Hang on a minute. I'll just take a look!'

'Hey!' she shouted, but in vain. Damian had darted behind the low wall which shielded the skip from the hotel. They followed, Emma annoyed and Matt rueful.

They arrived just as Damian, having swarmed up the side of the large metal container, scrambled into it. He stood atop a heap of black plastic rubbish sacks, surveying them with frustration clearly written on his face.

'Dozens of 'em!' he exclaimed. 'I don't even know which one my mag's in!' He crouched to pull at the nearest sack.

'Then come down, for goodness' sake!' Emma pleaded. 'Before anyone sees you!'

'Yes, hop down from there!' Matt said more crisply. 'That can't be the most hygienic spot. Don't rummage about! You might cut yourself!'

'Tetanus!' cried Emma immediately.

'I've had all my booster jabs,' came Damian's voice indistinctly. 'They gave them to us at school. Hullo, look . . .' His arm appeared above the rim, waving a metal object off which the sun glinted. 'A teapot! A perfectly good one. Why did they throw it out?'

'Get down, Damian, pronto!' Matt ordered.

'No, Damian, stay there!' Emma began to jump up and down in a vain attempt to see into the skip. 'Is there a cup and saucer, too?'

Damian duly hooted. 'Oh yes, very funny!'

'I mean it!' Emma called urgently. 'Sandra says a teapot, cup and saucer are missing from Sherwood's room! Give me a leg up, Matt. I want to take a look in there!'

'Have you gone quite crazy?' Matt demanded. 'This is taking things too far! I'm certainly not helping you climb into a rubbish skip, and not climbing in there myself, in case that idea's in your head!'

'It's not crazy!' She rounded on him. 'Hand me down that teapot, Damian!'

Damian dropped the teapot over the edge of the skip. Emma

caught it. 'See? Not even a dent!' She pushed it under Matt's nose. 'Why should anyone throw it out? I bet you anything you like, this is the one missing from Sherwood's room! Any broken china up there?'

Damian's face appeared. 'No, it may have fallen down to the bottom, between the sacks.'

Matt had taken the teapot from Emma and was examining it. 'It does seem undamaged. Must be a mistake.'

'We should take it to Loomis.'

Matt looked up. 'We'd look a couple of complete idiots.'

'Em's right.' Damian clambered out of the skip and jumped to the ground, dusting his hands. 'It's evidence! We'll go now!'

'You won't,' said his aunt. 'You'll go straight back inside and wash!'

'You can't leave me out of this!' he wailed. 'I found the teapot! It's not fair!'

'We'll wait for you,' Matt promised.

'Then we are going to take it to the police! I won't be long!' Damian raced back towards the hotel.

'Oh, no!' groaned Matt, grimacing. 'Emma – how am I going to explain this to Loomis? Evidence of what, for crying out loud?' He brandished the teapot in the air.

'You don't have to,' said Emma cheerfully, taking it from him. 'I'll do it.'

'Are you expecting me to make us all a cup of tea, then, Mrs King?' enquired Inspector Loomis.

He eyed the teapot which sat on his desk looking remarkably unsinister. 'I confess to being a little puzzled and not only as to

325

why you should consider this important. I also don't quite understand why the young man was clambering through a rubbish skip
in the first place!'

Emma ignored his ironic tone and explained about the missing
items from Sherwood's room.

Loomis tapped his fingers on his desk. 'I'll have a word with
the girl. Sandra, you say?' He made a note on a pad.

He then leaned back in his chair, placed the tips of his fingers
together and regarded Damian benignly. 'I mind when I was your
age, laddie. I was awful keen on cops and robbers, in the films
and on the telly, you know. Books too. Maybe that's what made
me join the force. Do you mind what made you join the police
force, King?'

'I sometimes wonder,' Matt growled. 'I must have thought
police work was a lot more straightforward than it is!'

Loomis chuckled. 'But, do you see,' he addressed Damian again.
'It's not like the films or the books, is it? With all due respect to
you, Mrs King! You write a very good yarn. My wife's very fond
of your books! But real life, d'you ken, is somewhat different. Is
that not right, King?'

'More than right!' Matt got to his feet. 'Thanks for giving us
your time. Emma! Come along. You, too, Damian!'

'Enjoy the rest of your holiday, now!' Loomis called as they
retreated.

But as soon as they'd left, Loomis's manner changed abruptly.
'Miller! Get in here!' he shouted.

Sergeant Miller appeared to find his boss standing by the
window, examining a metal teapot.

'Get this over to the lab.' Loomis held out the apparently harmless utensil. 'I've just learned one of these and some crockery are missing from that hotel room. You should have picked up on that, laddie! I don't take kindly to my inquiry being shown the way by a group of summer tourists! This pot turned up in a rubbish skip at the hotel. Get over there and go through that skip with a toothcomb! We're seeking a cup and saucer. And chase up the pathologist for a full post mortem report! I'm not having King go back to his Devon force thinking we're slow off the mark up here!'

'No, sir!' said Sergeant Miller, his face as red as his hair.

Outside by the car, Matt King, unaware of the hornet's nest just stirred up by his visit, lined up his unruly troops, both of them, and delivered a short speech.

'I feel a fool. I don't know why you talked me into that. But it's over and done. We gave the teapot to Loomis and it's up to him what he does. It's his case. We are now, all three of us, going to forget about it. Agreed?'

Silence greeted his question.

'Agreed!' yelled Matt.

Emma and Damian mumbled.

'Get in the car!' he ordered them, exasperated. 'We are going to spend a carefree, crime-free holiday, if it's the last thing I do.'

They set off to drive to Aberfeldy. The road was relatively free of traffic, winding its way through patches of woodland and open country. Damian was sunk in thought.

'Em,' he said at last. 'I wish you hadn't held out on me.'

'About what?' asked his aunt, trying not to sound guilty.

'Pretty well everything! You didn't tell me about the missing crocks until I found the teapot. You were just jolly lucky I picked it up! I could have left it in the skip and said nothing. I nearly did!'

'I'm sorry, Damian. Matt thought it wasn't important.'

'Go on, blame me,' said Matt resignedly.

'It's what you said!' Emma twisted in the front seat to face Damian, behind her. 'There's a couple of other things I didn't tell you. I overheard a quarrel of some sort between Sherwood and someone. And the evening you went for your walk, after dinner, I went straight upstairs. Although I didn't see anything, I heard a door click just before I turned the corner of the corridor and the fire doors were swinging. Someone had just gone through. I think someone had been searching Sherwood's room.'

'You only think!' said Matt aggravatingly. 'You don't know! This is complete fantasy, Emma! How did the mystery intruder get in and out of Sherwood's room so easily? Sherwood surely had the key on him in the dining room.'

'But there are other keys. Sandra's got a key to clean out the rooms.'

'Sandra wouldn't lend it to anyone! It would cost her her job.'

'She leaves her passkeys in the door,' Damian said. 'When she cleans a room. I noticed. She goes in and scrubs the bath and all the rest of it. Then comes out and moves on to the next room. It takes her fifteen or twenty minutes to do a room. All that time, her bunch of keys is hanging from the door and she can't see them.'

There was a silence. Matt grunted.

Emma spoke slowly, 'Someone could come along and take an impression, using warmed plasticine or a bar of softened soap. He could slip the key out of the door, take the imprint, and slide the key back.'

They rounded a bend. Matt raised an objection.

'That involves planning. The intruder, if he ever existed, would need time to prepare, watch for Sandra to be busy, take the impression, get away and get a duplicate key made up.'

More silence. Emma offered, 'Sherwood was already staying at the hotel when we arrived. He may have been there as long as a week and planning to stay longer. I heard the receptionists talking and one was saying that Sherwood came every year about this time. It was a regular rest-break for him. Perhaps he always had the same room? Perhaps the person who wanted to get into the room knew all this, and got himself a duplicate key ready for use if he should need it?'

'It's supposing a lot and you've no evidence. This is all conjecture!' Matt objected.

She was about to answer when a horn blared behind them. A green sports car swept past, overtaking dangerously near a bend, and disappeared.

'Idiot!' snarled Matt.

'That's him!' Damian exclaimed. 'That's the guy who nearly pushed me down the steps, the first night. I told you, Em! As I came back from my walk, a man – the driver of that car – hurried out of the hotel and shoved me aside. Then he ran towards the car park. I reckon he was up to no good!'

Damian leaned forward, grabbing the back of Matt's seat. 'Put your foot down, Matt!' he pleaded. 'Follow him! Let's see where he's going!'

'Certainly not!' said Matt. 'What do you think this is? One of those films Loomis talked of? If you think I'm screeching round country roads at that speed, you've got another think coming.'

'But—' Damian was not allowed to finish.

'And another thing!' Matt was now in full swing. 'You got the barest glimpse of that driver and I'm sure you can't identify him. Do you know, it's witnesses like you who cause endless bother. They swear to recognising a person when it turns out they only saw him in the half-light or from the back or in some cases, not at all! It was dark when you saw this fellow outside the hotel, was it?'

'Fairly,' Damian admitted. 'There was light over the door.'

'Shining on the fellow's face?'

'Well, no. He was running down the steps and had his back to it.'

'So his face was in shadow. And the driver of that car went past us at something like seventy miles an hour! Come on, Damian! How could you possibly link the two?'

'Oh, all right . . .' Damian grudgingly conceded temporary defeat. He slumped back in his seat.

At Aberfeldy, they parked by the riverside at the foot of the steep, wooded area called 'The Birks'. A twisting path led up through the trees, following the mountain stream. The way was made easier by a series of wooden bridges and handholds, and by a halfway halt to sit on the flat rock on which Robert Burns was reputed to have rested before penning his poem, 'The Birks of Aberfeldy'.

There they ate their fruit and crisps and watched the water as it rustled and splashed in its headlong race over the boulders to the foot of the hill.

In contrast to the expedition in Emma's company the previous day, Damian appeared full of energy. Now he was all animation, fizzing with excitement, and producing endless conjectures concerning the late Lawrence Sherwood.

Eventually, Emma, seeing that Matt was nearing explosion point, insisted they all keep off the subject, even though she was secretly as keen to discuss it as her nephew.

They continued on up to the falls. When they had made their way down again, some time later, they had tea at the old watermill in the town. Matt consulted the roadmap again and worked out a pleasant, if roundabout, drive back.

It was already evening. The sun was sinking and a warm glow spread over the landscape. Matt's route had taken them along a little-used road. Everywhere was quiet and peaceful. To their right was a wall which seemed to mark the boundary of a fairly large property. They had seen no sign of any other traffic, when they saw a notice warning of a concealed driveway ahead.

Matt slowed. There was a break in the boundary wall and an impressive pair of wrought-iron gates. Behind them, a wide drive could be seen, running between trees and, in the distance, a large and distinctive-looking house.

'Pull up a second, Matt,' Emma begged. 'That looks a lovely old house.'

Matt drove a little way past, then drew over to the side of the road where there was a convenient patch of flat ground under the trees. They all got out, walked back and pressed their noses to the wrought-iron gates.

'Like a set of Victorian country children spying on the squire in his manor!' said Matt, amused.

The house was of pinkish-grey granite. The architect had let his fancy guide him. Turrets and crenellations sprouted and decorated the façade and gave the house the look of a mini-castle.

Damian said quietly, 'There's that car.' He pointed.

So busy had the other two been with studying the house, that they'd failed to notice the green sports car parked before the main door.

'So now you know where he was going, Damian,' Matt said. 'Hope you're satisfied?'

But Damian had already wandered off and was following the boundary wall.

'Where do you think you're going?' Emma called after him.

'Just exploring. The wall turns a corner here. There's a path through the woods. We can just go a little way, can't we?'

Matt glanced at his wristwatch. 'We've got twenty minutes or so, then we really must get back.'

They followed Damian into the trees. Here it was uncannily silent, all sound smothered by the trees and the soft peat beneath their feet. To their left was the boundary wall. To their right, woodland. Once or twice a twig cracked in the undergrowth or a bird fluttered up into the branches. Otherwise they appeared to be alone in the deepening gloom.

Matt pointed to deep paired cuts imprinted into the earth. 'Deer around here somewhere. But we won't catch sight of them. They'll scent us.'

As he stopped speaking, the quiet was disturbed by the throaty roar of a powerful engine somewhere to the far left.

'That car!' Emma whispered, although there was no need to keep her voice down. 'He's leaving.'

They stood amongst the trees and listened as the engine noise dropped temporarily to a distant throb. There was a squeal of unoiled metal hinges, easily carried on the clear air. Then the car engine roared into life again and sped away.

'Drove down the drive. Stopped by the gates to open them up and has driven off back towards Aberfeldy,' Matt murmured.

'Will he have noticed our car?'

Matt looked undecided. 'Might not have done. He turned in the other direction to where we're parked. Not that it matters, anyway. Damian's probably wrong. There's no way he could identify the driver for sure, nor would it signify anything if he did. So the man ran out of the hotel. He was late for a meeting with someone else? He wanted to catch a bus? There could be any number of reasons and all of them innocent! Damian's letting this Sherwood business take over his imagination, and you encourage him, Emma! You're in danger of building a real house of cards, the two of you!'

This was blatantly unfair, but she didn't want to start an argument now. Damian had moved ahead. They'd lost sight of him completely. 'Where's he got to?' Emma fretted.

A few moments later, they saw him. On this secluded edge of the estate, the wall had crumbled and not been repaired. Damian had clambered over the fallen masonry and was some yards away, prowling through the bushes towards the distant house.

'Come back!' Emma called, instinctively muffling her voice.

'Damian!' Matt was not so prudent. 'Come out of there!'

Damian either didn't hear or affected not to.

'I'll go and get him. Stay here!' Matt hopped over the mound of stones and set off briskly after Damian. Emma scrambled after Matt.

They caught up with Damian about thirty yards in. He was standing at the edge of the trees, looking across open turf towards the east wing of the house.

'I heard the car start up,' he told them in a low voice. 'I jumped over the wall back there to see if I could get a glimpse. But it was too far away.'

The three of them stared towards the house. It looked deserted.

'It's Victorian,' said Matt decisively. 'It's in that Scots baronial style which Queen Vicky liked. It was probably built after she and Albert put Scotland in the forefront of fashion. Some wealthy sassanach, no doubt, deciding he'd like to play at being a laird!'

A pinpoint of light suddenly gleamed at a French window. It was briefly cut off and then showed again as a figure passed in front of it. The dark shadow slid across the window, not betraying whether it was a man or a woman who was within.

It must be getting gloomy indoors and someone had switched on a tablelamp, perhaps to read by, Emma thought.

At this reminder of evening drawing in, Matt touched Damian's shoulder. 'Come on.'

They made to turn but as they did, they heard a click and a dry voice ordered, 'Now, just stay right there.'

Emma squeaked. The three of them turned slowly and beheld a grizzled figure in tweeds, holding a shotgun in a meaningful way. A dog was at his heels, ears pricked, watching with the same hostile wariness as the man.

'Now, just a minute!' Matt exclaimed. The dog growled softly in its throat.

'No, laddie, you wait a minute!' The gamekeeper, or so Emma supposed him to be, jerked his head towards the house in the distance. 'And suppose you tell me just what you think you're doing, spying on the house?'

'I realise this is private property,' Matt began, 'and that we're trespassing. But it was just curiosity. The boy—'

'Curiosity? You were taking an awful close interest, that's for sure! Perhaps you should come and explain your curiosity to Mrs Frith.'

'Is she the owner?' Emma asked. 'Honestly, there's no need to bother her.'

'That's not her green sports car, though, is it?' Damian asked disastrously. 'Who was driving that?'

The gamekeeper's bushy eyebrows met in a scowl. 'My, you have been taking a good look at us! Full of questions, too. And just what would your interest be, I wonder? Go on!'

The barrel of the gun moved warningly. 'Just walk nice and slow now, ahead of me. And no tricks!'

'Oh, this is ridiculous!' Matt exclaimed. 'Look, I'm a pol—'

The gun barrel lifted. The dog gave a low bark.

'Do as he says, Matt!' Emma begged.

'I will never,' muttered Matt, 'live this down!'

They set off across the open ground towards the house, walking three abreast, uncomfortably aware that behind them walked a man with a gun.

To say nothing of the dog.

Part Three

Emma, Matt and Damian walked together in a straight line across the open turf towards the house, conscious of the gamekeeper, his gun and his dog, following behind.

The evening sun, sinking fast, caused the house to send a fantastical shadow across the ground on this side, creeping towards the little party. The curious turrets and the crenellations of the design were elongated and distorted, making the building appear more like something from a child's fairy tale than ever. But king's castle or ogre's lair? wondered Emma uncomfortably.

They reached the shadow and stepped out of warm sunlight into shade. As it fell over them, with its attendant chill, the French window ahead of them opened and a woman stepped out.

'What's all this, Duncan?' she called.

Emma's eyes had adjusted to the change in light. She could see that the woman was tall and perhaps sixty or a year or two less. Her hair was cut very short and her angular frame was neatly, even severely, clad in a long-sleeved dress in plain material. Its collar was hand crocheted in a Victorian touch which matched the house behind her. Otherwise, her only ornament was a small gold pin on the dress bodice.

'Mrs Frith?' Emma asked breathlessly. 'Do let us explain! We can, only the gamekeeper wouldn't let us.'

The woman's eyes moved to take in Emma in every detail. She said, 'I'm not Mrs Frith. I'm Jean Ross, Mrs Frith's housekeeper.' She had a pinched manner of speaking, the syllables clearly enunciated as if she were giving an elocution lesson.

The gamekeeper spoke up before Emma could reply. 'They were snooping about the house, Mrs Ross, and taking far too much interest for my liking! It seems they've been watching for a wee while. The young boy there was asking about Mr Alex's car!'

'Is that so?' Mrs Ross's suspicious gaze returned to Emma.

Emma flushed. 'No! We were walking through the woods by the wall over there.' She turned to point behind them and the distant boundary wall. 'Of course we were interested in the house. It's unusual. Damian tried to see closer . . .'

'You all climbed over the wall?' Mrs Ross seized on her words, her voice sharp.

'No! Well, yes, in a way, but not climbed. The wall has collapsed at one point. We just stepped over. We followed to fetch him back.'

The gamekeeper, sensing, perhaps, that some blame might attach to him in this respect, muttered, 'I've asked Jamie to come over and give me a hand to fix that wall.'

'I only asked about the car,' said Damian loudly, 'because I'm interested in sports cars.'

'And my husband is a police officer,' Emma added. 'So you can see we're not burglars or anything like that! Show her your identification, Matt.'

'I can't,' said Matt. 'I haven't got it on me.'

His wife turned on him in dismay. 'Why not? We need it!'

337

'Well, I didn't think I'd need it!' he protested crossly. 'Why on earth should I? I'm on holiday! I came out on a day trip. I didn't think I was going to be marched off by a madman with a shotgun!'

'You mind your words there!' rasped the gamekeeper.

'Yes, don't annoy him, for goodness' sake!' Emma hissed.

'Och, Duncan!' said Mrs Ross suddenly. 'Put the gun away, will you? You know as well as I do that it's not loaded!'

'Not loaded?' chorused Matt and Emma. They and Damian turned as one to stare at Duncan.

The gamekeeper lowered his weapon and rested the butt of the shotgun on the turf. He said sheepishly, 'Och, well, they weren't to know it, were they? And I didna' see them offering to come along and explain themselves unless I persuaded them.'

The dog, as if aware of its master's embarrassment, lay down on the turf and put its nose on its paws.

'I advise you,' said Matt fiercely, 'not to play such a trick again!'

'I wasna' to know,' said Duncan drily, 'that you were the polis!'

There was a movement in the room behind Jean Ross. A new voice, a woman's, called out, 'What is going on, Jean? Who are these people?'

'Now you've disturbed her!' Mrs Ross said to them, clearly annoyed. 'And I was hoping she'd take a nap before dinner! Now I've to bother her with this!'

'Bother me with what, Jean? What is this?'

Mrs Ross turned and moved back to the window to speak into the room. 'It's some people who came onto the property, interested to see the house. It's nothing for you to worry yourself about, Mrs Frith. Duncan and I can take care of it. It seems that the gentleman here is a police officer on his holidays, anyway!'

'Indeed?' There was a faint chuckle. 'Well, bring them in then, Jean. If I've visitors, I'd like to meet them!'

Although it was clearly not to the liking of either Mrs Ross or Duncan, Emma, Matt and Damian stepped through the French windows in response to the invitation. They found themselves in a comfortable drawing room, furnished with a great deal of heavy, dark, old-fashioned furniture. Emma wondered whether some of it was original to the building.

Mrs Ross had followed and switched on the main light to add to the lamp's glow. Emma blinked.

Mrs Frith was standing in the middle of the room, a small but commanding figure, leaning on a cane. Her bright eyes made a quick assessment of them. She addressed herself to Matt.

'I take it you're speaking the truth? To impersonate an officer of the law is an offence, as I understand it.'

'I'm a police officer,' Matt said. 'Inspector Matt King, on holiday here from Devon. This is my wife, Emma, and Damian.'

'Sit down, please. Jean, perhaps we could have a cup of tea?'

When Mrs Ross had left the room, still bristling with suspicion, their hostess lowered herself stiffly into a high-backed chair, rested her cane, and settled the skirts of her green silk dress round her knees.

'I'm Alice Frith,' she said. 'You must excuse Duncan if he was a little over-zealous. Both he and Jean are somewhat protective towards me!' She smiled. 'They mean well. Besides, this is a lonely house. Naturally, strangers can make us all a little nervous. I asked Duncan to mend that wall quite two weeks ago. Now, perhaps, he'll see to it!'

Obviously, Mrs Frith had been in the room and listening for a few minutes before she'd spoken. Emma, her curiosity aroused, studied her, trying not to appear rude.

Mrs Frith had turned her attention to Damian. 'And you're interested in sports cars, are you? Alex was the same at your age. Couldn't wait to get behind the wheel of his first car! That wasn't the present one, the one you saw. He's had three or four. Always changing. It seems to me a sad waste of money, but there, you're only young once!'

She turned back to Emma. 'Alex is my nephew, not my son. But I brought him up, here in this house. He's my sister's son.'

'Damian's *my* sister's son,' Emma told her. 'His parents are overseas.'

'In Africa,' Damian supplied.

'Indeed?' Mrs Frith evidently considered some bond had been forged between her and Emma by this joint circumstance. She smiled kindly at her.

The door reopened to admit Jean Ross with a tea trolley. Not only the tea itself was in evidence, but a plate of buttered home-made scones, shortbread, sultana cake and, for Damian, a can of orangeade.

Mrs Frith, indicating this last item, explained, 'We keep a supply of these canned drinks for Alex. When he's driving, he doesn't drink alcohol. He's a very reliable youngster in that way. It's a great relief to know it, the car being so powerful. But he's a good boy.'

It occurred to Emma that it was much in Alex's interest to show himself in his best light to his aunt. There was every sign that Mrs Frith was an indulgent relative and had probably paid for the succession of fast cars Alex liked driving around in. No doubt he was keen to impress her with his reliability. Emma hoped she wasn't being uncharitable.

But Mrs Frith was taking a closer interest in Emma, too. Now she put down her cup and said, 'Excuse me, my dear. But your face is very familiar. I'm quite sure I've seen you before, recently. Yet I seldom leave the house these days. I've an arthritic hip, as you see. So I can't imagine where it could have been. You're not on the television or any such thing, are you?'

'No,' Emma confessed. 'I'm a writer.'

'Ah!' Mrs Frith beamed at her and exclaimed triumphantly, 'Now I can place you! You're Emma Durrant! Why, I'm reading one of your books at the moment and your photo is on the cover! I'm a great fan of yours, you know!'

'Thank you,' Emma mumbled, scarlet in the face.

'I sleep badly. I read long hours into the night. I've an arrangement with a bookshop to send me new titles. He always sends me yours. Would you think I was imposing if I asked you, before you leave, to sign a copy for me?'

'Of course I will!' cried Emma.

'Just go over to the bookcase, will you?' Mrs Frith asked Damian. 'I'm sure some of your aunt's books are in that.'

Damian went to the tall oak Gothic-styled bookcase and duly returned with a copy of Emma's latest book, which she inscribed for Alice Frith.

Mrs Frith took it and patted the cover. 'Now, what I should really like, is if you could all come to dinner. I can't ask you to stay tonight as it wouldn't be fair on Jean to spring three extra at table on her without warning! But tomorrow? Then Alex will be here. He's mostly down in London these days, but is spending a couple of weeks up here with me. Entertaining him is always something of a problem. But a famous writer? That really is a chance not to be missed!'

She smiled. 'We'll have quite a little party. Will seven for seven thirty be in order?'

'That was really quite embarrassing!' said Matt as they drove back to Pitlochry.

'She was sweet. And she was so pleased to have visitors. She's lonely. Anyone can see that!' Emma argued. 'I know it was a little bit awkward, meeting in that way. But once she knew who we were she was delighted.'

'I'm not arguing with the fact that she's a charming lady. It's just that I feel we're imposing on her.'

'We're not! She told us, she's got her nephew there and it's a problem to find company for him. Now she's able to plan a dinner party and is as pleased as punch about it.'

'Wonder if *he'll* be as pleased?' said Damian from the back seat. 'When he sees us there.'

'He may think we've taken advantage of his aunt,' said Matt, ever the worrier.

'He may recognise me,' said Damian. 'After all, he did nearly push me over when he ran out of the hotel that evening. And don't say that it wasn't him, as I'm sure that it was!'

'Whatever you do,' Emma twisted in her seat to address him, 'don't mention that! We don't want to arouse his suspicions.'

'What suspicions?' demanded the exasperated Matt. 'There's nothing to be suspicious about! I do wish you two would stop all this nonsense.'

They drove into the hotel car park and set off towards the main entrance. As they came into the reception area, a figure standing by the desk, who had apparently been making some enquiry, turned to face them.

'Ah, there you all are!' said Inspector Loomis. 'I was just asking when you were expected back. Perhaps I could have a wee word?'

'I'm in the position of owing you some apology, Mrs King,' Inspector Loomis said in the privacy of the Kings' hotel room.

Damian, perched on the bed, exclaimed, 'The teapot!'

His aunt quelled him with a look but the inspector gave a wry smile.

'Indeed so! Examination of the teapot showed up some curious traces. We, ah, tried to find the cup and saucer which the girl said were also missing. Unfortunately, when Miller arrived at the hotel, he found the skip had just been removed! He tracked it down but its contents had been added to the general pile on the rubbish dump outside of town. I think our chances of finding a small amount of crockery amongst all that are slim. I've got men looking.'

Loomis sighed and continued. 'What's more, we have a further report from the pathologist. The heart attack which seems to have killed Sherwood was almost certainly precipitated by his having ingested some form of poison.'

'Poison!' cried the others in unison.

'Of herbal base.' Loomis glanced at Damian. 'You're not to speak of this, laddie, you understand?'

'Of course I do!' said Damian, offended.

Loomis transferred his severe gaze to the others. 'Poisoning isn't

343

always intentional. People poison themselves by accident. Picking the wrong mushrooms in the woods is a good example. The tea which the deceased seems to have drunk, and which precipitated his attack, may have been prepared by himself, using some home-gathered leaves, a herbal tisane, you know. But he picked the wrong ones.'

Three pairs of unconvinced eyes were fixed on him. Loomis insisted, 'Garden plants, several of them, yield up quite active poisons. Also common wild plants or so-called weeds. They vary in strength. The susceptibility of the victim varies also. Someone like Sherwood who, although he appeared a hale and hearty fellow, actually suffered quite a serious medical condition, would have been severely affected.'

'Perhaps,' said Emma crisply. 'But if you ask me, someone dosed his tea for him! That's why all the teabags were taken as well as the pot and cup. Someone got in and substituted spiked ones for the originals. Then returned and removed the evidence! I told you I was sure someone was snooping around that evening!'

'So you did. You told us about overhearing a quarrel, too. Can you remember any more about that?'

Beneath Loomis's gaze, Emma grew embarrassed and glanced at Matt.

Matt coughed. 'This is a bit awkward. Damian here, on the evening in question, saw someone leaving the hotel in a hurry. Today he thinks – only thinks, mind you – that he saw that person again.' He explained about Mrs Frith.

Loomis gave a low whistle. 'I know of Mrs Frith. She's something of a recluse. A very wealthy lady and utterly respectable. We can't go offending her!

'The nephew is Alex Carter. I've heard the odd tale or two about him. He sows his wild oats well away from here, and comes back, meek as a lamb, when the money runs out. That's what they say! He'll be the old lady's heir, there's not a doubt about it, and anxious to keep her sweet. As for Jean Ross and Duncan, they will both of them have been with Mrs Frith for years. I'm not well acquainted with Jean Ross, but I've come across Duncan Mackenzie from time to time. I'd describe him as an eccentric and liable to do things in his own way. I'll have a word with him about the gun when I see him next. He'll have a shotgun certificate for sure, and you said the weapon wasn't loaded. But that doesn't mean he can go around threatening people with it! Even intruders!'

Here Loomis gave them all a severe look. Matt coughed. 'We were in the wrong, I know.'

Loomis tapped his fingers on the arm of the chair. 'You're going to dine there tomorrow? You'll have to be very careful what you say. We don't know whether Alex Carter has anything to do with any of this. But we don't want to alarm him, if he does. Nor to upset Mrs Frith needlessly if he doesn't.'

The gates had been left open to admit the visitors the next evening when, at seven sharp, Matt turned the car into the drive.

They were not the first to arrive. Alex Carter's green sports car was already parked before the main door. Damian walked round it admiringly.

'Come on!' His aunt inspected him, tugging his jacket straight and smoothing a hand over his hair. 'Now, don't forget, Damian! Whatever you do, don't say anything about seeing Alex at the hotel that evening!'

345

'Especially,' said Matt doggedly, 'as we still don't know for certain that you did!'

'It was him!' said Damian ungrammatically but with complete confidence.

Mrs Frith received them in the room in which they'd had tea the previous day, dressed in black with pearls.

Emma was conscious of her own less formal attire. Matching pants, loose jacket and sleeveless blouse of silky material, comprised the most sophisticated outfit she'd brought, worn with medium-heeled sling-back shoes. She had made an effort with her hair, twisting it into a long rope which she'd coiled on top of her head and secured with a hastily purchased packet of hairpins.

'Will you have a glass of sherry?' Mrs Frith indicated a tray nearby with elegant little glasses and decanter, all of which appeared to be Victorian antiques. 'Alex will be down in just a moment. Damian, why don't you go along to the kitchen and see what kind of drinks Jean has in the fridge?'

'It's very kind of you to ask us,' Emma said.

'It's a pleasure to have the opportunity!' Mrs Frith insisted.

As she spoke the door opened. 'Ah,' she said. 'And here is Alex.'

Alex Carter must have been about twenty-five or -six. He was a good-looking young man, although Emma quickly decided that the rather petulant set of his mouth spoilt what otherwise was a fine set of features. He shook hands with them and expressed polite interest at meeting a well-known writer.

They had just exchanged all these pleasantries when Damian

346

returned, holding a glass of Coca-Cola. He entered the room behind Alex who had his back to him.

'And this is Damian,' said Mrs Frith.

Alex turned. His profile was towards Emma and she saw a muscle twitch in the young man's neck and his lips compress, as if he'd received some unwelcome surprise. But Alex said calmly enough, 'Hullo, Damian.'

'Hullo,' returned Damian politely.

Dinner was excellent. Emma had whispered to Jean Ross before leaving the previous day that she was a vegetarian. Thus, in addition to the succulent roast lamb which had been cooked for the others, Mrs Ross had produced a delicious tomato, garlic, herbs and courgette bake with a fluffy cheese and egg soufflé mixture as a topping, just for Emma.

'This is delicious!' Emma told Mrs Frith.

'We grow most of our own vegetables,' that lady replied, pleased.

'My aunt is quite a gardener!' Alex said with an affectionate grin at Mrs Frith.

'Not any longer, alas!' she said ruefully. 'My gardening is a question of supervising Duncan these days! I used to be a great one for digging and weeding, but the hip has put an end to all that. I've my greenhouse. I'm able to sit and mess around with pots of herbs and such in that. The tomatoes are from my greenhouse. I can claim some credit for those!'

They retired to the original drawing room for coffee. When they were settled there, Alex Carter asked casually, 'Will you be staying much longer in Pitlochry?'

'Till the end of the week,' Matt told him. 'Our holiday was nearly cancelled at one point. We had a few mishaps in the old house we're renovating back in Devon! And then I was held up by work.'

'You're a police officer, I hear?' Alex sipped his coffee, his gaze watchful.

'That's right. Emma and Damian came up to Scotland ahead of me and I followed on.'

'Such a long drive, my dear!' said Mrs Frith. 'For you to make alone.'

'It was really quite straightforward,' Emma assured her. 'We didn't have any mishaps.'

'Until we got here and Sherwood scratched the car door,' said Damian.

Silence fell. *Oh, Damian!* thought Emma in despair.

Damian had realised he'd blundered. He turned scarlet. 'It was just a bump in the car park. Not Em's fault. I mean, it didn't matter.'

Alex Carter set down his cup. 'Sherwood? Who is he?'

'A fellow guest at the hotel,' Emma said as nonchalantly as she could. 'It was only a scratch on the paintwork. Nothing to worry about.'

Mrs Frith said, 'That wasn't the poor man who dropped dead on the golf course? It was in the local paper. They said he was a summer visitor, staying at the hotel.'

'Yes, it was.' Emma was finding it difficult to keep up the nonchalant tone.

Some false note apparently struck Alex, who gave her a long, thoughtful stare, his dark eyes bright with curiosity.

'Did you talk to him at all?' he asked. 'Apart from the incident with your car? I mean, did he seem unwell?'

'No. I can't say I noticed. We didn't have much to say to each other. He was rather rude.'

With that the conversation moved on. Alex, however, took little part in it. After a while, he leaned towards his aunt. 'I must just put in a call to London, Aunt Alice, all right?'

'Yes, dear, of course.'

'Excuse me.' Alex nodded to the others and went out of the room.

Mrs Frith pulled a face. 'Making arrangements with his friends for when he shall get back, no doubt! I'm sure Alex finds life tedious here with me, though he does his best to hide it! He'll be wanting to get back to the city lights!' Sadness touched her face.

Alex returned some twenty minutes later with another apology for absenting himself.

All too soon, it was time for them to take their leave. It was now dark outside and Emma had noticed that Mrs Frith was showing signs of weariness. They thanked her effusively for her hospitality and thanked Jean for a fine dinner.

Alex escorted them to their car. He gave it an appraising look. 'Nice motor. New.'

'Yes.' Matt sounded pleased. 'It goes really well and all things considered, quite economically.' More modestly he added, 'It's not as showy as yours!'

Alex gave a short laugh. 'Mine's not a family car, but then, I'm not a family man.'

'It's got a good turn of speed, I dare say,' Matt said casually.

'You bet!' Alex's voice grew enthusiastic. 'On the open road, when I really put my foot down—' Too late he remembered he was talking to a policeman, even if one off duty. He broke off.

'You overtook us, not far from here, yesterday,' Matt said. 'On a bend, doing over seventy I reckoned. You were lucky to get round.'

'The steering's first rate!' Alex said shortly. 'It responds just to a touch. And I'm used to driving it. I've got the feel of the car. Goodnight.'

It was a fairly abrupt dismissal. They shook hands and Alex walked back indoors, leaving the visitors to set off home.

'He didn't like that,' Emma said as they rolled down the drive.

'My picking him up on his driving? Perhaps not the most courteous thing for a guest to do. But a word in time could save his life – or someone else's! I'm sure he thinks he's got full control of that car. But it only takes a moment's inattention or something unexpected and he'd lose it.'

The great wrought-iron gates still stood open, but as they approached, a figure emerged from the gloom. Duncan Mackenzie, waiting to close the gates and lock up as soon as the visitors had left. The dog was with him, at his heel. He probably, Emma guessed, made a last round of the grounds, late at night, to check all was well before turning in. She waved to him and Duncan raised a hand in farewell salute as they drove through.

'Sorry I put my foot in it!' groaned Damian as they drew away from the house.

'Couldn't be helped. It wasn't bad. I think it passed over pretty well,' said Emma optimistically. She hesitated. 'You know, Matt,

I'm almost sure that Alex was the person I overheard quarrelling with Sherwood. I listened to his voice very carefully. He looked a bit startled when he first saw Damian and when Sherwood was mentioned, he nearly jumped out of his seat. He really wanted to know how well we knew Sherwood.'

The headlights split the dark blue of the night, briefly illuminating trees and wayside verges. There were no other vehicles on this lonely stretch of road. It was perhaps not surprising that Alex had been tempted to put his foot down.

Matt said thoughtfully, 'If Sherwood ran gambling clubs and such places, a young man like Alex might well fall into his clutches and end up owing more money than he could hope to repay without going to his aunt. That would mean admitting how foolish he'd been. It would distress her considerably, quite aside from what it would cost her. She's not a well woman and she obviously believes Alex to be a paragon of virtue! Perhaps she's naive to expect so much of a young man, but she's isolated out there in that house. I doubt she knows much of what goes on outside. She'd be disillusioned, to say the least!'

'She might cut him out of her will,' Emma suggested.

'That would be extreme. I don't know. Something isn't right. I don't like this set-up, any of it. Even if Sherwood had some hold over Alex, would he be so stupid as to do Sherwood actual harm?'

'I liked her so much,' Emma sighed. 'I didn't know what to make of Alex. He looks weak. He was conceited about his driving. I think he could be stupid, just out of fear. He'd panic. Especially if Sherwood threatened him and I think that Sherwood did. Trying to remember exactly what I overheard is difficult. But the impression I got was that Sherwood had announced his intention of doing something. He might have said he'd go directly to Mrs Frith if Alex didn't get the money.'

The road made a sharp turn to the left. The car juddered. Matt muttered something beneath his breath. They were travelling downhill now, rather faster than Emma would have liked. She knew Matt for a cautious driver and was surprised, especially in view of the strictures he'd expressed to Alex not many minutes earlier.

It was at that moment she realised that Matt was attempting to brake – but nothing was happening in response to the increasingly frantic pressure of his foot.

Matt snapped, 'Hold on! Damian, you, too!'

The car leapt forward and swerved violently. They seemed to rise in the air, weightless. Emma grabbed at the dashboard. As Matt wrestled with the wheel, they headed towards the side of the road. The headlights picked out the formidable and solid barrier of trees. Somehow they missed the nearest trunk by a fraction, and plunged nose down into a ditch.

Part Four

In the wake of the impact came an eerie silence, broken by Matt's voice.

'Is anyone hurt? Emma? Damian?' He must have been worried, but he sounded cool and efficient.

Emma felt a surge of respect and love. Whatever the circumstances and whatever scrape she might get herself into, the one person she'd always want by her side was her husband. He might not share her fanciful imagination, but his practical common sense never let them down.

'I'm all right.' She pushed herself away from the dashboard and tried anxiously to see into the back of the car. 'Damian? Where are you? Matt, he's gone!'

Damian's head appeared from the well of the back seat. 'No, I haven't! I fell off the seat. I'm fine – but I bashed my knee.'

'Right, just take it easy. I'll get out first and then you two,' Matt instructed them.

All three managed to exit awkwardly but without too much difficulty from the car. Emma and Damian scrambled up the ditch to the road while Matt, armed with a pocket torch, made his way to the crumpled bonnet.

The impact had forced the bonnet upwards. Matt shone the torch into the depths beneath and reached in his hand. The car,

Emma could now see, was firmly wedged and there was no way it could be extricated without a breakdown truck. She put her arm round Damian's shoulders.

'All right there?' She tried to keep her voice bright and positive but she was shivering, she knew with shock rather than cool night air.

'Why was Matt driving so fast?' Damian asked hoarsely. 'Why didn't he brake as we got near the corner?'

'I think—' Emma wondered how to explain about the lack of response from the brakes.

Just then, Matt reappeared, climbing out of the ditch to join them on the roadside verge, and sparing her from the need to concoct some plausible explanation which wouldn't alarm.

'I can't see properly. It looks as if the brake pipe has—' He glanced at Damian. 'Has broken.'

'Broken?' Emma asked quietly.

'I told you, I couldn't see properly!' Matt's voice was sharp. More gently he added, 'I can't tell. Look, I'll have to go and raise some help. We're about a mile from town here. I can walk there. How about you two?'

'I've not got the right shoes for walking,' Emma said ruefully, 'and Damian has given his knee a bad knock. We'll wait here.'

'I shouldn't be too long. I'll leave you the torch.' Matt was clearly unhappy at the idea of abandoning his wife and her nephew on this lonely road.

'No, take the torch! You'll need it. Honestly, Matt, I'll worry if I know you're walking on the roadside without it. There's no footpath along here.'

The cloud cover flitted from the face of the moon. Its pale

light bathed the strip of road running steeply away downhill towards town, turning it into a silvery ribbon. The uptilted rear window of the crashed car glittered. Behind it, the trees were etched black against the sky.

Indecision showed on Matt's face. He stooped to give his wife a reassuring hug and a kiss. At the same time, he whispered into her ear, 'It may be sabotage but I'm not sure. Don't let the boy get that idea!'

He stretched out a hand and ruffled Damian's hair. 'Look after Em for me, now, won't you?'

'We're all right,' said Damian sturdily.

He limped away from them a little way in a manner which suggested he wasn't all right at all.

The sight seemed to decide Matt. Clearly Damian couldn't get far.

'I'll be as quick as I can!' he promised before setting off down the hill at a brisk pace.

Emma couldn't deny a moment's panic as she saw him go, her last glimpse of him a faint beam of torchlight. But when he was out of sight, she turned her attention to Damian. He was sitting on the roadside, examining his injured knee.

'It's swelling up like a balloon,' he observed, more out of pride than pain or distress.

'Let's have a look.' Emma stooped to examine the problem. The knee had certainly swelled alarmingly. She gave it a tentative prod. 'Can you flex it at all?'

Damian tried and gave a grunt. 'Yes, it's not broken or anything, Em. It's just going to be a whopper of a bruise and stiff. I've done the same sort of thing playing rugger. It'll go down in a day or two. But I won't be much good walking for a bit.'

Teasingly he added, 'So you and Matt will have to go on your hikes without me!'

'Yes, all right!' Emma gave a wry laugh. 'You'll be allowed to stay in with your computer games!'

Damian tugged his trouser leg down over his knee with some effort. 'What was Matt muttering to you?'

'Nothing much,' Emma said firmly.

'Has someone tampered with the car?'

'Don't start imagining things!' she ordered. Inwardly she gave a sigh. So much for preventing Damian getting suspicious!

'I reckon someone did. It could've been Alex!' Damian's voice grew animated. 'He left the room for a while, he said he needed to use the phone. He could have fixed the brakes then. He had plenty of time!'

'We don't know! I don't even want to think about it!' Emma hugged herself, wishing the silk top were warmer. She remembered that in the boot of the car was a large rug used for picnics. Fetching it would not only be practical but delay having to discuss the vexed matter of the brakes with Damian.

It was awkward to reach the boot catch, but not impossible. The lid flew up but the raised angle of the car meant she couldn't reach inside. Emma pulled herself up on the open rim. The car rocked dangerously, see-sawing back and forth.

'Hey, be careful!' Damian urged.

'It's all right, I can just reach the rug. Got it!'

She grasped it triumphantly, joined Damian on the roadside and draped the rug around them both.

'That's a lot better! We'll be all right now. Quite comfy!'

Damian said quietly, 'There's a car coming.'

So intent had she been on getting the rug, Emma hadn't heard it. Now powerful headlights split the night, illuminating the road. The throb of an engine came nearer, coming from the direction of the Frith house. Then it slowed to a dawdle as if the driver searched for something by the roadside.

The headlights swept over Emma and Damian and the car halted some feet away. From its low-slung outline, Emma guessed it to be Alex Carter's sports car. The driver was getting out. She wasn't surprised, when the dark silhouette approached them, to hear his voice.

'King? Mrs King?'

Picked out in the headlights' glare, Emma could do little but rise to her feet. Damian would have risen also, but she squeezed his shoulder, asking him to remain seated. If he stood up, Alex might notice the lameness of Damian's swollen knee. Instinctively, she didn't want Alex to know either of them was in any way injured.

He'd reached them now, sounding breathless and worried. 'Are you hurt?'

'No. We're both fine. What are you doing out here, Alex?'

Emma couldn't refrain from the barbed question, although it was probably unwise to provoke him.

The question certainly seemed to throw him off his stride. 'I – I was driving into town to the all-night chemist, something for my aunt.'

As a reason, Emma reflected, it was plausible enough. It could even be true. But somehow, she didn't think it was.

'Where's your husband?' He was looking around him, peering into the woodland beside the road.

'He'll be back shortly with some help,' Emma said with a confidence she didn't feel.

Alex appeared to hesitate. Emma would have liked to see his face more clearly, but the headlights were behind him.

He said quickly, 'You must come back with me, both of you! Three can just squeeze in the car. It's only a short drive, it won't matter.'

'I'm sure your aunt will be getting ready for bed by now,' Emma replied. 'I don't want to disturb her or frighten her with a story of an accident. Besides, if Matt comes back and finds us gone, he won't know what's happened.'

'I'll phone the breakdown garage from the house. Is he walking into town?' Alex moved to see past her, straining his gaze down the dim roadway ahead. 'Don't worry about Aunt Alice. She's already asleep.'

It didn't occur to him, Emma thought wryly, that this statement undermined his claim to be going into town to fetch some medicine or other from an all-night chemist for Mrs Frith. *So it wasn't true, Alex!* she thought to herself.

Alex was urging them to come with him, demolishing counter-arguments with fluent denials. 'She won't hear. She won't get up. We won't make any noise. She won't know anything about it.'

The last phrase struck Emma as particularly unfortunate. She had already noted that Alex had neither expressed any surprise at finding them in this predicament nor enquired as to the cause of the accident. In addition, he'd made no kind of reference to the fact that only a short time earlier, Matt had criticised Alex's own driving. She might have expected Alex, after initially establishing no one was hurt, to have made some remark. He had taken Matt's criticism badly.

'You can't stay here!' Alex's voice had risen. He sounded almost hysterical. 'You've got to come back with me!'

Nothing, now, would have persuaded Emma to get into Alex's car and she certainly wouldn't have allowed Damian to do so. It would be to place themselves entirely in his hands.

'We'll wait here!' she said with such authority that Alex seemed taken aback. He obviously realised it was pointless to argue.

'In that case . . .' Again he peered into the night, down the road. 'I'll drive on slowly and see if I can overtake your husband.'

This was even worse. Matt had no idea Alex was out on the roads. Matt, thought Emma in despair, who was walking by the roadside with only an inadequate pocket torch!

'He'll have reached the town by now!' she insisted.

But this time she was less successful at keeping anxiety from her voice.

Alex, himself sounding newly confident, said, 'He can't possibly have got there yet! I'll go after him.'

He turned and ran back to his car and before she could do anything to stop him, had driven off in the direction Matt had taken.

'Now what?' asked Damian.

In the darkness, the silence was overwhelming. Emma sank down on the verge beside her nephew. Damian reached out the blanket and draped her shoulders.

'Matt can take care of himself,' he offered.

'I just wish I had some idea what Alex will do.'

The pins had fallen from Emma's topknot and the coil of hair slid to frame her cheek, the end resting on her collarbone. She plucked at it absently. 'He could tell Matt anything. He could say he'd taken us back to Mrs Frith's house.'

'Matt will know we wouldn't go with him.' Damian sounded so decided that Emma was almost persuaded. But Damian's next words renewed her fears.

'I think he came to see if the job he'd done on our brakes had worked and we'd crashed. He was looking for us and he wasn't surprised to see us in that ditch, was he?'

'No,' Emma admitted. 'He wasn't. It was as if he'd expected it. Oh, Damian, do you think he really interfered with the brakes? Surely he couldn't do such a dreadful thing?'

'He's scared!' Damian sounded positive. 'He thinks we know more than we do. He thinks we talked to Sherwood and he told us something about Alex. I bet anything you like.'

'We could go after him, try and find Matt,' Emma said. 'But it's hopeless. Alex's car must find him first. Anyway, I've got the wrong shoes and you've got a gammy knee. Neither of us could make much speed!'

'Trust Matt!' Damian urged. 'He's not daft and he is a copper, after all.'

She could do little else. They sat by the road for a while, huddled together under the blanket.

'Em,' said Damian after a moment. 'This is a funny time to bring this up, but there's something I ought to say to you.'

'What's that?' Emma was puzzled.

'It's just I want to say I'm sorry.'

360

'What for?'

In the shadows she sensed, rather than saw, Damian turn his face away. 'I've been a bit – awkward lately. I know. I don't mean to upset you, Em.'

'Oh, Damian!' Emma gave him a hug. 'I know you don't.'

'But I just don't always want to do the things you want to do, Em.' He sounded exasperated. 'I mean, I do like coming on holiday with you, especially when interesting things happen, like this.'

'*This* is interesting?' Emma took a moment to assimilate this view of events. 'Damian, there are other things which are also very interesting and far less dangerous!'

'Those other things, other people do them on holiday. Things like this,' Damian pointed out with devastating frankness, 'only happen when I go on holiday with you. Or they always did happen. I was afraid that now you're married to a policeman, you'd change. You'd get stuffy and like other people. We wouldn't have any more fun.'

'Matt's fun!' Emma protested.

'He's fine. But he's a policeman and he can't just do as he likes. He has always to be thinking about his job. Now you, you're a writer. People expect you to do odd things.'

'Well, thanks!' said his aunt. She thought about it. 'Actually, I'm beginning to think I'm sometimes a bit irresponsible.'

'That's what makes you the sort of aunt I like,' he told her. 'Everyone at school envies me. Their aunts just take them out to tea or send them hopeless presents.'

'But your mum trusts me.' Emma pointed at the crashed car. 'I don't want to let down someone who relies on me as she does. She must never know about this! At least, not until it's all over.'

The last phrase was to tempt fate.

To Emma's horror, the sound of a car was again distantly audible.

Damian whispered, 'He's coming back! That's Alex's sports job. I recognise the engine.'

Emma made a snap decision. 'Come on, Damian! We can't get far but if we're in the woods over there, he'll have a job to find us at this time of night!'

They scrambled down the ditch and up the further side, past the car at its drunken angle, and into the fringe of trees. Damian hobbled gamely after her, uncomplaining. They had just managed to get a few yards in, when headlights again swept the verge and the car stopped.

A door slammed. They heard footsteps walking on the road surface. After a moment, Alex's voice called out, 'Mrs King?'

Emma and Damian crouched down amongst the resin-scented conifer trunks and held their breath.

'Emma! Damian!' Alex's voice was growing more agitated. 'Please, where ever you are, I have to talk to you!'

Emma gripped Damian's arm and he muttered, 'Ouch!' She forced herself to release her hold on him.

'I didn't find your husband!' Alex called more loudly. He had guessed they must be nearby. 'Please, where are you?'

He waited a while and they heard him enter the outer rim of trees. He began blundering about, muttering curses to himself. But he soon realised that he had little or no chance of finding them. The crack of twigs and sound of Alex's laboured breathing ceased and a few moments later, the car drove off with a now familiar roar.

Emma and Damian stood up.

'Phew!' Emma said. 'That was scary! Sorry I pinched your arm!'

'Think he was telling the truth about Matt?'

Emma considered. 'I think he was. Alex sounded scared. We've split up and he can't find any of us now. He's lost all three!'

'What do we do? Stay here?'

'I'm not sure what's best.' Emma deliberated. 'I think we ought to get away from the car. We can make our way through the edge of the trees, keeping parallel to the road. That way Alex won't see us if he decides to come back. If we hear the breakdown truck coming, I can run out and signal.'

They started slowly through the pines, making their way downhill. It was dark and obstacles littered the woodland floor, broken branches, trailing roots, unseen holes and hummocks. Damian was limping more obviously though he still didn't complain. However, after some five or six minutes, it was obvious that not only could they not hope to get very far, but they ran the risk of one or either of them tripping and becoming more injured.

'It won't do, Damian,' Emma gasped. 'We'll just sit here, near the edge of the trees. We can see the road.'

Damian collapsed thankfully onto the peaty ground, resting his back against a tree. Emma sat beside him. She was sweating profusely, despite the cool night. The silk suit clung to her body uncomfortably.

'What's that?' Damian touched her arm in the gloom. 'I thought I heard a different car, not Alex's.'

'Matt?' Emma exclaimed, making as if to rise.

Damian restrained her. 'No, wait! It wasn't coming from town.

And it's stopped, further up the road, just beyond where we left our car.'

She sank down again. 'Are you sure?'

'Pretty sure. Listen.'

Emma strained her ears. 'Perhaps it's someone driving towards town who's seen the crash and has stopped to investigate.'

They waited. If there were a stranger by the car, he was taking a long time to look around. He must have realised by now no one was there. Why didn't he drive on?

The wind rustled the boughs above their heads and caused odd noises to echo within the woodland. Her skin prickled, not with cooling perspiration, but with a sixth sense. Something was making its way through the trees, nearing them. Something alive.

Damian had sensed or heard it also. 'Something's coming, Em. What is it?' he murmured.

'Matt said there would be deer in the woods,' she whispered in reply, hoping against hope that this would prove the origin of the presence so near at hand.

A branch cracked. Panting breath was nearing them. There was a low yelp. A dog.

There was only one dog she'd seen around here so far.

Duncan Mackenzie's.

Matt had set off as fast as he dared to go in such poor light over uncertain terrain. He had no doubt in his own mind that the car brakes had been tampered with, weakening them. Leaving Emma and Damian by the roadside had been against all his instincts, but he'd noticed there was a garage with a breakdown service on the edge of town and, all being well, he should reach it before long.

The torch swept the verge ahead of him, occasionally picking out a startled rabbit. His own footsteps sounded unnaturally loud on the night air. He had to keep calm, to panic would be fatal. Matt began to plan, as coolly as he could, what to do, once the garage had been contacted.

Loomis next. Fortunately, the inspector had given Matt an emergency number before leaving them at the hotel the previous day. Matt suspected it was Loomis's own home phone number. The inspector would very likely be getting ready to go to bed by now if he wasn't there already.

The narrow torch beam picked up a turning to the left, not much more than a rough track, perhaps leading to a croft. Matt paused, head tilted, listening. An uneven growl and rattle was descending towards him as if someone rolled a giant tin full of dried beans along rocky ground. It had to be some kind of ancient four-wheel-drive vehicle. Lights glowed fitfully. Matt stepped into the road signalling furiously with the torch.

Bouncing and clanking, one of the oldest Land Rovers he'd ever set eyes on emerged from the turning onto the road and stopped.

'What's up there?' shouted a voice.

Matt ran over to it. 'We had an accident just up the road a way. Can you take me down to town, to the breakdown garage?'

'Surely,' said the voice placidly, as if this kind of thing happened all the time.

Matt climbed into the vehicle, apprehension mixed with his relief. The interior smelled as though it had been used for transporting sacks of potatoes and a faint but familiar odour of malt led him to suspect that his rescuer had taken a wee dram to see him on his way.

To his further discomfort, something warm and wet suddenly smothered Matt's ear. He gave a shout of surprise.

'Dinna mind the auld dog,' said the driver. 'She's always friendly.'

Matt turned his head and in the gloom could just make out a black and white face which pushed towards him again, tongue lolling, anxious to give the newcomer another welcoming lick.

'Good girl!' said Matt hastily, avoiding the canine caress.

With a roar and renewed rattling, they set off down the road.

Which was why, when Alex Carter passed that way little more than two minutes later, he failed to find Matt.

At the garage, Matt put in a hasty phone call to Loomis, explaining as briefly as he could what had happened, and apologising for disturbing the inspector so late.

'I'm no' in my bed,' came Loomis's voice down the line. 'I was watching the football, and rubbish it was. You go with the truck and I'll follow on behind you.' There was a pause and Loomis added with a touch of satisfaction, 'I'll fetch out Miller. He'll have been watching the football too, no doubt. If I'm to be up half the night on this business, then so can he be!'

The truck's headlights picked up the crashed car not much later.

'There's your vehicle,' said the driver. 'But I can't see your family.'

Matt leapt down, his heart in his mouth. 'Emma! Damian!'

His voice echoed around the treetops. No reply. He looked up and down the road in despair. Where could they have gone? They couldn't have got far, not on foot.

'No!' he muttered. 'Not on foot! But in a car . . .'

'There's another car parked up there,' the garageman pointed out.

Matt walked a little way up the road to where an elderly saloon he didn't recognise was parked under the trees. There was no sign of any driver. He peered through the rear window. There was a rough cloth of some sort on the back seat, as if some animal travelled there.

Two more vehicles were approaching. They decanted Loomis, a dishevelled Sergeant Miller and a constable.

'I shouldn't have left them here!' Matt said wildly, as Loomis approached.

'Calm yourself, man!' advised Loomis. 'They'll be in the woods yonder, I don't doubt.'

'And so is whoever drove this car here!' Matt declared.

At that moment, as he ceased speaking, a gunshot sounded from within the trees.

'Emma!' Matt yelled and plunged into the woodland in the direction of the noise.

'Alex went back to fetch the dog!' Emma had jumped to her feet, hauling Damian with her, as the reason for the snuffling breath and movement through the trees struck her.

'It's a gundog! He'll have let it sniff something from our car and it's tracking our scent!'

Instinctively they turned to run and stumbled through a few more trees and out into a small clearing. There they stopped.

Damian said with surprising calm, 'We can't outrun it.'

They both turned and stood, waiting, watching the trees behind them. The dog was clearly to be heard now and following behind it, a larger body, a man's. Twigs cracked relentlessly underfoot, like musket fire.

Without warning, the animal debouched from the trees into the small clearing where Emma and Damian stood. The moon chose that moment to emerge once more from the clouds and sent a white spotlight down on them all.

The dog had stopped, nose pointed towards them, a forepaw raised, motionless. Behind it, a man's voice called soft praise. It had done well. A burly figure emerged from the trees. Not Alex, but Duncan, and nursing his shotgun. A gun, Emma feared, which must this time be loaded.

Duncan stared at the two figures before him.

'Where's your man?' he demanded.

'Gone for help. He'll be back soon.' The words sounded brave but pathetic on the night air.

Duncan moved closer. 'You're a set of meddling fools. You should have left well alone. What business is it of yours anyhow?'

Emma said, 'You did it. You cut the brake pipe.'

Silently she bemoaned her earlier action of hiding from Alex. He had not been searching for them in order to harm them. Somehow he'd learned what Duncan had done, and had come looking for them to protect them.

'Why did you do it? To protect Alex?' she asked. She could only hope to keep him talking. Matt surely must get back soon.

'Asking questions, even now!' Duncan gave a snort of disgust.

'You're a sight too curious, lassie, and it's a bad thing, is curiosity. Poking and prying into other folks' affairs.'

'I haven't!' she protested. 'No one has. We don't know what happened.'

'Nor will you learn, now!' was the discouraging response.

Emma's heart leapt painfully. She moved to put herself between Damian and the man. There had to be something they could do. Where, oh where, was Matt?

'Duncan!'

The voice came unexpectedly from the trees. Duncan turned his head sharply.

There was movement in the shadows and Alex Carter stepped out into the clearing.

'Duncan, man, don't be an idiot! This can only make things worse. We're all of us getting in deeper and deeper. It's got to stop, right now!'

As he spoke, Alex was slowly walking across the clearing towards Mackenzie. The dog was obviously undecided. It knew Alex for a friend, but it sensed some dispute between the newcomer and its master. It waggled its stumpy tail uneasily, lowered its head and looked from one man to another, seeking guidance.

Duncan said gruffly, 'I'll not allow these people to cause grief to Mrs Frith!'

'Do you think this won't cause her grief?' Alex had almost reached the man with the gun. The dog growled softly at the fierce note that had entered Alex's voice.

'Duncan,' Alex's voice was again persuasive. The dog cocked its head, confused again. It whined in its throat.

'Let me have the gun, now,' Alex wheedled. 'What happened

before can't be undone. But this would be murder. It can't be, Duncan. It will come out and the knowledge of it would kill Aunt Alice. Only think!'

A momentary hesitation entered Duncan's manner. The gun wavered. Alex seized his chance, plunging forward and grabbing the arm holding the weapon.

It must be a recipe for disaster. Emma reacted instinctively. She launched herself at Damian, wrapping her arms round him. As they crashed full length together across the dry, rough turf of the clearing, the gun discharged with a deafening report.

Part Five

The gunshot echoed through the pinetops, sounding like a clap of thunder on the quiet night air. It succeeded in dislodging roosting pigeons, which flapped away into the night sky in a panic and a great clatter of wings.

Emma's first thought was for Damian. To her immense relief, he was unhurt.

A glance showed her that neither did the shot appear to have hit either of the two men. They grappled together in the moonlight in a desperate contest for possession of the gun. Duncan was fiercely retaining his grip on the weapon and the moonlight glinted off the barrel as it wavered to and fro between them.

Double barrelled, thought Emma. He fired once. There's another shot! The way the two men were behaving, the second barrel was likely to discharge at any moment and in almost any direction.

Duncan's dog, not understanding what was happening, had been driven into a frenzy. It circled the two men, barking furiously, rushing in and then darting back.

This was no place to linger. Emma seized her chance. They mightn't get another.

'Come on, now!' Emma grabbed Damian's arm and they made for the trees towards the sound of Matt's voice, yelling their names.

Despite his sore knee, Damian plunged over the open ground

and as they reached the first tree, Matt ran out and Emma flew into his arms.

He hugged her tightly to him. 'My God, Emma! Are you all right?'

'I'm fine – we're fine . . .' Emma, breathless, pressed her face to his chest. They clung together speechlessly for a moment, no words necessary to express how much this safe reunion meant to them both.

Then Emma blurted, 'Oh, Matt, it wasn't Alex who sabotaged the brake pipe, it was Duncan—'

'All right, now!' He smoothed back her tumbled hair, cradled her face in his hands and added in a hoarse whisper, 'Honestly, darling, I think I've just lived through the worst five minutes of my life!'

He looked over her shoulder towards Damian, who had panted to a halt a short distance away.

'I'm all right,' Damian said. 'But there's a fight going on back there!' He pointed back the way they'd come.

At that moment, Loomis and Sergeant Miller, closely followed by the uniformed constable, emerged from the trees, in time to catch Damian's words.

'I'll take care of that!' Loomis said grimly.

Matt seized his arm. 'Take care, the man's armed!'

'I've radioed for some back-up,' Loomis said. 'But by the time they get here, Duncan will either have done some mischief or made off into the woods. Incidentally, it seems a phone call has been received at the station from Mrs Frith! Leave this to me. Duncan knows me.'

He cupped his hands to his mouth and shouted, 'Duncan

Mackenzie! This is Inspector Loomis. Put that gun down, man! It's no use!'

As he spoke, the wrestling figures broke apart, Alex Carter stumbling back and falling to the ground. Duncan stood, still gripping the shotgun, staring towards Loomis and the others. For a moment his reaction hung in the balance. But as he realised the odds against him, a look of resignation crossed his face.

To everyone's relief, he tossed the weapon to the ground.

'There you are then, polis!' he called sourly.

Alex scrambled to his feet and stood sullenly as Miller and the constable ran forward.

Within seconds it was over, the two men were under arrest and the gun was being carried away as evidence. Duncan's dog, which appeared as relieved as anyone else that matters were settled, trotted after his master as the party made its way back through the woods.

'I can no' leave the dog,' shouted Duncan as he was being bundled into a police car. 'If I go, he'll have to come along too!'

'It makes a change!' said Loomis cheerfully to Emma. 'It's not often I have to arrest a dog!'

Emma had wanted to take Damian to the nearest hospital casualty department to have the knee X-rayed. But Damian wouldn't hear of it. After being involved in all that had gone before, he had no intention of being excluded at the end of the affair!

Thus they all sat, a little later, in the local police station, fortified with mugs of strong tea. The dog had been removed to the police kennels. Duncan Mackenzie sat silent in a corner, holding his cap in his hands and glowering at the assembled company.

As for Alex Carter, that young man bore almost no resemblance to his former cocksure self. He sat nervously nursing his mug of tea, his glance flickering from Matt and Emma to Loomis. There was a dried trickle of blood running from his lower lip down his chin. In the final tussle with Duncan he'd been struck in the mouth. From time to time, he ran the tip of his tongue over his split lip.

His restless gaze finally locked with Emma's accusatory stare. He raised his head and said with a touch of defiance, 'I didn't mean any harm to you, or to Damian, or any of you. I didn't mean any harm to anyone!'

Duncan Mackenzie stirred in his corner. 'It's as the lad says,' he growled. 'The business with the brake pipe was my doing.'

'And Sherwood? What about the poisoned tea?' Emma burst out, ignoring Matt's signals to be quiet and leave questions to Loomis.

Duncan scowled and pressed his lips together. He obviously had no intention of volunteering more information than he had to.

'That wasn't Duncan.' Alex looked away again.

'Your idea, was that, eh?' Loomis asked him.

Duncan opened his mouth and then closed it. Alex said nothing but his general air of misery increased.

Loomis eyed the pair of them, then turned to Miller. 'Take Mackenzie into the interview room, get his story and charge him.'

When Mackenzie had left, the atmosphere lightened a little. Alex's manner gained some confidence. He took a deep swig of tea, set the mug down and asked, 'If I tell you everything, will you take the circumstances into consideration?'

'What circumstances might those be?' Loomis asked him. His

manner suggested he'd heard all kind of excuses in his day and was unlikely to be impressed by any Alex might produce.

Alex flushed at the inspector's sarcastic tone. 'We're not criminals! None of us!'

'None of you?' Loomis squinted at him. 'So, who else is involved in this affair, apart from Mackenzie and yourself? You're saying Mrs Frith had a hand in things?'

'No!' Alex jumped out of his chair. The constable made a move towards him and Alex sat down again hurriedly. He leaned forward, his manner agitated.

'For goodness' sake! You can't believe Aunt Alice knew anything about any of this before tonight? That's madness! After I found your car crashed, King, I had to go back and just throw myself on her mercy. I explained Emma and Damian wouldn't come back with me and Matt was somewhere along the road into town. As for Duncan, I didn't know where he was, only that he'd got his dog and the gun . . .' Alex ran his hands through his dishevelled hair.

'Your aunt phoned the station after we'd left,' Loomis nodded. 'And in a rare state, I'm told! It seems to me that whatever you've been up to, you might have thought about her before you started it!'

'I know. You don't have to tell me!' Alex appeared near to tears.

Emma couldn't help feeling sorry for him, though he'd brought all his troubles on himself. She watched as Alex clasped and unclasped his hands nervously. She felt she was beginning to understand him. His was not a resolute character, but one of those easily swept along by events and influenced by stronger personalities than his own.

'It's all my fault!' he said wretchedly. 'But I haven't committed any crime. It was Duncan's and Jean Ross's doing. They wanted to help me but mostly to shield Aunt Alice from knowing about the trouble I was in. And Jean certainly didn't mean for anyone to die. Duncan did worse by tampering with your car, but he was always a crazy old fool!'

He was beginning to sound aggrieved. Emma thought Alex wanted to justify what had been done to appease his conscience. He saw the expression on her face and flushed crimson as he realised that she had so easily divined his mind.

'I admit it was all because of me!' he said angrily. 'I met Sherwood up here, some time ago. He believed the Scottish air was good for him. He came every year, never failed.' Alex grimaced. 'He invited me to go along to one of his clubs, when I should be in London. He said there would be gambling going on there but it was quite legal. I now realise he'd heard of Aunt Alice and thought that, as she was wealthy, I must have a lot of money, too. In fact, I don't!

'I started going to his clubs. Some of the people playing were well known. I recognised their faces. I thought it must be all right!'

Alex noticed the scepticism on the faces of his listeners.

'I know now that it was stupid. The regulars there were mostly experienced gamblers. They don't get in over their heads. I suppose, if I'm to be honest, I wanted to show off, impress others there. I must have been the typical mug!'

'Aye, you're not the first, nor will be the last!' Loomis told him.

Alex stiffened and something of his old arrogance returned. 'I'm prepared to make a full statement. But I want our Frith family solicitor present!'

'We'll fetch your lawyer,' Loomis nodded. 'But there'll be no walking away from what was done, Mr Carter.'

'I know,' Alex said quietly. 'I should have faced up to things at the beginning. I left it too late.'

The river splashed over the rocks at the Soldier's Leap, gurgling and chuckling. A group of children, who'd been standing listening to an adult tell the old tale of the fleeing Englishman and the pursuing Highlanders, turned and ran shrieking and laughing up the hill towards the Killicrankie tourist centre.

In the peace and solitude that followed, Matt King tossed a pebble into the sparkling water and rolled onto one hip to lean over his wife. She lay on the rug beside him, her upturned face to the sun. Her eyes were closed, her cheeks flushed pink. Matt picked a stem of grass and brushed it across her nose.

Without opening her eyes, she put up her hand to knock away the insect she supposed it to be.

He repeated the trick. Emma opened her eyes. 'I might have guessed!' she said.

'Enjoying the holiday?' he asked.

'Bliss!'

He kissed her and she wound her arms round his neck to pull his head down so that she could kiss him in return.

Matt leaned back when she'd released him, propped on one elbow. 'I phoned through to Devon this morning, before we left the hotel. I explained what had happened. I think there'll be no objection to my taking an extra few days to compensate.'

'Really?' Emma's face registered her delight.

377

'But I had to promise you'd behave! Absolutely swear, hand on heart, that you'd get us into no more scrapes!'

She sat up so suddenly she almost hit his nose with her head. 'You didn't! They didn't ask that, did they? The cheek!'

'Calm down!' Matt was laughing. 'No, they didn't. You rise to the bait very nicely, Mrs King!'

'I don't know why I let you get away with it! I should know by now when you're teasing!' Emma tossed back her hair, worn loose today. 'You don't need to worry, anyway. I don't want any more alarms. Not on this holiday at least!'

'Not on any holiday, please!' he begged.

But Emma was thinking of Damian's words, that holidays with her were interesting because the unexpected happened.

'Mmn . . .' she said absently.

'Emma . . .!'

'I'll try!' Her blue eyes fixed him guilelessly. 'I can't say more than that, can I?'

'Why do I have this awful premonition?'

She dismissed his fears briskly. 'You're hungry. It's an empty tum, not an awful forewarning! Do you think it's time we went and fetched Damian?'

Matt glanced at his watch. 'Yes. Come on. I hope he hasn't outworn his welcome!'

The wrought-iron gates stood wide, no Duncan to guard them today. The door to the Frith house was opened to them by a sturdy young woman in a pink checked overall.

'Oh, they're not indoors!' she said. 'They're out in Mrs Frith's greenhouse.'

So that was where they found Damian and Mrs Frith. They were seated side by side before a bench, potting up cuttings and chatting together like old friends. Damian's face was a study in concentration and he pressed the green shoots into the compost with careful fingers.

'I never thought he'd make a gardener!' Emma whispered to Matt.

Mrs Frith looked up as they entered. Emma saw for the first time Duncan's dog. It had been slumbering on a bed of old sacks in the warm greenhouse, close by the gardeners' feet. Now it trotted forward, sniffed at Emma's outstretched hand, and waggled its stump of a tail in welcome. It, too, was anxious to make peace.

'Have you come to take away my helper?' Mrs Frith smiled. 'Damian, run up to the house now and tell Morag to make a pot of tea. We'll have it in the garden, it's so lovely.'

Damian duly set off, not at a run because his knee was still stiff, but at a fast hobble.

'Thank you for lending me the young man,' Mrs Frith said quietly. 'He's been a great comfort.'

She wiped her hands on a cloth, picked up her stick and led the way to the greenhouse door. As they walked slowly across the lawn, the dog at their heels, Emma said, 'We are so sorry about everything. If Damian can cheer you up, it's the least we can do.'

'My dear! It's not your fault!' Mrs Frith raised her cane to point at the house ahead of them. Today its turrets and crenellations sparkled in the sunlight.

'This house,' she said, 'was built by my husband's great-grandfather. He had high hopes, so it's said, that it would be graced by a Royal Presence one day. Perhaps to take tea? He was over-ambitious, it seems, and Queen Victoria declined to stop off here on any of her travels in the area. Such a pity because he instructed his architect to build it in the style she admired! There is a tale, passed on in the family, that one day, hearing the Royal Party was to pass along this road, he lined up all the local people with flags and flowers. The royal carriage rattled into view to cheers and waving of banners. It stopped! Hearts were in mouths! My husband's ancestor hurried forward, bowing low. But it was John Brown, no less no more, the royal gillie and favourite, who descended to collect a few posies. The whole equipage drove off, while great-grandfather Frith was still bent double in homage. The Widow of Windsor had eluded him again.' She chuckled. 'We don't know if it's true, but the Highlands are full of tales and legends.'

She grew serious again. 'Jean Ross, Duncan and I have been together here so long we'd become a family. Alex has lived here from the age of seven. We all of us had a hand in bringing him up. I say that so that perhaps you'll understand something of why they acted as they did, although it can't be excused, I know. When I think of you, my dear . . .'

Mrs Frith touched Emma's arm. 'And the boy. What might have happened. How you could have been hurt when your car crashed! It will mean prison for Duncan, for sure. In due course, when he's released, I have doubts as to whether I can take him back here. I shall find it hard to overlook such an awful deed.'

They had reached a paved area to the side of the house where a table and chairs were set out ready for the tea. When they'd seated themselves, Mrs Frith looked at her stained hands and remarked, 'I shall just have to go up to the house and rinse these!

But I should like to tell you first what Alex told me, that dreadful evening. When he realised he'd lost track of you all, Emma, he returned home in a terrible state. I'd gone to bed, but he came to my room and begged me to listen to his story. He wanted to make a clean breast of everything.

'You'll know already how he gambled at those clubs and lost so much money. I'm hardly surprised!' She gave a rueful laugh. 'I'm sure he'd never done more before than sit in on a few hands of whist with me, Jean and some visitor! The sort of thing going on in that club, it was well out of his league! But he hadn't the sense to quit. Thought he'd look a fool, no doubt.'

Mrs Frith moved uncomfortably on her chair. 'He'd persuaded Sherwood to give him credit, assuring him I would always underwrite the boy's debts. Alex was sure that, sooner or later, he must hit a winning streak, as do all gamblers!

'But eventually, after he'd managed to put Sherwood off for a while, he had to admit he hadn't the money. Sherwood reminded Alex that he'd said I would fund him if things got tight.'

Alice Frith gave a little 'tsk' of exasperation. 'The silly boy wanted to gain time. He thought he could come up with some scheme to pay off the debts. He even, so he told me, considered selling the car. But I'd only just bought that car for his birthday and he was afraid of arousing my suspicions.'

She sighed. 'Apparently, Sherwood arrived here on his annual holiday. He told Alex if he didn't pay up, he would go to me, taking Alex's IOUs which he'd brought with him. He said it was a matter of principle that everyone paid him. He couldn't let one person off. The word would get round and no one would pay their debts!'

381

'That's the quarrel I overheard!' Emma exclaimed, unable to keep silent.

Mrs Frith looked surprised. 'You did? When?'

Emma had the grace to blush. 'From my bath. I mean, the party wall was very thin and Alex and Sherwood were shouting. I couldn't help but overhear.'

'I see. Sherwood succeeded in terrifying Alex. It's possible, I suppose, that he only meant to frighten him into paying. But Alex couldn't be sure. He'd made Sherwood angry, spoken to him in a way which was unwise. Sherwood wasn't a man to forget an insult.'

She drew a deep breath. 'Alex felt he couldn't talk to me about his troubles and for that I have to bear some responsibility. The boy should have thought he could come to me and not been afraid to do so.'

'It was because he loves you,' Emma said. 'And knew how hurt you'd be.'

'Perhaps. However, he had to talk to someone and he told Jean Ross. Poor Jean was worried Sherwood would appear at the house, demanding to see me. They discussed what they could do to put him off and hatched a lunatic plan. Jean knows a lot about medicinal plants and herbal remedies. Her grandmother used to be some kind of herbalist, years ago, in her village, during the last war. A sort of white witch, as far as I've ever been able to make out!' Mrs Frith spread out her earth-stained hands in a resigned gesture.

'Alex had told her how concerned Sherwood appeared to be about his health. He'd noticed he was a teetotaller, always drinking tea. It gave Jean the idea to concoct something to mix with tea leaves. She suggested she make up some special teabags and smuggle them into his room. They'd make him ill. Not seriously, but enough to put him off coming to see me. With luck, he'd go back to London to consult his own doctors. Alex had earlier obtained a duplicate key to Sherwood's room. He meant to search for the IOUs. If Sherwood had nothing he could show me, he'd be less likely to come here. But on the one occasion Alex did search, he couldn't find anything. Sherwood either kept them on him, or had put them in the hotel safe. Desperate, Alex listened to Jean's idea.' Mrs Frith leaned forward again urgently. 'Their intention was truly only to make Sherwood feel ill enough to return to London.

'Jean and Alex went to the hotel that evening. Naturally they were afraid of being seen. Jean peeked in the dining room to check Sherwood was at dinner. Then she went upstairs and substituted the teabags she'd made up for the ones in the room. She came back to where Alex waited in the hotel car park and told him it was done. Then she came home here. Later, when they heard of the poor man's death, Jean went back and hastily removed the evidence using the same duplicate key.

'As for Alex, he'd already begun to fear they'd be found out, the moment Jean said she'd made the switch. Suppose Sherwood went to a doctor here and the doctor sent samples for analysis? It was a stupid thing they'd undertaken. Alex decided to have one last talk with Sherwood. Make a last appeal.

'He met him in the lounge at the hotel. Sherwood refused to listen and Alex became angry. He thought, let him drink the wretched spiked tea! He ran out of the hotel in a rage.' Mrs Frith glanced at Damian. 'You were on your way in. He nearly sent you flying, I'm afraid.'

'I remembered him,' Damian said.

'Alex feared you might.' Mrs Frith made a visible effort to relate the final part of the sorry tale. Despite the stress caused to herself, she was obviously determined to tell it all.

'You know what happened. Sherwood drank the tea. But Jean hadn't allowed for his medical condition. It may have affected his heart. He went out playing golf and the extra strain, the exercise, was the last straw. It never occurred to them he'd play golf.'

'For some medical conditions, exercise is recommended, provided it's taken sensibly,' Matt observed.

She nodded. 'What I have to say now, will always cause me the greatest grief.' She looked up and met their combined gaze. 'You may recall Alex went out of the room to phone, after dinner?'

Matt, Emma and Damian all nodded.

She hunched her shoulders. 'He didn't really phone. He'd recognised Damian and was afraid he'd been recognised in return. He went down to the kitchen and told Jean. He also wasn't sure how well you, Emma, had known Sherwood. Jean was worried too. She was in her car, in the hotel parking lot, when there was the incident involving Sherwood and your car. She'd driven off at once, but she was also worried you might have noticed her. I fear our wretched pair of conspirators must have felt you were everywhere!

'Duncan was sitting in the kitchen having his supper as Jean and Alex discussed it. He took it into his head to sabotage your brakes. Alex swears he didn't know what he'd done until after you left. He was frantic! He jumped in his car and went out to see if you were safe and saw the car in the ditch! It was a dreadful moment! You and Damian, Emma, thank goodness, were unhurt, but obviously suspicious, refusing to come back to the house with him. And your husband had set out for town.'

Mrs Frith again threw out her hands in a despairing gesture. 'When Alex got back there was a row with Duncan, who decided to grab his gun and go looking for you and the boy! At that point what was left of Alex's nerve cracked. He ran upstairs to wake me and blurt out everything. I told him he must try to find Duncan before Duncan found you. When he'd left, I phoned the police. They said the inspector and the sergeant had already set out. Jean and I sat in the kitchen passing what was truly the worst night of both our lives. Poor Jean Ross blamed herself and I blamed myself. Oh, we were a sorry pair!'

'Well, Alex did find us,' Emma reassured her. Mrs Frith was becoming very agitated and Emma was anxious to soothe their elderly hostess. 'Not before Duncan found us, but in time, anyway. So it all ended all right.'

There was a silence. Mrs Frith appeared calmer and went on, 'Inspector Loomis called on me earlier today. He had some news he thought I ought to know. It seems medical opinion is now divided over how much effect that herbal brew of Jean's had on Sherwood. They think the poor man's health was so bad he could have gone at any time. It's debatable how much the poisoned tea hurried things along. It probably did no more than give him a severe stomach ache! So much for these old wives' potions! I am so glad, because Jean has been with me for so many years and I really couldn't face the thought she had become a murderess for my sake or Alex's. In her own wrong-headed but loyal way she tried to protect me. Since it's likely the charges against her will be reduced, I hope that she'll eventually be able to return here when it's all over.'

'That's good news,' Emma said.

'The good thing,' said Mrs Frith, 'is that you bear us no ill will. For that I thank you. I hope that now you'll be able to enjoy the rest of your stay in peace! And I pray that Alex has at least learned his lesson from this whole sad affair. Let's hope that now he'll settle down and eventually bring a wife to this house, and there will be children playing here once more.'

Figures were approaching, Morag with the tea tray and Damian lugging a garden parasol. Mrs Frith got up.

'I'll away and wash my hands. You'll help yourselves. Don't wait for me to come back.' Leaning forward she added in a mischievous whisper, 'Morag is my daily cleaner. A nice girl but no hand with pastry! However, don't worry! Jean being Jean,' Mrs Frith gave a wry smile, 'she at least left me a freezer full of home-baked cakes! Damian will be pleased about that, I think!'

She set off towards the house. Morag put down the tray and smiled brightly.

'There you are now. Eat hearty!'

When she'd gone, Emma, Matt and Damian surveyed the spread of cakes, scones and other delights.

'Jean Ross made these?' Matt peered at them. 'Let's hope there are no – er – added ingredients.'

'It doesn't worry me!' said Damian, helping himself to a scone and handing the plate to Emma.

'Nor me!' she said.

The Spirit of the Hearth

They moved into the house on a Monday, early in the spring. The cat arrived the following Saturday morning. As Margot opened the kitchen door, a dark shape, crouched low, squeezed past her and ran under the table. Startled, she let out a shriek.

Duncan shouted, 'What the devil—?' and began to chase the animal round the table. The cat nipped in and out of Duncan's feet and the furniture legs until Duncan stumbled and cracked his knee. He began to swear and curse in language which surprised Margot. Normally he had an unimaginative turn of phrase.

Eventually the cat streaked out through the door again.

'Poor thing, you frightened it!' said Margot reproachfully.

'Good!' retorted Duncan nastily, rubbing his bruised knee.

During the chase the porridge had congealed and the bacon burned to a crisp beneath the grill. It wasn't a good start to the weekend. But it was, thought Margot as she scraped the porridge pot, par for the course. But then, she hadn't wanted to move to this isolated house in the first place. A desolate neck of the woods, it appeared to her, offering not a soul for company. She clanged the pan against the side of the sink with unnecessary force.

The cat hadn't gone away. It crouched in the drizzling rain under the eaves of one of the two stone barns on the property, its eyes fixed on the house.

From the window, Margot asked, 'I wonder where it came from?'

Duncan, stomping around with hammer and nails, growled, 'I don't care. Just chase the brute away!'

'He's not a brute,' she said. 'He's rather handsome.'

DIY carpentry was Duncan's hobby and a new home offered him endless scope to indulge it. He specialised in putting up shelves, whether new shelving was needed or not, only satisfied when every available wall space bristled with lengths of pinewood. Margot pointed out that the shelves collected dust and made it impossible to reposition the furniture. But he ignored her.

When the rain stopped, and distant hammering indicated her husband was safely occupied, Margot went out and made friendly overtures to the cat.

He – for the newcomer was clearly a feline gentleman-adventurer – was black all over without a single white hair. He was fully grown and strongly made. If he had a fault, it was that his head was oddly shaped, broad and flat, and his smallish ears stuck outwards, on either side of his face, like a pair of lip handles on an urn. In compensation he had magnificent topaz eyes, gleaming against his jet fur.

Otherwise, he was in a sorry state. His coat was unkempt, he limped and looked as if he'd been living wild.

Throughout the day he continued to try to get into the house, growing ever more ingenious and desperate. Around four o'clock they were seated in the drawing room having a cup of tea. Duncan had just said, 'I could put some shelves either side of that hearth . . .' when they were startled by the shrill screech of claws scraping on glass.

Duncan nearly jumped out of his skin. A black shadow slithered through the open transom window and dropped to the floor with a thud. Enterprisingly, the cat had leapt from an emptied packing case deposited outside, to grab the window frame and scramble through the narrow aperture.

There was another Keystone Cops pursuit during which a Victorian card table which had belonged to Duncan's grandmother was knocked over and slightly marked.

The cat, ejected again, retired under the barn eaves and lay siege to the back door.

Eventually Margot took pity on him. She hunted in the larder for something a cat might eat and – while Duncan was measuring up for additional shelving in the linen cupboard – took a saucer of tuna fish outside. The cat watched her approach with suspicion, but he could smell the fish. As she put it down, he rubbed his wet fur against her leg before inspecting the offering. Then he ate it all. Margot felt absurdly pleased, like a mother whose infant had just managed a new skill.

'I do wish I knew where you came from,' she told him.

He gave her a cursory glance and set about cleaning himself up. He'd lost his air of desperation and there was a certain permanence about him, sitting there, polishing his whiskers. Wherever he'd come from, clearly he now meant to stay here.

He hung about for the next few days out of doors. Duncan swore at him and shied the occasional missile which the cat dodged. Margot surreptitiously bought cat food on her next shopping foray and fed him behind Duncan's back. The cat recognised her now and, when he saw her coming, would walk to meet her uttering chirrups of greeting. She called him 'Puss', because she didn't know what else to call him. She'd never kept a cat. Duncan disliked the idea of animals around the house.

They only ever did as Duncan wanted. Like moving to the Highlands. She'd been quite happy in Perth. But then Duncan had bought this former farmhouse, its stone outbuildings now converted into garaging. It was situated between Pitlochry and Aberfeldy and he announced he would commute from here into Perth, despite the long drive.

And all this, mind you, without a word of consultation. It didn't seem to occur to him that he took Margot away from all her friends, the many charitable concerns with which she'd been involved, the shops she knew and any form of entertainment, and plonked her down here in the middle of nowhere. On weekdays she was totally alone from after breakfast when he left till he returned for his supper in the evening. She could drive into either of the two towns, but they were small places and it would be difficult to spend more than an hour in either one of them.

At night, during much of the following week, the cat sat on a barn roof and yowled. The sound echoed eerily around the surrounding braes, sometimes sounding like a baby in distress and sometimes low and ominous as if some ancient being had stirred and called out to know who disturbed the sleep of centuries.

'Will you listen to that?' Duncan muttered, thumping the pillows. 'Like a blasted banshee!'

Margot crept out of bed and stood at the window. The sky was overcast but, as she watched, a paler, ink-blue patch lightened and the cloud cover slid aside to reveal a dead-white moon. In the pale light she thought she could distinguish a small shape perched on a ridge tile.

'He wants to come indoors,' she said.

'Over my dead body!' retorted her husband from the bed behind her.

The next morning, as Margot was settling the week's account with the milkman on the doorstep, the cat strolled round the corner of the house.

The milkman, a shaven-headed youth with an earring, said, 'Hullo, Hamish! I see they left you behind!'

'You know him?' Margot exclaimed.

'Aye. It's Mrs Frayne's cat, the lady who lived here before you.'

'But she moved miles away! He must have found his way back!' Margot stared at the cat, marvelling.

'Canny beasts, cats,' opined the milkman.

'Well, write to her!' Duncan ordered. 'Tell her we've got the creature and we'll put it in a basket and send it along by train.'

Margot wrote. Mrs Frayne wrote back to say she was glad Hamish was safe. She'd been worried. He'd run off from his new home within twenty-four hours. There didn't seem any point in returning him. He'd only run away again. Surely his attachment to his old house ought to be rewarded? Would they like to keep him?

'No!' snapped Duncan. 'Can you believe the effrontery of the woman?'

Margot heard herself say, loudly and firmly, 'I would like to keep him. He'll be company for me while you're away. In fact, I think I shall keep him.'

Duncan stared at her in surprise. She so seldom opposed him.

This time some new note in her voice told him her mind was made up.

'All right,' he said grudgingly. 'But keep it out of my way!'

Duncan needn't have worried about Hamish keeping out of his way. The cat refused to go anywhere near him. If Duncan came into the drawing room, Hamish would rise from his favourite place before the wide stone hearth, and stalk out, quivering disapproval. If forced to share room space with Duncan, Hamish could crouch immobile except for the very tip of his long black tail. This would twitch from time to time as if pent-up rage sent an electric charge running down his spine.

Having Hamish around made all the difference to Margot. She began to talk to him as she would a human companion. Every morning, just like a pair of human friends, they had elevenses together. Margot had coffee and Hamish had a saucer of milk. She had always bought semi-skimmed milk because Duncan worried about his cholesterol. But Hamish didn't care for semi-skimmed, so Margot began to buy one pint of full cream milk per week, just for Hamish.

She also bought a book on *Caring For Your Cat.*

To her alarm, the writer of the book was stern on the subject of feeding milk to cats. He insisted it was a food, not a drink, and played havoc with a cat's diet. He was against giving mature cats milk.

Margot read this bit out aloud to Hamish. He sat on a chair opposite her across the kitchen table, watching her with his tawny eyes and listening. When she'd finished, he directed a withering look at the book and his whiskers bristled. 'Much that fellow knows about cats!' he seemed to be saying. 'Calls himself an expert?'

* * *

As summer passed, Margot forgot Perth and her resentment at being removed from her former home. She began to understand Hamish's attachment to this present one.

The house was very old and built of a grey granite which, if you looked closely, was infused with shimmering echoes of slate-blue and mauve-pink.

Its great hearth, where Hamish liked to snooze, still had an iron hook from which a cauldron had once been suspended. The brickwork at the back of it was as black as Hamish's fur from a couple of hundred years of scorching flames.

It was beneath the stone flags of such hearths that, in olden times, the spirit of the house dwelt. The origins of this belief are long lost. Perhaps the spirit was a fire god. Or just a household deity of the sort worshipped from ancient Rome to the Far East. But he kept a watchful presence over his domain and could not be separated nor driven from it. Each new owner had first to placate him with small offerings of food and drink. Failure to do this would have resulted in ill fortune befalling the household for the spirit, true to his fiery nature, was easily made angry.

Perhaps, too, at some time the memory of the hearth spirit became confused with the legend of St Nicholas. Even now, hopeful children leave out offerings of mince pies and glasses of sherry for Father Christmas who, clad in his flame-red suit, enters the house via the chimney and will reward those who are true to him.

As for the house's twisting wooden staircase, that creaked with age as if its bones had set. Its banister was worn smooth by countless hands and its treads had warped and were uneven.

'This all needs replacing,' said Duncan, a manic gleam in his eye.

'Don't you dare!' cried Margot.

She was standing up for herself more and more these days and it seemed to puzzle him.

On the landing at the top of the stairs stood an ancient cupboard. Across the upper frame in brass studs was emblazoned the date 1788. Mrs Frayne had left it behind because, she said, it had been there when she came and, as far as she knew, had always been in the house. The top of this cupboard was another of Hamish's favoured retreats. He reached it by leaping first onto the newel post at the head of the stairs and thence to the cupboard top. Margot put a piece of old blanket up there for him.

Sometimes she and Hamish went for summer walks, climbing the steep path beside the rustling, splashing burn. Great boulders had rolled down from far above, who knew how many centuries before, and now lay strewn about. Densely growing trees shut out the sky. Hamish walked a little behind her in stately fashion and kept well clear of the water. If they met anyone – especially someone with a dog – he scrabbled up the nearest tree until the intruder had gone away. Dogs skirted the tree and Hamish with respect, very often in a shame-faced sort of way with their tails drooping. Only the bravest gave a nervous bark. Such was the power of Hamish's baleful topaz glare.

As autumn approached, the trees turned to glorious shades of flame-red, pale orange and golden-brown. It was so beautiful all around that every morning, when she got up, Margot threw open the window and just stood there, wondering at it all.

She realised she'd fallen in love for the very first time in her life. She was in love with this old house, the surrounding mountains and forests, everything. She loved it far more than she'd ever loved Duncan or anything else. She never wanted to leave it. She belonged here, just as Hamish felt he did. She and the cat together.

But something was going on. It had been going on all summer. To be quite honest, it had started before they left Perth, but Margot had ignored the signs.

More and more often, Duncan stayed late in Perth 'at the office'. But on several occasions, when she rang to see what she should do about supper, she only got the office cleaner who told her everyone had gone home ages earlier.

Then he began to ring late in the day to say he wouldn't be home at all that night. The pressure of work meant he had to stay on and it made better sense for him to stay over and return the following evening.

Next he bought some expensive new shirts and two or three rather bright ties, quite unlike his usual sober choice. He also took to using a scented aftershave.

At weekends – for goodness' sake – he started jogging. For this he bought a royal blue tracksuit with a white flash on the jacket. Clad in this startling outfit and large, clumsy white trainer shoes, he puffed up and down the hills and returned alarmingly purple in the face and sweating.

'Got to keep in trim!' he said. But didn't say why.

After a couple of weekends of this, his ankles ballooned and he developed painful shin splints. By Monday morning he could only hobble to the car, watched by Margot and Hamish in silence.

Then there were the phone calls. They came when Duncan was at home and he always dashed (or limped very fast depending on his fitness régime) to answer before she could get there. If she did pick the phone up first, the caller rang off as soon as Margot said, 'Hullo?'

'Hamish,' she said to the cat one morning across the kitchen table, 'a person can only be a fool for so long. He's got Another Woman!'

Hamish blinked his topaz eyes and looked wary.

'How long's it been going on, I wonder? Quite a while, I shouldn't be surprised. That's why he brought me all the way up here away from Perth! So as I shouldn't find out and he could have his fun undisturbed! I expect she's young and pretty. What on earth does she see in him?' Margot added in wonder.

He was, after all, of dour disposition and his sole passion to her knowledge had only ever been woodwork. Perhaps with his new lady-friend he was the life and soul of the party. It was hard to imagine. But on the other hand, perhaps she oughtn't to be surprised.

Margot was forty-six. Some women looked younger than their age but Margot had always looked hers. Even as a child she'd looked a year or two older than she was. ('Only five? And such a – er – bonnie lassie!') The spectacles didn't help. She'd always been short sighted. She'd tried contact lenses but hadn't got on with them. Fashionable clothes looked nothing on her and she stuck to skirts and sweaters. So that was it. Middle aged, bespectacled and plain.

'And about to be dumped!' she informed the cat. 'Traded in for a newer, flashier model, Hamish!'

Hamish looked as if he might argue.

'Now, I know what you're thinking,' Margot told him, 'but you're wrong. I don't mind Duncan finding me dull. Let the old goat make a fool of himself. I don't actually want him. What I do want is my home, here, and if I don't watch out, I'll lose it! And so, Hamish, will you! Both of us, out on our ears.'

Perhaps Hamish was sensitive about his rather small and oddly placed ears because he lowered them at this, and looked huffy.

But she'd told him the truth. She could lose the only thing she had which she loved with passion, the house. She had no money of her own. She had never had a career because Duncan hadn't wanted her to work. (A wife with a successful career, she had realised too late, would have been a threat to his ego.) They had no children. Everything was Duncan's.

She supposed, if they divorced, their finances would be divided, but knowing Duncan, he'd manage to fiddle it to his advantage. He was a lawyer, for goodness' sake. Even if she could persuade him to let her have this house, she wouldn't be able to afford to live here. Only think of the heating costs and the general maintenance! And she'd need to keep her little car, living way out here and the bus service so scarce. Soon it would be winter and the snow would lie on the ground. Then she'd really be cut off.

'When the weather turns bad, he'll get fed up with trying to commute to Perth. That's when he'll leave,' she said to the cat. 'We've got to do something before that, Hamish!' But she really didn't know what.

In the meantime, she polished and dusted and kept the old house immaculate. The fierce possessiveness grew in her. She wouldn't let it go, she wouldn't!

The phone continued to ring at intervals and when she answered, the line, as before, went dead. Duncan, heaven help them, bought a pair of jeans.

He also refused to eat red meat and took to crunching Ryvita instead of toast at breakfast.

'That, Hamish,' said Margot, 'is so that he can squeeze into the jeans! She'll be the death of him if he goes on like this.'

Hamish yawned widely, stretching his jaw and rolling back his upper lip to reveal needle-sharp teeth and a curled pink tongue. It was the nearest thing to a cat-sneer she'd ever seen.

One morning, when there was a real bite in the air, the milkman told her that snow had fallen the night before on the high ground. Winter was on its way.

Duncan announced that he had to go away for the weekend, to a business conference, in Edinburgh. But when she went into the bedroom on Friday morning he was packing his bright ties and expensive shirts and the jeans.

She hadn't meant to accuse him, because she had no real proof. But somehow, perhaps it was the sight of those hopelessly inappropriate clothes, she couldn't help it. It all poured out. She told him she knew he had someone else.

He didn't deny it. He just agreed, in a serenely pompous way, that he did. Fiona, her name was. She wasn't long out of law school, a bright girl and utterly charming. He told Margot all this with a smirking pride which was both repellent and ridiculous.

'And what,' asked Margot scornfully, 'does a bright, charming girl want with a humourless, balding, middle-aged man?'

Fiona, it seemed, found older men more interesting. She had told Duncan that she had never even considered a partner in her own age group. Young men were callow. Older men had experience.

'The only partnership she's interested in,' said Margot, 'is in the firm!'

Duncan said that was an unworthy remark. But, as it happened, he meant to offer Fiona a partnership in everything. Yes, he wanted a divorce. He trusted they could come to an agreeable settlement.

'Oh, do you? And what,' demanded Margot, her voice on edge, 'does an agreeable settlement mean? Agreeable to whom?'

Duncan said he hoped she wasn't going to be mean spirited. She ought not to deny him and Fiona happiness just because she was so discontented. He was disappointed she was being difficult. Perhaps she ought to see her doctor and get some pills or something? It was probably the menopause.

Margot rode roughshod over this. 'What about this house?' she asked, her voice cracking.

'We'll sell it, naturally,' Duncan said. 'And divide the money. You'll have enough to buy yourself a little flat somewhere.'

'I don't want a flat!' she yelled. 'I want my home!'

He said, 'Don't be silly. What would you do in a great empty house like this?' And with that, he walked out of the room onto the landing.

She flew after him and grabbed his arm. He tried to shake her off but Margot clung, shouting at him.

'For twenty years I've kept house for you, an unpaid housekeeper! For twenty years nothing but cooking and cleaning and shopping! A roof over my head is the only thing I had – and even then I had to earn it! What kind of partnership did you ever offer me? Our house wasn't something I shared with you! It was the place where I was employed – to look after you! Now you tell me it's something you think you can take back when you feel like it! Just as you took away my home in Perth, so now you want to take away this one, too! You shan't, do you hear? I won't let you, I won't!'

Duncan snapped back that it wasn't his fault if she hadn't found her life fulfilling. He'd always assumed she was perfectly happy and if she hadn't been, well, that wasn't his responsibility.

'Hypocrite!' she yelled, at which he uttered an exclamation of disgust and gave her a violent shove which loosened her grip and sent her spinning back.

She struck the wall behind her and slipped, ending up sitting on the floor with one leg crooked up and one out straight. Her glasses had fallen off and she had to scrabble around for them before she could do anything else. When she got them back on her nose, she saw that Duncan had started to walk downstairs, ignoring her plight. His back view was rigid with self-righteousness.

Neither of them had noticed the cat, so taken up were they with their own quarrel. Hamish had been crouched on top of the old cupboard on the landing as they argued, his ears flattened and his tail lashing. Now, without warning, he leapt.

To Margot, still sitting on the floor, the creature which launched itself from the cupboard wasn't Hamish at all. It was bigger, enormous, its jet fur bristling, yellow flames shooting from eyes like pits of molten gold, its sharp white teeth bared in a ferocious snarl. Its front legs were outstretched like bat's wings and, as it hurtled through the air, it let out a dreadful, blood-curdling hiss such as she'd never imagined from man or beast.

Duncan heard it and turned. For a second, only a brief moment, his face registered horror. He raised his arm to protect his face, but too late. The cat wrapped itself around his head. Scarlet lines appeared across the man's cheeks and brow. Blood spurted from the skin where the sharp claws dug in. Duncan staggered on the uneven old stairs as he tried simultaneously to push away the cat and grab at the banister.

He achieved neither. He fell, crashing down the whole length of the stairs, his body sliding helplessly from tread to tread, his head banging on the banister, man and cat locked together in an awful embrace.

They landed with an impact which made the whole stairway and landing shudder. Then there was a silence which was even worse.

Margot scrambled to her feet and hurried down the stairs. 'Hamish? Are you all right? Where are you?'

A low growl answered. She saw topaz eyes gleaming in the far corner of the hall. The cat crouched there, fur still bristling and tail thumping the ground. Duncan lay at the foot of the stairs, half turned onto his back. She knelt over him.

His eyes flickered up at her and his mouth moved but no sound came out. Thick, dark blood began to trickle from one ear and then from his nostrils and finally from his mouth. He made a sound at last, an indistinct mumbling. A desperate urgency entered his eyes but he didn't, or couldn't, move.

She jumped up and ran to the telephone. As she picked up the receiver, she heard another warning growl. From the corner Hamish's topaz eyes were fixed on her with mesmeric power, as if forbidding her to summon aid.

Obediently she put back the receiver and sat down on the chair by the telephone table. She sat there for perhaps a quarter of an hour. Then Hamish uncoiled himself and strolled away into the drawing room. Margot rose stiffly and went to where Duncan lay. His eyes gazed up, sightless.

She went back to the telephone and dialled for the ambulance.

Duncan was declared dead on arrival at hospital. A little later in the day, two police officers came, a man and a female colleague.

401

Both were very kind, but asked a lot of questions in a gentle, probing sort of way.

'The gentleman's face was severely lacerated,' the woman officer said. She glanced at Hamish who reclined in a shaft of pale sunlight, blinking sleepily. 'They appear to be animal claw marks. Is the cat – er – vicious?'

'Certainly not!' Margot said firmly.

'Could you tell us exactly what happened?'

'Unfortunately,' Margot began, 'I can't tell you exactly because I wasn't there when the accident occurred.'

What was this? She was the most truthful woman alive! How could she lie so easily? She heard her own voice, but somehow, it wasn't she who spoke. It was someone else who spoke through her, using her vocal cords. She wondered what on earth she was going to say next.

'What I suspect may have happened is this,' a voice – her voice – said. 'My husband was very fond of the cat . . .' The voice broke realistically. 'It used to ride round on his shoulder. It also sleeps on top of the cupboard up there on the landing. I think it must have been up there when Duncan started to go downstairs and it jumped onto his shoulder. Duncan hadn't expected it and reacted violently. The cat panicked and clung on and – and poor Duncan fell.'

The police officers exchanged glances. They asked if they might examine the staircase. She could hear them talking to one another as they did. The man said, 'The old stair's a death trap! It's a wonder one of them hasna' taken a tumble afore now!'

They came back and the woman observed, 'I see there's a suitcase by the bedroom door.'

'Yes, my husband was about to go on a business trip.' Margot's voice trembled. 'This has been such a terrible shock. We were married twenty years.'

They were very sympathetic. They made her a cup of tea and asked if there was anyone they could telephone who might come and stay with Margot.

'Because you shouldn't be alone, you really shouldn't,' the young woman officer said.

'I have friends in Perth,' Margot told her. 'I can ring one of them, if I find – if I find it too lonely.'

Hamish, before the log fire in the wide stone hearth, rolled onto his back and stretched himself into an elongated band of black fur.

The young woman went on hesitantly, 'I wonder if we could borrow the cat for a few hours? We'll take great care of him and bring him back tonight.'

They hadn't a cat basket so Margot found a wicker picnic basket and Hamish was shut up in that despite his plaintive miaows.

They brought Hamish back as promised. 'Forensics just wanted to take a wee look at his paws,' they explained.

Hamish had not enjoyed being transported in the picnic basket. He bristled with ruffled dignity and turned his back to Margot for almost an hour. Even so, she could see where a little fur had been clipped from between the pads of his paws. She supposed the police were looking for traces of Duncan's blood and wondered if they'd found any.

Very late that evening, after the police had gone, the phone rang and, when Margot picked it up, the line went dead, as before.

'She's wondering why he hasn't turned up, Hamish!' Margot said to the cat.

Hamish, the memory of the picnic basket fading, and feeling peckish after all the excitement, walked out into the kitchen and sat down before his dish. Margot gave him half a Weetabix mashed in tepid milk, a little treat to which he was partial.

The police returned the next morning and said they were sorry to bother her like this, but they'd like to take one more look. They climbed up to the top of the cupboard and saw Hamish's blanket. They measured the staircase. At last they expressed themselves satisfied.

'A tragic accident,' the male officer said. 'And to think the poor gentleman was so fond of the cat, too.'

Over the weekend, the phone rang three more times. The last time, when Margot picked it up, she didn't say 'hullo'. She just said, 'He won't be joining you. He's dead.'

There was a sharp intake of breath at the other end of the line. But Margot hung up before the caller could ask any questions.

'So, Hamish,' she said. 'That's that. Now we have the place to ourselves.'

With the cat at her heels, she went into the drawing room. There Margot settled with notepad and biro before the fire. It had occurred to her that the house, in such a picturesque tourist area, would be ideal for a summer bed-and-breakfast business. As she scribbled and planned, Hamish took up his rightful place before the hearth. The logs crackled and spat a little, but otherwise all was peace.

The Truth About Love

'Now then,' said Miss Garnett, putting up her hand to brush back a stray lock of brown hair and pin it firmly in place. 'Now we all make New Year resolutions, but we don't tell anyone what they are, do we?'

'No, Miss Garnett,' chorused Lucy and Edward.

'Do we, Sophie?'

'No, Miss Garnett,' mumbled Sophie, gazing out of the window to where she could see older members of the family returning from a walk to the village. Phoebe, at nineteen long released from the stifling confines of the schoolroom, was walking with Mr Michael Fulton with whom Sophie had been in love since she was ten.

And what love, what deep, searing passion tearing at the fibres of her being did she harbour for that handsome young man. What letters, never to be delivered, had been scrawled in secret on pages torn from exercise books, what tears had been shed when he was observed, covertly pressing Phoebe's hand behind the Christmas tree and whispering in her ear. What jealousy, what hatred, what longing, what despair had been suffered, turn and turn about, and were to be suffered still? Did he ever wonder where his left kid glove was? Probably not. It had been swiftly abstracted when it fell out of the hat he had deposited in the hall, and was hidden

405

amongst Sophie's hair ribbons. Hair ribbons! Nearly seventeen and not allowed to put up her hair. It was intolerable. Equally intolerable was the sight of Phoebe leaning winsomely on his arm. He was smiling down at her. The pain which transfixed Sophie's heart at the sight was so real she leaned forward, hunching up her shoulders.

'Pay attention, please, Sophie,' said Miss Garnett. 'And sit up straight. Why do we not tell anyone our New Year resolutions?'

Uneasy silence fell on the schoolroom. The fire crackled behind the stout wire screen and sent pink shadows dancing on the walls. Dancing, thought Sophie. Dancing at the New Year Ball. Phoebe dancing with Mr Fulton. It didn't bear thinking about.

'Because,' said Edward innocently, 'if we don't tell anyone, then no one will know if we don't keep them.'

'No, Edward,' said Miss Garnett taking a deep breath, 'it is because keeping a New Year resolution is a question of Inner Resolve. It is a question of Firmness of Character. Such as the admirable examples set us by the late Queen and – and the present King,' added Miss Garnett with less certainty.

'Papa says the King changes mistresses when he changes his socks,' said Sophie.

'Lucy and Edward, just carry on reading quietly,' said Miss Garnett. 'Sophie – just a word over here, please!'

Sophie followed the governess reluctantly to a far corner.

'Now then, Sophie, you know quite well that is not the sort of remark to make in front of the little ones! I don't care if your papa said it. I'm sure he didn't say it to you! I'm afraid you have been eavesdropping, Sophie. Eavesdropping is bad manners and remember, eavesdroppers hear no good of themselves! Please remember that at sixteen you have a responsibility towards your little brother and sister.'

'Yes, that's just it! I am sixteen!' burst out Sophie with a howl. 'And everyone treats me as if I were just Lucy's age! It isn't fair! Look!' She grasped her Holland pinafore and held it out. 'I have to hide from visitors – yes, hide! What would – what would anyone think who saw me in a pinafore?'

What would Mr Fulton think? He'd think she was just a child. He'd never give her a second glance. He'd go on holding Phoebe's hand and whispering in Phoebe's ear . . .

'Next year—' began Miss Garnett.

'How old are you, Miss Garnett?' Sophie demanded. She stared at the governess. Miss Garnett had always looked, to the children, incredibly old. But then, she wore such dull dresses and wore her hair scraped back so severely and never any jewellery. But she had, Sophie noticed with some surprise, very nice grey eyes and a fine skin, slightly flushed at the moment.

'I am thirty,' said Miss Garnett. 'Since you ask – though it's hardly polite to do so, Sophie.'

'Between sixteen and thirty isn't very long, is it?' Sophie's critical gaze swept over the governess. 'At sixteen here I am in a pinafore, not allowed to put up my hair or go to the New Year Ball, and in just fourteen years' time, I'll be like you.'

That was so horribly rude and cruel that even as the words came out, Sophie tried to catch them back again, but they floated away on the air beyond recall.

'Not quite like me, I dare say,' said Miss Garnett quietly. 'Because you will not be required to earn your living, as I have been required to do.'

'I'm very sorry,' said Sophie contritely. 'I didn't mean it the way it came out, you know. I just meant – there's never as much time as you think there is, is there?'

'No, Sophie,' said Miss Garnett in that same quiet voice. 'No, dear. There never is.'

'I mean, you've got to sort of grab your chances, and well, I'm never going to have any chances if I'm shut up in a schoolroom with Edward and Lucy.'

'Your time will come, dear,' said Miss Garnett, which was what people always said. But it would come far, far too late. Mr Fulton would be married to Phoebe by then.

That night the New Year Ball took place. Sophie was allowed to watch Phoebe dress and had to admit her sister looked beautiful, just like a princess in a picture book. The dress had a long train and a very low bodice and Phoebe's waist was laced in so tightly Sophie could almost, but not quite, put her hands around it. Mr Fulton could probably put his hands round it. Sophie shivered with a sense of awe at this frightening, fascinating, scandalous thought. What was it like to have a man's hands actually touch your body? Mr Fulton's hands, his fingers, running over your skin, her skin . . . Sophie's face burned scarlet at the thought.

'Shall you marry Mr Fulton, Phoebe?' she asked dolefully.

Phoebe, turning before the long mirror, opened out her ostrich feather fan experimentally and answered in an off-hand voice which would have fooled no one, especially Sophie, 'Oh, yes, I dare say – if he insists.'

Later that night, Sophie crept out of bed in her nightgown and hid on the stairs to listen to the music wafting up from below, the chatter of voices and the laughter. Strange exotic aromas mingled on the air, rising to the top of the house, perfume and champagne and all kinds of rich food. From her hiding place, Sophie could see the servants hastening back and forth with laden silver trays. Sometimes a lady passed through the hall below in glittering ballgown and a gentleman with starched shirtfront and tailcoat, hair centre parted and ruthlessly pomaded flat.

Then Sophie heard voices, not from the hall, but from much nearer at hand. Someone was just below her, out of sight, around the twist in the staircase, someone hidden in the shadows.

'But you know I love you!' said the man's voice passionately.

Sophie's heart almost stopped beating. Mr Fulton – she would recognise the beloved's voice anywhere. But the words, which she had so often dreamed would one day be addressed to her, were addressed to another.

A woman's voice murmured softly in reply. Phoebe, thought Sophie with rising anger, playing coy as usual. As if she didn't care a bit – and all the time she was just playing Mr Fulton as a fisherman plays a hooked salmon. Oh, why didn't he see through it? Why didn't he realise that elsewhere a heart beat true for him?

'But I want to marry you! I will marry you! I won't take no for an answer!'

Phoebe had said he would insist, and he was insisting. Unable to listen to any more, Sophie crept away and wept out her misery into her pillows.

The following day the whole household slept in late except for the children. Sophie got out of bed, dressed in warm clothes and went for a long lonely walk over the frosty ground. Her breath formed clouds in the cold air and her nose became numb. She stamped her feet and clapped her gloved hands as she climbed stiles and scrambled over iron-hard ruts in the ground, putting off the evil moment when she had to return to the house and where, sure as God made little fishes, as old Nanny used to say, Phoebe and Mr Fulton would announce to the world their New Year resolution, that they were engaged to be married.

At last Sophie trailed dejectedly homewards, resigned to hearing the heart-breaking news and with false words of congratulation prepared which surely, when spoken, must burn her lips.

But what was this? The house was in an uproar. Everyone was out of bed and in varying stages of undress. Papa in his quilted dressing gown was roaring at the servants and shouting, 'I'll follow him! I'll settle this! I'll bring the damn bounder back!'

Mama, looking quite dishevelled, which Sophie had never seen her, and accompanied by a female house-guest, was bending over yet another female form which had collapsed on a chair and was being ministered to with smelling salts and brandy.

To Sophie's amazement she saw, when Mama turned round, that the collapsed female was Phoebe, who lay back on the chair with white distraught face and wild eyes, repeating, 'He's gone . . . he's gone . . .'

'Who's gone?' asked Sophie of a young lady, a friend of Phoebe's, who stood nearby looking as if she'd like to wring someone's neck, hopefully not someone present.

'Michael Fulton!' said the young lady crisply. 'I knew he wasn't to be trusted!'

Sophie's heart rose. Mr Fulton, in the cold light of dawn, had thought better of his proposal and chosen dishonour rather than marriage to Phoebe. He was still free – still free for Sophie, one day . . .

'He's run away!' she exclaimed joyfully.

'Yes, he has!' said the young lady viciously. 'And he's run away with that governess of yours, Miss Garnett . . .'

Strange Dreams

They call Oxford 'the city of dreaming spires' because of its skyline of towers and pinnacles. It is a seductive city, especially if you're young and you've come up to study at one of the university's ancient colleges. A whole world of experience is unrolled before you. You are surrounded by the beautiful and the brilliant. Nothing ever again, anywhere, can ever rival that golden time.

I am one of those who arrived at nineteen with a box of books and a thirst to learn, and never left. There are a fair number of us who linger in the town long after student days are over, deluding ourselves that if we stay, somehow we'll be forever young. Alas, I'm no longer young. I'm a retired librarian from the university's Bodleian Library, where I was keeper of incunabula.

The Bodleian lies at the bottom of Broad Street (which locals call 'The Broad'). If you pass the Sheldonian Theatre with its circle of classical stone busts on plinths, you'll see a monumental arch at the top of a flight of steps. Go through it and you'll find yourself surrounded by the late fifteenth-century architecture of the venerable library. As a place to spend most of your life, it's not bad.

Over the years I saw countless youngsters visit the library. Sometimes they returned in later years to do some research. They looked older, fatter, balder, as the case may be, but essentially they hadn't changed. Oxford stamps its mark on you as a silversmith stamps his work. It stays for ever. Besides, I've a good memory for faces.

It was a particularly fine Sunday morning when I encountered one of these faces from the past. But it wasn't in the library, which is closed on a Sunday.

I had strolled down the Broad, past the library entrance and turned right into Catte Street. By turning my head to the left, I could see the Bridge of Sighs, an arched passageway spanning a narrow side road. A few steps further on and I was walking over the cobbles of Radcliffe Camera Square.

The 'Camera' itself is a baroque rotunda in the centre of the square. It functions as part of the library. To the south of the square lies the medieval university church of St Mary the Virgin. This was my first point of call because tucked into a vault on the side of the church facing the square is the Convocation Café. I fancied a cup of coffee and a piece of their truly delicious chocolate fudge cake.

Afterwards, I went into the church. I am fond of its curious memorial tablets. I'm told there is a fine view over Oxford from the top of its tower, but I have no head for heights. On the first Sunday of each month (January and August excepted) the German Lutheran congregation of Oxford borrows this church to hold a service.

I left the church through the south door, stepping out into the High Street. Here I turned left and set off in the direction of Magdalen College which lies on the left at the bottom of the High.

When I got there, I debated what to do next. Ahead of me lay

Magdalen Bridge, spanning the river Cherwell, one of Oxford's two rivers. The other river is the Thames, which at Oxford is called the Isis. I crossed the road with the original intention of entering the unversity's Botanic Garden which lies on the other side. But on a whim, I turned down Rose Lane just before the Garden.

Rose Lane is a short roadway. The wall of the Botanic Garden is on the left and it's blocked at the end by a metal gate. Pass through the pedestrian access at the side of the gate and you will be hard pushed to believe you are in the middle of a busy city. Here are the playing fields, open grassland and avenues of trees of Christchurch College meadows. The distant traffic roar is muted and soon forgotten. Skirt the back of the Botanic Gardens to your left and you'll come to a lovely shaded path along the bank of the river Cherwell.

This is where I found myself. There was hardly anyone about. The water rippled along, dappled in changing patterns of light and shade. Everywhere was calm, peace and rest for the eye. From time to time a punt passed downriver. A punt is a long, narrow, shallow, flat-bottomed craft, propelled by a long pole, on the same principle as the Venetian gondola. Punts are moored for hire below Magdalen Bridge.

I had reached a point on the bank opposite the grounds of St Hilda's College (a women's college) on the further side. There was at one time a do-it-yourself ferry there in the shape of a flat-bottomed boat. Strong wires on a pulley had run across the river from bank to bank and the idea had been to pull yourself across by this means. A notice had told you the ferry was private, and it had now gone altogether. To my surprise, I suddenly heard a fine tenor voice approaching, so it seemed, down the river towards me. Sure enough, a punt appeared. It was propelled by a young man. A girl sat in the bows and he was serenading her with some old-fashioned ballad. Not only did he have a good voice, but he was skilled with the punt pole, able to sing, gesture, propel the boat and keep his balance! The girl, I have to say, didn't appear to appreciate this at all but, red with embarrassment, begged him to stop. I watched until they sailed round the bend out of sight.

Absorbed by this little comedy, I had been oblivious to anything else. Now, as I looked up, I saw I was not alone. Under the trees, a short distance off, stood a man in his late thirties, clean shaven, casually dressed. He'd been watching the couple in the punt, as I had. Neither of us, I think, had been aware of the other. Now we stared at one another.

He turned quickly, as if to make off, but in that instant I remembered him and called, 'Wilson, isn't it?'

Unwillingly, he turned back and came a few steps towards me. 'Yes,' he said suspiciously. He was frowning. But then his brow cleared and he exclaimed, 'Why, it's Mr Carter, from the Bodleian.'

'No longer,' I said. 'Retired now and a gentleman of leisure! What about you? What's brought you back to Oxford? Or do you live here?'

I didn't think he could live in the city. I'd never seen him about. The centre of Oxford is a crowded, busy place where eventually you stumble over every acquaintance you've got in the town. As I asked, my mind threw up more facts. He'd been a brilliant student. But there'd been some sort of scandal and he'd quit the university without sitting his final examinations. A great pity. He'd been a fine-looking youth, but now the line of his jaw already sagged and he was carrying too much weight. I suspected he was a man rather too fond of his beer.

'I don't live here,' he answered my question. 'I'm visiting.'

An awkward silence fell. I couldn't ask him his reason if he didn't wish to tell me. I thought he might walk off, now we'd exchanged greetings. But he remained there, staring across the Cherwell to the spot where the chain ferry had been.

'You remember that old boat?' he asked suddenly. 'That's where Frank and I put the body.'

'Body?' I asked cautiously. I was startled, but puzzled too. I was sure that if anyone had ever discovered a body in the old ferry I should certainly have remembered.

He was shaking his head. 'It wasn't a real one, only a dummy. It was a joke. Frank was a student with me at Magdalen College. He knew a girl studying at St Hilda's.' He nodded towards the fringe of trees on the far bank and the college grounds beyond.

'The idea was to frighten the girl?' I guessed.

'That's right. Not a nice thing to do but I don't think we were particularly nice young men. It was the end of term and we were all celebrating. Frank fixed with this girl to meet her and a friend of hers at midnight, down there by the old ferry. The girls couldn't get out of their college grounds at that time of night unseen, but the riverbank was in their grounds. We reckoned on staying out all night from Magdalen and slipping back in the morning. We planned to steal a punt from below the bridge, float down here and rendezvous. We'd bring a couple of bottles of champagne. I forget what they were going to bring.'

'And the body?'

He grinned and for a moment he looked like the youngster I remembered. 'We made it from some pillows and dressed it in old clothes. Its head was a white balloon with features drawn on it. It looked pretty ghastly in daylight. At night, when we were punting down the river with it as passenger, its white balloon head gleaming in the moonlight, it looked downright gruesome.

'We got to the rendezvous early, pulled the punt up on the bank over there, propped our dead friend in the old ferryboat and hid in the trees.'

He stopped at this point. I hadn't noticed but we'd begun walking back as he told his story. We'd reached the open area at the beginning of the river path.

Wilson asked me, 'Which way?'

I suggested we cut across the grass towards Merton College and the town centre.

So we set off again and Wilson resumed his tale.

'Things went wrong from the start. To begin with, the girl was late and came alone. We found out later the other girl had decided she was scared of the dark. She was right. If we'd all had enough sense to be scared, none of it would've happened.

'Then we saw torchlight. The girl scrambled through the undergrowth towards the bank, calling Frank's name. She sounded nervous, poor kid. We, miserable pair, waited. We'd drunk one bottle of the champagne by then, I should say.

'She walked towards the old ferryboat, the torch flashing on the way ahead of her. Suddenly she gave a dreadful scream.

'"She's seen it!" whispered Frank. He chuckled.

'But suddenly I felt sorry for her and sorry for my own part in it. I stood up and called, "We're over here!" We both got up and went towards her. I called out there was nothing to be scared of. We had only done it for a joke.

"'A joke?" she shouted. "YOU KILLED HIM FOR A JOKE?" Then she turned and ran like the wind, crashing through brambles, shrieking, into the college grounds and away. I shouted after her that it was only a dummy. But she was too far away already to hear us and in no mood to listen in any case.

"'Come on!" urged Frank. "We've got to catch her. If she goes back and tells everyone we've killed someone and left the body in the old ferryboat, we'll have half the college down here, to say nothing of the police."

'So we began to run after her but as the darker outline of St Hilda's College showed on the midnight-blue skyline, I grabbed Frank's arm and made him stop. I pointed out that in the first place, we couldn't catch her. She was almost at the college. Secondly, if we were discovered chasing a screaming girl student through the grounds at night, we'd be accused of goodness knows what dire intention. "It's bad enough we're going to be accused of murder," I said, "without being accused of attempted rape as well."

'So we turned back and made our way towards where we'd left our punt. I could hear the water lapping. Twigs cracked under our feet. The clock of Magdalen chimed one in the distance. My toe stubbed against something large, soft and heavy. I didn't know what it was, but I swear, Mr Carter, my blood ran cold. I told Frank to shine our torch down. He did and we both saw it. Another body lay in the undergrowth by the river's edge, but this one was real.'

* * *

'We told each other to stop panicking and tried to work out what had happened. The body belonged to an old vagrant wearing a dirty raincoat tied round the middle with string. His hair and beard were long, grey and tangled. Rigor had frozen his face in a dreadful grimace, but there was no sign of violence. He appeared simply to have lain down there and died. How he got there, goodness knows. This was the body the poor girl had seen and no wonder, when I spoke of "doing it for fun", she had been so appalled and run away.

'Frank said he wasn't waiting there for the St Hilda's college porter to come and find us with a real body. He suggested we weight our dummy with stones, drop it in the river, punt back to Magdalen Bridge, return our stolen craft, and make for the safety of our college. Better to be caught by Magdalen's porter sneaking in, than caught here with a corpse.

'I told him he was mad. To begin with, we had to keep our dummy to prove our story. We had to leave it where it was in the ferryboat.

'But Frank disagreed. We argued drunkenly. Time was getting short. The girl would be back soon with other people. Then Frank had his idea. It was simple. We put the old tramp in our punt. We take our dummy out of the ferryboat and put it where the old tramp's body had been. Then we punt downriver with our grisly cargo and tip the tramp's body overboard.

'"You see," said Frank. "When the girl comes back with help, all they'll find is the dummy. She'll have to admit she made a mistake in the dark. Come on, she'll believe it herself, when she sees the dummy. No dead tramp. We'll be away from here. All's well that ends well."

'So I'm sorry to say, that's what we did. We lifted our dummy onto the bank. The balloon head burst as we did, unfortunately, so it was a headless figure we placed near the dead vagrant. We picked up the old man. I found it difficult. I'd never seen a dead man before, much less touched one. I was terrified. He was very heavy and smelled bad. I felt vomit rise in my throat and forced it back. We put him in the punt, floated downriver and tipped him out after putting the empty champagne bottle in his coat pocket. That was Frank's idea, too. "They'll think he fell in while drunk."

'I pointed out that homeless tramps didn't usually drink champagne. Frank's reply was that we didn't have to explain how he got it. "Maybe he stole it?" he suggested.

'We made our way back to the punt moorings at Magdalen Bridge and returned our borrowed craft. Then we crept back to the college. I was violently sick in the gateway, to the fury of the porter. We knew we'd be in trouble with the college authorities in the morning, but that was the least of our worries. Frank, of course, insisted we didn't have any worries any more. He was always an optimist.'

Wilson stopped talking at this point. 'Well?' I asked impatiently. 'What happened next?'

'Oh,' he said. 'The girl returned with St Hilda's night-porter and they found the dummy. She accepted she'd made a mistake. The real body, the tramp, was hauled out of the river two days' later. It had lost the champagne bottle in its pocket, and floated a long way downstream to where the Cherwell joins the Isis. So the body was actually found in the Isis and no one connected it. It was only an old vagrant, after all. They said he must have fallen in drunk. No one was much bothered.

'Frank and I got into deep trouble for being out of college at night, playing the joke on the St Hilda's girl, breaking into St Hilda's grounds at night, returning to college drunk, you name it. We were afraid we'd be rusticated.'

He meant suspended from residence at the university for a short time by way of punishment.

'But in the end, it didn't go as far as that. So we were lucky, I suppose. Or Frank was. He seemed able to put the escapade behind him. I couldn't forget the smell of that old man, the weight of his body, his tangled hair, his open mouth and staring eyes. I began to think how badly the poor old fellow had been treated by life. And how had we treated him in death? Even worse. We'd broken every ancient law of respect for the dead (to say nothing of not reporting our find to the police). I became ill. I had a breakdown. I left college and never came back.'

It's sometimes the way with brilliant brains. The mind teeters on a knife-edge. It's easily knocked off-balance by shock or stress. I told Wilson I was very sorry, and I meant it.

He shrugged. 'That young chap in the punt just now, the one serenading his girl, he'll have better memories than I do of my time here. Or I hope he does.'

We parted company at that. As he walked off I reflected that Oxford is indeed the city of dreaming spires. But not all dreams are happy ones.

A Question of Trust

A four-part serial featuring crime writer Emma King

Part One

'Tell me,' ordered the fierce young woman, 'do you get a lot of *satisfaction* out of killing people off?'

Emma gazed at her, perplexed. She had agreed to be interviewed at home by someone from the local press despite some misgivings. She enjoyed talking about her work. It was the 'at home' bit which had disconcerted her.

As she'd explained to her husband Matt, 'I'm used to being interviewed. I'm a writer. It goes with the job. But I value my private life – *our* private life. Anyway,' she had concluded, 'the house looks a bit of a mess right now.'

'The publicity couldn't do you any harm, surely?' Matt had replied. 'The readers would probably be interested to know a well-known crime writer has come to live in their midst.'

Emma had given in. So here was the reporter sitting on Emma's sofa, pen and notebook in hand, waiting. Emma considered the question.

'No,' she said. 'Not really. It is all only in a book, you know.'

The young woman wasn't so easily deflected. She leaned forward eagerly. 'Do you ever put real people into a book? I mean, if it was me, I'd be tempted to get my own back on a few people, you know what I mean?'

'Well, you aren't me,' retorted Emma, nettled. 'No, I've never put a real person in a book. A book's a work of fiction. Real people don't belong in it.'

The interviewer was scribbling. Emma studied her. The girl was eight or nine years younger than Emma herself, which would make her about twenty. Obviously the paper didn't consider Emma warranted a senior reporter. She'd got the cub. The knowledge that this girl was just practising on her didn't help. The girl had strangely coloured short spikey hair, a sort of reddish-orange. The edge of one ear was festooned with studs, from the lobe to the top. She wore a short skirt with black tights, a scarlet sleeveless sweater and laced ankle boots. On one bare upper arm was tattooed a small rose. Her leather jacket lay where she'd thrown it – on the carpet, by her bag. Her name was Polly Owen, which suited her very well. She did put Emma in mind of a brightly coloured macaw.

Emma considered her own outfit. She was wearing new jeans (in honour of the occasion), one of her nephew Damian's discarded shirts and a multi-hued waistcoat she'd bought in a charity shop. She had fancied it gave her the bohemian look, suitable for a writer. But perhaps it was a bit old-hat. She wondered what Matt would say if she came home with her ear pierced all the way up, like Polly.

'Did it hurt?' she heard herself asking.

Polly looked up in surprise. 'Did what hurt?'

'Sorry, thinking aloud. I was wondering about having your ear pierced like that. I've got pierced ears, but only one hole in the lobes.'

Polly fingered her row of studs. 'It hurt a bit when it got towards the top.'

Emma decided she was a coward. Matt wouldn't like it, anyway.

'It must help, being married to a policeman,' said Polly. 'A real detective.'

'Not really!' returned Emma, rather more sharply than she intended. To soften the reply, she added, 'Well, of course, it means I can ask him whether it's all right for my detective, in my book, to do something, if it's correct procedure. Generally Matt says it isn't but I let my detective do it, anyway.'

Matt, though appreciative of his wife's achievements in the literary line, was generally scornful of fictional detectives and their doings.

'Besides,' Emma added briskly. 'I was a writer before I ever met my husband.'

It was an irritating fact that since she had married, people who previously had happily assumed Emma capable of creating any amount of mayhem in a book totally unaided, now assumed Matt helped her. To his credit, Matt staunchly denied it. In fact, he was horrified at the very idea.

'What would they say at the station if word got round I had anything to do with your books? I mean, it'd be downright embarrassing.'

Emma had been torn between replying, 'That's not very polite', and retorting, 'Quite right, too!'

They had only been married a little over a year and were still finding running two separate careers had its challenges. Especially as in Emma's case, according to Matt, her books gave people quite the wrong idea as to what he did for a living.

'People think I'm like *him*!' he protested regularly.

'Him' or rather 'he' was Felix Watts, Emma's fictional sleuth. Felix had detected his way through four books with growing success. An increasing band of readers had become fascinated by his lifestyle, which included living in a converted oast house with a springer spaniel called Bert, travelling around by vintage motor-cycle with Bert in a sidecar and making regular forays into foreign climes, leaving Bert behind with Felix's loyal secretary, Jemima. Felix was six foot three, very athletic and left handed.

'Why?' Matt had asked, as to the last.

'I don't know,' Emma had replied truthfully. 'When I invented him, he came out left handed all by himself. Characters do things like that.'

Polly wasn't giving up easily. 'You don't get ideas from his cases?' Emma thought she sounded a little wistful but hardened her heart.

'No. He doesn't discuss his work with me. My ideas come out of my own head.'

Oh dear, that was a mistake. Now she knew what the next question was going to be. It was.

'Where do you get your ideas from?'

'Oh, almost anywhere. Would you like some more coffee?'

'No, thanks. Got to go on somewhere else and they'll probably offer me a drink, too. Can you give me an example? Our readers really like to know this sort of thing.'

Emma thought furiously. 'I overheard some people talking on a bus once, and it got me thinking. Just something one of the women said.'

'On – a – bus.' Polly wrote it down and then, thank goodness, closed her notebook and pushed it with the pen into her capacious bag. 'I think that should do it,' she said. 'The photographer will be over to take some pics, probably tomorrow morning, okay?' She slumped back on the sofa and stuck her boots out, crossed at the ankle.

'It will have to be morning,' said Emma, 'because my nephew is arriving to spend half-term with us in the afternoon.'

Polly still showed no sign of going. She was staring at Emma as if making up her mind about something.

Please, prayed Emma, *don't let her have written a six-hundred-page novel and will I just glance through it?* She eyed Polly's bag. Did it look as if it had a bulky manuscript stuffed in it?

'Funny things do happen, don't they?' said Polly.

'Yes, they do. Life is full of oddities. A writer doesn't really have to look very far, just keep her ears and eyes open.'

'Journalists have to do that, too, looking for a story, you know.' Polly chewed her lower lip. 'But things aren't always what they seem, are they? A writer, like a journalist, has to check things out. You spoke of overhearing conversations. But what you hear doesn't have to be right.'

She leaned forward. Emma held her breath.

'For example, the old woman who lives next door to my parents thinks someone is trying to murder her.' Polly delivered this unexpected statement and gazed at Emma, waiting for a reply.

'Ah,' said Emma. 'People do sometimes take fancies into their heads. Your parents will just have to learn to live with it. I presume she thinks your parents are the guilty parties?'

'Oh, no!' Polly looked shocked. 'She thinks it's poor Jeremy, which is ridiculous! Or if it's not Jeremy, it's Guy or Lucinda.'

This already sounded far too complicated for Emma to want to hear any more. But Polly was now steaming ahead, obviously determined to get the story out before Emma could interrupt.

'Let me explain. The woman, she's in her sixties—'

'Sixties isn't so old,' Emma interrupted.

'No, I suppose not. My mum is forty-three.'

'Is she?' Emma managed, just, not to sound both horrified and despondent. Did this whippersnapper look upon her, Emma, as an older woman? The impulse to rush to the nearest mirror and look for grey hairs was strong.

'Her name,' Polly was saying, blithely unaware of having filled her hostess with gloom, 'is Mrs Myra Carter. Her husband was fearfully rich. I mean, you know, mega rich. Rolling in it. Her house is a big one. It makes my parents' place look really titchy. She lives in it all on her own with just a daily cleaner coming in. I think,' said Polly with the unconscious arrogance of youth, 'that's immoral.'

'I expect the daily woman doesn't think so, it's her job,' Emma pointed out.

Polly amended her statement. 'I mean, to have so *much* and to be so *mean.*'

'Is she mean?'

'Gosh, and how! You'd think she made all the money herself, but she didn't, her husband did, Henry Carter. Guy and Lucinda and Jeremy are his nephews and niece. Mrs Carter hasn't got any kids of her own. You'd think she'd want to help her husband's sister's children. He was awfully fond of them. Their own father was a bit of a loser.'

'How old,' asked Emma, 'are Guy, Lucinda and—'

'Jeremy,' said Polly with a suspicious breathlessness. 'Their surname is Bryant. Lucinda is the eldest, she's twenty-five and not got a job. She did have one, awfully well paid in the city. But the firm went bust or something. Guy's twenty-four and he's started up his own business. He's a headhunter.'

'As in Borneo?' Emma couldn't resist.

'No, as in city top jobs – oh, I see, you're making a joke.' Polly looked reproachful. 'Honestly, none of it is funny. Jeremy is the youngest, he's had several jobs. He wants to be a sports coach but it's an awfully difficult business to break into. At the moment he's a rep for a sportswear firm.'

'And Myra Carter thinks one or all of the Bryants is trying to bump her off?'

'Yes, as if they would! I don't much like Lucinda and Guy but they're all right. They wouldn't go round killing people. Jeremy,' again a suspicion of breathlessness entered Polly's voice, 'Jeremy is really nice.' She turned as red as her sweater. 'He's teaching me to surf, down at Newquay.'

'He lives in the area, then?'

'He's got a tiny fisherman's cottage. I don't mean the fisherman was tiny, I mean the cottage.' Polly's journalistic training had alerted her to an editorial pitfall. 'But the original inhabitants must've been pretty small because the ceilings are so low. The other two have flats in London.'

So Polly had actually been in Jeremy's cottage. Emma told herself firmly that this was the point at which she should utter a few well-chosen words and stop this line of conversation stone-dead. Instead she went on, 'Why does Mrs Carter think she's the object of a homicidal plot?'

'Because things have been happening. But they've all been either genuine accidents or have happened because she's muddled things up herself. Like the tablets. She took the wrong sort of tablets. She thought they were the right sort, but she got ill and it turned out they were tablets for treating heart disease, which she hasn't got. She said one of them had swopped her real tablets for these heart ones. But it wasn't like that at all. The heart ones were old ones belonging to Uncle Henry that had been left lying around the house, which you shouldn't let old tablets do. You see, she's a bit vain. She doesn't like to be seen taking pills so she tips them out of their proper bottles and puts them in things like old face-cream jars. No wonder they get muddled up! Then she fell down the stairs and said someone had loosened the carpet runner. No, they hadn't. She jolly well needs a new carpet and won't pay for one.'

'And you,' said Emma, 'are keen to keep any suspicion away from Jeremy.'

'It's not that I'm keen on Jeremy,' Polly lied ineptly. 'I just want to be fair.'

'So why do you refer to the late Mr Carter as Uncle Henry? He isn't your uncle. I think it's because Jeremy's been telling you all this and you're taking his part.'

There, Felix Watts would've been proud of that bit of deduction!

'Even if I am,' said Polly with dignity, 'someone should stop her going round saying these things. They're not true.'

'Look, Polly, I shouldn't think any listener would take her seriously. It is a pretty wild tale. It sounds as though she's a little, well, eccentric.'

'You haven't met her,' said Polly despondently. 'She's very forceful. She knows lots of important people. She's the sort of person people do believe and – and the worst of it is, she's told

Jeremy and his brother and sister that she intends going to the police. Your husband's a police inspector, isn't he? I thought if you told him what I've told you, the police would realise she's got it all wrong.'

So that was what Polly's tale was leading up to! Annoyed, Emma said, 'The police, if she does go to them, will check her out and find out about her habit of switching pill bottles for cream jars.'

Polly looked downcast.

Emma's heart softened. 'If I get a chance, I'll mention it.'

She hoped this was the end of it. Upstairs, in her study, a half-finished chapter flickered on the screen of the VDU, tugging Emma back to it. Felix Watts, for all his fictional abilities, was incapable of making a move without his creator.

Polly drew a deep breath. 'I was actually hoping you'd do a bit more than mention it to your husband. I thought you might talk to Mrs Carter. You write about murder. She might listen to you if you tell her that it's all in her imagination.'

Emma was horrified. 'No! I couldn't! Anyway, I don't know her.'

Polly began hunting in her bag again. 'I wrote out her address. I was hoping you'd be the sort of nice person I could ask to do it. She's my parents' neighbour so I thought you could go out there to see them and sort of strike up an acquaintance with Mrs C. The houses are on the clifftop near Rock. You can't miss them. Here's my business card. You can always leave a message at the newpaper's offices and I've scribbled my home number on the back. I'll call my parents and tell them you might drop by. They're both crime-fiction fans and would be over the moon if you did. You can call me and tell me when you've done it.'

'Polly,' Emma began, 'I don't intend to get personally involved in this. Let me make that quite plain. I'm a busy full-time writer. I've got a young visitor coming for a week to stay tomorrow, and on Monday the plumbers are coming to start installing a new bathroom. You saw the mess,' she added.

Polly had nipped upstairs early in her visit and had ample opportunity to observe the walls stripped of their original tiles, revealing flaking plaster. The floor was down to the boards up there. The existing rust-stained cast-iron bath, though still *in situ* until Monday, had been deprived of its side panel. This had revealed a number of electrical cables and a sinister hole in the floor.

It was a pity the plumbers could only manage this coming week, when Damian would be there. It was either that or they spoke vaguely of some unspecified date in the future. Then when the plumbers moved out, the tilers would move in, if all went to plan.

'Bird in the hand,' Matt had said. 'Get them to come on Monday. You and Damian can manage.'

'But the water will be turned off.'

'You won't be hanging around the house, will you? With Damian here? You can't work with the plumbers bashing things around. Take Damian out for the day. Or two days.'

'It's not asking much,' Polly was saying with that reproachful look in her eyes again, like a puppy that can't get anyone to play with it. 'Jeremy and I would be really grateful.'

Recalled sharply to the present, Emma managed a firm, 'No, Polly! I'll mention the situation to Matt, but that's as far as I'll go.'

Polly slung her bag over her shoulder. 'Well, perhaps you'll change your mind.' She gave Emma a dazzling smile and, at long last, took herself off.

Emma went upstairs and tried to concentrate on Felix Watts's latest case. Elderly ladies prone to conspiracy theories did *not* come into it.

Matt King, Emma's husband, was a detective inspector, CID, with the Devon and Cornwall Constabulary. When he and Emma had met, his area had been in Devon. Recently he'd been moved further west, into Cornwall, which was why they had bought this old house in Wadebridge and were busy renovating it.

'How did you get on with the reporter?' Matt asked when he got home that evening.

'Pretty well.' Emma hesitated. She'd promised Polly she'd tell him about Mrs Carter but Matt had had a long day. This wasn't the right moment.

Matt had noted the hesitation and was waiting, eyebrows raised.

'She was very young,' said Emma.

'Oh?' Matt had a wicked gleam in his eye. 'Feeling your age, old girl?'

'She did make me feel sort of mature.'

'Wait till Damian gets here tomorrow,' warned Matt. 'Then we'll both feel like a couple of ancient mariners!'

Emma poked at the mushroom risotto simmering on the stove and asked, 'You don't mind Damian coming?'

'Of course I don't!' Matt sounded astonished. 'He's a great kid.'

'That's okay, then. I'm his guardian in this country while Bridget and her husband are away in Africa.'

Emma's sister and brother-in-law were both doctors employed by a medical charity.

Matt moved closer. His wife had twisted her long brown hair up into a knot secured by a big clasp. Matt stooped and kissed the nape of her neck where there was a cluster of curls too short to catch up in the clasp. She squeaked and waved her wooden spoon at him. 'That tickles!'

In reply he grabbed her waist, which brought forth a squawk and 'Not while I'm cooking!'

'All right, Mrs King, I can wait!' Matt helpfully began grating cheese. 'Look, you had Damian with you when I met you. I know you're his guardian. I'm more than happy to be his uncle, right?'

'He likes you,' said Emma. 'You're sort of his hero.'

'I hope not!' Matt sounded alarmed. 'That's a responsibility too far.'

'He wants to be a policeman, a detective, like you.'

'I don't mind that,' said Matt. 'So long as he doesn't want to be a detective like Felix Watts.'

Emma ignored that. 'I wish I knew what I'm going to do with Damian all next week. He doesn't like just lolling around on beaches.'

'You'll find something . . .' said Matt.

The photographer promised by Polly turned up the next morning, Friday. He took pictures of Emma in the garden, Emma at her desk, Emma in the kitchen chopping carrots.

'Old house, this,' he said.

'Yes, we're renovating it.'

'Got your work cut out, I reckon,' said the photographer

433

deflatingly. 'I don't go on these old places myself. Give me a nice new house on an estate with all mod cons.'

'Nothing wrong with that,' said Emma politely. 'We just fancied doing up this one.'

'Have you had the drains tested?' asked the photographer. 'These old houses often have dodgy drains.'

'Do you want any more pictures?' This chap was wearing out his welcome fast. Emma tapped the carrot knife on the chopping board.

'Got all I need, thanks. Cheers.' He left.

Emma stared at the pile of sliced carrots and decided to make vegetable soup. She was a vegetarian herself but Matt was a meat-eater. Damian, on his last visit, had lived on a diet of hamburgers, pizza, and sausage sandwiches. The coming week would see some juggling of menus.

That afternoon, Emma drove to Bodmin to collect Damian off the train. His boarding school insisted that boys travel in uniform. That might be all right for the smaller ones but Emma had to admit, Damian had a point in grumbling about older pupils being made to mix with the public in school garb.

Teenagers were sensitive creatures (certainly as far as their own feelings were concerned. They could, Emma had learned, be oblivious to the sensitivity of others). Damian had shot up over the last twelvemonth. Between thirteen and fourteen he had turned from a boy into a youth. She could see him coming towards her down the platform, lugging his holdall and a plastic carrier. His grey flannels flapped round his legs. His tweed jacket (at least older boys weren't condemned to a blazer) was of the conservative cut and style which, apart from senior boarding school pupils, was only worn nowadays by retired colonels and country vets. He appeared to have had a recent haircut of the short back and sides variety. He wore his tie, but had pulled the knot down to his chest so that the tie hung round his neck like a halter. His face was red with effort, embarrassment and frustration.

'Hello!' Emma waved to attract his attention. He saw her, brightened up, and quickened his step.

Emma went to meet him and remembered in time to greet him with a simple pat on the arm. 'Do not,' Matt had warned, 'kiss him in public. I had an aunt who used to do that to me. It's all right when you're four but not at fourteen.'

'Nice to see you,' said Emma. 'No problems on the journey?'

'Apart from being dressed up like a refugee from some old fifties film, I suppose not,' said Damian grumpily. 'This is the last, positively the last time I'm travelling down kitted out like this. They can expel me. I don't care. The next time, I'm changing out of this school rubbish at Paddington Station!'

'Don't worry about it,' Emma mistakenly urged. 'I'm sure no one noticed.'

'Everyone noticed!' Damian's voice rose in a wail and sounded, for a moment, much younger than his fourteen-year-old status would have liked. 'A whole bunch of kids at Paddington laughed their heads off at me. Look at it, Em. This outfit is hardly *cool*.'

Emma couldn't resist replying, deadpan, 'No, it looks a bit hot.' Then, seeing horror and dismay on his face, she added hastily, 'Only pulling your leg, Damian. As soon as we get home, you can change and forget all about it for a week.'

'They made me have a haircut,' Damian went on as they made

their way to the car park. His tone suggested the procedure had been carried out by the Spanish Inquisition.

'It'll grow,' consoled Emma.

'It'll grow a bit in time for me to go back to school and then they'll make me have it cut again!'

'Damian,' said Emma, slamming the boot on the holdall and plastic bag. 'Are you going to grumble non-stop for the next week or is there any chance of us having any fun?'

Damian had the grace to look abashed. 'Sorry, Em. I oughtn't to grouse to you. Not your fault.' In a change of tone, he asked with formal courtesy, 'How are you? How is Matt? Keeping well, I hope?'

'Very well, thank you.' Emma struggled to keep a straight face.

Damian abandoned etiquette to ask in what she thought of as his old, enthusiastic way, 'Has he got any good cases at the moment? You know, like gold-bullion robberies or murder?'

'Sorry, don't think so.'

Damian looked disappointed. 'How about in your books? Is old what's his name still solving things?'

'You mean Felix Watts,' Emma said, letting in the clutch and lurching forward.

'Has he still got that dog in a sidecar?' asked Damian. Emma's car was growling its way up a hill as if it had some sort of animal trapped beneath the bonnet. 'Give the poor bloke a proper car.'

'I can't,' objected Emma, grinding through the gears. 'I gave him a motorbike and sidecar in the first book so I'm stuck with it, and so is he. The readers wouldn't like it if I changed him.'

'I say,' said Damian, 'not meaning to be rude or anything, but this car of yours has about had it, hasn't it?'

'Yes, it has. But unless I get the latest book finished and earn some money, there's not a chance of replacing it. At the moment, we're paying for a new bathroom and after that, it's the turn of the kitchen to be refitted. Matt wants to put down a patio and barbeque area and the old prefab garage has developed a list to one side.'

'Bad luck,' commiserated Damian at this tale of woe. 'Hey, Em! Someone's waving at you!'

Emma glanced across and, to her surprise, saw Polly the reporter gesticulating furiously from the pavement. She slowed and drew in.

Polly came scurrying up and crouched at the passenger window, which Damian obligingly lowered.

'Hello! This is a bit of luck. I heard a car rattling along and turned my head to see who it was and it was you.'

Damian looked mortified at being seen, especially by a young person, in a car that audibly announced its progress. He slumped down in his seat, arms folded, and stared out through the windscreen, doing an impression of someone who wasn't there.

'Won't hold you up,' went on Polly breathlessly. Today she wore a royal-blue fleece over an orange sweatshirt and black leggings. With her crested head, she looked more than ever like some kind of exotic bird. 'Just thought I'd ask whether you'd had a chance to mention you know what to your husband.'

'Sorry,' Emma admitted guiltily. 'Not yet. I'll mention it to Matt tonight, okay?'

To her relief, Polly seemed satisfied and waved them on their way.

'Who's that?' Damian, interested, straightened in his seat.

'A journalist. She interviewed me the other day. She had something she wanted me to tell Matt.'

Damian clearly wanted to ask what it was, but nobly put good manners first. Probably he reckoned on finding out later.

They had reached the open road. Emma and the car both cheered up. They were now purring along quite nicely with only the occasional strange clunk from somewhere under the bonnet. Emma returned to the conversation they were having before Polly's appearance.

'The plumbers are coming in on Monday and the water will be turned off for at least a couple of days. After that the tilers will move in. It's all right for Matt, he's at work. I don't know how you and I are going to manage.'

But when Matt got home that evening it turned out he had the answer.

'Cottage!' he announced and dropped a bunch of keys on the kitchen table.

'What cottage?' asked Emma ungrammatically.

'Where?' asked Damian, ever practical.

'Near Daymer Beach. A really nice secluded setting, a stone's throw from the sea and clifftop paths for rambles. A colleague owns it as a weekend place but he's lending it to us, or rather you, for the coming week. I told him about Damian being here and the plumbers and all the rest of it and he came up with the idea straight away. Very nice of him.'

'You mean, we're all going to go, you too?' asked Emma. 'Someone's got to be here to let the plumbers in.'

'That's me. I can't take a week off work but I can take a couple

438

of half-days to keep an eye on the plumbing work. You two can take off for the whole week and enjoy yourselves.'

'Sounds pretty good,' said Damian.

'It's very kind of your colleague,' said Emma, 'but plumbing aside, I was hoping to do a bit of work on the book, at least in the evenings.'

Matt placed his palms on the table and leaned over it. 'What was my Christmas present to you?'

'The laptop,' said Emma meekly.

'Which I haven't yet seen you use much. The whole idea was that you'd be free to go anywhere and still be able to dash off a few hundred words on old Felix's latest exploits.'

'You know,' said Emma, 'I really wish I knew what both you and Damian have against my sleuth.'

'Actually,' said Damian, 'having an aunt who writes whodunnits is pretty cool.' ('Cool' was obviously the word of the moment. Emma suspected she was going to hear it several times a day for the following week.)

'Yes, well,' said Matt. 'I am actually very proud of my wife.' When Emma, startled by the open admission (and before a witness) blushed, he added, 'Only I wouldn't want her to get big headed.'

'Fat chance,' said Emma. 'With you two around.'

So it was agreed that on Monday, Matt would be left to oversee the plumbers and Emma and Damian would rattle off to the cottage in Emma's runabout, provided it didn't conk out on the hills before they got there.

Damian then remembered that his plastic carrier bag contained presents for both Matt and Emma. He produced a squashed box of chocolates for his aunt and a box of golf balls for Matt.

'You do still play?' he asked anxiously.

'When I get the chance,' said Matt, looking martyred.

Damian had remembered something else. 'Em, Polly wanted you to give a message to Matt.'

'Oh, yes,' said Emma guiltily. 'Polly, the kid who interviewed me the other day, is worried that her boyfriend's aunt thinks he – or his brother and sister – is trying to murder her.'

'Why, what's he done?' asked Matt simply.

'Polly says he hasn't done anything. His aunt sounds a bit daffy. She's got a lot of money, though, and won't shell out to help Jeremy, that's the boyfriend, and the other two. Why should she? I mean, she oughtn't to go round accusing them, but—' Emma paused. 'Polly says the aunt has threatened to go to the police. She wanted you to know that you need to take what she'll tell you with a pinch of salt.' Emma explained about the wrong tablets.

'This aunt wouldn't be called Mrs Myra Carter, by any chance?'

If Matt had expected a reaction to this query, he must have been more than satisfied.

'She *has* been to see you!' cried Emma.

'No, she's coming to see me tomorrow. Thank you for the information, but if you see Polly again, tell her we are more than capable of dealing with this sort of thing. We won't arrest her precious Jeremy or any of the others without any proper evidence.'

'I told her that,' said Emma.

'Well, then, nothing to worry over. Just relax and enjoy yourselves in the cottage.'

'Daymer Beach,' mused Emma. 'It's not far from Rock, is it?'

* * *

Emma and Damian set off on Monday morning, just as the plumbers' van drew up.

'I ought,' said Emma to Damian, 'to feel guilty at leaving Matt alone, but I don't. After all, he's quite capable of coping without me.'

'Of course he is,' said Damian in such a matter-of-fact way that Emma wondered if that was quite what she'd meant to suggest.

'Dealing with plumbers, anyway,' she said. 'And there's lots of food in the freezer. Anyway, he's hoping to get off early tomorrow and drive down and stay overnight with us. We'll see him then.'

The cottage was tucked away at the end of a path running off a long lane down to the beach. It was very small and a mix of stone and blue-painted clapboard. Inside, though on a mini-scale, it had everything a short-stay visitor could want. Downstairs it was open-plan with a big hearth containing a stove. There was also a microwave oven to satisfy the more modern cook. A large old scrubbed deal table served as both kitchen and dining table. Comfortable armchairs and a sofa were arranged around a TV. Upstairs were two tiny bedrooms under the eaves. The bathroom was an extension downstairs, reached from the kitchen.

'Great,' said Damian and clattered up the wooden stairs to unpack.

Emma set the laptop down carefully on the deal table and looked around. It was a lovely place. Poor Matt, left to divide his days between a waterless house and his usual daily grind as a police detective. Perhaps, thought Emma, later on his friend might lend us the cottage again and Matt and I can have a lovely, secluded, romantic weekend here.

'Em,' said Damian, clattering downstairs again. 'I think this cottage has got bats.'

'If so,' warned Emma, 'we mustn't disturb them. They're protected.'

'They might bite our necks as we sleep and we'll wake up mad.'

'You're thinking of Dracula,' said Emma firmly. 'I've never heard of vampires in Cornwall.'

She pushed the car keys into her jeans pocket and her fingers encountered a scrap of paper. She took it out. It was the note Polly had given with the details of Myra Carter's address.

'Well, well,' said Emma, sitting down. 'How about that?'

'What?' asked eager Damian, scenting something interesting.

'Mrs Carter's house isn't far from here, on the clifftop near Rock. And what's more,' she went on, 'at low tide, it's a nice walk along the beach to Rock, or one can go along the cliff or over the dunes if the tide is in. A nice healthy stroll would do us good.'

'And maybe we'll find this house where there's been strange goings-on!' exclaimed Damian, eyes shining.

'Not prying, you know,' murmured Emma.

'Of course not! Look, I've got this,' said Damian, producing a piece of paper of his own. 'Matt gave it to me before we left. His mate gave it to him, the cottage owner. It's the times of the tides this week. And look, we can go this afternoon.'

'It's so beautiful,' said Emma.

They had gone down to the beach and were setting out towards Rock across the sands. The tide was far out but water channels crisscrossed their route. They had taken off their shoes and walked barefoot. The firmness of the shell-strewn sand was illusory. Each footstep sank in at least an inch and left a print which quickly filled with water and was erased. Higher up, towards the cliffs, where the tide didn't reach, the sand was piled up in soft dunes held together by clumps of dry grasses. The cliffs themselves formed a towering backdrop, glittering in the early summer sun with shimmering hues of grey, blue, pink and turquoise. Rocks which had tumbled down in ages long past reached out towards the sea as if scattered by a giant. At high tide they would be covered. The rock pools left by the retreating tide would disappear, the slippery seaweed strands float free again and anyone rash enough to be caught down here be left with virtually nowhere to go. This was a coast where once upon a time, shipwrecks had been common and, even now, the fishing and other boats far out would have to negotiate their course with care.

They reached Rock and gazed across the inlet towards Padstow on the further side.

'There's a ferry,' said Damian, reading a wooden board. 'It says if you want it to come over for you, you've got to wave this flag.' He pulled a yellow flag from a holder and brandished it.

'Don't wave it now!' urged Emma.

'It's all right, the ferry's coming anyway.' Damian pointed out to sea.

They stood and watched as the sturdy craft drew near and anchored. A gangplank was pushed out and several people got off. One of them was evidently well known to the ferry's skipper.

'Cheerio, Jeremy. See you again!' he called.

Both Emma and Damian stepped forward and then, unwilling to be thought gawking, pretended to be looking elsewhere.

443

It had to be Jeremy Bryant, thought Emma. He was an athletic-looking young man of middle height in shorts and a T-shirt, with sun-bleached fair hair. He took no notice of Emma and Damian and set off purposefully towards a path leading cliffward.

After a discreet moment they followed him.

It was easy to trail Jeremy. They could see him ahead, striding onward. He didn't appear to be aware he was being followed, but why should he? There were plenty of other walkers up here, even though it wasn't yet the tourist season proper. There were local people with dogs, ramblers, early holidaymakers. Occasionally their quarry disappeared behind a rise in the ground or a clump of windswept trees, only to reappear. Suddenly, he vanished and didn't come back into view.

'Where's he gone?' cried Damian in alarm.

'Don't panic, there must be a turning.' Emma was proved right. When they got to the spot they saw a stony track, wide enough to take a car, running inland. At the far end it must meet a proper road. There were three or four houses along it at irregular intervals. Jeremy wasn't in sight and must have turned into one of them.

Emma and Damian picked their way up the track until they reached two houses standing closer together than the others. One was very small, an older building of white-washed stone. The other was more modern and clearly architect designed. The accommodation was split-level with windows looking out to sea, a magnificent view. There was a double garage with wide up-and-over doors. It was the home of someone wealthy, as Polly had described. The garden was laid to lawn on which three or four little rabbits gambolled unafraid. There was a movement on the other side of some French windows. Emma glimpsed Jeremy and a tall woman in blue. Then they moved out of sight.

At that moment, a woman in slacks and sweatshirt emerged from the white-washed house. She looked towards the strangers, shielding her eyes.

On impulse, Emma called, 'Hello! Are you Mrs Owen, by any chance?'

'Yes.' The woman came closer.

'You don't know me,' Emma explained. 'In private life, my name's Emma King. But professionally I'm Emma Durrant and I'm a writer. Your daughter Polly interviewed me the other day.'

'Oh yes, she phoned us and told us all about it! She was so excited to meet you. She did say you might call round. What a pity Robert, my husband's, not here at the moment,' said Mrs Owen. 'He'll be so sorry to have missed you. Do come in.'

A little later, over tea, Emma told her she and Damian were staying not far away. When she heard that, Frances Owen urged them to come again. 'Robert would love to meet you. He's a great whodunnit fan. And to be honest, we don't get many callers up here.'

'We followed someone, a young man, up here from the ferry,' Emma said. 'He turned in next door.'

Mrs Owen looked a little wry. 'Oh, that will be one of the Bryants visiting his aunt, probably Jeremy.' She frowned. 'Polly hasn't been telling you about that, has she?'

'If you mean the pills and the accidents, yes, she has,' Emma confessed.

'She really shouldn't have done that. But I'm not surprised. Polly does get involved in things. We weren't surprised she chose journalism for a career! I think,' added Frances Owen confidentially, 'my daughter is rather keen on the young man.'

'Do you mind?' asked Emma.

'He's a nice enough boy, well mannered, always pleasant. Which, I might say, isn't always true of his aunt, who can be quite difficult as a neighbour. Jeremy is certainly an improvement on some of the young men Polly's fallen for in the past!'

'What about Guy and Lucinda?' asked Emma. 'Do you know them?'

'I've met them when they come to visit their aunt. I admit I'd be concerned if Polly had fallen for Guy, who's rather a flashy sort of chap, all talk and no substance, if you ask me. Lucinda seems a capable girl if with rather grand ideas. But, you know, families do fall out especially over money. I've told Polly, it's really most unwise of her to get involved in any squabbles.'

Matt, thought Emma, couldn't have put it better. Then she remembered that Mrs Carter herself was due to visit Matt that morning. Was that why Jeremy was visiting her this afternoon? To find out what she'd told the police? She was sorry not to have had a closer look at Myra Carter. A shadowy figure behind glass only intrigued.

But she was to see Mrs Carter closer to hand. As they walked by the big house on leaving Frances Owen, they heard shouting voices. Suddenly the French windows burst open. Jeremy appeared, jumped down a couple of steps onto a terrace, then turned to face the house.

'You've absolutely no right! You're causing trouble for all of us, Guy, Lucinda and me!' Every line of his body trembled with rage.

Mrs Carter appeared framed by the windows. 'I shall do as I like, young man. The money, I would remind you, is legally mine. If necessary, by which I mean if there's any more nonsense, I shall change my will.'

Jeremy gasped, 'You can't do that! Uncle Henry wanted us to inherit!'

'Henry didn't know how you three would turn out!' snapped back his aunt. 'You're a charming boy when you want to be, Jeremy, but frankly, you're also an idle layabout. Guy and Lucinda are really no better, just playing at having careers. Well, if there are any more "little accidents", as you choose to call them, I shall be seeing my solicitor!'

She went back indoors. The young man stormed down the path to the gate, rushed past Emma and Damian without even noticing them, and was soon out of sight.

There was a silence. Then Damian spoke.

'I don't know what's going on,' he said, 'but I don't think she ought to have threatened that she might change her will. Not if one of them does need the money badly. That guy Jeremy is bound to tell the others.'

Emma nodded. 'Yes, if one of them was impatient before, he or she will be desperate on hearing that news. I know Polly thinks it's Mrs Carter's imagination, but I confess I am beginning to wonder!'

Part Two

Inspector Matt King carefully moved three biros lying on his desk so that they were lined up like guardsmen. This wasn't because he was obsessed by neatness but because he was giving himself time to think.

His visitor, observing the manoeuvre, asked tartly, 'Well?'

Matt sighed and raised his eyes to meet the frankly hostile gaze of the woman sitting opposite.

'Mrs Carter,' he began, 'although murder hits the headlines in the press and on TV, the reason it does so is because it's a comparatively rare crime in Britain.'

'It's going on all the time,' said his visitor, dismissing this.

'No,' Matt persisted gently, 'it isn't. Per head of population there are remarkably few murders.'

Mrs Carter leaned forward slightly. 'You mean, there are comparatively few the police choose to investigate.'

'However suspicious a death may look, Mrs Carter, unless there is evidence of the involvement of another party—'

Mrs Carter made a sound which Matt had seen written in books as 'Pshaw!'

He felt he was on a losing wicket here. To begin with his visitor was an imposing woman of uncertain age. She was large, not fat, just a big woman, tall, broad shouldered, carrying herself well.

Her hands, one of which he'd shaken on her arrival, were as big as many a man's and the clasp equally as strong. She was dressed in a loose blue cotton shift, sleeveless, and reaching to her ankles. Round her neck were several gold chains. Her hair, though grey, was thick and worn in a shoulder-length bob. Her skin was tanned and he suspected that a lifetime of sunbathing had contributed to the crazing of fine lines. Her gaze was mesmerising. Or at least, Matt felt himself, like the proverbial rabbit in a car's headlights, unable to move out of danger.

There were other contributory factors to the spell she cast over him. He was listening to her today, to this barmy notion she had of being a designated murder victim, at the personal request of the Assistant Chief Constable. Apparently she was a member of his bridge club. Matt suspected she would be an excellent bridge player, well used to the complex calculations and adept manipulations of the game. She certainly didn't conform to the usual image of a victim. She looked well able to take care of herself.

Diverted, Matt recalled that Rock, where she lived, was not far from the cottage to which he'd that morning dispatched his wife and her nephew for a week while plumbers were in their house. Oh yes, the plumbers . . .

Matt forced his drifting mind away from the situation which had arisen at home within an hour of Emma's departure. A situation he was determined his wife shouldn't find out about. Not yet, anyway, not until it had been fixed. In the meantime, there was Mrs Carter.

The Assistant Chief Constable's voice echoed in his head. 'Best to humour her. She's an utterly respectable woman and she genuinely believes this nons—' The ACC had coughed and continued, 'genuinely believes she is the object of a malicious campaign. She, er, could be classed as a trifle eccentric.'

Eccentricity, Matt thought, could often be a euphemism for just plain nuts. Sometimes, as he suspected was now the case, it meant his visitor was rich and independent enough to do just as she wished and not care what anyone else thought of her actions. Here was a woman who, after her husband's death, had run his business interests until only a few years ago. Matt had this information from the ACC. It meant she was accustomed to giving orders and seeing others jump to obey. Even the ACC hadn't been exempt. He had sounded distinctly shifty when phoning his request to Matt. Even senior officials can be bullied by someone like Mrs Carter. Bridge, thought Matt again, is a power game.

'What,' asked Mrs Carter impatiently, 'are you going to *do*?'

Matt pulled a notepad towards him. 'Right then, suppose you tell me exactly why someone should wish to kill you?'

'Money,' said Mrs Carter succinctly.

'Right . . .' Matt obediently wrote this down. He didn't need to, but she obviously expected some sort of action. He hoped it showed he was taking her seriously.

'Is there any particular person who might, er, see your demise as benefitting his financial position?'

'Good Lord!' said his visitor. 'Do you always talk like that? If you mean, does anyone come into the loot if I drop off the twig, why not say so?'

'All right,' retorted the goaded inspector. 'Does anyone?'

'Three of 'em,' returned Mrs Carter. 'Two nephews and a niece.'

'And you've named these three people as beneficiaries of your will?'

'Haven't I just said so?' she retorted.

'I mean, do they know that?'

'Of course they know it!' said Mrs Carter irritably. 'They're not thick. Well, Jeremy's not too bright but he goes in for things like bungee-jumping, so he is a man of action.'

Clearly Mrs Carter approved of action. But not, it seemed, in every instance.

'It would be just the daft sort of thing Jeremy might dream up, to drop a rock on my head from a clifftop. If you ask me, all that bouncing up and down at the end of a rope hasn't done his brain any good. What with that and the surfing. Sea water in the ears, I shouldn't be surprised. Of course, Guy's more of a plotter.'

Matt held up his hand to interrupt. 'Before we get to the individuals themselves, you say they're aware they're the beneficiaries of your will. Surely that means they wouldn't wish to upset you? People in your situation have been known to take umbrage and leave everything to, say, a charity.'

'Do I look like the sort of person who leaves good money to a cats' home?' demanded Mrs Carter.

'No,' admitted poor Matt.

'Then don't suggest such a thing. I don't have much time for my late husband's relatives, but I do have a strong sense of duty.'

There was a fierce gleam in her eye. Boadicea, thought Matt, must have been a lot like this. He could easily imagine Mrs Carter driving a chariot, knife blades on the wheels scything through the ranks of her enemies. Such people often had many enemies. He wasn't keen on her himself.

His visitor leaned forward and placed her large clasped hands on his desk. On one finger she wore a ring with a stone the size of a canary egg.

'Listen to me, young man,' she said. 'All the money was made by Henry, my late husband. He, too, had a strong sense of family duty. His sister married, very unwisely, a spineless chap without a cent to his name. A musician. Henry paid the school fees of all three of her children. It was understood that should Henry predecease me before their education was complete, I would continue to honour the arrangement. In the long term, I would, in turn, leave any of his fortune remaining at my death to the three of them.'

'Why did your husband not leave money to them under his will, say in a trust?'

'When he made his will the children were still young and in education. He saw no need for a trust. Why let the money be swallowed up in administration costs? My husband considered me to be the most reliable person to take care of matters and certainly the most capable steward of his fortune! There would be business decisions to be made and I was the one to make them! We decided all this before he died and Henry knew that I was a woman of my word. I told him I'd see the children got the money eventually and he knew that I would.'

Matt sat back in his chair and contemplated her. He was beginning to lose his awe of her but admitted she commanded a certain respect. He still didn't think her a particularly pleasant person but she was certainly one of iron principles. To speak of duty had become a slightly old-fashioned thing. But he didn't doubt she meant every word.

That didn't mean she was right that one of the legatees might not be willing to wait. He was strongly inclined to agree with Polly Owen that Mrs Carter had got a bee in her bonnet quite erroneously. The trouble with a woman like this was shifting the *idée fixe*, an almost impossible task. She'd see it as surrender.

'One, or two, or all of them, is trying to kill me.' Mrs Carter was not giving anyone the benefit of the doubt. 'They all need money. Lucinda had some sort of high-powered job but the firm crashed and she found herself out in the cold. She has a very expensive lifestyle, that girl. If she thought I'd finance it, she's found out she was wrong.

'Guy runs his own business but I know that's in trouble because he's asked me to bail him out. I refused, incidentally. Although Henry wished me to look after them, he didn't wish me to mollycoddle them. They've got to find out how to manage their own problems. They mustn't start thinking they can just run to me for the money every time life gets tough. Don't you agree?'

'Er – well, that's your decision, of course. What about the remaining nephew – Jeremy?' Matt had been scribbling furiously on his pad as she talked.

'He's a nice enough lad,' Mrs Carter's voice softened.

Matt wrote '*her favourite?*' and moved his in-tray so that she wouldn't be able to lean across and read it.

'He works for a sportswear manufacturer, goes round persuading shops and clubs to stock or recommend the goods. He is quite a persuasive boy,' Mrs Carter added.

'So he doesn't need money?'

'He wouldn't,' said Mrs Carter, 'if he didn't have so many expensive hobbies. He flew out to Africa last year just so he could bungee-jump off the Victoria Falls bridge.'

'But what has made you think one of them means you harm?' Matt persisted.

'Things have happened,' Mrs Carter retorted belligerently. 'They always look like accidents or the sort of thing which might just happen anyway. For example, someone polished the parquet under a rug in the hall. I nearly fell.'

'Your cleaner?'

'Nonsense. She knows better than to do a stupid thing like that. I asked her. She said she didn't do it. She's cleaned for me for fifteen years. I believe her. After that, someone loosened the stair carpet. These incidents haven't been confined to the house. I was walking on the beach at the foot of the cliffs and some rocks fell and just missed me by inches. I referred to that just now. I reported it to the council who investigated and could find no damage or unsafe area on the clifftop. Of course, they told me that it can always happen with cliffs. But it's very odd it should have happened when I was passing underneath and it hasn't happened again recently to anyone else!'

She paused. 'Someone switched my tablets. And please don't repeat that nonsense about my making a mistake because I'd transferred the pills to another pot. I knew exactly which tablets were in which container. I always do. I've never made a mistake and I didn't on that occasion. Someone got in and changed them.'

'Do any of the Bryant family have independent access to your house?'

'Pah!' The expression burst from her lips. 'Do you mean, have they got a key? I wish you wouldn't speak in police-jargon. Yes, they've all got keys. They might need to open up in an emergency.'

'So why not change the locks?'

She leaned forward again. "That is tinkering with details. I want you to sort out the fundamental situation. I want you to investigate. Interview them all. Find out who's lying and who's been doing it.'

'We are very busy!' said Matt, fed up with all this. 'My advice to you is to change the locks and don't take medicines out of their original containers.'

Mrs Carter rose to her feet and towered over him. 'You are an impertinent young man and I shall complain to your superiors!'

She sailed out.

'You do that!' muttered Matt, once he was sure she was out of earshot. He'd done his best. Even the ACC couldn't expect more.

That evening Matt rang Emma to say that he would still be coming over on Tuesday to see them. 'But not in the afternoon, I'm afraid. I'll be along later and stay over. I'll drive back after breakfast on Wednesday morning.'

Emma was getting used to this and learning fast that being married to a detective meant one could never make hard and fast plans.

'How about the plumbers?' she asked.

'Getting on,' said Matt enigmatically. 'See you tomorrow.'

On Tuesday, in honour of the reunion that evening, Emma drove into Polzeath and bought some beautiful fresh sea bass, caught that morning.

'I thought you didn't eat any meaty things,' said Damian.

'This isn't meat, it's fish and I do sometimes eat fish if it's exceptionally nice, like this.'

'That's not being a veggie,' argued Damian. 'That's being a demi-veggie.'

'Don't split hairs,' said Emma.

She was concerned to see, when Matt arrived, that he looked tired. But he seemed cheerful and assured her that the bathroom was coming along just fine, but taking a bit longer than first thought. 'Nothing to worry about.'

This convinced Emma that some major catastrophe had occurred but she was obliged to take Matt's word it hadn't. She had another matter on her mind, too.

'Did Mrs Carter come to see you?'

'She did. Tell Polly not to worry.'

'It's all sorted out? I have been wondering. I've seen one of the suspects, Jeremy, and I caught a glimpse of Mrs Carter.'

'He is not a suspect,' said Matt. 'No one is trying to murder her.'

Damian said in dire tones, 'We heard her threaten to change her will.'

Matt looked startled. 'Did she? She gave me to understand she wouldn't go back on a promise made to her late husband. Still, if she really believes . . .' Matt broke off and frowned.

'If she is going to change her will,' Emma reminded him, 'it strengthens any motive someone might have and it means they've got to act double-quick!'

After Matt had driven back to Wadebridge on Wednesday morning, Emma made a valiant attempt to get to grips with the laptop and the ongoing adventures of Felix Watts. It didn't go well. It was one thing to sit indoors at a desk and work. It was quite another to sit out here on a day of drowsy warmth. The branches overhead threw dappled shade on the grass. Birds twittered, insects buzzed, and from nearby came the soft splash of the incoming tide. It was made even more difficult by Damian, who'd taken himself off earlier. He reappeared at lunchtime, sweaty, red faced and happy, demanding, 'What's for lunch?'

'Make yourself a sandwich!' said his aunt crossly.

'Okay, shall I make you one?'

Emma sighed and switched off the computer.

'Not going well?' asked Damian sympathetically when she joined him in the kitchen. He was buttering bread enthusiastically.

'Not too much for me,' she said, eyeing the large amounts being slapped on. 'No, it's not going well. I'm getting a bit fed up with Felix, between you and me.'

Damian completed a doorstop of a cheese and tomato sandwich and handed it to her. 'I don't think you ought to be working on that book while we're here, Em. I'm not just saying this because I'm here. I think you need a break.'

Even Damian, thought Emma, struggling to chew a wodge of bread, was seeking to take care of her as if she couldn't do it for herself. A kind of role reversal was taking place. He, too, probably thought she was getting old – older.

'Get out this afternoon for a nice walk,' said her nephew kindly. 'We'll go over the dunes. It's just like the Sahara up there.'

It was a very hot afternoon. The deep sands on the dunes didn't make for easy walking. There was a path but in places it disappeared or had broken away. They were heading in the general direction of Rock. Emma had suggested they might take the ferry across to Padstow.

'Pity Matt can't get time off,' said Damian. 'But he can't, not with the plumbers in your house and everything.'

'I think there's been a problem with those plumbers,' confided Emma. 'There's definitely something Matt isn't telling me.'

The path now dropped down a steep sandy bank. Just as Emma and Damian reached the spot, someone struggled up the other side and arrived, panting, at the top, facing them.

It was an extraordinarily beautiful girl. She had long blonde hair in the sort of cut that cost a hundred pounds a go. She wore abbreviated shorts and what Emma judged a pure silk shirt in sugar pink. Her legs were long, shapely and the sort of beautiful honey tan to which Emma aspired but seldom managed to achieve. Her own sunbathing efforts generally had patchy results with the fronts of her legs always browner than the backs. The blonde's sunglasses were perched fashionably on top of her head, another style Emma had never managed with any success. Hers always fell off.

It was hard to say who was the most surprised to find someone else on the path. Then the blonde pulled her sunglasses down over her nose and stepped forward with the confidence of one who was sure others would make way for her. Damian did so politely and Emma had little choice but to follow his example.

'Good afternoon!' she said to the blonde, but got no reply other than a toss of the well-coiffed mane.

'Whoa!' said Damian appreciatively when the blonde had gone.

'Start daydreaming about girls like that when you've made a million, not before!' advised Emma.

'Miaow!' retorted Damian.

They finally emerged onto the strip of land at the sea's edge at Rock, just in time to see the ferry departing towards Padstow.

'Perhaps it would be better to go tomorrow, in the morning, make a day of it?' suggested Emma. 'What shall we do now?'

Damian's gaze had wandered towards the path that led up to the clifftop along which they'd followed Jeremy Bryant on their first day. 'We could go and have another look at that house.'

They climbed up the path and made their way along to where the track turned off, leading to the houses. To their surprise a white vehicle of familiar design was grinding its way away from them, down the track to the far end and access to a proper road.

'It's an ambulance!' cried Damian, starting to run forward.

Emma followed him. As they reached Mrs Carter's house, they saw Polly's mother, Frances Owen, standing by the gate, gazing anxiously after the ambulance.

'What's happened?' gasped Emma.

'It's poor Myra Carter. She's had another accident. She slipped in the kitchen. Someone had spilled water on the tiled floor and not mopped it up. She hit her head against a cupboard corner.'

Frances gestured wildly at the house behind her. 'I found her but it was only by chance. Her cleaner goes home at midday. We're not what you might call friendly, Myra and I, but I try to keep on neighbourly terms. A friend who keeps beehives gave me a couple of pots of honey. I took a pot round to Myra. The kitchen door was ajar. I pushed it open and called out to her. There was no reply, so I thought I'd put the honey jar just inside. I knew there was a dresser there. But the minute I pushed the door open

459

a little further, I saw her sprawled on the floor. Her head was covered in blood. I thought at first she was dead. But she was breathing though unconscious. I called the ambulance. Only imagine, if I hadn't chanced to go round there, she might have bled to death!'

She broke off and gazed at them, perplexed. 'How could this sort of thing keep happening? The daily woman is so careful, she'd never leave spilled water on a tiled floor. I suppose Myra herself . . .'

Frances pushed back her brown hair. 'I must go and phone one of the family, let them know. I've got Jeremy's number somewhere. Do excuse me . . .'

Damian and Emma watched her hurry away.

'What do you think, Em?' asked Damian.

'I think it's one accident too many,' Emma said firmly. 'Whatever Polly says, and of course she's keen to protect Jeremy Bryant, it's beginning to look very fishy.'

Damian cleared his throat. 'The kitchen door's still open.'

'So it is.' Emma drew a deep breath. 'We must go and close it, Damian. Obviously Frances has forgotten in her haste to phone one of the family.'

They approached the open door both attempting to feel like good citizens and less like prying interlopers.

With evidence in mind, Emma avoided the handle and made to push the door with her elbow. She paused.

'Go on,' urged Damian. 'Just a quick look. It wouldn't do any harm.'

They inched inside. It was a large kitchen, tiled as Mrs Owen had indicated. On the floor, the patch of water was drying fast.

But it was impossible to miss the sticky red stain on the corner of a cupboard.

'She fell that way,' said Emma, pointing. 'She came into the kitchen from the hall, rounded the table there on her way to the sink. I expect she was going to fill the kettle for tea. She slipped and fell there . . .' She touched Damian's arm. 'Come on, we shouldn't be here.'

They went outside. Emma picked up a twig and, using it as a hook over the handle, pulled the kitchen door shut.

'Are you going to tell Matt about this?' asked Damian as they walked home.

'Of course. The poor woman went to see him on Monday morning to complain someone was trying to kill her. You and I both heard her threaten to change her will. Now she's in hospital. I'm beginning to think we should all have been taking her more seriously, and even Matt will have to agree after this!'

A strange car almost as old as Emma's was parked outside the gate of their cottage. As they reached it, Polly Owen jumped out.

She greeted them with, 'Awful news! Jeremy's Aunt Myra's in hospital!'

'I know,' said Emma. 'We were there as the ambulance left. We spoke to your mother. More to the point, how do you know?'

'Mum rang Jeremy and Jeremy rang me. He's so upset. He's really scared. The police are bound to think it's one of the family. But it was just another accident, it's bound to be. But you wait, as soon as Mrs Carter regains consciousness, she'll accuse the family. She never admits she's responsible herself.' Polly waved her hands in despair.

'Come and have a cold drink,' Emma invited. 'And calm down.'

Beneath the trees with a jug of Emma's home-made lemonade, Polly's agitation gave way to dejection. 'Everything's conspiring against Jeremy. Did you tell your husband what I told you?' She gazed at them anxiously.

Emma nodded. 'I believe Mrs Carter did go to see him.'

'I knew she would, mean old bat,' said Polly.

'Come on,' said Emma. 'She's a very worried woman. You say Jeremy is scared. Perhaps you should consider Mrs Carter's feelings.'

Polly gave a snort. 'You don't know her! She isn't the sort who scares easy!' She sat back. 'You know what will happen now? She'll come out of hospital and the first thing she'll do is change her will. You'll see. She's already told Jeremy she means to.'

'Perhaps,' Emma said gently, 'from Jeremy's point of view – and the point of view of his brother and sister – that would be the best thing she could do. It would remove their motive.'

'Right,' retorted Polly. 'Let me tell you what Jeremy and I think! We think she wants an excuse to change her will. She's bound by this promise to Jeremy's uncle Henry. But she really wants to leave the money to someone or something else, right? So she wants a really cast-iron excuse to go against Henry Carter's last wishes.'

'I hardly think,' protested Emma, 'that she'd go to the lengths of cracking her own head open.'

Polly made a dismissive gesture. 'No, of course not. I don't say she did. What I am saying is, every time something like this happens, she tells everyone it's an attempt to kill her and points the finger at the family. She's building a case against them all. When she's got everyone thinking it's true, then she can change her will and no one will blame her.'

Polly stood up. 'I'm going to meet Jeremy at the hospital. Guy and Lucinda are driving down from London. Tell your husband, they didn't have anything to do with it!'

'Whew,' observed Damian when Polly's car had bounced away. 'She's really keen on that Jeremy guy.'

'Yes, so keen she won't admit even the possibility Mrs Carter might be right about these incidents. As Polly's own mother indicated, there are far too many of them.'

Emma sat back and fell into deep thought. After a while, Damian couldn't bear the silence any longer and prompted her.

'Well? What have you decided?'

Emma looked slightly embarrassed. 'Don't make fun of this – and don't tell Matt! But I was wondering how Felix Watts would interpret all this. Now, I know he isn't real, I invented him. But he is a detective, so if I put myself in his mind, I start thinking like a detective, too. Do you follow?'

'Absolutely, Em!' said Damian, rapt.

'Right, here goes. Someone else could have been in the house, someone Myra Carter might not even have known was there. It doesn't have to be one of the family. Let's just say someone else got in. The weather's very warm. The houses down that track are isolated. People living there probably don't bother to keep doors shut in hot weather. Or remember those French windows? Someone, banking on easy access, slipped in.'

'Makes sense so far,' encouraged Damian.

'So this person followed her to the kitchen, struck her or pushed her so she fell and then spilled water deliberately on the tiles. The assailant could have arranged her like that, with her head by the cupboard, and smeared a little blood on the wood.'

463

'Then, when she comes round, she might remember who it was,' Damian offered.

'Not necessarily, not if she didn't see him or her,' Emma mused. 'On the other hand, the assailant can't be sure of that and must be pretty scared. In which case, whoever it was, will definitely try again and next time won't leave anything to chance. I don't think Myra Carter's at risk in the hospital. It'll be when she returns home. But can I convince Matt of that?'

Part Three

Late Thursday morning, much to Emma's surprise, Matt turned up at the cottage unannounced.

'I thought you'd be too busy to take a day off!' she exclaimed, throwing her arms round his neck with enthusiasm.

'I am,' said her husband, returning her welcoming kiss and then disentangling himself. 'But it so happens it's official business that's brought me out here.'

'Myra Carter's accident!' cried Emma at once. 'You're investigating. You think someone did try to kill her.'

Matt held up his hands. 'Whoa! I don't think anything. Yes, I have been out to her house to have a look at the scene of the accident. I've spoken to the neighbour who found her.'

'That's Polly's mother,' put in Damian.

'And I've also spoken to the three Bryant siblings. They turned up at the hospital where their aunt is, so I was able to corner all three in one go which was helpful.'

'And?' chimed Emma and Damian together.

'Lucinda and Guy both say they were in London at the time of the accident. Guy waved his personal organiser at me and claimed to be able to account for every moment of his day until contacted by his brother with news of Mrs Carter's hospitalisation. He then cancelled his appointments, leapt in his car, and drove to her bedside. Most commendable.

'Lucinda went to her health club in the afternoon to swim and was on her way home to get ready for an evening dinner date when she received a call from Jeremy on her mobile phone to tell her the news. She, like her brother Guy, immediately dropped all other plans and drove down to see Auntie.

'Meanwhile, Jeremy was busy selling swimwear to stores along the North Cornish coast until he got a call on his mobile from Mrs Owen. He drove at once to the hospital. He is the only one who admits to being in the area, but denies he had time to go to the house at Rock and set up an "accident". That, however, isn't quite true.

'The strongest point in their favour is that there's absolutely no sign that any one of them was anywhere near Rock. The plain fact of the matter is, we've been over that house with a fine-tooth comb and nothing suggests that between the daily cleaner leaving at noon and Mrs Owen, the neighbour, finding Myra Carter on the kitchen floor at around four there was any other person in the house.'

'But you do admit this accident, following on after all the others, looks suspicious?' Emma asked anxiously.

Inspector King looked unhappy. 'Yes, yes – it looks very odd to me. It'd look odd to anyone. But I'm not that detective of yours, Felix Watts. He goes off at the drop of a hat and spends his entire time chasing down a hunch. A real-life copper can't do that. I need evidence, signs of a break-in, a witness who saw one of the suspects, that sort of thing. As I've nothing to go on, I'm afraid this is going to have to be put down as a household accident.'

All three of them sat in silence for a while until Damian got up and switched on the kettle.

'What about Mrs Carter herself?' asked Emma. 'How is she?'

'Doing fine, but she's got a sore head, a couple of stitches in it, and concussion. She'll be in hospital for a day or two.'

'So you haven't been able to talk to her about it?'

Matt shook his head. 'Not properly. But according to a nurse, she got very agitated when the Bryants arrived to see her and the nurse had to ask them to leave. When I arrived there, I found all three in a corridor arguing fit to bust. So it looks as though she intends to blame them, or one of them. I'm afraid she isn't a woman who'll even consider she might have spilled water herself or tripped on a loose carpet runner because she hadn't had it fixed.'

'Then she'll carry out her threat to change her will,' Emma said soberly, accepting a mug of coffee from Damian.

'We did hear her make that threat, Matt,' Damian said. 'She shouted it out to Jeremy and he told Polly.' He placed a steaming mug in front of Matt, who mumbled his thanks.

'And there's another thing, Matt,' Emma went on. 'You didn't see the patch of water on the floor. I did. Although it was drying, it was still quite big and there was no sign of a skid mark.'

'And what,' asked Matt suspiciously, 'were you and Damian doing inside the house?'

'We went to close the back door!' said Emma virtuously. 'It had been left open. That was very careless of the ambulance men.'

'And we just went inside a step or two,' added Damian. 'Not right through the place!'

Matt decided to accept the explanation but still had a question.

'Wouldn't a skid mark, formed by the layer of water being dispersed, dry first?'

'It might,' Emma admitted unhappily.

Matt frowned. 'And as you said, I didn't see it... and perhaps you just didn't notice it? After all, you said your prime interest was to close the back door.'

Emma thought furiously. 'What did you mean about it not being true that Jeremy had no time to go to Rock?'

Matt, stirring his coffee, said slowly, 'He admits to being in the area at the time and there's a gap in his timetable for the day around one o'clock. He says he was sitting on the seafront at Newquay, watching the surfers and eating a Cornish pasty. The man's entitled to a lunchbreak, I suppose. He isn't, however, able to produce any witnesses. It's just conceivable he could have driven to his aunt's house, parked well away from it, and approached it over the clifftop. There's a little-used footpath which passes near the rear of Mrs Carter's garden.'

'Polly will never accept that Jeremy is prime suspect,' Emma pointed out.

'With respect,' said her husband, 'Polly's judgement is skewed by the fact that she's besotted with the young man, or so you say.'

'I didn't say besotted,' objected Emma. 'I said in love.'

'In love, then. Either way, of course she believes in his innocence. But have you considered that Jeremy Bryant might be using Polly? Let's say, just for argument's sake, he's been arranging these accidents. He knows his aunt is going to tell everyone about them and knowing her character, he's pretty sure she'll blame him or his brother or sister. So, Jeremy gets in first. Before Myra Carter can go to the police, he tells Polly that his aunt is an eccentric bully who is going round slandering him and his brother and sister. Perhaps Polly had already told him she was going to interview you, Emma? Jeremy has done his homework. He knows you're married to me and that if his aunt goes to the police, it's very likely I'm the officer she'll speak to. So he tells Polly, Polly tells you and asks you to tell me. You do tell me. By the time Mrs Carter arrives in my office I'm already prejudiced against anything she might say.'

'Gosh!' said Damian, deeply impressed.

Matt looked gratified and Emma folded her arms, looking glum. 'If that turns out to be true, it'll break poor Polly's heart. He wouldn't use her like that, would he? She loves him, with or without the money!'

'Just remember,' Matt said, 'that Jeremy Bryant has been brought up in expectations of inheriting a third share of a fortune. Perhaps Polly doesn't care about the money. But you can bet Jeremy Bryant does! And Guy and Lucinda. I told you I met them in the hospital corridor. When they realised I was a copper they virtually mobbed me. Guy says his aunt is dotty. Lucinda claims a third party is poisoning her aunt's mind against them. Jeremy just keeps repeating none of them did it and his aunt is being unfair. What a family!'

Matt slapped his hands on the tabletop. 'It's all academic, anyway. I've no evidence anyone tried to do anything and as far as police investigations are concerned, that's it. We've examined the scene of the accident and we've spoken to the relatives. We simply can't do any more. Now, I've really got to get back. I'll see you at the weekend.'

'Matt,' Emma asked, following him out to his car, 'everything's all right at the house, isn't it? I mean the plumbers—'

'The bathroom's coming along just fine!' he assured her and

slammed the door before she could reply. He blew a kiss at her through the window and drove off.

'No, it isn't!' yelled Emma after him. 'I know something's gone wrong!' She knew he couldn't hear her but it helped to let off frustration.

'We could drive back to Wadebridge and take a look at the bathroom for ourselves,' Damian suggested.

Emma was tempted but resisted. 'No, if Matt says everything's fine, I've got to take his word for it. I mustn't go checking up on him. Suppose everything is all right? The plumbers would be bound to tell him I was there, asking. Trust, Damian. It's all about trust.'

'Well, stop worrying about it, then,' said Damian.

After Matt had left, Emma and Damian made what turned out to be a bad decision. Despite Damian's constantly urging her not to dwell on what Matt had said about Polly, it preyed on her mind and Emma suggested a good long walk. So they set out in a new direction, towards Trebetherick and from there along the cliff path to Polzeath. But the fresh air failed to blow away the main thing occupying both their minds.

'I like Polly,' said Emma. 'She's really keen on Jeremy. She'd believe anything he told her. She could innocently be allowing him to use her to discredit his aunt. I can see that.'

'I'm just glad no one in our family's got a fortune,' said Damian. 'Not if it makes all that trouble. But I've been thinking too, Em. Polly claimed that Mrs Carter wants a reason to change her will. Matt told us Mrs Carter is a bridge player. We've got a bridge club at school. I joined for a bit but it wasn't my scene. The thing is, bridge is all about getting people to play the cards in the order you and your partner want them. Making people do what you want, you see? So perhaps Mrs Carter is manipulating her nephews and her niece. Okay, from what Matt said they sound a gruesome threesome. But that doesn't make them villains, does it?'

Emma looked doubtful.

'Think about it, Em,' urged Damian. 'If she wants to change her will, then who does she want to leave it all to?'

'To whom . . .' corrected Emma automatically.

Damian hissed in exasperation. 'Honestly, Em. Who cares about grammar when we're talking about murder? Who's the mystery person? That's what we ought to be thinking about!'

'I'm not convinced she's looking for an excuse to change her will. I can't believe she'd injure herself or make herself ill by taking the wrong medication. No, Damian, it doesn't add up. Someone's out to harm her. But if the three Bryants are innocent then we're certainly looking for a mystery person,' Emma mused.

They had turned and were making their way home. The stiff breeze which had buffeted them all the way there had gained in force. Neither of them had brought waterproof garments and Emma was unhappily aware of the gathering dark clouds. Below them, the tide was in and the sea crashed angrily on the rocks. Then the first flurry of rain hit their faces and before they knew it, the skies opened above them.

There was no shelter and nowhere to go but onward through driving rain. They bent their heads and hurried as fast as they could. The mounting wind caught them maliciously broadside on and caused them both to stagger. The edge of the cliff seemed far too near for comfort but to leave the path and walk on the uneven turf was dangerous. Damian grasped his aunt's hand and hauled her along. She realised that, although so much younger than she was, he was certainly as strong and somehow solider. They must play a lot of sport at that school of his, she found herself thinking. Water found its way down her neck and inside her clothing so that she was soon as wet inside as out. Not another living soul was in sight. Out at sea all craft had fled to the shelter of the harbour. No one else, thought Emma, had been so daft as to be caught out like this.

After what seemed an eternity, they battled their way back to the cottage through driving rain and staggered inside, dripping wet and breathless.

'I thought we might get blown over the cliff edge!' gasped Damian, running his hands over his hair, squeezing out water.

'Go and have a bath,' advised his aunt. Her own long brown hair hung in rat's tails round her face. Her shoes were sodden and her shirt and jeans clung unpleasantly to her body. She kicked off her shoes. 'Go on, Damian, do. I can't let you get pneumonia. Your mum and dad would never forgive me. The school would be pretty annoyed as well.'

'No, you go,' said Damian robustly. 'I'm okay. I'll just take off these wet things. I won't get cold or anything. At school they make us play rugby in all weathers. Even when it's freezing. The sports master digs the heel of his boot into the pitch and if it makes even the slightest dent, we play.'

'Being cold is one thing. Being cold and wet is another,' countered his aunt.

But being sent off to take a bath was clearly seen by Damian as being treated like a small child. They were still wrangling over it when there came a loud rat-tat at the cottage door.

472

They looked at one another. Rain still beat against the window-panes. Who could be out in this weather? Had Matt come back?

Emma went to the door, leaving a trail of wet footprints on the flagged floor. She pulled it open. Outside a familiar figure stood holding a folded newspaper over her head.

'Polly!' she exclaimed.

'May we come in?' asked Polly, and Emma became aware of a larger figure looming up in the grey mist. 'We're getting awfully wet. You haven't met Jeremy, have you?'

Fifteen minutes later saw them all settled round the electric fire, hands clasping mugs of cocoa, enjoying the comforting heat. Emma had changed her clothes and lent Polly a dry sweater. Damian had changed, too. Only Jeremy Bryant was in his original gear and steamed gently before the bars of the electric fire.

Emma was interested to get a closer look at him. He was an attractive young man, she thought, with a pleasant, open face, though just now his forehead was puckered in a worried frown.

'You know all about my aunt being in the hospital?' he asked.

Emma nodded. 'How is she?'

'She's doing well. She's pretty tough. The thing is, she's also in a rotten mood. She won't let any of us sit with her. Lucinda lost her rag and flounced off back to London. She says she'll come back when Aunt Myra can speak to her without making vile accusations. That's Luce's expression, by the way, the "vile accusations" bit. I have to admit, Aunt Myra's attitude is hurtful. She and I haven't always seen eye to eye. She doesn't approve of my hobbies, for a start. But generally, I've always got on well with her. Or I did,' added Jeremy gloomily, 'before she started having all these accidents. She's got this bee in her bonnet that one of us is trying to bump her off. Nothing any of us can say makes any difference.'

'What about your brother, Guy?' Damian asked. 'Has he gone back to London?'

'As far as I know. Polly and I have been to see Polly's parents. Polly said you might know— well, she wanted me to come and meet you so we started to walk here. Then we got caught in the rain.'

'All of us got caught in the rain,' said Emma. 'I am pleased to meet you, Jeremy. Polly's told us a lot about you.'

Suddenly, she liked him and was inclined to believe him in his innocence. 'You know my husband is a police inspector and that your aunt went to see him?'

'Oh, I know that. Polly told me and I met him myself at the hospital. Goodness knows what he thought of us. We were all so upset we fell out with each other and were having a real barney in the corridor. But it isn't because we're all three heartless and grasping. It's because we care about Aunt Myra. Your husband's been out to Auntie's house looking around, hasn't he? He didn't find anything sinister or he hasn't said so, if he did.' Here Jeremy looked enquiringly at Emma.

'I understand he found no evidence of foul play,' said Emma carefully. This was why Polly and Jeremy were here, she thought. They wanted to know Matt's thoughts and hoped Emma would enlighten them.

She could hardly explain that, although Matt had closed his enquiry into Myra Carter's accident for lack of evidence, he did have his private theories, and in them, Jeremy Bryant figured as prime suspect!

*   *   *

The rain had stopped. Although a watery sun was doing its best to dry things up, too much water dripped from the trees for them to eat out in the garden. Emma produced an early-evening meal of hot lentil soup, cheese, salad, French bread and Damian's favourite, cold cooked pork sausages. A bottle of wine she'd meant to keep for Matt's next visit was opened in honour of visitors. They all four gathered round the kitchen table and tucked in with healthy appetites.

'You know, Jeremy,' said Emma tactfully when everyone was well fed and had relaxed. 'Perhaps we're all taking too narrow a view of this. Suppose someone is engineering these accidents? I don't mean you or your brother or sister. Has your aunt any other relatives?'

'Don't think so,' said Jeremy. 'We're the only ones in the frame.'

'What about old friends, then? Someone who might think she would leave everything to them if she changed her will?'

'Aunt Myra hasn't got any old friends,' he said. 'She's fallen out with them all over the years. She falls out with everyone. She's always changing solicitors, accountants, doctors, you name it. Uncle Henry was the same. He and my mother fell out over her marriage to my father. He never spoke to my father that I'm aware of. He took over us kids because he believed our parents incapable. Looking back, it seems high handed, but he meant well.

'Then our father left and our mother died and Uncle Henry became our guardian. It suited him fine. He could really organise us! He just steam-rollered over people and the wise ones got out of the way. I suppose that's why he did so well in business. He had a partner once and fell out with him. There was some sort of court case over it which Uncle Henry won. I remember the partner vaguely. I was only a kid but I met him when he and Uncle Henry were still big pals. His name was Erwin Berg and he came to see my uncle with his wife and baby daughter a few times. They seemed a nice family, as far as I could judge, though I was only a kid. Anyway, after they fell out, it didn't do to mention his name in front of either Uncle Henry or Aunt Myra. With Uncle Henry you were "in" or "out". Aunt Myra's much the same.'

Polly said eagerly, 'All that's in Jeremy's favour, isn't it? She didn't mind the Bryants when they were children because she and her husband controlled their lives. Now they've grown up, Uncle Henry's dead, and she's still trying to control Jeremy and the others. But she's found she can't do it and so she's fallen out with them, just like all the others.'

'Give her her due,' protested Jeremy, 'she's been quite straight with us until now. She doesn't approve of our lifestyles, especially mine. But she's been all right, just stingy. I know Guy asked her for money. His business is up the creek. She wouldn't come across. I warned him beforehand she wouldn't. Lucinda's probably a bit short of cash now she's out of a job, but on the other hand, the sort of boyfriends Luce has, she never has to pay for anything.'

'For her flat, presumably?' Emma pointed out.

'Yes, but that's about it. She gets asked out to dinner virtually every day by someone. She holidays on other people's yachts. Blokes have given her some really nice jewellery over the years. She could always hock that.'

Possibly, thought Emma disapprovingly. She didn't like the sound of Lucinda's lifestyle and she certainly didn't agree with Jeremy that his sister didn't need money. Rich friends might invite her out so long as she was able to keep up with them. They'd soon drop an impoverished freeloader. She didn't say this to Jeremy.

Instead she asked, 'And you, Jeremy? I don't mean to pry. But has she recently refused you, as well as Guy?'

'No!' he said indignantly. Then, reddening, added, 'I did ask her for a few quid last year. I needed new skis. It was only a few hundred but I didn't get it. I hadn't really expected to. I don't hold it against her, for goodness' sake! It was only for skis. Now poor old Guy has sunk everything into setting up that firm of his—'

Jeremy broke off as he realised what he was saying. 'Guy was angry when she turned him down but he wouldn't harm her. Believe me.'

Not the sort of family, as Damian had said, that you'd want as your own, thought Emma with a sigh. Even pleasant Jeremy seemed to see nothing wrong with his attitude or that of his sister or brother. She hoped Polly's friendship would straighten him out.

A little later Polly and Emma were clearing away the supper dishes when they heard the clunk of a car door, followed by the creak of the gate.

'Another visitor!' Damian sang out from the window. 'Tall chap. Gosh, he drives a Porsche—'

Polly spun round from the sink and nearly dropped the dish she was holding. Emma caught it in the nick of time. Jeremy also looked startled. He joined Damian at the window.

As a knock sounded at the door, he turned a bewildered face to Polly. 'Guy's here,' he said. 'I thought he was back in London. How did he find us?'

'Open the door, Damian,' Emma said quickly. 'Ask him in.'

* * *

Guy Bryant was taller and slimmer than his brother, an altogether more dashing figure in expensive casual wear. He had that air of confidence in himself and his own abilities which always annoyed Emma in similar brash young men. He certainly didn't seem to share Jeremy's pleasant nature. Or, if he did, he was hiding it well now! He walked past Damian and gave Emma only a cursory nod of acknowledgement when introduced.

'I asked Frances if she knew where you were. She told me you and Polly had probably come here.' His words were directed at his brother and his tone was critical.

Jeremy flushed. 'I thought you were back in town, Guy.'

'Did you?' said his brother disagreeably. 'I got back to London last night and realised that I should have stayed here until matters are sorted. Too many things have been happening behind my back.'

Here Guy gave his brother a meaningful look and glanced round the cottage. So he didn't approve of Polly and Jeremy being here, thought Emma. Tough. The youngsters were free agents. It seemed to her Guy had inherited Uncle Henry's desire to control others.

'So I'm back,' Guy went on. 'And I've taken a room in a hotel just down the road. I can tell you that with things the way they are for me just now, I can ill afford the time away from my office and certainly can't be driving up and down between the West Country and the city every other day! But things can't be left as they are, can they? I don't suppose,' Guy added sarcastically, 'that I can rely on you to sort things out.'

Polly said hotly, 'Hey! We're doing our best. We've been talking about it with Emma and Damian—'

'We?' Guy interrupted. 'This is what I suspected. This is Bryant family business, no one else's. I don't know what you've been saying,

Jerry, but I certainly don't fancy being discussed behind my back with people I don't know and I can't see have any legitimate interest in this.'

'My husband,' said Emma loudly, 'is Detective Inspector King who's been investigating these accidents your aunt has had.'

Guy turned to her and surveyed her with more interest than he'd shown so far. 'Is he, indeed? Well, you tell your husband that "accidents" are exactly what Aunt Myra's had. No one is trying to kill her. If she maintains any differently, it's because she's losing her marbles.'

There was a brief silence. Guy turned back to his brother. 'In my opinion, she's no longer competent to run her affairs. One of us should apply to the courts for power of attorney. Lucinda wouldn't be any good at it, she'd mess things up. You can't say you've got a business brain, Jerry. So it'll have to be me. You agree?'

'Well, I—' Jeremy began unhappily.

Polly reached out and took his hand. 'We don't think things are anywhere near as bad as that. At least, I don't and I've seen a lot of your aunt over the years. I know her well. My parents know her even better. We don't know why she's doing this, accusing you all. Perhaps she's mistaken or perhaps—' She broke off.

Guy raised his eyebrows. 'Do favour us with your opinion, Polly.'

Polly glanced guiltily at Jeremy. 'You won't mind me telling Guy this, Jeremy? Guy, we've been wondering whether she's looking for an excuse to disinherit you all.'

'I've been wondering that, too,' said Damian eagerly. 'But Em doesn't agree.'

'Why?' asked Guy coldly.

Polly wasn't fazed by his attitude. 'So she can leave the money to someone else. After all, it is her money in law, even though Henry made it in his business. She can leave it to someone else if she chooses.'

Guy placed his palms flat on the tabletop and leaned forward. 'And that someone,' he said nastily, 'wouldn't just turn out to be you, would it?'

'Me?' gasped Polly.

'Polly? You're barmy!' snapped Jeremy.

'Yes, her!' Guy snapped back. Unexpectedly he burst into a snatch of song. '"Pretty little Polly Perkins of Paddington Green . . ." Only, in this case,' he added in a normal voice, 'it's little Polly Owen, the girl next door. The girl who's known Aunt Myra all her life, right? Whose parents are Aunt Myra's neighbours and about the only people she hasn't quarrelled with!'

'Don't be daft, Guy!' Jeremy argued. 'Polly wouldn't have suggested it if she thought she might be the alternative beneficiary.'

'Wouldn't she?' Guy retorted. 'Never heard of a double bluff? Incidentally, Polly's got easy access to Aunt Myra's house. Perhaps it's time someone – ' He turned to Emma, 'your husband, for example – asked Polly about Aunt Myra's accidents!'

Part Four

'Guy Bryant is ghastly,' declared Emma into the phone. 'Honestly, Matt, there's no other word for him. He wants his aunt declared unable to run her affairs so he can run them. We can all guess what that would mean! Even worse, in my mind, he made a dreadful accusation about Polly.'

She explained what Guy had said about Polly hoping to replace the Bryants as beneficiary of Mrs Carter's will.

'I doubt the courts would agree to give Guy Bryant power of attorney,' Matt replied. 'He's whistling in the wind there. She's perfectly compos mentis as far as I can see. She's just extremely cantankerous and has got hold of the idea one of them is trying to kill her. I repeat there's no evidence to suggest one of them is, but now you've met two of the three, you'll understand why she's got pretty fed up with them.'

'But for Guy to suggest that Polly—' Emma spluttered to a halt in rage.

At the other end of the phone she could hear Matt clearing his throat in the way that meant he was going to contradict her somehow.

'I didn't like Guy Bryant, either. However, face it, Emma. Elderly people have taken a fancy to a young neighbour or friend before now and cut the family out of the will. The Bryants would be able to contest it, of course. But as they aren't blood relatives, well . . .'

'I won't hear a word against Polly!' cried Emma into the phone.

'Oy, mind my eardrums, won't you? I'm sorry,' Matt went on. 'I know you like Polly but she does sound an impetuous sort of kid and she is in love with Jeremy. Let's say Guy is wrong about Polly's aims. There's still a possibility Polly and Jeremy are in it together in an attempt to hasten Jeremy's inheritance.'

'Well, I don't believe it of Polly,' declared his wife. 'Okay, she might, just might, be Jeremy Bryant's dupe, but she wouldn't be his knowing accomplice.'

'It's happened before,' Matt's voice, aggravatingly reasonable, said into her ear. 'Nice girl meets handsome, dashing young guy and falls for him like a ton of bricks. "We could get married and go off and live happily ever after," says the boyfriend, "if my rich auntie would cough up some cash. But she won't. She's a thoroughly unpleasant woman and no one would grieve if a rock fell on her head while she was walking under the cliffs or if she fell downstairs in her own house." So they get together to arrange something.'

'I still don't believe Polly would agree,' said Emma obstinately.

'Nevertheless, nasty Guy has made a fair point. Polly's parents live next door to Myra Carter. Polly visits them regularly. No one is surprised to see her around there, least of all Mrs Carter, who knows the girl well. It would be the easiest thing in the world for Polly to slip into Mrs Carter's house—'

'No!' Emma interrupted. 'Polly may be hot headed, but she's a thoroughly nice kid and not stupid. I don't think money means anything to her. I've told you before. She's far more likely to tell

Jeremy not to worry about the money. They can manage without it.'

'And I've pointed out to you before that Jeremy has grown up expecting one day to inherit a sizeable amount. The Bryants look upon that money as theirs by moral right. Their uncle made it. He was their guardian. He intended they should have it all eventually.' Matt paused. 'Are we quarrelling about this, by any chance?'

'No.' Emma was taken aback. 'We're discussing it.'

'Good, just so I know. Can we leave the subject now?'

'I can't just forget about it, Matt! I'm sure whoever is trying to kill Myra Carter will try again as soon as she leaves the safety of the hospital.'

'That will be on Saturday,' said Matt unexpectedly.

'What?'

'Saturday, she's being discharged on Saturday.'

'She can't be!' wailed Emma.

'She's been judged fit to go home and she's champing at the bit to leave. I disagree that she's in danger. With so much suspicion being directed at all three Bryants, they'd be mad to try anything.'

'But if it's not one of them? If it's—?'

'Emma!' Matt was beginning to sound exasperated. 'There is no one else, except Polly, and you won't hear of that! Now, let it go, will you?'

'I've just got one more question,' Emma said quickly. 'And then I'll shut up, I promise. I've met Guy and Jeremy. But I haven't met Lucinda. What's she like? What does she look like?'

'Tall girl, long blonde hair, good figure.' Matt's voice gained a suggestion of amusement. 'Not getting jealous, are you? You needn't

483

be. I'd sooner tackle a nest full of angry wasps than be around Lucinda Bryant! Why do you want to know?'

'Just curious,' said Emma. 'You know me.'

'I know you, too,' said Damian when Emma had put down the phone. 'Why do you want to know about Lucinda Bryant?'

'Do you remember the day Myra Carter had the accident which put her in the hospital? You and I walked over the dunes to Rock and we met a tall blonde coming away from Rock? One with a surly disposition, too! That could have been Lucinda, returning from her aunt's house where she'd set up the "accident".'

'But Lucinda was in London that day, at her health club,' objected Damian. 'Jeremy rang her mobile to tell her about it. She cancelled her dinner date and drove down.'

'How did Jeremy know she was at her health club?' Emma sat back expectantly.

Damian frowned. 'Well . . . because she told him so.'

'Exactly!' crowed his aunt. 'If you call someone on an ordinary phone, they have to be there to pick it up and speak to you. But a mobile? The person can say she's anywhere. If she's a regular at that health club she probably has a season card and just walks in and out. It'd be hard for anyone to say for certain they saw her there on any particular day. And because she cancelled the dinner date, the people there no longer expected to see her. She has no alibi, Damian! When Jeremy rang her she could have been anywhere between Rock and London. Jeremy seems a nice chap but I wouldn't say he—' Emma broke off in some embarrassment.

'He was the owner of a megawatt brain?' suggested Damian helpfully.

'Thank you. Awfully nice. Not awfully bright. Fortunately Polly is bright enough for both of them. Come on, Damian!'

'Where are we going?' asked Damian as he hurried after her to the car.

'We're going to pay a hospital visit – on Mrs Myra Carter!'

They found Mrs Carter in the hospital dayroom. She was wearing her loose blue dress and sitting by a window, leafing through a magazine. Even in these circumstances she presented a formidable figure, a sturdy woman, outwardly in no way frail or vulnerable. At Emma's approach, she dropped the magazine to the floor and waited in silence, fixing her visitor with sharp if faded blue eyes.

Nervously Emma explained who she was.

'Your husband,' retorted Mrs Carter disagreeably, 'has been next to useless.'

'It's very difficult for him when there are no clues!' Emma defended Matt.

'Isn't his job to find clues? Or am I wrong about what a detective does?'

'Matt says I'm wrong,' Emma told her. 'You see I write detective stories and—'

She was interrupted. 'Who is that young man?' Mrs Carter pointed at Damian, doing his best to lurk inconspiciously in the background. 'You look rather young to be his mother.'

'I'm not his mother, I'm his aunt,' explained Emma. 'And his guardian in this country. His parents are overseas.'

Mrs Carter's unwelcoming manner relaxed at this information, as Emma had rather hoped it would. 'Nephew, eh? And you're

485

his guardian. My husband and I had the guardianship of his nephews and niece. I hope that young man doesn't turn against you the way mine have turned against me.'

'Em hasn't got any money,' said Damian tactlessly. 'I mean, I wouldn't, anyway.'

'Damian,' said Emma, 'I believe the hospital League of Friends run a cafeteria. Why don't you pop along and get yourself a drink?'

Damian retired with alacrity.

Mrs Carter had a sardonic smile on her face. 'Why did you bring him along? To impress me?'

'In a way, yes,' Emma admitted. 'Look, Mrs Carter, I believe you – about the accidents not being real accidents. What's more, without wanting to frighten you—'

'I don't frighten easily!' interrupted Mrs Carter. 'You are going to say that once I return home, I shall be in danger again. I have already thought of that for myself, thank you!'

'Tell me,' urged Emma. 'What do you remember about the accident which put you in here?'

'Precious little!' snorted Mrs Carter. 'I went into the kitchen, walked towards the sink and the next I knew, I was in here, in a bed, with the wretched Lucinda, Guy and Jeremy all hovering like vultures around me! I chased 'em out!'

'But more memory may return at any time, don't you see? So the attacker must be worried and he or she hasn't got much time now. I think, if anything is tried, it'll be as soon as you return home. So that's why I've thought of a plan to flush out whoever it is.' Emma sat back and waited, holding her breath.

'You say you write detective stories,' said Mrs Carter. 'Plans and plots are up your street, I imagine. Go on, then. Tell me.'

Emma tried to control a sigh of relief. She'd been afraid Mrs Carter wouldn't let her get this far. 'It's like this,' she began. 'Everyone knows you are to be discharged tomorrow, right?'

The other woman nodded, stony faced.

'So my idea is that instead of going home you go instead to a small hotel or bed and breakfast. I'll book you into one. We don't tell anyone, certainly not the Bryants. I'll go to your house. I believe there's a hill path down to the rear of the property which will take me in unseen. I've got a blue dress, just as you have. I'll wander round the house wearing it so that anyone looking through the window will see someone in blue. Of course, I won't get too close to the window. And I'll wait . . .'

Mrs Carter folded her hands in her lap and leaned back in her chair. 'Wouldn't all this be rather dangerous for you?'

'Ah,' Emma produced her trump card. 'But if you agree, and I set it up, Matt – my husband – will certainly come along and hide in the house, ready to leap out and protect me, you know.'

'But he knows nothing about this?' Mrs Carter sounded faintly amused.

'Er – no, not yet,' admitted Emma nervously. 'But if I tell him first, he'll do his best to stop me. So it's better I arrange it all first and, well, persuade him afterwards. He isn't going to like it very much!' she concluded honestly.

'So I imagine,' said Mrs Carter drily.

'*What?*' yelled Matt when Emma appeared in his office later and explained her brilliant idea. 'Have you taken leave of your senses?'

'No, and don't shout. Everyone will hear and it's got to be a secret. I'm sure you're cross—'

'You could say that!' interrupted her husband, breathing heavily. 'I'd prefer the word furious.'

'Furious, then. But if you'll just calm down, you'll see what a good plan it is.'

'It's barmy.'

'No, it is not!' Emma insisted. 'Mrs Carter has no memory of the attack—'

'If it was an attack! There's no sign it was.' Matt's voice was icy.

That, thought Emma, was rather worse than Matt shouting. She gathered up her courage.

'I believe it was and I also believe I can prove it to you and flush out who did it. Incidentally, I believe it was Lucinda.'

To Matt's query as to why, she explained as she had to Damian. 'Damian and I saw that girl on the dunes. I'm sure it was Lucinda. Mrs Carter could remember something at any moment. Lucinda must be panicking.'

'You didn't tell me,' said Matt angrily, 'that you saw anyone on the dunes that day.'

'It's not unusual. There are always people walking on the dunes. I didn't think much of it myself until later, after I'd heard Jeremy describe his sister's lifestyle. It just seemed to fit the girl I saw. Then I remembered you'd said Jeremy rang her on her mobile.'

Matt tapped his fingernails on his desk. 'If I take part in this,' he said, 'it's on the understanding that *you* don't. A policewoman can do it.'

'It's my idea!' argued Emma. 'Besides, just think. If you put a policewoman in there, it makes it official and then, if nothing happens, you'll look foolish. And Mrs Carter thinks it's going to be me. She doesn't mind me wandering round her house. She might not agree to a policewoman. You know how awkward she is.'

'We'll ask her,' said Matt.

To Matt's annoyance and Emma's satisfaction, Mrs Carter came down firmly on the side of Emma taking the role. Her reasoning was unfair but typical.

'A policewoman looks like a policewoman. Even glimpsed through a window. Let your wife do it. She's probably a better actress.'

'It's too dangerous,' said Matt obstinately.

'But you don't believe anything is going to happen,' pointed out his wife.

'I'm doubtful. But I don't rule it out. I'll take a policewoman along anyway for extra security. She can hide upstairs in the bedroom in case the attack comes at night. I'll hide downstairs and hope to nab any intruder before he or she gets upstairs.'

It was one thing to hatch the plan, another actually to put it into effect. Emma couldn't help but be nervous as she wandered round Mrs Carter's house in her blue dress on Saturday afternoon.

But nothing happened, other than Frances Owen knocked at the back door and, receiving no answer, slipped a note under it.

Understand you don't want visitors today. Will call tomorrow.

Emma watched her from an upstairs window, walking back to her own house. 'Whatever happens,' she prayed, 'don't let it be Polly we catch!'

489

The evening drew on and eventually Emma announced that she was going to bed.

'Only not properly. I'll just lie down fully dressed under the duvet.'

'I'll be in that big old wardrobe,' said Sergeant Brenda Mayhew, a tall athletic girl. 'If anyone gets in the bedroom, I'll be out in a flash.'

'I'll be downstairs in the hall cupboard,' added Matt. He heaved a sigh. 'I've an awful idea I'll never live this down!'

'Don't worry, sir,' consoled Sergeant Mayhew. 'I think it's a great idea – even if it doesn't work.'

Emma had never realised a night could drag on so. The illuminated digits on the bedside clock-radio changed at agonisingly long intervals, surely more than a second? Occasionally there was a clunk from the roomy Edwardian wardrobe where Brenda Mayhew huddled, Emma hoped not too uncomfortably. It was reassuring to know she was still awake. Emma wondered about Matt, downstairs in the hall cupboard with little more room than Brenda had in the wardrobe.

She must have dozed off. Emma opened her eyes suddenly. *Drat!* she thought. *I didn't mean to drop off like that.* She wondered if Brenda had also nodded off. She turned her head on the pillow. The clock read 3.45 a.m. Not much longer. It really looked as if nothing would happen. *Suppose it doesn't?* mused Emma. *I'll have to think up another plan. Matt won't go along with a second idea of mine, not if this one doesn't work out. He'll never forgive me for making him spend an entire night in a hall cupboard.*

As happens when one awakes in the middle of the night, Emma next began to fancy she needed to get up and go to the bathroom.

She told herself she didn't, but mind over matter didn't work. Cautiously, she swung her legs to the ground and padded to the wardrobe.

'Brenda?'

No reply. Brenda had dozed off too. Emma tapped on the door. There was a rustle within and it opened a crack.

'I'm going to the bathroom,' Emma whispered.

'Right . . .' came the faint reply.

Emma trotted down the dimly lit corridor to the bathroom. Ahead of her, moonlight beaming through a window at the far end sent a splash of white light onto the carpet by the bathroom door. But just before that, in the nook formed by an arch, there was a pool of inky blackness. Emma hesitated. Was it imagination or did she really hear breathing? Not her own, not Brenda in the wardrobe and certainly not Matt downstairs in the hall cupboard. She reached out a hand to the light switch she remembered was just about here. Before she could reach it, however, there was a movement and a figure leapt towards her.

Whoever it was cannoned into her with such force that Emma fell flat on her back with a tremendous thump! The other person had unbalanced, too, and collapsed on top of her. Whoever it was, was now struggling to get up. Emma reached up and grabbed. Her hand caught a hank of long hair. She hung on.

Her assailant let out a cry of pain and then a long hiss of annoyance. She grabbed Emma's wrist to force her to release the hair. As they tussled, feet pounded along the corridor from the direction of the bedroom. Another figure appeared, looming above them, and grabbed Emma's opponent, hauling her off Emma and upright. The mystery woman let out a yell.

'Let go!' shouted Brenda Mayhew.

Emma realised she was still hanging on to her assailant's hair. She released it, scrambled to her feet and switched on the light.

Before her, her arms held behind her back in Brenda Mayhew's firm grasp, was a panting, flushed, dishevelled but still beautiful blonde.

'So it is you!' cried Emma. 'I saw you on the dunes the day you fixed your aunt's accident! You attacked me thinking I was your aunt!'

'I didn't attack you!' snapped the blonde, shaking hair from her eyes. 'You were going to switch on the light. I'd already seen from your height and shape you weren't Myra. I realised it was a set-up. I pushed you out of the way so that I could get out of the house!'

As she spoke, Emma realised that she could still hear pounding. A tremendous racket was coming from downstairs.

Clipping handcuffs on the blonde, Brenda Mayhew gasped, 'That sounds like the inspector! He's in some sort of fix.'

'Matt!' cried Emma. She ran downstairs. The cupboard door in the hall shuddered from repeated blows and from behind came the clear sound of Matt expressing his frustration.

Emma stretched out her hand to the key in the outside of the lock and turned it. The door flew open and Matt shot out.

'What's going on?' he yelled.

'She locked you in,' said Emma.

'Who?' howled Matt.

'Lucinda Bryant. It's all right, Brenda's got her safe upstairs.'

Matt raced up the staircase, taking the treads two at a time. Emma followed close behind but he reached the landing first and when she got there she bumped into him.

'There!' Emma gasped, peering round him and pointing triumphantly at the blonde. 'I told you so. I told you it was Lucinda!'

Matt turned his head to give her an exasperated look. 'That's not Lucinda Bryant!'

'Then who is it?' asked Emma in bewilderment. She stared at the blonde who now had a sardonic smile on her face. 'Who are you?' Emma demanded.

'I'm Sonia Berg,' said the blonde.

There was a moment's silence, then Emma cried, 'You're Erwin Berg's daughter! Matt, Erwin Berg was Henry Carter's business partner! They quarrelled and—'

Sonia Berg interrupted. 'They didn't quarrel! Henry Carter cheated my father. That business was founded on my father's ideas. Henry waited until it was thriving and then he ousted my father!'

'I thought there was a court case and your father lost?' returned Emma.

'My father didn't get justice!' shouted Sonia. 'He returned home to Sweden a broken man. He set up several business but they all failed. My mother, a beautiful, fun-loving, fashionable woman was reduced to living in a tiny flat, deprived of foreign travel, theatre trips, all the things she loved. I watched her fade. Last year they both died within weeks of one another. They should have been living in a big house like this one, enjoying the money made from my father's ideas!'

'Hang on a moment,' Matt's reasonable voice broke in. 'Did you set up these accidents to Myra Carter?'

'Some of them,' Sonia said defiantly. 'But I didn't muddle the pills!' Sonia snorted. 'Myra did that herself. Look, I didn't want to kill her! I just wanted her to suspect the Bryants and cut them out of the will.'

'But cutting them out wouldn't put you in,' argued Emma.

'I didn't do it for myself,' Sonia stormed at her. 'I just wanted to get the money out of the hands of that wretched family! They're Henry Carter's relatives. I couldn't stop Henry, when he was alive, or Myra now enjoying the money, but at least I could try and keep it out of the hands of the rest of the family!'

Unexpectedly Sonia smiled. 'You needn't think this will ever come to court. The last thing Myra Carter wants is for me to tell the world my story! She'd just hate the publicity.'

'So, that's it then,' said Damian. 'What will happen now?'

Their stay in the cottage was over and Emma was driving them back to Wadebridge.

'To Sonia? I don't know,' she confessed. 'She's changed her tune and is denying she arranged any accidents.'

'But all three of you heard her say she did!' Damian protested.

'A confession on its own is no good these days. There's no other evidence connecting her apart from our sighting of her on the dunes, which in itself doesn't mean she was in the house. She can't deny she broke into the house Saturday night, of course, when Matt, Brenda and I were there and caught her. But she still denies she attacked me. She says she was just shoving me out of the way. The reason she was there at all, she now says, was that she meant to search the place to see if there were any papers there which might show, even at this late stage, that her father was unfairly treated. She wants, she says, to restore honour to his memory.'

'Even so, now she's been rumbled, she'll have to stay away,' observed Damian.

Emma nodded. 'In any case, Matt says Myra should be able to get an injunction forbidding Sonia from going anywhere near her. Sonia was right, by the way. Myra Carter isn't keen to see Sonia in a courtroom. Myra's a pretty tough woman and not afraid of much but she doesn't want a lot of questions asked about her late husband's business dealings! So Sonia was quite correct in claiming Myra would shun any publicity.

'Myra's playing all the episodes down now, saying that probably most of the accidents were just that, ordinary mishaps, nothing to do with Sonia at all. She's told Matt she's withdrawing her claim that someone has tried to harm her.'

'Crumbs,' said Damian. 'That's a turnaround!'

'Isn't it? Matt's really fed up after all the fuss she made. I gather the Assistant Chief Constable is pretty miffed as well. I think Myra just lost a bridge partner.'

'What about the Bryants?' asked Damian.

'According to Matt, Myra Carter is sorry she suspected them and she's going to help Guy with his business and find a way of helping the other two as well to make it up.'

'Not bad,' commented Damian.

'I admit, it does seem rather more than they deserve, but on the other hand, it seems clear that the late Henry Carter was very fond of those children and would probably have helped them had he still been alive.'

'Polly will be happy, anyway,' Damian said.

'Polly is delirious. All she ever wanted was for Jeremy Bryant to be declared innocent of any wrong-doing. She didn't give a hoot about the other two. She called me and if I'm interpreting our phone conversation right, then she and Jeremy are about to become engaged.'

'Guy Bryant won't like that,' said Damian.

'He probably doesn't care now Myra Carter's going to bail out his business.'

Emma turned into their home street. 'But I tell you what, Damian, if I were Polly I'd think twice before marrying into that family!'

They drew up before the house and as they climbed out of the car, they got a surprise. Matt, whom Emma had assumed would be at work, opened the front door and stood there, grinning at them.

'I didn't know you'd be here!' cried Emma.

'I couldn't miss your face when you saw the brand new bathroom,' he returned.

Emma ran upstairs and threw open the bathroom door. 'Oh, Matt! It's lovely! They've done a beautiful job!' She paused and added doubtfully, 'Isn't that a different window glass? The pattern's not the same.'

'Ah, well,' Matt mumbled. 'I couldn't get the same glass.'

'Matt!' She turned to him. 'Why did you need to replace the glass? You've got to tell me what happened! I know something did!'

'I didn't want to worry you,' he began. 'But when they came to remove that heavy old cast-iron bath, they decided they'd do too much damage to the hall walls getting it downstairs. The stairwell is very narrow. They couldn't imagine how the original plumbers got a bath that size up there! So they took a hammer to it, to break it up where it was and carry it out in bits. Only when they hit it, a piece flew off and went straight through the window. It was only single glazed, as you know.'

'Oh,' said Emma.

'And after it went through the window it landed on the roof of that prefabricated garage and went through that as well. So that had to be patched up.'

'I see,' said Emma.

'And, um, after it fell through the garage roof it landed on the top of my car and made a dent which had to be knocked out.' Matt reflected on the event. 'It was a bit like a meteorite whizzing in and demolishing all before it. Fortunately no living creature got in the way.'

Emma drew a deep breath. 'It's probably just as well I wasn't here. I understand why you didn't want to tell me. I would have been in a terrible tizz out there in the country. It was nice of you to spare my feelings and keep it from me. All's well that end's well.'

Matt looked his relief. He put his arm round her. 'Now I know why I love you, Mrs King. Welcome home!'

Rhubarb Pie

Mother was a wonderful cook. She was a gardener, too, with a true green thumb. She grew all our fruit and vegetables in the long narrow garden behind the cottage. She could grow almost anything, but most of all, I remember the rhubarb and how fascinated I always was by its rose-pink sticks and large green leaves which acted as umbrellas or parasols, depending on the weather. I can smell and taste in memory Mother's rhubarb pies, tarts, puddings, mousses, jams . . . You name it: Mother made it. She was a tiny woman but full of energy. She never walked anywhere, but scurried along like a terrier on the scent, eager to be at the next task. Or so it seemed to me then. As you get older, you get wiser, and see things you didn't when you were a kid. Or maybe you just see them differently.

As for my father, he was quite different. He was a brooding presence in our household, a lanky man with a face like a week of wet Sundays and a surly way with him at the best of times. He'd always had a name for being a bit difficult, but as time went by, he got worse. He fell out with everyone: neighbours, work-mates, shopkeepers. He fell out of one job after another, and eventually out of work altogether, because no one could or would work with him. He said there was a conspiracy against him in the village. It was then he rented the lonely cottage about a mile from everyone else and Mother started her garden.

There was little money coming in. You didn't get much government help then. It was work or starve, and as Father didn't work, we might well have gone very hungry but for Mother. Eventually she dug up every square inch of land around the cottage to squeeze in another row of beans or potatoes, or a gooseberry or blackcurrant bush. She did sometimes say she wished she could spare the ground for a few flowers, but they were a luxury and we didn't have luxuries. Economy was our watchword.

No freezers in those days. She made jams and chutneys, pickled onions and beetroot. The green beans were sliced and packed in jars of salt. The salt came in blocks which had to be crushed with a rolling pin. That was my job. She kept chickens too, so we had fresh eggs and when a hen got past laying, it went in the pot and that was a real feast.

From spring till the year's end, Mother was up at first light and out in her garden. I'd wake in my little room up under the thatch, with the sun poking its fingers through the dormer windows, and hear the sound of Mother's hoe scratching at the weeds. She also earned extra money cleaning in the bigger houses around. After breakfast – having already done an hour's work in the garden – she'd get on her old bike and pedal off to polish folks' floors and windows. Then she'd pedal back home to polish her own. Even as a nipper I realised she didn't mind working for others, because it gave her a chance to get out of the cottage and meet and talk with other people. We didn't have friends. Father wouldn't have allowed any visitors.

He spent his days tinkering with anything in need of repair or listening to the radio. He'd done odd jobs for other people at first to earn a bit of money, but his bad temper soon meant that offers of those dried up. At first when we moved there, he'd walk into the village on fine days and read newspapers and periodicals in the little library, presided over by Miss Nibbs, the librarian. She was a kindly woman, short sighted with a pince-nez, and played the harmonium of a Sunday at the Wesleyan chapel.

Needless to say, Father soon fell out with Miss Nibbs. She admitted that from the start he'd made her nervous, sitting there all day. But the final break came because he took to striking out, with a stub of red pencil, anything in the papers he didn't agree with. Miss Nibbs said she appreciated he had strong views. She held quite strong views herself. But one of her views happened to be that people shouldn't write on the papers and books in her library. So he was barred.

After that Father sat at home, remembering every quarrel and disagreement he'd ever had with anyone, polishing his hatred as Mother polished windows.

One day when I was about eleven, I came back from school and walked into our kitchen to find Mother standing before her store cupboard, studying the jars and bottles. As I came up, she said, not looking at me, 'It can't go on. Something's got to be done.'

I asked her, 'What can't?' But she didn't answer and I think she spoke more to herself than to me.

The next day, amongst all the pans bubbling on the kitchen range, was one containing stewed greens. They smelled bitter so I wasn't sorry when Mother said, 'There's not much of that, Stevie, so we'll let Dad have it.'

I accepted the reasoning because when food was in short supply, Dad's plate was still kept filled. Mine was pretty well filled. Mother didn't eat much.

However, perhaps she thought I might be disappointed, because she went on, 'But there's stewed rhubarb for pudding. You like that, don't you, Stevie?'

I'd already seen the pink and green rhubarb stalks, lying on the kitchen table.

Mother kept a compost pit going at the bottom of the garden and all peel and waste went in it. That evening, I took the waste down to the compost pit, and as I tossed it in, it crossed my mind the rhubarb leaves weren't amongst it. But I didn't think anything of it.

The fact was I was in love at the time with a girl called Winifred Pearce. She had the longest plaits of any girl in the class. She could sit on them. She was bright, too, always top of the form and could spell any word. She let me sharpen pencils for her.

Lots of times after that I saw the little pot of dark green leaves boiling on the stove and the contents would appear in a glistening heap on Dad's plate, along with the spuds and carrots. Once or twice he muttered, 'I don't think much of this spinach, Jeanie!'

Then Mother would say, 'It contains iron, does spinach. Of course, if you don't fancy it, I could send Stevie to the village to buy a tin of peas . . .'

At that Dad would snap, 'You'll do no such thing! Waste not, want not!' And he'd gobble up the greens determinedly.

I noticed that, in the store cupboard, a new row of jars of crushed salt appeared. They contained not cut green beans, but dark shreds of leaves. She was preserving the new kind of spinach against the winter.

Late in the summer I was sitting with Winifred on the bank at the back of the school field. She was making a daisy chain and I was picking the daisies for her, as fast as I could find them. Suddenly she said, 'Your mother told my mother that your father is going up north to look for a job, next spring, perhaps.'

I was flabbergasted. To begin with, we never discussed family business with anyone and that Mother could have casually mentioned such a thing to anyone was quite shocking. But not as shocking as the idea that my father meant to stir himself and look for work again, and as for travelling . . .

However, I didn't want to look a fool in front of Winifred, so I said airily, 'That's right!'

So it got round the village and a couple of people said to me, 'I hear your dad is thinking of going up north come springtime, Stevie.'

I asked Mother about it and she said, yes, but not to say anything to Dad because he'd hate it if he thought we'd gossiped. So I said nothing to him and, needless to say, he said nothing to me. He wasn't one for conversation.

Father wasn't a healthy-looking fellow at the best of times, but by the end of that summer he was looking worse. He complained of stomach aches, headaches, dizziness and nausea. His complexion had got a yellowish tinge to it. Mother mixed him up bicarbonate of soda.

He got worse over the winter and by spring, he was sleeping downstairs to be near the bathroom. Our cottage being old, the bathroom and toilet were late additions, tacked onto the side as an extension. Father had to get up in the night regularly now and so he had to be near the facilities.

Our doctor was Dr Briggs, but Father had fallen out with him long ago and called him a quack. Dr Briggs knew it and so wasn't keen on Father, either. Eventually, when the pains in his stomach got really bad, Father had to go and consult the doctor. He got short shrift. Dr Briggs pointed out it couldn't be his appendix because Father had had his appendix out as a boy. Dr Briggs's opinion was that Father was a malingerer. The doctor said that if he (Father) thought that he (Dr Briggs) was going to write any letters to the authorities, certifying Father was unfit for steady work, then he was mistaken, especially if Father was trying to get out of going up north.

Father came home saying Dr Briggs was a charlatan, and barmy besides, talking about going up north or something. Father couldn't make head or tail of it but one thing he did know, he wasn't going back there again.

So Mother went down to the library and Miss Nibbs found her the medical handbook. Mother read it up and came home and told Father that symptoms like his could be caused by stress and depression. Father said anyone would be depressed and stressed with gut ache like he'd got and no help on hand but a barmy doctor wittering about going north.

Mother said he'd feel better in the spring. But by spring he was worse again. He'd become lethargic, his ankles and hands swollen and puffy, the stomach aches permanent.

I woke early one morning, just before it got light, and heard him stumbling about downstairs; he was groaning, swearing and retching by turns. Then he gave a sharp cry and shouted out, 'Jeanie!' in a terrible voice.

I scrambled out of bed, but as I put my head through the door, Mother came running along the passage. She pushed me back in the room, saying, 'You go back to bed, Stevie. It's only Dad having one of his turns!'

I lay there, listening to them moving about downstairs. I thought I heard Father mumbling as if he was delirious but then he went quiet. There was still a lot of moving about, though.

I got up and got dressed and was wondering what I should do, afraid to go downstairs, when Mother came back. She was still in her nightclothes, nightdress and worn old dressing gown, and her hair was braided into a single long plait hanging over her shoulder. She seemed very calm. She sat on the edge of the bed, took my hand and said, 'Stevie, your dad has passed away. I've laid him out properly. Do you want to come and see him?'

So I went downstairs and there he was, laid out in his bed. She'd washed him and shaved him, too, and changed his sheets for nice clean ones. He looked peaceful and, to tell the truth, happier than he'd done when he was alive.

Then Mother said, 'Now, Stevie, you remember how Dad told us how important it is to mind economy in all things. Funerals are a very expensive business and he'd hate to think we'd spent a lot of money on one. So how about we bury Dad in the garden? Down where the compost pit is? I was going to start a new rhubarb bed there anyway. Only you'll have to give me a hand and not tell anyone. The vicar might grumble, feeling he'd been cheated out of his fee and there's the undertaker who won't like us not buying one of his coffins.'

So that's what we did. We made a good and decent job of it. Dad was wrapped in a blue counterpane and we put him in the grave we'd dug out, nice and straight. Then we covered him over with earth very tidily, Mother taking as much care to get it all looking nice when it was finished, just as she did when she put the pastry over one of her pies. Then we held hands and said a prayer. I don't think the vicar could have done it better.

'When the earth's settled a bit, I'll plant something here,' she said to me. 'To make it look nice.'

Mother went into the village and dropped the word that Dad had gone up north, as he'd said he would, to look for a job. A couple of people told me they hoped my father had luck.

The untruth made me feel awkward now with Winifred. I began to avoid her and she was offended. When she needed her pencils sharpened, she took them to a big ginger-haired lout whose father kept pigs.

After a few weeks, Mother went down to the village and shed a few tears in the shop. When she'd got a concerned little crowd round her she sniffled out just a hint . . . but it was enough.

Next time I heard people talking about my father it was in whispers. They were telling one another that Norman Yarrow had found another woman up north and wouldn't be coming back to his wife and son. They said, 'If you ask me, Jeanie and the boy are better off without him. He was always a miserable cuss and work-shy. His fancy woman is welcome to him!'

No one mentioned Father again. About a year after that, turning the pages of Mother's *Gardener's Book of Knowledge* one rainy afternoon, I came across a paragraph on rhubarb. It told me rhubarb stalks are safe to eat but not the leaves which are poisonous and 'on no account to be ingested'. I closed up the book and put it back on the shelf and said nothing to Mother.

When I got old enough to leave school I got a job and with money coming in there was no need for Mother to go cleaning any more, and she could spare space for flowers in her garden. Winifred went to the high school in town and became a librarian. I told you she was bright. She took over from Miss Nibbs at our library, until it was closed down. Then she went away to work somewhere and I heard she married a teacher.

All that happened over forty years ago. Mother died fifteen years ago come Christmas. I still live in the cottage. It's not lonely now because they built houses all round it. The fellow next door is a friendly sort. He leans over the fence when I'm out in the garden and chats, admiring my fruit and veg.

'My, you've got some champion rhubarb there, Mr Yarrow! You'd win a prize with that in any show. I've never seen rhubarb like yours!' he says, pointing at the bed at the end of the garden.

I don't suppose he has. The stalks are three foot long, thick as my wrist, and the leaves as big as palms.

Only I never pull it to eat. I don't seem to fancy it.

Time Tracks

I ought to begin this letter 'To whom it may concern', but that sounds formal and I'm not a formal sort of person. I suppose, if I were, I wouldn't have let myself get caught up in this at all. I'm not even sure who will read it, perhaps only Felix, but I want everyone to know just how it all came about. I want it to be my story, my version of events, and not what anyone else thinks I did or saw or heard.

I knew, when I set eyes on the house, it was what Felix and I had been seeking for months. We'd begun to get discouraged. It wasn't that we couldn't *find* what we wanted. It was that we could never afford what we liked, and what we could afford, we didn't want.

Our flat in London was cramped and noisy. It wasn't in a good area or even one becoming gentrified, but sat above run-down shops and a litter-strewn pavement on a busy street. We'd bought it because it had been cheap and we'd been broke. Felix had then been earning a pittance from his writing. My job as a legal secretary at Partington's kept us.

That was five years ago. Then things got better. Felix's novels started to 'take off'. Hollywood was showing interest at the time. We'd make quite a bit of money if everything worked out. I was

507

keen to leave my job. Nice old Mr Partington had retired and I was working for Andy Wilkes, who was bright but irritating.

We decided to sell up and move to the country. Felix could write undisturbed and I might even concentrate on my painting.

Don't get the wrong idea. I'm no Renoir. But I'd managed to sell a few illustrations for children's books. I thought I might make a go of it. At least, I could try. We began to look for a property.

Felix was too busy to go house-hunting. He had a deadline to meet. The Hollywood offer was frustratingly on hold. The traffic outside was worse. All in all, it left him tetchy. He's best left on his own when things get to this pitch and come to that, so am I. I told Andy I was going to take the Friday off. He didn't like this much but I'd put in a lot of unpaid overtime lately and he couldn't refuse.

Felix mumbled, 'Fine, Jess, a weekend in the country will do you good. I'll be all right. Is there anything to eat in the freezer?' All of this without taking his eyes off the screen.

I left him tapping away and drove off early Friday morning, down to Sussex. I chose Sussex because I'd holidayed there as a child. I found a reasonably priced hotel in Chichester as my base and started house-hunting straight away.

It was midsummer, and on a warm, golden evening I made my way inland, following impulse. It led me to a village I'd never visited before. It had a meandering main street with a post office/general store, three pubs, a garage and an antiques shop. I wasn't surprised to see the antiques shop since tourism is always catered for. I was more surprised to see a general store. I parked the car and wandered about until, down a side street, I spotted a 'For Sale' notice.

After months of searching I was conditioned like one of Pavlov's dogs. I trotted towards it, mouth watering in anticipation.

I admit, when I got there, my hopes took a knock. The house was red brick with steep gables and pointed windows in Gothic style, probably mid-Victorian. It stood alone, odd man out in a row of elderly bungalows. The sale notice had clearly been there for ages and tilted sadly. Nettles grew round its base. But the front garden was a riot of colour with mauve, pink and white cosmos plants which had seeded themselves everywhere. They reached out over the path and I had to push them aside to reach the front door.

I peered through cobwebby panes. The rooms were a desolate sight, with peeling wallpaper, blotched flaking plaster, rotten skirting boards. No one could have done anything to the place for years. Yet it felt absolutely right, as if it had been waiting here for me and I had come at last.

The back garden was as overgrown as the front but less pictur-esque, just weeds. Starlings were settling to roost in a tree, quarrelling amongst themselves. Using a stick, I hacked my way to the far end where, almost buried in long grass, I found a seat of wooden slats on an iron frame with a rust-pitted inscription. I could make out one word: *Railway.* I supposed someone had bought it at a sale.

Then, all at once, I had the oddest sensation. My surroundings receded, leaving me encapsulated in a sort of bubble. The mild evening sun had become the bright light of midday. The noisy birds were silenced and replaced by a patter of footsteps and confused babble of voices as if I were surrounded by people, yet I could see no one. Above it all was a grinding as if some huge piece of machinery were cranking itself into life.

Just as suddenly, the moment was gone. I was back in the garden, with the old house and the screeching starlings, just as before. No voices, no groan of metal joints. I put the experience down to one of those mental blips which happen when you're tired or hungry, made worse by excitement. I was all of those things.

I noted the estate agents' details and returned to the high street where I ordered a meal in one of the pubs. It was far from busy, and the woman who brought my chicken and chips seemed inclined to linger, so I asked if she knew the empty house.

'Oh, that's Railway Cottage!' she said. 'Proper eyesore. There used to be a branch line here years ago, and that was the station master's cottage. They tore the line up in the fifties and built those bungalows. An old woman lived there, never did anything to the place . . . No one's daft enough to buy it.' She eyed me. 'You're not interested, are you?'

'I might be,' I said cautiously. 'We've been looking for a place to renovate.'

'Renovate?' She laughed. 'You'd need to pull the whole thing down and rebuild it!'

Halfway through my meal, I happened to look up and saw the woman whispering to the landlord and nodding towards me. He looked concerned.

He must have kept an eye on me after that because as soon as I'd finished, he came over. He picked up my plate and hovered, a lanky man with limp hair and fish-grey eyes.

'Need anything else?'

'No, thanks,' I said. 'I've got to get back to Chichester.'

'You live there?' he asked in a prying way I didn't like.

I told him, no, I lived in London, but knew Sussex well from my childhood.

'Brenda says,' he glanced at the woman behind the bar, 'you're interested in Railway Cottage. That right?'

I felt annoyed with Brenda, but it was my own fault for asking her. I assured him it was only passing curiosity.

'Real old dump,' he said. 'Wouldn't suit you.'

That did it. Now I was determined Felix and I would buy Railway Cottage and make something of it, if only to show Brenda and this man that we could. I thanked him for the meal, got up and left.

I rang Felix from the hotel, told him about the cottage and urged him, despite his protests, to leave everything and come down.

Saturday morning I went to the estate agents. The woman there also appeared surprised at my interest. She seemed nervous as she handed me the prospectus, as if not sure what to do about me. We could just make the asking price if we found a buyer for the flat. My heart rose and I asked if I could have the keys to look over the property.

'Now?' she asked. 'I'll have to ask the manager.'

'Well, is he here?' I asked impatiently.

She trailed into some inner sanctum and after much furtive whispering, reminding me of the previous evening in the pub, she came back accompanied by a cadaverous man who really did remind me of the landlord, he was so gloomy. I wondered if they represented some local physiognomy, hitherto unnoticed by me. He handed over the keys reluctantly.

'I should tell you the property is in very bad shape,' he bleated.

I received this with a bright smile, just to annoy him.

I met Felix off the midday train and we drove straight to

Railway Cottage. It looked even more delapidated today. I wondered if I'd been wrong to assume Felix would love the place as I already did.

But I wasn't wrong. He fell for its decrepit charms just as I'd done. We prowled around inside and out. It really was a mess, but there was nothing that couldn't be fixed. It would take money and time and we had more of the latter than the former, but we'd do it.

It was as we were preparing to leave, Felix already in the car, that I heard an odd sound originating, it seemed to me, at the rear of the property.

I stooped by the open car window and asked, 'Did you hear that?'

'Hear what?' asked Felix, fiddling with the ignition key.

'I don't know,' I said doubtfully. 'It was like a loud sigh or steam coming out of a pressure cooker. It reminded me of something.'

But Felix was anxious to get back to London and said he hadn't heard a thing.

We drove home and, dog tired, turned in early. But you know how it is when an unsolved riddle nags at your subconscious. You wake in the middle of the night and the answer leaps out at you. This is what happened to me.

'Felix?' I whispered. 'That sound I heard just before we left Railway Cottage. It sounded like an old steam engine standing in a station.'

But Felix was asleep.

We bought Railway Cottage, despite an attempt by the estate agent to hike the price. He said the executors of the old woman's estate wanted more, but I had the feeling he was just trying to put us off. Andy Wilkes, who'd agreed to handle the legal side for us, unexpectedly turned up trumps. Faced with stiff letters from him, the estate agent and the unknown executors surrendered. We got Railway Cottage at the first price. The sale of the London flat went through without a hitch. We spent every free moment down in Sussex, trying to make the cottage habitable.

As moving day neared, we decided to take quilts and sleep there over the weekend, so we could finish decorating before the furniture arrived.

We worked hard all Saturday and turned in on the bedroom floor. Felix can sleep anywhere and went out like a light. I found the floor too hard, dozed fitfully and woke up in the early hours. As I lay awake, I heard, quite distinctly, the distant whistle of a steam train.

I scrambled out of my quilt and ran to the window.

It was full moon and the back garden was bathed in silver light. It was as weed infested as ever, but I could see right down to the far end, and the old slatted seat.

There was someone sitting on it. My first thought was, 'Blooming cheek! Some kids are fooling about in our garden!' I would have thrown open the window but the sash frame was stuck.

As I stood there undecided whether to wake Felix or just take the torch and tackle the trespassers myself, I realised there was only one intruder.

The woman sat all alone, very still, on the seat. She was very formally dressed, as I could see well in the silvery light. She wore a frock or suit with square shoulders. Tilted over her forehead was a hat with a crown like an upturned flowerpot and wide brim. I got the impression of a net veil. My grandmother was married in a similar outfit in 1944. Beside the woman on the seat was a large bag or suitcase.

I knew then with absolute certainty that she wasn't an intruder. Felix and I were the intruders. The woman had every right to be down there on the railway bench. She was waiting for her train and, as I stood there, I heard its distant whistle again and the clackety-clack of its wheels coming ever closer.

I ran back into the bedroom and shook Felix awake. He started up, mumbling, 'Whazzat?' as I began to tug him towards the door and explain to him at the same time. He stumbled after me, protesting until we got to the window.

'There!' I said excitedly.

He peered out. 'There what?' he asked disagreeably.

There was nothing. I stared disbelievingly out at the garden. I could see right down to the far end and the old seat, but no one sat on it and there was no sound on the night air.

'Imagination,' said Felix, stomping back to his sleeping bag. 'Moving to Sussex has set you remembering your grandparents and old family snapshots. They took on life in your dreams.'

I would have argued but I was hardly in a position to do that with no evidence, so I had to give way, privately telling myself that I hadn't been dreaming and I knew what I'd seen.

We spent the next couple of months working non-stop on the house, trying to do all the major jobs before winter set in. It gave us little time for a social life, but even so, it was obvious to me that there wasn't much going on in that line in the village. The inhabitants seemed intent on keeping themselves to themselves, although the woman at the shop was friendly, happy to have a new customer, I suppose. Nor did we have good neighbours. On one side the property was boarded up and seemed to be used as a storage facility, no one there at all. On the other side was a bungalow lived in by an elderly man who seldom appeared and when he did, didn't respond to my overtures of friendship. I decided he was deaf. At the time, we were too busy for this to matter much.

Then Felix had to go away for three or four days and, for the first time, I found myself alone in Railway Cottage. The nights were starting to get cooler. I lit a fire in the hearth and settled down in front of it that evening, feeling cosy and relaxed. I started to read but all the physical hard work recently was taking its toll and I dozed off.

I woke up just after eleven. The fire had burned down to a few glowing remnants of logs which rustled as the ash settled. I was stiff from the awkward position I'd slept in and made my way into the kitchen to make a cup of tea. As I went to the tap, I heard it again . . . that low, gusting sigh of a steam engine.

I relinquished the kettle and dashed to the window. The night was not so clear as on the previous occasion and I couldn't see so well. But as I strained my eyes into the darkness, my ears caught the slow powerful sound of great wheels beginning to turn as a steam train pulled out of a station.

I couldn't leave it at that, I had to know. I wrenched at the back door and ran out into the garden. I was halfway towards the garden seat before I stopped and asked myself if I was being quite wise. I hadn't even brought a torch. The train sound had faded away and the night air touched my face and legs with chill fingers. I shivered. Then the moon came out from behind clouds and in the interlude of pale light, he appeared. A man in the uniform of an old-style railway porter. He walked right in front of me, from left to right, and disappeared into the hedge between us and the old man whom I thought deaf.

For a moment I was frozen to the spot. Then, heart pounding, I ventured forward a little and peered about me. Nothing. Only the old railway seat and a pile of rubbish we'd created in clearing out the house. There was nothing to suggest how I might have imagined it. And I had, surely, imagined it?

I hurried back to the cottage, glad of its warm welcome, slept badly and was awake with the birds. I lost no time going to investigate again, this time by daylight, but it left me no wiser. The hedge at the point where the 'porter' had disappeared was thin. I peered through but there was just a neglected jungle on the other side and a collapsing wooden shed. My elderly neighbour was no gardener.

I went back indoors and wondered what, if anything, I should tell Felix. At first I decided I wouldn't tell him, but in the end, I couldn't keep it to myself and when he returned, I blurted it all out.

His reaction was predictable. 'Look, Jess, you admit you'd dozed off in front of the fire. You were dreaming again. You're letting the history of this place get to you.'

'I wasn't,' I said stubbornly. 'I admit I woke up and heard the train, but when I saw the porter, I was in the garden, wide awake. He passed only feet away from me. I saw him, Felix!'

Felix stood in front of me, frowning, seeking a flaw in my argument. 'What were you reading before you dozed off on the sofa?'

I said, as far as I could remember, it had been an Agatha Christie.

'There you are!' he said triumphantly. 'I bet there was someone travelling on a train in it. It's all of a period. You've got the forties on the brain. Moonlight plays tricks. It was a moving shadow.'

He sounded so sure I began to think he must be right. I can't say I'd ever believed or disbelieved in ghosts before that. I'd never thought much about it.

'You've been overdoing it,' said Felix kindly.

And perhaps he was right, at that.

But the next time I saw the porter, it was broad daylight. Needless to say, Felix was away again. He'd driven into Chichester for something and I had decided to tackle the back garden. It was a nice afternoon, cool but sunny. I worked away happily for a while before straightening my aching back and thinking I'd done enough for one day. I gathered up a heap of weeds and set off towards our rubbish heap – and there he was. The porter appeared as he'd done before. He took not the slightest notice of me, just walked in front of me from one side of the garden to the other, and vanished into the hedge.

I let out a yell, dropped my bundle of weeds, and ran towards the spot. This time I pushed right through the hedge into my neighbour's garden and looked eagerly around. There was no railway porter, but my elderly neighbour was there, poking about in the overgrown tangle with a stick. He wore baggy corduroys and an ancient tweed jacket over a knitted pullover and he glared at me, as well he might. I was trespassing and had probably given him a fright.

'Excuse me—' I began.

'What?' He cupped his hand to his ear. 'What are you doing there? You come through my hedge?' He raised the stick to point it threateningly at me.

'I'm sorry!' I yelled. 'I thought I saw—' I hesitated. 'I thought I saw someone in my garden. He went through the hedge here.'

'No one never come through here,' said the old man. 'Or I'd have seen him, wouldn't I? You've got no business in my garden, you haven't.'

So much for that. I could only bawl more apologies and retreat. But now I was angry because I might have been dreaming once, or even twice, but not three times.

When Felix came back I was ready for him. I wouldn't take any refusals. I knew I'd seen something. Oddly enough, Felix didn't dismiss it as before.

He put his hands on my shoulders. 'Calm down, Jess. I agree with you. You saw – heard – something. But I don't believe in ghosts and I'm going to phone Andy about it.'

'Andy Wilkes?' I gaped at him. 'What's Andy going to do? He's in London.'

'Andy knows a private detective. Someone is giving us the runaround, Jess, and I don't like it any better than you do.'

Funnily enough, once Felix believed me, and once I knew someone was investigating it all, I also started to think it must be some kind of hoax. I didn't know why, but the more I thought it over, the more I decided that we – or rather I – was the victim of an unpleasant practical joker. But who and why?

As if to confirm my new belief, there were no more sounds of steam engines nor sightings of the phantom porter nor of the woman on the bench.

'Whoever the blighter is,' said Felix, 'he knows Andy's man is asking questions, and he's lying low. With luck, we've frightened him off for good. But I'd still like to know who it was.'

Andy appeared a week later, roaring through the village in his red Porsche and sweeping to a halt before Railway Cottage.

'Hullo, country-lovers!' he greeted us. 'I've come to see this ideal home of yours.' He raised a bottle of wine in salute. 'House-warming gift.'

We showed him around with some pride, pointing out all the work we'd done.

'Well,' said Andy a little later, lounging on our sofa. 'It's all very nice, though it wouldn't suit me. You're going to get it looking great. So I suppose,' he added, 'you'd like to know who's been frightening Jess here out of those clumping great boots she's taken to wearing?'

'You know?' Felix and I exclaimed together.

He tapped the side of his nose. 'Leave it to your uncle Andy. The trouble with you two, you've got too much imagination. Me, I'm a practical guy. As soon as Felix told me that the property on one side of you was boarded up and the other side belonged to a very elderly gent, I smelled developers.'

We gazed at him in silence.

Our awestruck response was just what he'd wanted and he

smiled smugly. 'I checked out who owns the properties to either side, and surprise! They both belong to the same person.'

'The old man next door!' I cried.

'No, he's a tenant and he's going to be moving out shortly. Going to live with his daughter in Bournemouth. The chap who owns both properties is the same one who owns the local pub here. He was hoping to get this property too, cheap, until you came along. Once he'd got all three, he'd apply for planning permission. These old places all have huge gardens, there's a lot of land here. Get a nice little estate on it. So he, with the help of the barmaid, tape-recordings of steam engines and an old porter's uniform, set up the whole thing. He targeted Jess, because if you'd both seen or heard these things, you'd have been suspicious. As it was, when Felix didn't see or hear anything, Jess, it encouraged you to think you'd seen something supernatural.'

'Well, I'm blowed,' said Felix. 'Sorry, Jess, I didn't believe you the first time.'

I was thinking it over. 'The first time I heard the engine,' I said, 'was when I brought Felix to see the house. The landlord wouldn't have had time to set it up.'

Andy shrugged. 'That probably was a mistake on your part, Jess.'

'What about the old man next door?' I persisted. 'When I followed the porter through the hedge, the old man said he'd seen no one.'

'The old boy is the landlord's uncle. Your "porter" was hiding in that rickety shed and the old chap was ready and waiting to tell you he'd seen nothing. It was all set up, Jess. Incidentally, the estate agent is another relative.'

'They made a fool of me!' I said furiously.

'Well, you won't have any more trouble,' Andy assured us.

I should have been happy. I should have left it at that. But perhaps I'm a romantic or I long for adventure. Somehow when Andy had left, I felt profoundly disappointed. I wanted to believe that I'd been offered a glimpse down a tunnel in time. I resented the whole thing being taken away from me and a prosaic explanation being offered.

'You're never satisfied,' said Felix only yesterday. 'First you wanted to believe it was ghosts. Then you were happy to think it might be a hoax. Now you've found it was a hoax, you want it to be ghosts again.'

I didn't say anything but I've made my plans. It's full moon again tonight, just as it was the night I saw the woman sitting on the old railway seat, waiting for her train. There's only one way I can settle this. Tonight, when Felix is asleep, I'm going to creep out, go down the garden and wait on that seat myself. If I don't see anything, I'll be satisfied at last. If I do, it'll be my secret. I won't tell Felix. But on the other hand, I will leave this letter. I don't believe anything will harm me. I'll come back in the early morning, retrieve this letter and destroy it. Felix will never know. It's just a precaution.

'No news?' Andy Wilkes stood by his red Porsche, staring anxiously towards the cottage door. 'I came as soon as I got your message.'

Felix came slowly to meet him. 'None. The police are working on the theory she's had some sort of breakdown. She's been under a lot of stress. All that business of the train she heard and the things she saw – they say she's probably wandering around somewhere suffering from amnesia. I gave them that letter she left and they reckon she got obsessed by the history of the cottage and she's . . . just lost touch with reality. But it's been over a week and someone should have seen some sign of her. Where's she sleeping? What's she doing for food, for money?' His voice rose desperately.

'Look, old chap,' Andy said awkwardly. 'They'll find her.'

Felix interrupted him sharply. 'Not if it wasn't all a hoax!'

Andy blinked. 'What do you mean?'

The other man hesitated. 'There's something you ought to know. Something I haven't told, haven't shown, anyone.' He led Andy into the cottage and went to a drawer. 'I didn't ask you down here just for your sympathy. I want your advice. Tell me what to do about this.'

He put a small oblong card down on the kitchen table.

Andy picked it up. 'It's an old rail ticket,' he said in surprise. 'A local branch line ticket into Chichester. Where did you get this?'

'I found it on the garden seat on the morning— the morning I woke up and found Jess gone. Look at the date on it, Andy.'

The solicitor peered at the card. 'It's the date she disappeared – only, good Lord, the year is 1943!' He looked up, bewildered. 'What does it mean?'

'It means,' Felix said softly, 'Jess went down her tunnel in time. She waited for the train that night and it came. She stepped aboard. And now, there's no tunnel back.'

Auntie, Are You There?

Lorna stood on the doorstep and fiddled nervously with the button of her plush-trimmed coat. She twisted her head to see if the seams were straight in her brand new taupe lisle stockings and noticed with dismay that the Louis heels of her button-over shoes were muddy – she must have stepped in a puddle but couldn't remember doing so. Lorna sighed and pressed the bell push.

The door was opened by a parlourmaid in an over-large apron and cap who asked, 'Yus?'

At least, Lorna guessed that was what she said. Being slightly deaf was becoming more and more of a handicap. It had never seemed so serious when living in Torquay all those years with Auntie, because Auntie had shouted all the time. In Lorna's head the dreaded voice was still quite audible.

'Lorna! Buck up and go down to the circulating library! I want new books – it's not raining much. Put on your galoshes and don't be such a weakling!'

Auntie had never known of Lorna's hearing problem because Lorna had carefully concealed it from her, knowing that it would only feed the scorn in which the old lady held her niece. But since moving to London the deafness became ever more troublesome. Lorna had even considered buying an advertised deaf aid. But they were so cumbersome and obvious. Two long wires dangling from one's ears attached to the large square control box with its buttons and dials. No, not yet, anyway.

'I have an appointment with Madame Eva,' said Lorna with as much aplomb as she could muster. 'My name is Miss Harris.'

The girl, plainly bored, led Lorna through a cramped ill-lit hall which smelled of lavender polish and abandoned her in a front parlour, rather a modest one, furnished with well-polished but old furniture and Benares brass. In the window stood a small table covered with an oriental shawl, chairs either side of it inviting confidences. Lorna's heart sank.

It was Jane's idea that she should come. 'You must see a medium, Lorna dear. Lots of my friends have consulted Madame Eva. She explains everything so well and her ability to get in touch with the Other Side is wonderful!'

Lorna and Jane had been at school together years ago before the Great War. Neither had married, Lorna because there had been Auntie to care for and Jane because she was a believer in Free Love. Not, as Lorna understood it, that very much in the way of Free Love had come Jane's way. But it was the principle of the thing. Jane believed in it. She also believed in Madame Eva.

'I have attended a seance conducted by her,' Jane confided, georgette draperies a-quiver, her bundle of grey-streaked hair escaping from a crocheted silk snood in fluttering tendrils. 'She called up several spirits. One felt their presence most distinctly although only Madame Eva could see them, you understand.'

But Lorna was beginning to think the whole thing a mistake. This house, the parlourmaid, the net curtains, the Benares brass and ageing furniture: it was just like being back in Torquay. Surely the spirit world did not regularly commune with someone who lived in such an ordinary way?

Yet Lorna herself was ordinary and incredible things had been happening to her. This morning as she waited at the tube station, she had rehearsed her account of her experience calmly and logically. Now she couldn't remember a word she had meant to say. The station was near the flat, one of the amenities which had attracted Lorna to the area in the first place. It was a brand new station, above ground, which was so much nicer, on a brand new extension to the line which dived underground into a dark tunnel after a few hundred yards and brought Lorna into the bustle of central London in an incredibly short time.

The flat itself was part of the new suburbia, only three years old and so reasonable in price. The first time Lorna had put her own key in her own front door she had felt reborn. And now? Every hope had been dashed. She felt numb, unable to comprehend why she should have been singled out by fate to suffer such cruel disappointment.

She did not hear the door click behind her. Without warning, a small dark woman appeared, attended by a bright-eyed white poodle which jumped up at Lorna, endangering the new lisle stockings.

'M-madame Eva?' Lorna asked with a gulp, fending off the enthusiastic greeting of the poodle.

'It is I!' declared the little lady. She spoke in a high-pitched crystal-clear voice which penetrated Lorna's deafness and filled her with gratitude.

She now saw that Madame Eva was old. But her shrivelled face was heavily powdered and rouged and her hair dyed an aggressive ginger. She wore a faded velvet tea-gown and a lot of foreign-looking jewellery and peered up into Lorna's face with bright, inquisitive eyes very like the poodle's.

'How do you do?' said Lorna. 'What a dear little dog.'

Madame Eva lifted a bejewelled forefinger. 'He is more than a dog, dear Miss Harris! He is the most recent temporal form of the Pharoah Thutmose the Third! He is quite indispensable to me!' Madame Eva leered in an unnerving way. 'He is my contact – with Them! Now let us sit down!' she continued brightly. 'And you shall tell me of your little problem, Miss Harris!'

Hearing Madame Eva describe it so, Lorna felt, for the first time in weeks, a rise of her heart and a dawning optimism. They took seats either side of the table. The medium placed the tips of her bedizened fingers together and smiled encouragingly at Lorna. Thutmose III climbed into a dog basket and settled down with his nose on his paws.

'I lived until recently in Torquay with my aunt. I had no money of my own and Auntie needed a companion . . .' Lorna's voice faded away. Madame Eva nodded. It was a commonplace situation. 'I do write a little,' continued Lorna nervously. 'Stories which I sometimes sell to ladies' journals. But I couldn't live on that.'

Madame Eva smiled sympathetically. Thutmose III began to snore.

'Auntie – I know one ought not speak ill of the dead – that is, of – of Them . . .' Lorna glanced nervously about the room. Lord knows who stood in the shadows, waiting and listening to this conversation, unseen except by Madame Eva. 'Auntie was a little difficult . . . However, when she died, just over a year ago in

1926, she left me her bungalow and everything. It gave me a chance to get away and start a new life.' Lorna drew a deep breath. 'I am thirty-five. I really didn't want to spend the rest of my life in Torquay. Jane – Miss Fanshawe, she recommended you to me – she suggested I sell up, buy a little flat in outer London and start afresh.'

Lorna's voice tailed away dismally. It had all seemed too wonderful to be true. Free of Auntie and her perpetual criticism and nagging. Free of Torquay and its bridge parties peopled by retired colonels and wealthy widows. Enough money invested, after the purchase of the flat, to bring in an annual income of two hundred and fifty pounds. Enough to live on modestly, with the occasional supplement from selling a story. Freedom and independence for the first time in Lorna's life.

She pulled herself together. 'I found the flat through an advertisment in a newspaper. It seemed just the thing. Only three years old in a small block, near the new underground station and not far from shops. Oh, it was ideal!' Lorna's voice rose in despair. 'And then, not long after I moved in, that is to say about six weeks ago, things started happening.'

'Yes?' encouraged Madame Eva. Thutmose stirred in his basket and uttered a squeak. He was dreaming. Of the palm-fringed Nile? Or of next door's cat? Impossible to know.

'I have to tell you,' Lorna said bravely, 'that I am just a trifle hard of hearing. I first found a broken vase. I thought I must have placed it too near the edge of a windowsill. But other things keep falling and breaking, for no reason. Then there was the painting . . .' Now Lorna could not get the words out fast enough, eager to share the horror she had experienced. 'I found it leaning against the wall underneath where it had been hanging. The picture nail was still firmly in place. The cord wasn't broken. Nor was the picture glass. It just seemed to have unhooked itself. It was only a very ordinary little watercolour of Torbay. But it belonged to Auntie and hung in the bungalow. I kept it when I sold all the other things because she was so fond of it and would have been so cross . . .'

'Oh, yes . . .' said Madame Eva with deep satisfaction. 'They feel very deeply about their possessions.'

'So that,' said Lorna loudly and baldly, 'was when I began to think that it might be Auntie doing these things. That she had somehow followed me, angry because I sold the bungalow and that – oh, Madame Eva! I think she wants to persecute me now, even after her death, just as she did when she was alive. I shall never be free of her, never!'

On this wild cry, Lorna fell silent. Madame Eva leaned across the table and patted her hand consolingly.

'Dear Miss Harris, do not distress yourself! Your experience is far from uncommon. Sadly, many people refuse to admit such things. But you are obviously sensitive.'

'Auntie used to say I had too much imagination,' said Lorna dolefully. 'She disliked my writing my stories. She said it was unhealthy. I was so happy at first in my flat. Now I'm terrified all the time I'm in it. I sense things. Every so often I feel a shudder run through me. I know she's there.'

'Oh, yes, I do believe she is,' said Madame Eva calmly.

'But can't I get her to go away?' demanded Lorna hysterically. 'Will she continue to follow me everywhere I go? I stay out of the flat as much as I can. I go to museums and art galleries and libraries and walk round shops. When it's fine I sit in the park. I take all my writing materials with me and try to write my stories in the library – but it has become so difficult to concentrate. I keep thinking eventually I shall have to go home and find – what? Some new thing broken or moved? Sometimes the change of position is slight but I know a thing has moved. It's not my imagination, truly!'

'Of course not,' said Madame Eva serenely. 'You have a spirit visitor. People talk of the supernatural. But this is all quite natural. The spirit world is just as real as this one and there is not the slightest need to be afraid of it. I believe the cause of your little problem to be this. When you lived with your aunt, you were not happy. Your aunt was not quite kind to you. Now she is sorry. She wishes to tell you so. You must establish contact with her.'

'But I don't want to,' objected Lorna. 'I want her to go away.'

'First you must discuss things with her, face to face,' said Madame Eva firmly. 'I could call up the spirit of your aunt here . . .'

Lorna glanced over her shoulder and Thutmose opened one beady eye.

'But since she is already in your flat and trying so hard to contact you, you must first try there. The next time you feel her presence, welcome her loudly to your home. Assure her you bear her no ill will and think of her with affection. Tell her you are sorry if she is distressed because you sold her bungalow, but you felt like a change and hope she understands and will forgive. Mutual forgiveness will set both your minds at rest. Once she is assured that all is well, she will not trouble you any more.'

'Are you sure?' asked Lorna doubtfully.

'Absolutely!' said Madame Eva with confidence. 'Let me know how you get on.'

Lorna stood up and Thutmose woke up and jumped out of his basket. On a sideboard lay an empty saucer. Madame Eva's eye seemed to stray towards it. Lorna, taking the hint, put a pound note in it. They parted amicably.

When Lorna returned to the flat it looked cheerful and normal. No broken ornaments. No moved furniture. Pictures all on the walls. The sun shone in with an end-of-day golden glow and sent a splash of light across a polished table and the vase of large white daisies. Lorna heaved a sigh of relief and went to make a cup of tea. She felt so much better, now she had spoken to Madame Eva. Not that she relished making contact with Auntie, but if Madame Eva were right, Auntie wanted to be friends and 'make up', although such a thing was quite out of the old lady's character since Auntie had always been one to harbour a grievance. But Passing Over had presumably changed her.

Late that night, Lorna awoke suddenly. It was very dark. A shiver ran through her and she felt quite sure she was not alone.

Panicking, she rolled over and fumbled for the switch of the bedside lamp, the sweat breaking out on her body. The room appeared quite normal. The wardrobe door, half open, showed a glimpse of her coat hanging above her shoes. She could see her hatbox, her library book.

Hairs prickling on the nape of her neck, Lorna got out of bed and pulled on her dressing gown. She peered into the wardrobe and moved the clothes about, then she stepped out into her tiny hall and switched on the light. Nothing would satisfy her but to examine every room, every nook and cranny.

Lorna opened the door of her tiny drawing room, switched on the light and immediately gave a cry of dismay. The vase with the daisies had rolled over onto its side, spilling flowers and water across the tabletop and onto the floor. Auntie was playing her destructive, malicious tricks again.

Lorna made an effort not to give way to complete hysteria. She must make contact. There was nothing Lorna wanted to do less. However, she cleared her throat and stammered, 'Auntie? Auntie – are you there?'

There was no reply, by sound or sign. Lorna heaved a sigh of relief and decided to make a cup of tea. The kitchen was the only room she had not examined and as the door slid noiselessly open beneath her hand a breath of ice-cold air blew round her shoulders and brushed her cheek.

Lorna screamed. It was in there! In the kitchen! She scrabbled for the light switch.

The kitchen was empty – but the window stood open. 'Oh my goodness!' exclaimed Lorna. Such a simple explanation. She crossed the room, half crying and half laughing, and closed it.

Imagination after all! *Now then, my girl, a cup of tea with a drop of brandy in it, that's what you need!* Lorna took down a cup and saucer and stood them on the worktop. It was as she reached for the kettle that it happened.

The cup rocked all by itself and with no human agency, rattling in its saucer though Lorna could not hear it, only watch it with fascinated horror-filled eyes as it danced a silent jig. A shudder ran through her. Lorna clutched at the neck of her dressing gown.

'Auntie? Auntie, if you are there, do please let me see you!'

The exact nature of the apparition, should it choose to materialise before her, now filled her with a new horror. With dread Lorna waited for the familiar and hated figure of her aunt to appear – in what shape she could not guess. A human form, however ghastly pale and ethereal, would be infinitely more bearable than some hideous deformity or amorphous floating mass of ectoplasm, essentially formless and changing its weird shapelessness into ever more terrifying and unrecognisable manifestations. It might grow and swell until it filled the kitchen, enveloping Lorna in its suffocating embrace. Alternatively, it might be light and gossamer, binding her with invisible chains as when one walked unwarily into a cobweb. Or Auntie might just appear as she had always been, sitting there on a kitchen chair, iron-grey hair scraped into a tight bun, gold pince-nez clamped on the high bridge of her narrow nose, gimlet eyes glittering. Again she would hear the dreaded voice. 'Lorna! Why did you sell the bungalow and move to this vulgar flat? Lorna! You have been scribbling those ridiculous tales again!'

Nothing. When, after a long wait, Lorna moved, she was stiff and cold and so miserable she did not know what to do. Tears began to run down her cheeks.

'Auntie? It's not fair, really it's not. I did everything you wanted for years! Can't I lead a life of my own, ever?'

'Not while I can stop you!' Auntie's voice seemed to echo in her head.

'I hate you!' Lorna suddenly shouted as loudly as she could. She ran out into the hall, opened all the doors one at a time and repeated her cry into every room. 'You're a horrid old woman!

You always were and you always will be! You're not welcome here! I'm glad I sold the bungalow! I don't forgive you! So there!'

Silence mocked her. Her anger faded and a deep, aching misery was left. She abandoned her attempt to make tea and hadn't the courage to return to bed. She scrambled onto her sofa and huddled in one corner of it, too deep in despair to move.

She was there when dawn came. The sun crept over the sill, touching her still form with curious pale yellow fingers. Cold and aching in every limb, Lorna unwound her arms from her knees and got up. She picked up the spilled flower vase and set out for the kitchen.

Because she could not hear a normal doorbell buzz, Lorna had had a large shop-door bell on a spring installed when she moved into the flat. As she crossed the hall, it leapt wildly and jangled.

Lorna froze, her heart lurching painfully. But spirits did not ring doorbells. Lorna peered through a crack and recognised the woman standing outside as living in the flat beneath. Although she was still in her dressing gown, the need for human company was so overwhelming that she pulled the door open wide and begged, 'Oh, do please come in!'

The woman sat down in the drawing room and mouthed at Lorna.

'I'm sorry,' Lorna apologised. 'I'm hard of hearing, you'll have to speak up.'

'I'm Mrs Belling,' the visitor repeated loudly, pulling her mouth into exaggerated shapes and leaning forward, anxious to make Lorna understand. 'I live in the flat below. I do apologise for calling so early. I wondered if you were quite well . . . I see you are in your dressing gown. I do hope I didn't get you out of bed?

I thought I heard you cry out during the night. These flats are not very solidly built. One hears . . .' A dusky flush crossed her face as she realised she was being tactless and that the other woman could not hear. 'I mean, I've been meaning to call. I wanted to give you time to settle in first.'

'Thank you,' said Lorna in a shaking voice.

'Can I make you a cup of tea?' asked Mrs Belling. 'You look very pale.'

Lorna shook her head. 'I'm all right.'

'You don't look all right,' said Mrs Belling doubtfully. 'However, as you wish. There is something, Miss Harris, about which I have been intending to call. I speak on behalf of all the other residents. Will you join us in writing to the council? If we all sign the letter . . .'

'What about?' asked Lorna, prepared to listen to anything provided it kept the visitor there a little longer.

'About the nuisance from the underground railway. The entrance to the tunnel is only a short way from here and it runs right under the block. The foundations are not what they should be and surely, Miss Harris, you've noticed? Haven't you felt the vibrations from the trains?'

'Trains . . .?' echoed Lorna slowly.

'Yes, sometimes quite violent. Can't you hear – oh dear, no, I do apologise. I suppose you can't. But haven't you noticed anything? I've had ornaments quite literally fall off my mantelshelf, I've even had things move. We have all suffered similar inconvenience and believe we are entitled to compensation. Miss Harris?' Mrs Belling leaned forward in alarm. 'You look dreadfully ill! Do let me fetch you a glass of water!'

She rose to her feet but Lorna leapt up and grasped her arm. Her grip was so fierce and her eyes glittered so wildly that Mrs Belling blanched.

'T-trains . . .!' stuttered Lorna. 'You mean, the trembling – it's the trains? The – the things falling?' She began to cry in loud unlovely sobs. Between them could be heard the words, 'Trains – vase – Auntie – tunnel – deaf – trains . . .'

Mrs Belling wrenched herself free and fled.

Alone, Lorna wiped her eyes and ran to the window, throwing it open. A lovely, wonderful day! She had been unchained from a nightmare. No ghosts, no Auntie, only sunshine and freedom! She would call on Jane and suggest lunch, over which she would explain about the trains and rebuke her friend for believing in Madame Eva's nonsense.

It was as Lorna stood before the mirror, humming and pulling on her cloche hat, that she saw, reflected behind her, a favourite little carriage clock just jump off the mantelshelf and crash to the floor. She was annoyed but even this damage to a treasured possession could not destroy her new happiness. 'There!' she said. 'Those trains again! I really shall sign Mrs Belling's letter. Something must be done about the vibrations!'

Lorna hurried out and down the pavement. Her heart was as light as air and her feet almost danced along. Before the entrance to the tube station she stopped. The iron gates were closed and affixed to them was a notice:

'Works on the Line. No Trains Today.'

THRILLINGLY GOOD BOOKS FROM CRIMINALLY GOOD WRITERS

CRIME FILES BRINGS YOU THE LATEST RELEASES FROM TOP CRIME AND THRILLER AUTHORS.

SIGN UP ONLINE FOR OUR MONTHLY NEWSLETTER AND BE THE FIRST TO KNOW ABOUT OUR COMPETITIONS, NEW BOOKS AND MORE.